Beloved Vietnam

Volume 2

Pham ThuDzung

Beloved Vietnam

Volume 2

Virtual Reality

BELOVED VIETNAM • VOLUME 2
Author: ThuDzung Pham
Printed in the United States of America
Cover design by ThuDzung Pham
Print book interior design by Xpress Print
First Edition: May 2022
ISBN: 978-1-62988-512-4

CONTENTS

FORE WORD

"Yesterday, I called, but you didn't pick up the phone. What were you doing, ThuDzung?"

"Oh, Papa! I was thoroughly absorbed in the Tell-Tale Heart of Edgar Allen Poe, the Master of mystery, suspense, and horror…. I didn't hear the phone ring."

Smiling, the father said, "The majority topics of Mystery focus on the enigmatic, puzzling of the problems creating the curiosity of the audience to guess who was the culprit. The skillful authors [Arthur Conan Doyle/ Sherlock Homes; Agatha Christie/ Hercules Poirot and R. D. Rowling/Harry Potter….] often surprise us by the most unnoticeable character in the anecdote was the killer. In those murderous scenes, usually there is one or a few victims were murdered…Should we figure out the real identity of persons that people followed and even worship them - are they the superheroes in real life?"

"Whom are you talking about, Papa?" the girl asked

"Ah…. Let's take a look at the life of South Vietnam President, Ngô Đình Diệm and the life of Hồ Chí Minh- a Marxist–Leninist-Chairman and First Secretary of the Workers' Party of Vietnam, Prime Minister of North Vietnam from 1945 to 1955 and President from 1945 until his death in 1969.

…

Turn the pages with me, would you?

1

Đi trong lịch sử dân ta
Luống nghẹn ngào
When I read Vietnam history,
I cry with painful tears...

Ngô Đình Diệm

He was the final prime minister of the State of Vietnam (1954–55), and then served as President of South Vietnam (Republic of Vietnam) from 1955 until he was captured and assassinated during the 1963 military coup. Ngo Dinh Diem - Wikipediahttps://en.wikipedia.org › wiki ›

Ngô Đình Diệm (3 January 1901 – 2 November 1963) was a Vietnamese politician.

Diệm was born into a prominent Catholic family, the son of a high-ranking civil servant, Ngô Đình Khả. He was educated at French-speaking schools and considered following his brother Ngô Đình Thục into the priesthood, but eventually chose to pursue a civil-service career. He progressed rapidly in the court of Emperor Bảo Đại, becoming governor of Bình Thuận Province in 1929 and interior minister in 1933. However, he resigned the latter position after three months and publicly denounced the emperor as a tool of France. Diệm came to support Vietnamese nationalism, promoting an anti-communist and anti-colonialist "third way" opposed to both Bảo Đại and communist leader Hồ Chí Minh. He established the Can Lao Party to support his political doctrine of Person Dignity Theory.

After several years in exile, Diệm returned home in July 1954 and was appointed prime minister by Bảo Đại, the head of the Western-backed State of Vietnam. The Geneva Accords were signed soon after he took office, formally partitioning Vietnam along the 17th parallel. Diệm soon consolidated power in South Vietnam, aided by his brother Ngô Đình Nhu. After a rigged referendum in 1955, he proclaimed the creation of the Republic of Vietnam, with himself as president. His government was supported by other anti-communist countries, most notably the

United States. Diệm pursued a series of nation-building schemes, emphasizing industrial and rural development. From 1957, he was faced with a communist insurgency backed by North Vietnam, eventually formally organized under the banner of the Việt Cộng. He was subject to a number of assassination and coup attempts, and in 1962 established the Strategic Hamlet Program as the cornerstone of his counterinsurgency effort.

Diệm's favoritism towards Catholics and persecution of South Vietnam's Buddhist majority led to the "Buddhist crisis" of 1963. The violence damaged relations with the United States and other previously sympathetic countries, and his regime lost favour with the leadership of the Army of the Republic of Vietnam. On 1 November 1963, the country's leading generals launched a coup d'état with assistance from the CIA. He and his younger brother Nhu initially escaped, but were recaptured the following day and assassinated on the orders of Dương Văn Minh, who succeeded him as president. Diệm has been a controversial historical figure in historiography on the Vietnam War. Some historians have considered him a tool of the United States, while others portrayed him as an avatar of Vietnamese tradition. At the time of his assassination, he was widely considered to be a corrupt dictator.

Ngô Đình Diệm was born in 1901 in Quảng Bình, a province in the central Vietnam. His family originated in Phú Cam Village; a Catholic village adjacent to Huế City. His clan had been among Vietnam's earliest Catholic converts in the 17th century. Diệm was given a saint's name at birth, Gioan Baotixita (a Vietnamized form of Jean Baptiste), following the custom of the Catholic Church. The Ngô-Đình family suffered under the anti-Catholic persecutions of Emperors Minh Mạng and Tự Đức. In 1880, while Diệm's father, Ngô Đình Khả (1850–1925), was studying in British Malaya, an anti-Catholic riot led by Buddhist monks almost wiped out the Ngô-Đình clan. Over 100 of the Ngô clan were "burned alive in a church including Khả's parents, brothers, and sisters." Ngô Đình Khả was educated in a Catholic school in British Malaya, where he learned English and studied the European-style curriculum. He was a devout Catholic and scrapped plans to become a Roman Catholic priest in the late 1870s. He worked for the commander of the French armed forces as an interpreter and took part in campaigns against anti-colonial rebels in the mountains of Tonkin during 1880. He rose to become a high-ranking Mandarin, the first headmaster of the National Academy in Huế (founded in 1896) and a counselor to Emperor Thành Thái under the French colonial regime. He was appointed minister of the rites and chamberlain and keeper of the eunuchs. Despite his collaboration with the French colonizers, Khả was "motivated less by Francophilia than by certain reformist ambitions". Like Phan Châu Trinh, Khả believed that independence from France could be achieved only after changes in Vietnamese politics, society and culture had occurred. In 1907, after the ouster of emperor Thành Thái, Khả resigned his appointments, withdrew from the imperial court, and became a farmer in the countryside.

After the tragedy of his family, Khả decided to abandon preparation for the priesthood and married. After his first wife died childless, Khả remarried and had twelve children with his second wife, Phạm Thị Thân (in a period of twenty-three years) of whom nine survived infancy – six sons and three daughters. These were Ngô Đình Khôi, Ngô Đình Thị Giao, Ngô Đình Thục, Ngô Đình Diệm, Ngô Đình Thị Hiệp, Ngô Đình Thị Hoàng, Ngô Đình Nhu, Ngô Đình Cẩn and Ngô Đình Luyện. As a devout Roman Catholic, Khả took his entire family to Mass each morning and encouraged his sons to study for the priesthood. Having learned both Latin and classical Chinese, Khả strove to make sure his children were well educated in both Christian scriptures and Confucian classics. During his childhood, Diệm labored in the family's rice fields while studying at a French Catholic primary school (Pellerin School) in Huế, and later entered a private school started by his father, where he studied French, Latin, and classical Chinese. At the age of fifteen he briefly followed his elder brother, Ngô Đình Thục, who would become Vietnam's highest-ranking Catholic bishop, into seminary. Diệm swore himself to celibacy to prove his devotion to his faith, but found monastic life too rigorous and decided not to pursue a clerical career. According to Moyar, Diệm's personality was too independent to adhere to the discipline of the Church, while Jarvis recalls Ngô Đình Thục's ironic observation that the Church was "too worldly" for Diệm. Diệm also inherited his father's antagonism toward the

French colonialists who occupied his country. At the end of his secondary schooling at Lycée Quốc học, the French lycée in Huế, Diem's outstanding examination results elicited the offer of a scholarship to study in Paris. He declined and, in 1918, enrolled at the prestigious School of Public Administration and Law in Hanoi, a French school that prepared young Vietnamese to serve in the colonial administration. It was there that he had the only romantic relationship of his life, when he fell in love with one of his teacher's daughters. After she chose to persist with her vocation, entering a convent, he remained celibate for the rest of his life. Diệm's family background and education, especially Catholicism and Confucianism, had influences on his life and career, on his thinking on politics, society, and history. According to Miller, Diệm "displayed Christian piety in everything from his devotional practices to his habit of inserting references to the Bible into his speeches"; he also enjoyed showing off his knowledge of classical Chinese texts.

Early career: After graduating at the top of his class in 1921, Diệm followed in the footsteps of his eldest brother, Ngô Đình Khôi, joining the civil service in Thừa Thiên as a junior official. Starting from the lowest rank of mandarin, Diệm steadily rose over the next decade. He first served at the royal library in Huế, and within one year was the district chief in both Thừa Thiên and nearby Quảng Trị province, presiding over seventy villages. Diệm was promoted to be a provincial chief (Tuần phủ) in Ninh Thuận at the age of 28, overseeing 300 villages. During his career as a mandarin, Diệm was known for his workaholism and incorruptibility, and as a Catholic leader and nationalist. Catholic nationalism in Vietnam during the 1920s and 1930s facilitated Diệm's ascent in his bureaucratic career. Diệm's rise was also facilitated through Ngô Đình Khôi's marriage to the daughter of Nguyễn Hữu Bài (1863–1935), the Catholic head of the Council of Ministers at the Huế court and also supported the indigenization of the Vietnamese Church and more administrative powers to the monarchy. Nguyễn Hữu Bài was highly regarded among the French administration and Diệm's religious and family ties impressed him and he became Diệm's patron. The French were impressed by his work ethic but were irritated by his frequent calls to grant more autonomy to Vietnam. Diệm replied that he contemplated resigning but encouragement from the populace convinced him to persist. In 1925, he first encountered communists distributing propaganda while riding horseback through the region near Quảng Trị. Revolted by calls for violent socialist revolution contained in the propaganda leaflets, Diệm involved himself in anti-communist activities for the first time, printing his own pamphlets. In 1929, he was promoted to the governorship of Bình Thuận Province and was known for his work ethic. In 1930 and 1931, he helped the French suppress the first peasant revolts organized by the communists. According to Fall, Diệm put the revolution down because he thought it could not sweep out the French administration, but might threaten the leadership of the mandarins. In 1933, with the ascension of Bảo Đại to the throne, Diệm accepted Bảo Đại's invitation to be his interior minister following lobbying by Nguyễn Hữu Bài. Soon after his appointment, Diệm headed a commission to advise on potential administration reforms. After calling for the French administration to introduce a Vietnamese legislature and many other political reforms, he resigned after three months in office when his proposals were rejected. Diệm denounced Emperor Bảo Đại as "nothing but an instrument in the hands of the French administration," and renounced his decorations and titles from Bảo Đại. The French administration then threatened him with arrest and exile.

For the next decade, Diệm lived as a private citizen with his family in Huế, although he was kept under surveillance. He spent his time reading, meditating, attending church, gardening, hunting, and in amateur photography. Diệm also conducted extensive nationalist activities during those 21 years, engaging in meetings and correspondence with various leading Vietnamese revolutionaries, such as his friend, Phan Bội Châu, a Vietnamese anti-colonial activist, whom Diệm respected for his knowledge of Confucianism and argued that Confucianism's teachings could be applied to a modern Vietnam. With the start of the World War II in the Pacific, seeing an opportunity for Vietnam to challenge French colonization, he attempted to persuade the Japanese forces to declare independence for Vietnam in 1942 but was ignored. Diệm also tried to establish relationships with Japanese diplomats, army officers, and intelligence operatives who supported Vietnam's independence. In 1943, Diệm's Japanese friends helped him to contact Prince Cường Để, an anti-colonial activist, who was in exile in Japan. After contacting Cường Để, Diệm formed a secret political party, the Association for the Restoration of Great Vietnam (Việt Nam Đại Việt Phục Hưng Hội), which was dominated by his Catholic allies in Hue. When its existence was discovered in the summer of 1944, the French declared Diệm to be a subversive and ordered his arrest. He flew to Saigon under Japanese military protection, staying there until the end of WWII. In 1945, after the coup against French colonial rule, the Japanese offered Diệm the post of prime minister in the Empire of Vietnam under Bảo Đại, which they organized on leaving the country. He declined initially, but reconsidered his decision and attempted to reverse the refusal. However, Bảo Đại had already given the post to Trần Trọng Kim. In September 1945, after the Japanese withdrawal, Hồ Chí Minh proclaimed the Democratic Republic of Vietnam, and in the Northern half of Vietnam, his Việt Minh began fighting the French administration. Diệm attempted to travel to Huế to dissuade Bảo Đại from joining Hồ, but was arrested by the Việt Minh along the way and exiled to a highland village near the border. He might have died of malaria, dysentery, and influenza had the local tribesmen not nursed him back to health. Six months later, he was taken to meet Hồ, who recognized Diệm's virtues and, wanting to extend the support for his new government, asked Diệm to be minister of the interior. Diệm refused to join the Việt Minh, assailing Hồ for the murder of his brother Ngô Đình Khôi by Việt Minh cadres. During the Indochina War, Diệm and other non-communist nationalists had to face a dilemma: they did not want to restore colonial rule and did not want to support the Việt Minh. Diệm proclaimed his neutrality and attempted to establish a Third Force movement that was both anti-colonialist and anti-communist In 1947, he became the founder and chief of the National Union Bloc (Khối Quốc Gia Liên Hiệp) and then folded it into the Vietnam National Rally (Việt Nam Quốc Gia Liên Hiệp), which united non-communist Vietnamese nationalists. He also established relationships with some leading Vietnamese anti-communists like Nguyễn Tôn Hoàn (1917–2001), a fellow Catholic and political activist. His other allies and advisors were dominated by Catholics, especially his family members and their friends. Diệm also secretly maintained contact with high-ranking leaders of the Democratic Republic of Vietnam, attempting to convince them to leave Hồ Chí Minh's government and join him. At the same time, he lobbied French colonial officials for a "true independence" for Vietnam, Diệm was disappointed when in June 1948, Bảo Đại signed an agreement to grant Vietnam status as an "associated state" within the French Union, which allowed France to maintain its diplomatic, economic, and military policies in Vietnam. In the meantime, the French had created the State of Vietnam and Diệm refused Bảo Đại's offer to become the Prime Minister. On 16 June 1949, he then published a new manifesto in newspapers proclaiming a third force different from Vietminh and Bảo Đại, but it raised little interest and further, his statement provided evidence to both the French and Việt Minh that Diệm was a dangerous rival. In 1950, the Việt Minh lost patience and sentenced him to death in absentia, and the French refused to protect him. Hồ Chí Minh's cadres tried to assassinate him while he was traveling to visit his elder brother Thục, bishop of the Vĩnh Long diocese in the Mekong Delta. Recognizing his political status, Diệm decided to leave Vietnam in 1950. According to Miller, during his early career, there were at least three ideologies which influenced Diệm's social and political views in the 1920s and 1930s. The first of these was Catholic nationalism, which Diệm inherited from his family's tradition, especially from Bishop Ngô Đình Thục, his brother, and Nguyễn Hữu Bài, who advised him to "return the seal" in 1933 to oppose French policies. The second was Diệm's understanding of Confucianism, especially through his friendship with Phan Bội Châu who argued that Confucianism's teachings could be applied to a modern Vietnam. Lastly, instructed by Ngô Đình Nhu, Diệm began to examine Personalism, which originated from French Catholicism's philosophy and then applied this doctrine as the main ideology of his regime.

Exile: Diệm applied for permission to travel to Rome for the Holy Year celebrations at the Vatican. After gaining French permission, he left in August 1950 with his older brother, Bishop Ngô Đình Thục. Before going to Europe, Diệm went to Japan, where he met with Prince Cường Để, his former ally, and discussed Cường Để's efforts to return to Vietnam and his capacity to play some roles in his homeland. Diệm's friend also managed to organize a meeting between him and Wesley Fishel, an American political science professor at the University of California, who was working for the CIA in Japan. Fishel was a proponent of the anti-colonial, anti-communist third force doctrine in Asia and was impressed with Diệm and helped him organize connections in the United States. In 1951, Diệm flew to the United States to seek the support of government officials. Nevertheless, Diệm was not successful in winning US support for Vietnamese anti-communists. In Rome, Diệm obtained an audience with Pope Pius XII at the Vatican before undertaking further lobbying across Europe. He also met with French and Vietnamese officials in Paris and sent a message indicating that he was willing to be the Prime Minister of the State of Vietnam to Bảo Đại. But Bảo Đại then refused to meet him. Diệm returned to the United States to continue building support among Americans. Nonetheless, to Americans, the fact that Diệm was an anti-communist was not enough to distinguish him from Bảo Đại and other State of Vietnam leaders. Some American officials worried that his devout Catholicism could hinder his ability to mobilize support in a predominantly non-Catholic country. Diệm recognized that concern and broadened his lobbying efforts to include a development focus in addition to anti-communism and religious factors. Diệm was motivated by the knowledge that the US was enthusiastic in applying their technology and knowledge to modernize postcolonial countries. With the help of Fishel, then at Michigan State University (MSU), Diệm was appointed as a consultant to MSU's Government Research Bureau. MSU was administering government-sponsored assistance programs for cold war allies, and Diệm helped Fishel to lay the foundation for a program later implemented in South Vietnam, the Michigan State University Vietnam Advisory Group. The Americans' assessments of Diệm were varied. Some were unimpressed with him, some admired him. Diệm gained favor with some high-ranking officials, such as Supreme Court Justice William O. Douglas, Roman Catholic cardinal Francis Spellman, Representative Mike Mansfield of Montana, and Representative John F. Kennedy of Massachusetts along with numerous journalists, academics, and the former director of the Office of Strategic Services William J. Donovan. Although he did not succeed in winning official support from the US, his personal interactions with American political leaders promised the prospect of gaining more support in the future. Mansfield remembered after the luncheon with Diệm held on 8 May 1953, he felt that "if anyone could hold South Vietnam, it was somebody like Ngô Đình Diệm". During Diệm's exile, his brothers Nhu, Cẩn, and Luyện played important roles in helping him build international and internal networks and support in different ways for his return to Vietnam. In the early 1950s, Nhu established the Cần Lao Party, which played a key role in helping Diệm attain and consolidate his power.

Becoming Prime Minister and consolidation of power: Until 1953, the State of Vietnam was nominally independent from Paris. Since dissatisfaction with France and Bảo Đại was rising among non-communist nationalists, and support from non-communist nationalists and Diệm's allies was rising for his "true independence" point of view, Diệm sensed that it was time for him to come to power in Vietnam. In early 1954, Bảo Đại offered Diệm the position of Prime Minister in the new government in Vietnam. In May 1954, the French surrendered at Điện Biên Phủ and the Geneva Conference began in April 1954. On 16 June 1954, Diệm met with Bảo Đại in France and agreed to be the Prime Minister if Bảo Đại would give him military and civilian control. On 25 June 1954, Diệm returned from exile, arriving at Tân Sơn Nhứt airport in Saigon. On 7 July 1954, Diệm established his new government with a cabinet of 18 people. In the first period of his premiership, Diệm did not have much power in the government; he lacked control of the military and police forces, and the civil system's key positions were still held by French officials. He also could not control the Bank of Indochina. Besides, Diệm had to face massive obstacles: refugee issues; the French colonists wanting to remove Diệm to protect France's interest in South Vietnam; general Nguyễn Văn Hinh, a Francophile, the leader of National Army was ready to oust Diệm; the leaders of the Hòa Hảo and Cao Đài sectarian armies wanted positions in Diệm's cabinet and complete administrative control over the areas in which they had large numbers of followers; and the major threat of Bình Xuyên, an organized crime syndicate that controlled the National Police led by Lê Văn Viễn, whose power was focused in Saigon. In summer 1954, the three organizations controlled approximately one-third of the territory and population of South Vietnam. In that situation, besides his own political skills, Diệm had to trust in his relatives and the backing of his American supporters to overcome the obstacles and neutralize his opponents.

Partition-Main article: Operation Passage to Freedom: On 21 July 1954, the Geneva Accords temporarily partitioned Vietnam at the 17th parallel, pending elections in July 1956 to reunify the country. The Democratic Republic of Vietnam controlled the north, while the French-backed State of Vietnam controlled the south with Diệm as the Prime Minister. Diệm criticized the French for abandoning North Vietnam to the Communists at Geneva, claimed that the terms did not represent the will of the Vietnamese people, and refused French suggestions to include more pro-French officials in the government. The Geneva Accords allowed for freedom of movement between the two zones until October 1954; this put a large strain on the south. Diệm had only expected 10,000 refugees, but by August, there were more than 200,000 waiting for evacuation from Hanoi and Hải Phòng. Nevertheless, the migration helped to strengthen Diệm's political base of support. To deal with the refugee situation, Diem's government arranged for their relocation into fertile and under-populated provinces in the western Mekong Delta. The Diệm regime also provided them with food and shelter, farm tools, and housing material. The government also dug irrigation canals, built dikes, and dredged swamp-lands to help stabilize their lives.

Establishing Control: In August 1954, Diệm also had to face the "Hinh crisis" when Nguyễn Văn Hinh launched a series of public attacks on Diệm, proclaiming that South Vietnam needed a "strong and popular" leader. Hinh also bragged that he was preparing a coup. However, at the end of 1954, Diệm successfully forced Hinh to resign from his post. Hinh had to flee to Paris and hand over his command of the national army to general Nguyễn Văn Vy. But the National Army officers favored Diệm's leadership over General Vy, which forced him to flee to Paris. Despite the failure of Hinh's alleged coup, the French continued to encourage Diệm's enemies in an attempt to destabilize him. On 31 December 1954, Diệm established the National Bank of Vietnam and replaced the Indochinese banknotes with new Vietnamese banknotes. In early 1955, although American advisors encouraged Diệm to negotiate with the leaders of the political-religious forces who threatened to overthrow his position and to forge an anti-communist bloc, he was determined to attack his enemies to consolidate his power. In April 1955, Diệm's army forces took most of Bình Xuyên's posts in Saigon after a victory in the Battle of Saigon. Within a few months, Diệm's troops wiped out the Bình Xuyên's remnants, leaving only a few small bands, who then joined forces with the communists. The failure of Bình Xuyên marked the end of French efforts to remove Diệm. After the defeat of Bình Xuyên, the authority and prestige of Diệm's government increased. Most of the Cao Đài leaders chose to rally to Diệm's government. Diệm then dismantled the private armies of the Cao Đài and Hòa Hảo religious sects. By the end of 1955, Diệm had almost taken control of South Vietnam, and his government was stronger than ever before. In April 1956, along with the capture of Ba Cụt, the leader of the last Hòa Hảo rebels, Diệm almost subdued all of his non-communist enemies, and could focus on his Vietnamese communist opponents. According to Miller, Diệm's capacity in subduing his enemies and consolidating his power strengthened US support of his government, although the US government had planned to withdraw its backing from Diệm during his early difficult years of leadership.

Presidency (1955–1963): [Establishment of the Republic of Vietnam] *1955 State of Vietnam referendum*

In South Vietnam, a referendum was scheduled for 23 October 1955 to determine the future direction of the south, in which the people would choose Diệm or Bảo Đại as the leader of South Vietnam. During the election, Diệm's brother Ngô Đình Nhu and the Cần Lao Party supplied Diệm's electoral base in organizing and supervising the elections, especially the propaganda campaign for destroying Bảo Đại's reputation. Supporters of Bảo Đại were not allowed to campaign, and were physically attacked by Nhu's workers. Official results showed 98.2 per cent of voters favored Diệm, an implausibly high result that was condemned as fraudulent. The total number of votes far exceeded the number of registered voters by over 380,000, further evidence that the referendum was heavily rigged. For example, only 450,000 voters were registered in Saigon, but

605,025 were said to have voted for Diệm. On 26 October 1955, Diệm proclaimed the formation of the Republic of Vietnam, with himself as its first President, although only until 26 October 1956. The first Constitution provided articles to establish the republic and organize the election of its president. The 1954 Geneva Accords prescribed elections to reunify the country in 1956. Diệm refused to hold these elections, claiming that a free election was not possible in the North. According to Taylor, Diệm's rejection of the Geneva accords was a way of objecting to the French colonization of Vietnam. Diệm's disposition of Bảo Đại and the establishment of the First Republic of Vietnam was a way to claim Vietnamese independence from France. At the same time, the first Constitution of the Republic of Vietnam was promulgated. According to the Constitution, Diệm had almost absolute power over South Vietnam. His governance style became increasingly dictatorial over time. Diệm's rule was authoritarian and nepotistic. His most trusted official was Nhu, leader of the primary pro-Diệm Can Lao political party, who was an opium addict and admirer of Adolf Hitler. He modeled the Can Lao secret police's marching style and torture styles on Nazi designs. Cẩn was put in charge of the former Imperial City of Huế. Although neither Cẩn or Nhu held any official role in the government, they ruled their regions of South Vietnam, commanding private armies and secret police. His youngest brother Luyện, was appointed Ambassador to the United Kingdom. His elder brother, Ngô Đình Thục, was the archbishop of Huế. Despite this, Thuc lived in the Presidential Palace, along with Nhu, Nhu's wife and Diệm. Diệm was nationalistic, devoutly Catholic, anti-Communist, and preferred the philosophies of personalism and Confucianism. Diệm's rule was also pervaded by family corruption. Can was widely believed to be involved in illegal smuggling of rice to North Vietnam on the black market and opium throughout Asia via Laos, as well as monopolizing the cinnamon trade, amassing a fortune stored in foreign banks. With Nhu, Can competed for U.S. contracts and rice trade. Thuc, the most powerful religious leader in the country, was allowed to solicit "voluntary contributions to the Church" from Saigon businessmen, which was likened to "tax notices". Thuc also used his position to acquire farms, businesses, urban real estate, rental property and rubber plantations for the Catholic Church. He also used Army of the Republic of

Vietnam personnel to work on his timber and construction projects. The Nhu's amassed a fortune by running numbers and lottery rackets, manipulating currency and extorting money from Saigon businesses. Luyen became a multimillionaire by speculating in piasters and pounds on the currency exchange using inside government information. The Can Lao Party played a key role in Diệm's regime. Initially, the party acted secretly based on a network of cells, and each member only knew the identities of a few other members. When necessary, the Party could assume the role of the government. After 1954, the existence of the party was recognized, but its activities were hidden from public view. In the early 1950s, Diệm and Nhu used the party to mobilize support for Diệm's political movements. According to the decree 116/BNV/CT of the Republic of Vietnam, the Can Lao Party was established on 2 September 1954. Personalism (*Vietnamese: Chủ nghĩa nhân vị*) officially became the basic doctrine of Diệm's regime since the Constitution's preface declared that "Building Politics, Economy, Society, Culture for the people based on respecting Personalism".

ELECTION: 1956 South Vietnamese Constitutional Assembly election and 1959 South Vietnamese parliamentary election

According to Miller, democracy, to Diệm, was rooted in his dual identity as Confucian and Catholic, and was associated with communitarianism and the doctrine of Personalism. He defined democracy as "a social ethos based on certain sense of moral duty", not in the US sense of "political right" or political pluralism and in the context of an Asian country like Vietnam, Confucian values were relevant to deal with contemporary problems in politics, governance, and social change. In this sense, Diệm was not a reactionary mandarin lacking an interest in democracy as he has been portrayed by some scholars. His way of thinking about democracy became a key factor of his approach to political and administrative reform.[75] On 4 March 1956, the elections for the first National Assembly were held. On this occasion, non-government candidates were allowed to campaign, but the government retained the right to ban candidates deemed to be linked to the communists or other 'rebel' groups, and campaign material was screened. The police were also used to intimidate opposition candidates, and military personnel were driven around to cast multiple ballots for regime

14

members. However, Diệm's regime of "democratic one-man rule" faced increasing difficulties. After coming under pressure from within Vietnam and from the United States, Diệm agreed to hold legislative elections in August 1959 for South Vietnam. But in reality, newspapers were not allowed to publish names of independent candidates or their policies, and political meetings exceeding five people were prohibited. Candidates who ran against government-supported opponents faced harassment and intimidation. In rural areas, candidates who ran were threatened using charges of conspiracy with the Việt Cộng, which carried the death penalty. Phan Quang Đán, the government's most prominent critic, was allowed to run. Despite the deployment of 8,000 ARVN plainclothes troops into his district to vote, Đán still won by a ratio of six to one. The busing of soldiers to vote for regime approved candidates occurred across the country. When the new assembly convened, Đán was arrested. In May 1961, U.S. Vice President Lyndon B. Johnson visited Saigon and enthusiastically declared Diệm the "Winston Churchill of Asia." Asked why he had made the comment, Johnson replied, "Diệm's the only boy we got out there." Johnson assured Diệm of more aid in molding a fighting force that could resist the communists.

Socio-Economic Policies: During his presidency, Diệm imposed programs to reform Saigon society in accordance with Catholic and Confucian values. Brothels and opium dens were closed, divorce and abortion were made illegal, and adultery laws were strengthened.[79] Additionally, Diệm's government established many schools and universities, such as the National Technical Center at Phú Thọ in 1957, the University of Saigon (1956), the University of Hue (1957), and the University of Dalat (1957).

Rural Development: During Diệm's rule setting up a democratic basis and to promote a rural and material rearmament among the people". Civic Action was considered a practical tool of Diệm's government to serve "the power vacuum" and make a rural influence for Diệm's government in countryside due to the departure of Việt Minh cadres after the Geneva Accords (1954). Steward's study provides a clearer picture of Diệm's domestic policies and a further understanding of his government's efforts in reaching and connecting with local communities in South

Vietnam that shows "an indigenous initiative" of the government in building an independent and viable nation.

Land Reform: In South Vietnam, especially in Mekong Delta, landholdings in rural areas were concentrated in small number of rich landlord families. Thus, it was urgent to implement land reform in South Vietnam. Diệm had two attempts to control the excesses of the land tenancy system by promulgating the Ordinance 2 on 28 January 1955 to reduce land rent between 15% to 25% of the average harvest and the Ordinance 7 on 5 February 1955 to protect the rights of tenants on new and abandoned land and enhancing cultivation. In October 1956, with the urge from Wolf Ladejinsky, Diệm's personal adviser on agrarian reform, Diệm promulgated a more serious ordinance on the land reform, in which he proclaimed a "land to the tiller" (not to be confused with other Land reform in South Vietnam like Nguyễn Văn Thiệu's later 'Land to the Tiller" program) program to put a relatively high 100 hectares limit on rice land and 15 hectares for ancestral worship. However, this measure had no real effect because many landlords evaded the redistribution by transferring the property to the name of family members. Besides, during the 1946–54 war against the French Union forces, the Việt Minh had gained control of parts of southern Vietnam, initiated land reform, confiscated landlords' land and distributed it to the peasants. Additionally, the ceiling limit was more than 30 times that allowed in Japan, South Korea, and Taiwan, and the 370,000 acres (1,500 km2) of the Catholic Church's landownings in Vietnam were exempted. The political, social, and economic influences of the land reform was minimal. From 1957 to 1963, only 50 percent of expropriated land was redistributed, and only 100,000 out of approximately one million tenant farmers in South Vietnam benefited from the reform.

Resettlement: According to Miller, Diệm, who described tenant farmers as a "real proletariat" and pursued the goal of "middle peasantization", was not a beholden to large landowners, instead of vigorously implementing Land Reform, Diệm had his own vision in Vietnamese rural development based on resettlement, which focused on redistribution of people (rather than land), could reduce overpopulation and lead to many benefits in socio-economic transformation as well as military affairs and security, especially anti-communist infiltration. Moreover, Diệm was ambitious to envision Resettlement as a tactic to practice the government's ideological goals. The differences between the US and Diệm over nation building in countryside shaped the clashes in their alliance. The Cái Sắn resettlement project: In late 1955, with the help of US material support and expertise, Diệm's government implemented the project Cái Sắn in An Giang province, which aimed to resettle one hundred thousand northern refugees.

Land Development Program (*Khu dinh điền*): In early 1957, Diệm started a new program called the *Land Development* to relocate poor inhabitants, demobilized soldiers, and minority ethnic groups in central and southern Vietnam into abandoned or unused land in Mekong Delta and Central Highlands, and cultivating technological and scientific achievements to transform South Vietnam and ensure security and prevent communist infiltration. Diệm believed that the program would help improve civilians' lives, teach them the values of being self-reliant and hard working. At the end of 1963, the program had built more than two hundred settlements for a quarter of a million people. Nevertheless, the lacks of conditions in these areas along with the corruption and mercilessness of local officials failed the program.

Agroville Program (*khu trù mật*): During late 1959 and early 1960, motivated by the idea of population regroupment, Diệm introduced the Agroville Program, which he intended to physically relocate residents who lived in remote and isolated regions in Mekong delta into new settlements in "dense and prosperous areas"—proposing to offer them urban modernity and amenities without leaving their farms, and to keep them far away from the communists. Nonetheless, by late 1960, Diệm had to admit that the program's objective failed since the residents were not happy with the program and the communists infiltrated it, and he had to discard it. According to Miller, the disagreement between the US and Diệm over agrarian reform made their alliance "move steadily from bad to worse".

Counter-Insurgency: 1960 South Vietnamese coup attempt and 1962 South Vietnamese Independence Palace bombing- During his presidency, Diệm strongly focused on his central concern: internal security to protect his regime as well as maintain order and social change: staunch anti-subversion and anti-rebellion policies. After the Bình Xuyên was defeated and the Hòa Hảo, Cao Đài were subdued, Diệm concentrated on his most serious threat: the communists. Diệm's main measures for internal security were threats, punishment and intimidation. His regime countered North Vietnamese and communist subversion (including the assassination of over 450 South Vietnamese officials in 1956) by detaining tens of thousands of suspected communists in "political re-education centers." The North Vietnamese government claimed that over 65,000 individuals were imprisoned and 2,148 killed in the process by November 1957. According to Gabriel Kolko, by the end of 1958, 40,000 political prisoners had been jailed. By the end of 1959, Diệm was able to entirely control each family and the communists had to suffer their "darkest period" in their history. Membership declined by two thirds and they had almost no power in the countryside of South Vietnam. Diệm's repression extended beyond communists to anti-communist dissidents and anti-corruption whistleblowers. In 1956, after the "Anti-Communist Denunciation Campaign", Diệm issued Ordinance No. 6, which placed anyone who was considered a threat to the state and public order in jail or house arrest. Nevertheless, Diệm's hard policies led to fear and resentment in many quarters in South Vietnam and negatively affected his relations with the US in terms of counter-insurgent methods. On 22 February 1957, when Diệm delivered a speech at an agricultural fair in Buôn Ma Thuột, a communist named Hà Minh Tri attempted to assassinate the president. He approached Diệm and fired a pistol from close range, but missed, hitting the Secretary for Agrarian Reform's left arm. The weapon jammed and security overpowered Tri before he was able to fire another shot. Diệm was unmoved by the incident. The assassination attempt was the desperate response of the communists to Diệm's relentless anti-communist policies. As opposition to Diệm's rule in South Vietnam grew, a low-level insurgency began to take shape there in 1957. Finally, in January 1959, under pressure from southern Viet Cong cadres who were being successfully targeted by Diệm's secret police, Hanoi's Central Committee issued a secret resolution authorizing the use of armed insurgency in the South with supplies and troops from the North. On 20 December 1960, under instructions from Hanoi, southern communists established the Viet Cong (NLF) in order to overthrow the government of the south. On 11 November 1960, "a failed coup attempt against President Ngô Đình Diệm of South Vietnam was led by Lieutenant Colonel Vương Văn Đông and Colonel Nguyễn Chánh Thi of the Airborne Division of the ARVN (ARVN)". There was a further attempt to assassinate Diệm and his family in February 1962 when two air force officers—acting in unison—bombarded the Presidential Palace.

South Vietnamese "Strategic Hamlet": In 1962, the cornerstone of Diệm's counterinsurgency effort – the Strategic Hamlet Program (*Vietnamese: Ấp Chiến lược*), "the last and most ambitious of Diem's government's nation building schemes", was implemented, calling for the consolidation of 14,000 villages of South Vietnam into 11,000 secure hamlets, each with its own houses, schools, wells, and watchtowers supported by South Vietnamese government. The hamlets were intended to isolate the National Liberation Front (NLF) from the villages, their source for recruiting soldiers, supplies, and information, and to transform the countryside. In the end, because of many shortcomings, the Strategic Hamlet Program was not as successful as had been expected and was cancelled after the assassination of Diệm. However, according to Miller, the program created a remarkable turnabout in Diệm's regime in their war against communism.

Religious Policies & the Buddhist crisis: In a country where surveys of the religious composition estimated the Buddhist majority to be between 70% and 90%, Diệm's policies generated claims of religious bias. Diem was widely regarded by historians as having pursued pro-Catholic policies that antagonized many Buddhists. Specifically, the government was regarded as being biased towards Catholics in public service and military promotions, as well as the allocation of land, business favors, and tax concessions. Diệm also once told a high-ranking officer, forgetting that he was a Buddhist, "Put your Catholic officers in sensitive places. They can be trusted." Many officers in the Army of the Republic of Vietnam converted to Catholicism in the belief that their military prospects depended on it. The distribution of weapons to village self-defense militias intended to repel Việt Cộng guerrillas saw weapons only given to Catholics. Some Buddhist villages converted en masse to Catholicism in order to receive aid or to avoid being forcibly resettled by Diệm's regime, with Buddhists in the army being denied promotion if they refused to convert to Catholicism. Some Catholic priests ran their own private armies, and in some areas forced conversions, looting, shelling, and demolition of pagodas occurred. The Catholic Church was the largest landowner in the country, and the "private" status imposed on Buddhism by the French required official permission to conduct public Buddhist activities and was never repealed by Diệm. Catholics were also *de facto* exempt from the *corvée* labor that the government obliged all citizens to perform; US aid was disproportionately distributed to Catholic-majority villages. The land owned by the Catholic Church was exempt from land reform. Under Diệm, the Catholic Church enjoyed special exemptions in property acquisition, and in 1959, Diệm dedicated his country to the Virgin Mary. The white and gold Vatican flag was regularly flown at all major public events in South Vietnam. The newly constructed Hue and Dalat universities were placed under Catholic authority to foster a Catholic-skewed academic environment. Nonetheless, Diệm had contributed to Buddhist communities in South Vietnam by giving them permission to carry out activities that were banned by French and supported money for Buddhist schools, ceremonies, and building more pagodas. Among the eighteen members of Diệm's cabinet, there were five Catholics, five Confucians, and eight Buddhists, including a vice-president and a foreign minister. Only three of the top nineteen military officials were Catholics. The regime's relations with the United States worsened during 1963, as discontent among South Vietnam's Buddhist majority was simultaneously heightened. In May, in the heavily Buddhist central city of Huế, where Diệm's elder brother was the Catholic Archbishop, the Buddhist majority was prohibited from displaying Buddhist flags during Vesak celebrations commemorating the birth of Gautama Buddha when the government cited a regulation prohibiting the display of non-government flags. A few days earlier, however, white and yellow Catholic papal flags flew at the 25th anniversary commemoration of Ngô Đình Thục's elevation to the rank of bishop. According to Miller, Diệm then proclaimed the flag embargo because he was annoyed with the commemoration for Thục. However, the ban on religious flags led to a protest led by Thích Trí Quang against the government, which was suppressed by Diệm's forces, and unarmed civilians were killed in the clash. Diệm and his supporters blamed the Việt Cộng for the deaths and claimed the protesters were responsible for the violence. Although the provincial chief expressed sorrow for the killings and offered to compensate the victims' families, they resolutely denied that government forces were responsible for the killings and blamed the Viet Cong. According to Diệm, it was the communists who threw a grenade into the crowd.

The Buddhists pushed for a five-point agreement: freedom to fly religious flags, an end to arbitrary arrests, compensation for the Huế victims, punishment for the officials responsible, and religious equality. Diệm then banned demonstrations and ordered his forces to arrest those who engaged in civil disobedience. On 3 June 1963, protesters attempted to march towards the Từ Đàm pagoda. Six waves of ARVN tear gas and attack dogs failed to disperse the crowds. Finally, brownish-red liquid chemicals were doused on praying protesters, resulting in 67 being hospitalized for chemical injuries. A curfew was subsequently enacted. The turning point came in June when a Buddhist monk, Thích Quảng Đức, set himself on fire in the middle of a busy Saigon intersection in protest of Diệm's policies; photos of this event were disseminated around the world, and for many people these pictures came to represent the failure of Diệm's government. A number of other monks publicly self-immolated, and the US grew increasingly frustrated with the unpopular leader's public image in both Vietnam and the United States. Diệm used his conventional anti-communist argument, identifying the dissenters as communists. As demonstrations against his government continued throughout the summer, the special forces loyal to Diệm's brother, Nhu, conducted an August raid of the Xá Lợi pagoda in Saigon. Pagodas were vandalized, monks beaten, and the cremated remains of Quảng Đức, which included his heart, a religious relic, were confiscated. Simultaneous raids were carried out across the country, with the Từ Đàm pagoda in Huế looted, the statue of Gautama Buddha demolished, and the body of a deceased monk confiscated. When the populace came to the defense of the monks, the resulting clashes saw 30 civilians killed and 200 wounded. In all 1,400 monks were arrested, and some thirty were injured across the country. The United States indicated its disapproval of Diệm's administration when ambassador Henry Cabot Lodge Jr. visited the pagoda. No further mass Buddhist protests occurred during the remainder of Diệm's rule. Madame Nhu Trần Lệ Xuân, Nhu's wife, inflamed the situation by mockingly applauding the suicides, stating, "If the Buddhists want to have another barbecue, I will be glad to supply the gasoline." The pagoda raids stoked widespread public disquiet in Saigon. Students at Saigon University boycotted classes and rioted, which led to arrests, imprisonments, and the closure of the university; this was repeated at Huế University. When high school students demonstrated, Diệm arrested them as well; over 1,000 students from Saigon's leading high school, most of them children of Saigon civil servants, were sent to re-education camps, including, reportedly, children as young as five, on charges of anti-government graffiti. Diệm's foreign minister Vũ Văn Mẫu resigned, shaving his head like a Buddhist monk in protest. When he attempted to leave the country on a religious pilgrimage to India, he was detained and kept under house arrest.

At the same time that the Buddhist crisis was taking place, a French diplomatic initiative to end the war had been launched. The initiative was known to historians as the "Maneli affair", after Mieczysław Maneli, the Polish Commissioner to the International Control Commission who served as an intermediary between the two Vietnams. In 1963, North Vietnam was suffering its worst drought in a generation. Maneli conveyed messages between Hanoi and Saigon negotiating a declaration of a ceasefire in exchange for South Vietnamese rice being traded for North Vietnamese coal. On 2 September 1963, Maneli met with Nhu at his office in the Gia Long Palace, a meeting that Nhu leaked to the American columnist Joseph Alsop, who revealed it to the world in his "A Matter of Fact" column in the *Washington Post*. Nhu's purpose in leaking the meeting was to blackmail the United States with the message that if Kennedy continued to criticize Diem's handling of the Buddhist crisis, Diem would reach an understanding with the Communists. The Kennedy administration reacted with fury at what Alsop had revealed. In a message to Secretary of State Dean Rusk, Roger Hilsman urged that a coup against Diem be encouraged to take place promptly, saying that the mere possibility that Diem might make a deal with the Communists meant that he had to go. There have been many interpretations of the Buddhist crisis and the immolation of Thích Quảng Đức in 1963. Relating the events to the larger context of Vietnamese Buddhism in the 20th century and looking at the interactions between Diệm and Buddhist groups, the Buddhist protests during Diệm's regime were not only the struggles against discrimination in religious practices and religious freedom, but also the resistance of Vietnamese Buddhism to Diệm's nation-building policies centered by a personalist revolution that Buddhists considered a threat to the revival of Vietnamese Buddhist power. Until the end of his life, Diệm, along with his brother Nhu still believed that their nation-building was successful and they could resolve the Buddhist crisis in their own way, like what they had done with the Hinh crisis in 1954 and the struggle with the Bình Xuyên in 1955.

Diệm, accompanied by US Secretary of State John Foster Dulles, arrives at Washington National Airport in 1957. Diệm is shown shaking hands with US President Dwight D. Eisenhower.

Foreign Policy: Ngô Đình Diệm presidential visit to Australia and Ngô Đình Diệm presidential visit to the United States: The foreign policy of the Republic of Vietnam (RVN), according to Fishel, "to a very considerable extent", was the policy of Ngo Dinh Diem himself during this period. He was the decisive factor in formulating foreign policies of the RVN, besides the roles of his adviser – Ngô Đình Nhu and his foreign ministers: Trần Văn Đỗ (1954–1955), Vũ Văn Mẫu (1955–1963) and Phạm Đăng Lâm (1963) who played subordinate roles in his regime. Nevertheless, since Diệm had to pay much attention to domestic issues in the context of the Vietnam War, foreign policy did not receive appropriate attention from him. Diệm paid more attention to countries that affected Vietnam directly and he seemed to personalize and emotionalize relations with other nations. The issues Diệm paid more attention in foreign affairs were: the Geneva Accords, the withdrawal of the French, international recognition, the cultivation of the legitimacy of the RVN and the relations with the United States, Laos (good official relations) and Cambodia (complicated relations, especially due to border disputes and minority ethnicities), and especially North Vietnam. Besides, the RVN also focused on diplomatic relations with other Asian countries to secure its international recognition. Diệm's attitude toward India was not harmonious due to India's non-alignment policy, which Diệm assumed favored communism. It was not until in 1962, when India voted for a report criticizing the communists for supporting the invasion of South Vietnam, that Diệm eventually reviewed his opinions toward India. For Japan, Diệm's regime established diplomatic relations for the recognition of war reparations, which led to a reparation agreement in 1959 with the amount of $49 million. Diệm also established friendly relations with non-communist states, especially South Korea, Taiwan, the Philippines, Thailand, Laos and the Federation of Malaya, where Diệm's regime shared the common recognition of communist threats. The RVN established diplomatic relations with Cambodia, India, Burma, Indonesia, Hong Kong, Singapore, Australia, New Zealand, Brazil, Argentina, Mexico, Morocco, and Tunisia. Regarding the relations with communist North Vietnam, Diệm maintained total hostility and never made a serious effort to establish any relations with it. In relations with France, as an anti-colonialism nationalist, Diệm did not believe in France and France was always a negative factor in his foreign policy. He also never "looked up on France as a counterweight to American influence". Concerning relations with the US, although Diệm admitted the importance of the US-RVN alliance, he perceived that the US's assistance to the RVN was primarily serving its own national interest, rather than the RVN's national interest. Keith Taylor adds that Diệm's distrust of the US grew because of its Laotian policy, which gave North Vietnam access to South Vietnam's border through southern Laos. Diệm also feared the escalation of American military personnel in South Vietnam, which threatened his nationalist credentials and the independence of his government. In early 1963, the Ngô brothers even revised their alliance with the US. Moreover, they also disagreed with the US on how to best react to the threat from North Vietnam. While Diệm believed that before opening the political system for the participation of other political camps, military, and security matters should be taken into account; the US wanted otherwise and was critical of Diệm's clientelistic government, where political power based on his family members and trusted associates. The Buddhist crisis in South Vietnam decreased American confidence in Diệm, and eventually led to the coup d'état sanctioned by the US. Ultimately, nation-building politics "shaped the evolution and collapse of the US-Diem alliance". The different visions in the meanings of concepts – democracy, community, security, and social change – were substantial, and were a key cause of the strains throughout their alliance.

Coup and assassination - 1963 South Vietnamese coup, and Arrest and assassination of Ngô Đình Diệm

As the Buddhist crisis deepened in July 1963, non-communist Vietnamese nationalists and the military began preparations for a coup. Bùi Diễm, later South Vietnam's Ambassador to the United States, reported in his memoirs that General Lê Văn Kim requested his aid in learning what the United States might do about Diệm's government.[141] Diễm had contacts in both the embassy and with the high-profile American journalists then in South Vietnam, David Halberstam (*New York Times*), Neil Sheehan (United Press International), and Malcolm Browne (Associated Press).

The coup d'état was designed by a military revolutionary council including ARVN generals led by General Dương Văn Minh. Lieutenant Colonel Lucien Conein, a CIA officer, had become a liaison between the US Embassy and the generals, who were led by Trần Văn Đôn. They met each other for the first time on October

2, 1963 at Tân Sơn Nhất airport. Three days later, Conein met with General Dương Văn Minh to discuss the coup and the stance of the US towards it. Conein then delivered the White House's message of American non-intervention, which was reiterated by Henry Cabot Lodge Jr., the US ambassador, who gave secret assurances to the generals that the United States would not interfere. The coup was chiefly planned by the Vietnamese generals.[143] Unlike the coup in 1960, the plotters of the 1963 coup knew how to gain broad support from other ARVN officer corps. They obtained the support of General Tôn Thất Định, General Đỗ Cao Trí, General Nguyễn Khánh, and the I Corps and II Corps Commanders. Only General Huỳnh Văn Cao of IV Corps remained loyal to Diệm. On November 1, 1963, Conein donned his military uniform and stuffed three million Vietnamese piastres into a bag to be given to General Minh. Conein then called the CIA station and gave a signal indicating that the planned coup against President Diem was about to start. Minh and his co-conspirators swiftly overthrew the government. With only the palace guard remaining to defend Diệm and his younger brother Nhu, the generals called the palace offering Diệm exile if he surrendered. That evening, however, Diệm and his entourage escaped via an underground passage to Cha Tam Catholic Church in Cholon, where they were captured the following morning. On November 2, 1963, the brothers were assassinated together in the back of an M113 armored personnel carrier with a bayonet and revolver by Captain Nguyễn Văn Nhung, under orders from Minh given while en route to the Vietnamese Joint General Staff headquarters. Diệm was buried in an unmarked grave in a cemetery next to the house of the US Ambassador. At the time of his assassination, he was widely considered to be a corrupt dictator.

Hồ Chí Minh

Ho Chi Minh - Wikipediahttps://en.wikipedia.org › wiki › (19 May 1890 – 2 September 1969), born Nguyễn Sinh Cung, also known as Nguyễn Tất Thành, Nguyễn Ái Quốc, Bác Hồ, or simply Bác ('Uncle', pronounced, was a Vietnamese revolutionary and politician. He served as Prime Minister of North Vietnam from 1945 to 1955 and President from 1945 until his death in 1969. Ideologically a Marxist– Leninist, he served as Chairman and First Secretary of the Workers' Party of Vietnam.

Hồ Chí Minh led the Việt Minh independence movement from 1941 onward, establishing the Communist-ruled Democratic Republic of Vietnam in 1945 and defeating the French Union in 1954 at the Battle of Điện Biên Phủ, ending the First Indochina War. He was a key figure in the People's Army of Vietnam and the Việt Cộng during the Vietnam War, which lasted from 1955 to 1975. The Democratic Republic of Vietnam was victorious against the Republic of Vietnam and its allies, and was officially reunified with the Republic of South Vietnam in 1976. Saigon, the former capital of South Vietnam, was renamed Ho Chi Minh City in his honor. Ho officially stepped down from power in 1965 due to health problems, and died in 1969. The details of Hồ Chí Minh's life before he came to power in Vietnam are uncertain. He is known to have used between 50 and 200 pseudonyms. Information on his birth and early life is ambiguous and subject to academic debate. At least four existing official biographies vary on names, dates, places and other hard facts while unofficial biographies vary even more widely. Aside from being a politician, Ho was also a writer, a poet and a journalist. He wrote several books, articles and poems in French, Chinese and Vietnamese.

Early Life: Hồ Chí Minh was born as Nguyễn Sinh Cung in 1890 in the village of Hoàng Trù (the name of the local temple near Làng Sen), his mother's village. Although 1890 is generally accepted as his birth year, at various times he used four other birth years: 1891, 1892, 1894 and 1895. From 1895, he grew up in his father Nguyễn Sinh Sắc (Nguyễn Sinh Huy)'s village of Làng Sen, Kim Liên, Nam Đàn, and Nghệ An Province. He had three siblings: his sister Bạch Liên (Nguyễn Thị Thanh), a clerk in the French Army; his brother Nguyễn Sinh Khiêm (Nguyễn Tất Đạt), a geomancer and traditional herbalist; and another brother (Nguyễn Sinh Nhuận), who died in infancy. As a young child, Cung (Ho) studied with his father before more formal classes with a scholar named Vuong Thuc Do. He quickly mastered Chinese writing, a prerequisite for any serious study of Confucianism, while honing his colloquial Vietnamese writing. In addition to his studies, he was fond of adventure and loved to fly kites and go fishing. Following Confucian tradition, his father gave him a new name at the age of 10: Nguyễn Tất Thành ("Nguyễn the Accomplished"). His father was a Confucian scholar and teacher and later an imperial magistrate in the small remote district of Binh Khe (Qui Nhơn). He was demoted for abuse of power after an influential local figure died several days after having received 102 strokes of the cane as punishment for an infraction. His father was eligible to serve in the imperial bureaucracy, but he refused because it meant serving the French. This exposed Thành (Ho) to rebellion at a young age and seemed to be the norm for the province. Nevertheless, he received a French education, attending Collège Quốc học (lycée or secondary education) in Huế. His disciples, Phạm Văn Đồng and Võ Nguyên Giáp, also attended the school, as did Ngô Đình Diệm, the future President of South Vietnam (and political rival).

First sojourn in France: Previously, it was believed that Thành (Ho) was involved in an anti-slavery (anti-*corvée*) demonstration of poor peasants in Huế in May 1908, which endangered his student status at *Collège Quốc học*. However, a document from the Centre des archives d'Outre-mer in France shows that he was admitted to *Collège Quốc học* on 8 August 1908, which was several months after the anti-*corvée* demonstration (9–13 April 1908). The exaggeration of revolutionary credentials was common among Vietnamese Communist leaders, as shown in North Vietnamese President Tôn Đức Thắng's falsified participation in the 1919 Black Sea revolt. Later in life, he claimed the 1908 revolt had been the moment when his revolutionary outlook emerged, but his application to the French Colonial Administrative School in 1911 undermines this version of events, in which he stated that he left school to go abroad. Because his father had been dismissed, he no longer had any hope for a governmental scholarship and went southward, taking a position at Dục Thanh school in Phan Thiết for about six months, then traveled to Saigon. He worked as a kitchen helper on a French steamer, the *Amiral de Latouche-Tréville*, using the alias Văn Ba. The steamer departed on 5 June 1911 and arrived in Marseille, France on 5 July 1911. The ship then left for Le Havre and Dunkirk, returning to Marseille in mid-September. There, he applied for the French Colonial

Administrative School, but his application was rejected. He instead decided to begin traveling the world by working on ships and visited many countries from 1911 to 1917.

In the United States: While working as the cook's helper on a ship in 1912, Thành (Ho) traveled to the United States. From 1912 to 1913, he may have lived in New York City (Harlem) and Boston, where he claimed to have worked as a baker at the Parker House Hotel. The only evidence that he was in the United States is a letter to French colonial administrators dated 15 December 1912 and postmarked New York City (he gave as his address Poste Restante in Le Havre and his occupation as a sailor) and a postcard to Phan Chu Trinh in Paris where he mentioned working at the Parker House Hotel. Inquiries to the Parker House management revealed no records of his ever having worked there. Among a series of menial jobs, he claimed to have worked for a wealthy family in Brooklyn between 1917 and 1918 and for General Motors as a line manager. It is believed that while in the US he made contact with Korean nationalists, an experience that developed his political outlook. Sophie Quinn-Judge states that this is "in the realm of conjecture". He was also influenced by Pan-Africanist and Black nationalist Marcus Garvey during his stay, and said he attended meetings of the Universal Negro Improvement Association.

In Britain: At various points between 1913 and 1919, Thành (Ho) claimed to have lived in West Ealing and later in Crouch End, Hornsey. He reportedly worked as either a chef or dishwasher (reports vary) at the Drayton Court Hotel in West Ealing.[18] Claims that he trained as a pastry chef under Auguste Escoffier at the Carlton Hotel in Haymarket, Westminster are not supported by documentary evidence. The wall of New Zealand House, home of the New Zealand High Commission which now stands on the site of the Carlton Hotel, displays a blue plaque. During 1913, Thành was also employed as a pastry chef on the Newhaven–Dieppe ferry route.

Political Education in France[1921] From 1919 to 1923, Thành (Ho) began to show an interest in politics while living in France, being influenced by his friend and Socialist Party of France comrade Marcel Cachin. Thành claimed to have arrived in Paris from London in 1917, but the French police only had documents recording his arrival in June 1919. In Paris he joined the *Groupe des Patriotes Annamites* (The Group of Vietnamese Patriots) that included Phan Chu Trinh, Phan Văn Trường, Nguyễn Thế Truyền and Nguyễn An Ninh. They had been publishing newspaper articles advocating for Vietnamese independence under the pseudonym Nguyễn Ái Quốc ("Nguyễn the Patriot") prior to Thành's arrival in Paris. The group petitioned for recognition of the civil rights of the Vietnamese people in French Indochina to the Western powers at the Versailles peace talks, but they were ignored. Citing the principle of self-determination outlined prior to the peace accords, they requested the allied powers to end French colonial rule of Vietnam and ensure the formation of an independent government. Prior to the conference, the group sent their letter to allied leaders, including Prime Minister Georges Clemenceau and President Woodrow Wilson. They were unable to obtain consideration at Versailles, but the episode would later help establish the future Hồ Chí Minh as the symbolic leader of the anti-colonial movement at home in Vietnam. Since Thành was the public face behind the publication of the document (although it was written by Phan Văn Trường), he soon became known as Nguyễn Ái Quốc, and first used the name in September during an interview with a Chinese newspaper correspondent. Many authors have stated that 1919 was a lost "Wilsonian moment", where the future Hồ Chí Minh could have adopted a pro-American and less radical position if only President Wilson had received him. However, at the time of the Versailles Conference, Hồ Chí Minh was committed to a socialist program. While the conference was ongoing, Nguyễn Ái Quốc was already delivering speeches on the prospects of Bolshevism in Asia and was attempting to persuade French socialists to join Lenin's Communist International. In December 1920, Quốc (Ho) became a representative to the Congress of Tours of the Socialist Party of France, voted for the Third International and was a founding member of the French Communist Party. Taking a position in the Colonial Committee of the party, he tried to draw his comrades' attention towards people in French colonies including Indochina, but his efforts were often unsuccessful. While living in Paris, he reportedly had a relationship with a dressmaker named Marie Brière. As discovered in 2018, Quốc also had relations with the members of Provisional Government of the Republic of Korea like Kim Kyu-sik, Jo So-ang while in Paris. During this period, he began to write journal articles and short stories as well as running his Vietnamese nationalist group. In May 1922, he wrote an article for a French magazine criticizing the use of English words by French sportswriters. The article implored Prime Minister Raymond Poincaré to outlaw such Franglais as *le manager*, *le round* and *le knock-out*. His articles and speeches caught the attention of Dmitry Manuilsky, who would soon sponsor his trip to the Soviet Union and under whose tutelage he would become a high-ranking member of the Soviet Comintern.

In the Soviet Union and China: In 1923, Quốc (Ho) left Paris for Moscow carrying a passport with the name Chen Vang, a Chinese merchant, where he was employed by the Comintern, studied at the Communist University of the Toilers of the East and participated in the Fifth Comintern Congress in June 1924 before arriving in Canton (present-day Guangzhou), China in November 1924 using the name Ly Thuy. In 1925–1926, he organized "Youth Education Classes" and occasionally gave socialist lectures to Vietnamese revolutionary young people living in Canton at the Whampoa Military Academy. These young people would become the seeds of a new revolutionary, pro-communist movement in Vietnam several years later. According to William Duiker, he lived with a Chinese woman, Zeng Xueming (Tăng Tuyết Minh), whom he married on 18 October 1926. When his comrades objected to the match, he told them: "I will get married despite your disapproval because I need a woman to teach me the language and keep house". She was 21 and he was 36. They married in the same place where Zhou Enlai had married earlier and then lived in the residence of a Comintern agent, Mikhail Borodin.

Hoàng Văn Chí argued that in June 1925 he betrayed Phan Bội Châu, the famous leader of a rival revolutionary faction and his father's old friend, to French Secret Service agents in Shanghai for 100,000 piastres. A source states that he later claimed he did it because he expected Châu's trial to stir up anti-French sentiment and because he needed the money to establish a communist organization. In Ho Chi Minh: A Life, William Duiker considered this hypothesis, but ultimately rejected it. Other sources claim that Nguyễn Thượng Huyện was responsible for Chau's capture. Chau, sentenced to lifetime house arrest, never denounced Quốc. After Chiang Kai-shek's 1927 anti-Communist coup, Quốc (Ho) left Canton again in April 1927 and returned to Moscow, spending part of the summer of 1927 recuperating from tuberculosis in Crimea before returning to Paris once more in November. He then returned to Asia by way of Brussels, Berlin, Switzerland and Italy, where he sailed to Bangkok, Thailand, arriving in July 1928. "Although we have been separated for almost a year, our feelings for each other do not have to be said to be felt", he reassured Minh in an intercepted letter. In this period, he served as a senior agent undertaking Comintern activities in Southeast Asia. Ho Chi Minh worked as a cook all over the world from 1911 to 1928, also in Milano. This plaque in Via Pasubio, on the left next to "Antica Trattoria della Pesa", remembers one of his work places.

Quốc (Ho) remained in Thailand, staying in the Thai village of Nachok until late 1929, when he moved on to India and then Shanghai. In Hong Kong in early 1930, he chaired a meeting with representatives from two Vietnamese Communist parties to merge them into a unified organization, the Communist Party of Vietnam. In June 1931, Ho was arrested in Hong Kong as part of a collaboration between the French colonial authorities in Indochina and the Hong Kong Police Force; scheduled to be deported back to French Indochina, Ho was successfully defended by British solicitor Frank Loseby. Eventually, after appeals to the Privy Council in London, Ho was reported as dead in 1932 to avoid a French extradition agreement; it was ruled that, though he would be deported from Hong Kong as an undesirable, it would not be to a destination controlled by France. Ho was eventually released and, disguised as a Chinese scholar, boarded a ship to Shanghai. He subsequently returned to the Soviet Union and in Moscow studied and taught at the Lenin Institute. In this period Ho reportedly lost his positions in the Comintern because of a concern that he had betrayed the organization. However, according to Ton That Thien's research, he was a member of the inner circle of the Comintern, a protégé of Dmitry Manuilsky and a member in good standing of the Comintern throughout the Great Purge. In 1938, Quốc (Ho) returned to China and served as an advisor to the Chinese Communist armed forces. He was also the senior

Comintern agent in charge of Asian affairs. He worked extensively in Chungking and traveled to Guiyang, Kunming and Guilin. He was using the name Hồ Quang during this period.

Independence movement: In 1941, Hồ Chí Minh returned to Vietnam to lead the Việt Minh independence movement. The Japanese occupation of Indochina that year, the first step toward invasion of the rest of Southeast Asia, created an opportunity for patriotic Vietnamese. The so-called "men in black" were a 10,000 member guerrilla force that operated with the Việt Minh. He oversaw many successful military actions against the Vichy France and Japanese occupation of Vietnam during World War II, supported closely yet clandestinely by the United States Office of Strategic Services and later against the French bid to reoccupy the country (1946–1954). He was jailed in China by Chiang Kai-shek's local authorities before being rescued by Chinese Communists. Following his release in 1943, he returned to Vietnam. It was during this time that he began regularly using the name Hồ Chí Minh, a Vietnamese name combining a common Vietnamese surname (Hồ, 胡) with a given name meaning "Bright spirit" or "Clear will" (from Sino-Vietnamese 志明: Chí meaning "will" or "spirit" and Minh meaning "bright"). His new name was a tribute to General Hou Zhiming (侯志明), Chief Commissar of the 4th Military Region of the National Revolutionary Army, who helped release him from a KMT prison in 1943.

Hồ Chí Minh (third from left, standing) with the OSS in 1945

In April 1945, he met with the OSS agent Archimedes Patti and offered to provide intelligence, asking only for "a line of communication" between his Viet Minh and the Allies. The OSS agreed to this and later sent a military team of OSS members to train his men and Hồ Chí Minh himself was treated for malaria and dysentery by an OSS doctor. Following the August Revolution (1945) organized by the Việt Minh, Hồ Chí Minh became Chairman of the Provisional Government (Premier of the Democratic Republic of Vietnam) and issued a Proclamation of Independence of the Democratic Republic of Vietnam. Although he convinced Emperor Bảo Đại to abdicate, his government was not recognized by any country. He repeatedly petitioned President Harry S. Truman for support for Vietnamese independence, citing the Atlantic Charter, but Truman never responded. In 1946, future Israeli Prime Minister David Ben-Gurion and Hồ Chí Minh became acquainted when they stayed at the same hotel in Paris. He offered Ben-Gurion a Jewish home-in-exile in Vietnam. Ben-Gurion declined, telling him: "I am certain we shall be able to establish a Jewish Government in Palestine". In 1946, when he traveled outside of the country, his subordinates imprisoned 2,500 non-Communist nationalists and forced 6,000 others to flee. Hundreds of political opponents were jailed or exiled in July 1946, notably members of the Nationalist Party of Vietnam and the Dai Viet National Party after a failed attempt to raise a coup against the Viet Minh government. All rival political parties were hereafter banned and local governments were purged to minimize opposition later on. However, it was noted that the Democratic Republic of Vietnam's first Congress had over two-thirds of its members come from non-Việt Minh political factions, some without an election. Nationalist Party of Vietnam leader Nguyễn Hải Thần was named vice president. They also held four out of ten ministerial positions.

Birth of the Democratic Republic of Vietnam: Following Emperor Bảo Đại's abdication on 2 September 1945, Hồ Chí Minh read the Declaration of Independence of Vietnam under the name of the Democratic Republic of Vietnam. In Saigon, with violence between rival Vietnamese factions and French forces increasing, the British commander, General Sir Douglas Gracey, declared martial law. On 24 September, the Việt Minh leaders responded with a call for a general strike. In September 1945, a force of 200,000 National Revolutionary Army troops arrived in Hanoi to accept the surrender of the Japanese occupiers in northern Indochina. Hồ Chí Minh made a compromise with their general, Lu Han, to dissolve the Communist Party and to hold an election which would yield a coalition government. When Chiang forced the French to give the French concessions in Shanghai back to China in exchange for withdrawing from northern Indochina, he had no choice but to sign an agreement with France on 6 March 1946 in which Vietnam would be recognized as an autonomous state in the Indochinese Federation and the French Union. The agreement soon broke down. The purpose of the agreement, for both the French and Vietminh, was for Chiang's army to leave North Vietnam. Fighting broke out in the North soon after the Chinese left. Historian Professor Liam Kelley of the University of Hawaii at Manoa on his Le Minh Khai's SEAsian History Blog challenged the authenticity of the alleged quote where Hồ Chí Minh said he "would rather smell French shit for five years than eat Chinese shit for a thousand," noting that Stanley Karnow provided no source for the extended quote attributed to him in his 1983 Vietnam: A History and that the original quote was most likely forged by the Frenchman Paul Mus in his 1952 book Vietnam: Sociologie d'une Guerre. Mus was a supporter of French colonialism in Vietnam and Hồ Chí Minh believed there was no danger of Chinese troops staying in Vietnam (although this was the time when China invaded Tibet). The Vietnamese at the time were busy spreading anti-French propaganda as evidence of French atrocities in Vietnam emerged while Hồ Chí Minh showed no qualms about accepting Chinese aid after 1949. The Việt Minh then collaborated with French colonial forces to massacre supporters of the Vietnamese nationalist movements in 1945–1946, and of the Trotskyists. Trotskyism in Vietnam did not rival the Party outside of the major cities, but particularly in the South, in Saigon-Cochinchina, they had been a challenge. From the outset, they had called for armed resistance to a French restoration and for an immediate transfer of industry to workers and land to peasants. The French Socialist leader Daniel Guérin recalls that when in Paris in 1946 he asked Hồ Chí Minh about the fate of the Trotskyist leader Tạ Thu Thâu, Hồ Chí Minh had replied, "with unfeigned emotion," that "Thâu was a great patriot and we mourn him, but then a moment later added in a steady voice 'All those who do not follow the line which I have laid down will be broken.'" The Communists eventually suppressed all non-Communist parties, but they failed to secure a peace deal with France. In the final days of 1946, after a year of diplomatic failure and many concessions in agreements, such as the Dalat and Fontainebleau conferences, the Democratic Republic of Vietnam government found that war was inevitable. The bombardment of Haiphong by French forces at Hanoi only strengthened the belief that France had no intention of allowing an autonomous, independent state in Vietnam. The bombardment of Haiphong reportedly killed more than 6000 Vietnamese civilians. French forces marched into Hanoi, now the capital city of the Socialist Republic of Vietnam. On 19 December 1946, after the Haiphong incident, Ho Chi Minh declared war against the French Union, marking the beginning of the Indochina War. The Vietnam National Army, mostly armed with machetes and muskets immediately attacked. They assaulted the French positions, smoking them out with straw bundled with chili pepper, destroying armored vehicles with "lunge mines" (a hollow-charge warhead on the end of a pole, detonated by thrusting the charge against the side of a tank; typically a suicide weapon) and Molotov cocktails, holding off attackers by using roadblocks, landmines and gravel. After two months of fighting, the exhausted Việt Minh forces withdrew after systematically destroying any valuable infrastructure. Ho was reported to be captured by a group of French soldiers led by Jean Étienne Valluy at Việt Bắc in Operation Léa. The person in question turned out to be a Việt Minh advisor who was killed trying to escape. According to journalist Bernard Fall, Ho decided to negotiate a truce after fighting the French for several years. When the French negotiators arrived at the meeting site, they found a mud hut with a thatched roof. Inside they found a long table with chairs. In one corner of the room, a silver ice bucket contained ice and a bottle of good champagne, indicating that Ho expected the negotiations to succeed. One demand by the French was the return to French custody of a number of Japanese military officers (who had been helping the Vietnamese armed forces by training them in the use of weapons of Japanese origin) for them to stand trial for war crimes committed during World War II. Hồ Chí Minh replied that the Japanese officers were allies and friends whom he could not betray, therefore he walked out to seven more years of war. In February 1950, after the successful removal of the French border blockade, he met with Joseph Stalin and Mao Zedong in Moscow after the Soviet Union recognized his government. They all agreed that China would be responsible for backing the Việt Minh. Mao Zedong's emissary to Moscow stated in August that China planned to train 60,000–70,000 Viet Minh in the near future.[69] The road to the outside world was open for Việt Minh forces to receive additional supplies which would allow them to escalate the fight against the French regime throughout Indochina. At the outset of the conflict, Ho reportedly told a French visitor: "You can kill ten of my men for everyone I kill of yours. But even at those odds, you will lose and I will win". In 1954, the First Indochina War came to an end after the decisive Battle of Dien Bien Phu, where more than 10,000 French soldiers surrendered to the Viet Minh. The subsequent Geneva Accords peace process partitioned North Vietnam at the 17th parallel. Arthur Dommen estimates that the Việt Minh assassinated between 50,000 and 100,000 civilians during the war. By comparison to Dommen's calculation, Benjamin Valentino estimates that the French were responsible for 60,000–250,000 civilian deaths.

Becoming President: The 1954 Geneva Accords concluded between France and the Việt Minh, allowing the latter's forces to regroup in the North whilst anti-Communist groups settled in the South. His Democratic Republic of Vietnam relocated to Hanoi and became the government of North Vietnam, a Communist-led one-party state. Following the Geneva Accords, there was to be a 300-day period in which people could freely move between the two regions of Vietnam, later known as South Vietnam and North Vietnam. During the 300 days, Diệm and CIA adviser Colonel Edward Lansdale staged a campaign to convince people to move to South Vietnam. The campaign was particularly focused on Vietnam's Catholics, who were to provide Diệm's power base in his later years, with the use of the slogan "God has gone south". Between 800,000 and 1,000,000 people migrated to the South, mostly Catholics. At the start of 1955, French Indochina was dissolved, leaving Diệm in temporary control of the South. All the parties at Geneva called for reunification elections, but they could not agree on the details. Recently appointed Việt Minh acting foreign minister Pham Van Dong proposed elections under the supervision of "local commissions". The United States, with the support of Britain and the Associated States of Vietnam, Laos and Cambodia, suggested United Nations supervision. This plan was rejected by Soviet representative Vyacheslav Molotov, who argued for a commission composed of an equal number of communist and non-communist members, which could determine "important" issues only by unanimous agreement. The negotiators were unable to agree on a date for the elections for reunification. North Vietnam argued that the elections should be held within six months of the ceasefire while the Western allies sought to have no deadline. Molotov proposed June 1955, then later softened this to any time in 1955 and finally July 1956. The Diem government supported reunification elections, but only with effective international supervision, arguing that genuinely free elections were otherwise impossible in the totalitarian North. By the afternoon of 20 July, the remaining outstanding issues were resolved as the parties agreed that the partition line should be at the 17th parallel and the elections for a reunified government should be held in July 1956, two years after the ceasefire. The Agreement on the Cessation of Hostilities in Vietnam was only signed by the French and Việt Minh military commands, with no participation or consultation of the State of Vietnam. Based on a proposal by Chinese delegation head Zhou Enlai, an International Control Commission (ICC) chaired by India, with Canada and Poland as members, was placed in charge of supervising the ceasefire. Because issues were to be decided unanimously, Poland's presence in the ICC provided the Communists with effective veto power over supervision of the treaty. The unsigned Final Declaration of the Geneva Conference called for reunification elections, which the majority of delegates expected to be supervised by the ICC. The Việt Minh never accepted ICC authority over such elections, insisting that the ICC's "competence was to be limited to the supervision and control of the implementation of the Agreement on the Cessation of Hostilities by both parties". Of the nine nations represented, only the United States and the State of Vietnam refused to accept the declaration. Undersecretary of state Walter Bedell Smith delivered a "unilateral declaration" of the United States position, reiterating: "We shall seek to achieve unity through free elections supervised by the United Nations to ensure that they are conducted fairly".

Between 1953 and 1956, the North Vietnamese government instituted various agrarian reforms, including "rent reduction" and "land reform", which were accompanied by significant political repression. During the land reform, testimonies by North Vietnamese witnesses suggested a ratio of one execution for every 160 village residents, which if extrapolated would indicate a nationwide total of nearly 100,000 executions. Because the campaign was mainly concentrated in the Red River Delta area, a lower estimate of 50,000 executions was widely accepted by scholars at the time. However, declassified documents from the Vietnamese and Hungarian archives indicate that the number of executions was much lower than reported at the time, although it was likely greater than 13,500.

The Vietnam War: As early as June 1956 the idea of overthrowing the South Vietnamese government was presented at a politburo meeting. In 1959, Hồ Chí Minh began urging the Politburo to send aid to the Việt Cộng in South Vietnam; a "people's war" on the South was approved at a session in January 1959, and this decision was confirmed by the Politburo in March. North Vietnam invaded Laos in July 1959 aided by the Pathet Lao and used 30,000 men to build a network of supply and reinforcement routes running through Laos and Cambodia that became known as the Hồ Chí Minh trail. It allowed the North to send manpower and material to the Việt Cộng with much less exposure to South Vietnamese forces, achieving a considerable advantage. To counter the accusation that North Vietnam was violating the Geneva Accord, the independence of the Việt Cộng was stressed in Communist propaganda. North Vietnam created the National Liberation Front of South Vietnam in December 1960 as a "united front", or political branch of the Viet Cong intended to encourage the participation of non-Communists. At the end of 1959, conscious that the national election would never be held and that Diem intended to purge opposing forces (mostly ex Việt Minh) from the South Vietnamese society, Hồ Chí Minh informally chose Lê Duẩn to become the next party leader. This was interpreted by Western analysts as a loss of influence for Hồ, who was said to actually have preferred the more moderate Võ

Nguyên Giáp for the position. From 1959 onward, the elderly Ho became increasingly worried about the prospect of his death, and that year he wrote down his will. Lê Duẩn was officially named party leader in 1960, leaving Hồ to function in a secondary role as head of state and member of the Politburo. He nevertheless maintained considerable influence in the government. Lê Duẩn, Tố Hữu, Trường Chinh and Phạm Văn Đồng often shared dinner with Hồ, and all of them remained key figures throughout and after the war. In the early 1960s, the North Vietnamese Politburo was divided into the "North first" faction who favored focusing on the economic development of North Vietnam, and the "South first" faction, who favored a guerrilla war in South Vietnam to reunite Vietnam in the near future.

Between 1961 and 1963, 40,000 Communist soldiers infiltrated into South Vietnam from the North. In 1963, Hồ purportedly corresponded with South Vietnamese President Diem in hopes of achieving a negotiated peace.[97] During the so-called "Maneli Affair" of 1963, a French diplomatic initiative was launched with the aim of achieving a federation of the two Vietnams, which would be neutral in the Cold War.[98] The four principle diplomats involved in the "Maneli affair" were Ramchundur Goburdhun, the Indian Chief Commissioner of the ICC; Mieczysław Maneli, the Polish Commissioner to the ICC; Roger Lalouette, the French ambassador to South Vietnam; and Giovanni d'Orlandi, the Italian ambassador to South Vietnam. Maneli reported that Ho was very interested in the signs of a split between President Diem and President Kennedy and that his attitude was: "Our real enemies are the Americans. Get rid them, and we can cope with Diem and Nhu afterward". At a meeting in Hanoi held in French, Ho told Goburdhun that Diem was "in his own way a patriot", noting that Diem had opposed French rule over Vietnam, and ended the meeting saying that the next time Goburdhun met Diem "shake hands with him for me". The North Vietnamese Premier Phạm Văn Đồng, speaking on behalf of Ho, told Maneli he was interested in the peace plan, saying that just as long as the American advisers left South Vietnam "we can come to an agreement with any Vietnamese". On 2 September 1963, Maneli met with Ngô Đình Nhu, the younger brother and right-hand man to Diem to discuss the French peace plan. It remains unclear if the

Ngo brothers were serious about the French peace plan or were merely using the possibility of accepting it to blackmail the United States into supporting them at a time when the Buddhist crisis had seriously strained relations between Saigon and Washington. Supporting the latter theory is the fact that Nhu promptly leaked his meeting with Maneli to the American columnist Joseph Alsop, who publicized it in a column entitled "Very Ugly Stuff". The mere possibility that the Ngo brothers might accept the peace plan helped persuade the Kennedy administration to support the coup against them. On 1 November 1963, a coup overthrow Diem, who was killed the next day together with his brother. Diem had followed a policy of "deconstructing the state" by creating a number of overlapping agencies and departments who were encouraged to feud with one another in order to disorganize the South Vietnamese state to such an extent that he hoped that it would make a coup against him impossible. When Diem was overthrown and killed, without any kind of arbiter between the rival arms of the South Vietnamese state, South Vietnam promptly disintegrated. The American Defense Secretary Robert McNamara reported after visiting South Vietnam in December 1963 that "there is no organized government worthy of the name" in Saigon. At a meeting of the plenum of the Politburo in December 1963, Lê Duẩn's "South first" faction triumphed with the Politburo passing a resolution calling for North Vietnam to complete the overthrow of the regime in Saigon as soon as possible while the members of the "North first" faction were dismissed. As South Vietnam descended into chaos, whatever interest Ho might have in the French peace plan ended as it become clear it was possible for the Viet Cong to overthrow the government in Saigon. A CIA report from 1964 stated the factionalism in South Vietnam had reached "almost the point of anarchy" as various South Vietnamese leaders fought one another, making any sort of effort against the Viet Cong impossible, which was rapidly taking over much of the South Vietnamese countryside.

As South Vietnam collapsed into factionalism and in-fighting while the Viet Cong continued to win the war, it became increasingly apparent to President Lyndon Johnson that only American military intervention could save South Vietnam. Though Johnson did not wish to commit American forces until he had won the 1964 election, he decided to make his intentions clear to Hanoi. In June 1964, the "Seaborn Mission" began as J. Blair Seaborn, the Canadian commissioner to the ICC, arrived in Hanoi with a message from Johnson offering billions of American economic aid and diplomatic recognition in exchange for which North Vietnam would cease trying to overthrow the government of South Vietnam. Seaborn also warned that North Vietnam would suffer the "greatest devastation" from American bombing, saying that Johnson was seriously considering a strategic bombing campaign against North Vietnam. Little came of the back channel of the "Seaborn Mission" as the North Vietnamese distrusted Seaborn, who pointedly was never allowed to meet Ho. In late 1964, People's Army of Vietnam (PAVN) combat troops were sent southwest into officially neutral Laos and Cambodia. By March 1965, American combat troops began arriving in South Vietnam, first to protect the airbases around Chu Lai and Da Nang, later to take on most of the fight as "[m]ore and more American troops were put in to replace Saigon troops who could not, or would not, get involved in the fighting". As fighting escalated, widespread aerial and artillery bombardment all over North Vietnam by the United States Air Force and Navy began with Operation Rolling Thunder. On 8–9 April 1965, Ho made a secret visit to Beijing to meet Mao Zedong. It was agreed that no Chinese combat troops would enter North Vietnam unless the United States invaded North Vietnam, but that China would send support troops to North Vietnam to help maintain the infrastructure damaged by American bombing. There was a deep distrust and fear of China within the North Vietnamese Politburo, and the suggestion that Chinese troops, even support troops, be allowed into North Vietnam, caused outrage in the Politburo. Ho had to use all his moral authority to obtain the Politburo's approval. According to Chen Jian, during the mid-to-late 1960s, Lê Duẩn permitted 320,000 Chinese volunteers into North Vietnam to help build infrastructure for the country, thereby freeing a similar number of PAVN personnel to go south. There are no sources from Vietnam, the United States, or the Soviet Union that confirm the number of Chinese troops stationed in North Vietnam. However, the Chinese government later admitted to sending 320,000 Chinese soldiers to Vietnam during the 1960s and spent over $20 billion to support Hanoi's regular North Vietnamese Army and Việt Cộng guerrilla units.

To counter the American bombing, the entire population of North Vietnam was mobilized for the war effort with vast teams of women being used to repair the damage done by the bombers, often at a speed that astonished the Americans. The bombing of North Vietnam proved to be the principal obstacle to opening peace talks as Ho repeatedly stated that no peace talks would be possible unless the United States unconditionally cease bombing North Vietnam. Like many of the other leaders of the newly independent states of Asia and Africa, Ho was extremely sensitive about threats, whether perceived or real, to his nation's independence and sovereignty. Ho regarded the American bombing as a violation of North Vietnam's sovereignty, and he felt that to negotiate with the Americans reserving the right to bomb North Vietnam should he not behave as they wanted him to do, would diminish North Vietnam's independence. In March 1966, a Canadian diplomat, Chester Ronning, arrived in Hanoi with an offer to use his "good offices" to begin peace talks. However, the Ronning mission foundered upon the bombing issue, as the North Vietnamese demanded an unconditional halt to the bombing, an undertaking that Johnson refused to give. In June 1966, Janusz Lewandowski, the Polish Commissioner to the ICC, was able via d'Orlandi to see Henry Cabot Lodge Jr, the American ambassador to South Vietnam, with an offer from Ho. Ho's offer for a "political compromise" as transmitted by Lewandowski included allowing South Vietnam to maintain its alliance with the U.S, instead of becoming neutral; having the Viet Cong "take part" in negotiations for a coalition government, instead of being allowed to automatically enter a coalition government; and allowing a "reasonable calendar" for the withdrawal of American troops instead of an immediate withdrawal.[120] Operation Marigold as the Lewandowski channel came to be code-named almost led to American-North Vietnamese talks in Warsaw in December 1966, but collapsed over the bombing issue.

In January 1967, General Nguyễn Chí Thanh, the commander of the forces in South Vietnam, returned to Hanoi, to present a plan that became the genesis of the Tet Offensive a year later. Thanh expressed much concern about the Americans invading Laos to cut the Ho Chi Minh Trail, and to preempt this possibility, urged an all-out offensive to win the war with a sudden blow. Lê

Duẩn supported Thanh's plans, which were stoutly opposed by the Defense Minister, General Võ Nguyên Giáp, who preferred to continue with a guerrilla war, arguing that the superior American firepower would ensure the failure of Thanh's proposed offensive. With the Politburo divided, it was agreed to study and debate the issue more. In July 1967, Hồ Chí Minh and most of the Politburo of the Communist Party met in a high-profile conference where they concluded the war had fallen into a stalemate. The American military presence forced the PAVN to expend the majority of their resources on maintaining the Hồ Chí Minh trail rather than reinforcing their comrades' ranks in the South. Ho seems to have agreed to Thanh's offensive because he wanted to see Vietnam reunified within his lifetime, and the increasingly ailing Ho was painfully aware that he did not have much time left. With Ho's permission, the Việt Cộng planned a massive Tet Offensive that would commence on 31 January 1968, with the aim of taking much of the South by force and dealing a heavy blow to the American military. The offensive was executed at great cost and with heavy casualties on Việt Cộng's political branches and armed forces. The scope of the action shocked the world, which until then had been assured that the Communists were "on the ropes". The optimistic spin that the American military command had sustained for years was no longer credible. The bombing of North Vietnam and the Hồ Chí Minh trail was halted, and American and Vietnamese negotiators held discussions on how the war might be ended. From then on, Hồ Chí Minh and his government's strategy, based on the idea of not using conventional warfare and facing the might of the United States Army, which would wear them down eventually while merely prolonging the conflict, would lead to eventual acceptance of Hanoi's terms, materialized.

In early 1969, Ho suffered a heart attack and was in increasingly bad health for the rest of the year. In July 1969, Jean Sainteny, a former French official in Vietnam who knew Ho secretly relayed a letter to him from President Richard Nixon. Nixon's letter proposed working together to end this "tragic war", but also warned that if North Vietnam made no concessions at the peace talks in Paris by 1 November, Nixon would resort to "measures of great consequence and force". Ho's reply, which Nixon received on 30 August 1969 made no concessions, as Nixon's threats apparently made no impression on him.

Personal life

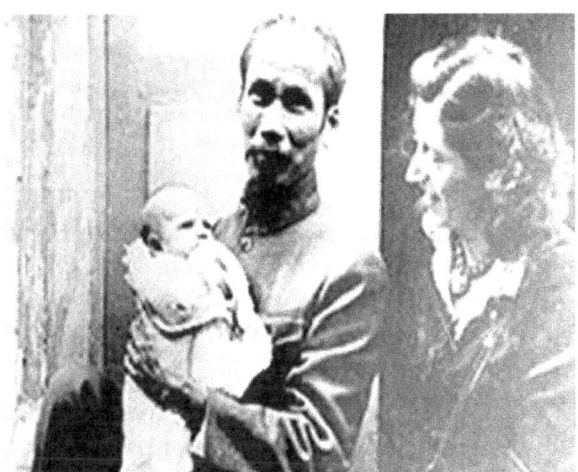

*Hồ Chí Minh holding his god-daughter, baby Elizabeth (Babette) Aubrac,
with Elizabeth's mother, Lucie, 1946*

In addition to being a politician, Hồ Chí Minh was also a
writer, journalist, poet and polyglot. His father was a scholar
and teacher who received a high degree in the Nguyễn
dynasty Imperial examination. Hồ was taught to master Classical
Chinese at a young age. Before the August Revolution, he often
wrote poetry in Chữ Hán (the Vietnamese name for the Chinese
writing system). One of those is *Poems from the Prison Diary*,
written when he was imprisoned by the police of the Republic
of China. This poetry chronicle is Vietnam National Treasure
No. 10 and was translated into many languages. It is used in
Vietnamese high schools. After Vietnam gained independence
from France, the new government exclusively promoted Chữ
Quốc Ngữ (Vietnamese writing system in Latin characters)
to eliminate illiteracy. Hồ started to create more poems in the
modern Vietnamese language for dissemination to a wider range
of readers. From when he became president until the appearance
of serious health problems, a short poem of his was regularly
published in the newspaper *Nhân Dân* Tết (Lunar new year)
edition to encourage his people in working, studying or fighting
Americans in the new year.

Because he was in exile for nearly 30 years, Hồ could speak
fluently as well as read and write professionally in French,

English, Russian, Cantonese and Mandarin as well as his mother tongue Vietnamese. In addition, he was reported to speak conversational Esperanto. In the 1920s, he was bureau chief/editor of many newspapers which he established to criticize French Colonial Government of Indochina and serving communism propaganda purposes. Examples are *Le Paria* (The Pariah) first published in Paris 1922 or *Thanh Nien* (Youth) first published on 21 June 1925 (21 June was named by The Socialist Republic of Vietnam Government as *Vietnam Revolutionary Journalism Day*). In many state official visits to the Soviet Union and China, he often talked directly to their communist leaders without interpreters especially about top secret information. While being interviewed by Western journalists, he used French. His Vietnamese had a strong accent from his birthplace in the central province of Nghệ An, but could be widely understood throughout the country. As President, he held formal receptions for foreign heads of state and ambassadors at the Presidential Palace, but he personally did not live there. He ordered the building of a stilt house at the back of the palace, which is today known as the Presidential Palace Historical Site. His hobbies (according to his secretary Vũ Kỳ) included reading, gardening, feeding fish (many of which are still living) and visiting schools and children's homes. He is believed by some to have married Zeng Xueming, although only being able to live with her for less than a year. Hồ Chí Minh remained in Hanoi during his final years, demanding the unconditional withdrawal of all non-Vietnamese troops in South Vietnam. By 1969, with negotiations still dragging on, his health began to deteriorate from multiple health problems, including diabetes which prevented him from participating in further active politics. However, he insisted that his forces in the South continue fighting until all of Vietnam was reunited regardless of the length of time that it might take, believing that time was on his side.

Death: With the outcome of the Vietnam War still in question, Hồ Chí Minh died of heart failure at his home in Hanoi at 9:47 on the morning of 2 September 1969; he was 79 years old. His embalmed body is currently on display in a mausoleum in Ba Đình Square in Hanoi despite his will which stated that he wanted to be cremated. The North Vietnamese government originally announced Ho's death as 3 September. A week of mourning for his death was decreed nationwide in North Vietnam from 4 to 11 September 1969. His funeral was attended by about 250,000 people and 5,000 official guests, which included many international mourners. Representatives from 40 countries and regions were also presented. During the mourning period, North Vietnam received more than 22,000 condolences letters from 20 organizations and 110 countries across the world, such as France, Ethiopia, Yugoslavia, Cuba, Zambia, and many others, mostly Socialist countries.

Hồ Chí Minh watching a football game in his favorite fashion, with his closest comrade Prime Minister Phạm Văn Đồng seated to Ho's left (photo right)

It was said that Ho's body was hidden, and carried a long way among forests and rivers in a special-designed coffin until Ho Chi Minh Mausoleum was built. He was not initially replaced as president; instead, a "collective leadership" composed of several ministers and military leaders took over, known as the Politburo. During North Vietnam's final campaign, a famous song written by composer Huy Thuc [vi] was often sung by PAVN soldiers: "Bác vẫn cùng chúng cháu hành quân" ("You are still marching with us, Uncle Ho"). During the Fall of Saigon in April 1975, several PAVN tanks displayed a poster with those same words on it. The day after the battle ended, on 1 May, veteran Australian journalist Denis Warner reported that "When the North Vietnamese marched into Saigon yesterday, they were led by a man who wasn't there".

Legacy Ho Chi Minh remains a major figure in modern contemporary history: The Socialist Republic of Vietnam still praises the legacy of Uncle Ho (*Bác Hô*), the Bringer of Light (*Chí Minh*). It is comparable in many ways to that of Mao Zedong in China and of Kim Il-sung and Kim Jong-il in North Korea. There is the embalmed body on view in a massive mausoleum, the ubiquity of his image featured in every public building and schoolroom, and other displays of reverence, some unofficial,

Hô Chí Minh statue and a yellow star as depicted in the Vietnamese flag

that verge on "worship". (Ho Chi Minh's image appears on some family altars, and there is at least one temple dedicated to him, built in then-Việt-Cộng-controlled Vĩnh Long shortly after his death in 1970).

Hô Chí Minh statue outside Hô Chí Minh City

In *The Communist Road to Power in Vietnam* (1982), Duiker suggests that the cult of Ho Chi Minh is indicative of a larger legacy, one that drew on "elements traditional to the exercise of control and authority in Vietnamese society." Duiker is drawn to an "irresistible and persuasive" comparison with China. As in China, leading party cadres were "most likely to be intellectuals descended [like Ho Chi Minh] from rural scholar-gentry families" in the interior (the protectorates of Annam and Tonkin). Conversely, the pioneers of constitutional nationalism tended to be from the more "Westernized" coastal south (Saigon and surrounding French direct-rule Cochinchina) and to be from "commercial families without a traditional Confucian background".

Ho Chi Minh Mausoleum, Hanoi

Shrine devoted to Hồ Chí Minh: In Vietnam, as in China, Communism presented itself as a root and branch rejection of Confucianism, condemned for its ritualism, inherent conservatism and resistance to change. Once in power, the Vietnamese Communists may not have fought Confucianism "as bitterly as did their Chinese counterparts", but its social prestige was "essentially destroyed." In the political sphere, the puppet son of heaven (which had been weakly represented by the Bảo Đại) was replaced by the people's republic. Orthodox materialism accorded no place to heaven, gods, or other supernatural forces. Socialist collectivism undermined the tradition of the Confucian family leader (*gia truong*). The socialist conception of social equality destroyed the Confucian views of class. Yet Duiker argues many were to find the new ideology "congenial" precisely because of its similarities with the teachings of the old Master: "the belief in one truth, embodied in quasi-sacred texts";

in "an anointed elite, trained in an all-embracing doctrine and responsible for leading the broad masses and indoctrinating them in proper thought and behavior"; in "the subordination of the individual to the community"; and in the perfectibility, through corrective action, of human nature. All of this, Duiker suggests, was in some manner present in the aura of the new Master, Chi Minh, "the bringer of light," "Uncle Ho" to whom "all the desirable qualities of Confucian ethics" are ascribed. Under Ho Chi Minh, Vietnamese Marxism developed, in effect, as a kind of "reformed Confucianism" revised to meet "the challenges of the modern era" and, not least among these, of "total mobilization in the struggle for national independence and state power."

This "congeniality" with Confucian tradition was remarked on by Nguyen Khac Vien, a leading Hanoi intellectual of the 1960s and 70s. In *Confucianism and Marxism in Vietnam* Nguyen Khac Vien, saw definite parallels between Confucian and party discipline, between the traditional scholar gentry and Ho Chi Minh's party cadres. A completely different form of the cult of Hồ Chí Minh (and one tolerated by the government with some uneasiness) is his identification in Vietnamese folk religion with the Jade Emperor, who supposedly incarnated again on earth as Hồ Chí Minh. Today Hồ Chí Minh as the Jade Emperor is supposed to speak from the spirit world through Spiritualist mediums. The first such medium was one Madam Lang in the 1990s, but the cult acquired a significant number of followers through another medium, Madam Xoan. She established on 1 January 2001 Đạo Ngọc Phật Hồ Chí Minh (the Way of Hồ Chí Minh as the Jade Buddha) also known as Đạo Bác Hồ (the Way of Uncle Hồ) at đền Hòa Bình (the Peace Temple) in Chí Linh-Sao Đỏ district of Hải Dương province. She then founded the Peace Society of Heavenly Mediums (Đoàn đồng thiên Hòa Bình). Reportedly, by 2014 the movement had around 24,000 followers. Yet even when the Vietnamese government's attempt to immortalize Ho Chi Minh was also met with significant controversies and opposition. The regime is sensitive to anything that might question the official hagiography. This includes references to Ho Chi Minh's personal life that might detract from the image of the dedicated "the father of the revolution", the "celibate married only to the cause of revolution". William Duiker's *Ho Chi Minh: A Life* (2000) was candid on the matter of Ho Chi Minh's liaisons. The government sought cuts in a Vietnamese translation and banned distribution of an issue of the *Far Eastern Economic Review* which carried a small item about the controversy.

Depictions of Ho Chi Minh: Busts, statues and memorial plaques and exhibitions are displayed in destinations on his extensive world journey in exile from 1911 to 1941 including France, Great Britain, Russia, China and Thailand. Many activists and musicians wrote songs about Hồ Chí Minh and his revolution in different languages during the Vietnam War to demonstrate against the United States. Spanish songs were composed by Félix Pita Rodríguez, Carlos Puebla and Alí Primera. In addition, the Chilean folk singer Víctor Jara referenced Hồ Chí Minh in his anti-war song "El derecho de vivir en paz" ("The Right to Live in Peace"). Pete Seeger wrote "Teacher Uncle Ho". Ewan MacColl produced The Ballad of Ho Chi Minh in 1954, describing " a man who is father of the Indo-Chinese people, And his name it is Ho Chi Minh." Russian songs about him were written by Vladimir Fere and German songs about him were written by Kurt Demmler. Various places, boulevards and squares are named after him around the world, especially in Socialist states and former Communist states. In Russia, there is a Hồ Chí Minh square and monument in Moscow, Hồ Chí Minh boulevard in Saint Petersburg and Hồ Chí Minh square in Ulyanovsk (the birthplace of Vladimir Lenin, a sister city of Vinh, the birthplace of Hồ Chí Minh). During the Vietnam War the then West Bengal government, in the hands of CPI(M), renamed Harrington Street to Ho Chi Minh Sarani, which is also the location of the Consulate General of the United States of America in Kolkata. According to the Vietnamese Ministry of Foreign Affairs, as many as 20 countries across Asia, Europe, America and Africa have erected statues in remembrance of President Hồ Chí Minh.

Hồ Chí Minh is considered one of the most influential leaders in the world. *Time* magazine listed him in the list of 100 Most Important People of the Twentieth Century (*Time* 100) in 1998. His thought and revolution inspired many leaders and people on a global scale in Asia, Africa and Latin America during the decolonization movement which occurred after World

War II. As a communist, he was one of the international figures who were highly praised in the Communist world. In 1987, UNESCO officially recommended that its member states "join in the commemoration of the centenary of the birth of President Hồ Chí Minh by organizing various events as a tribute to his memory", considering "the important and many-sided contributions of President Hồ Chí Minh to the fields of culture, education and the arts" who "devoted his whole life to the national liberation of the Vietnamese people, contributing to the common struggle of peoples for peace, national independence, democracy and social progress".

Yes, this is the truth. Ho Chi Minh/Ho Quang (Chinese) was born 1901. Nguyen Ai Quoc (Vietnamese) was born 1890. This is a fact now.

A Vietnamese professor teaching in Taiwan named Hồ Tuấn Hùng has popularized this theory in his 2008 book Hồ Chí Minh Sinh Bình Khảo. Why has it gained traction? Because the current tension in the South China Sea / East Sea as well as contentious issues related to Chinese bauxite mines in Vietnam has brought increased attention to the Vietnamese Communist Party's close relationship with the Chinese

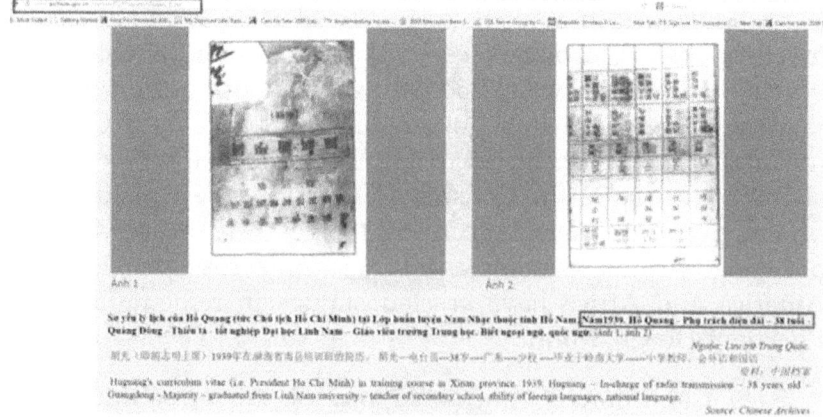

Sơ yếu lý lịch của Hồ Quang (tức Chủ tịch Hồ Chí Minh) tại Lớp huấn luyện Nam Nhạc thuộc tỉnh Hồ Nam [Năm1939. Hồ Quang - Phụ trách điện đài - 38 tuổi] Quảng Đông - Thiếu tá - tốt nghiệp Đại học Linh Nam - Giáo viên trường Trung học. Biết ngoại ngữ, quốc ngữ. (Ảnh 1, ảnh 2)

Nguồn: Lưu trữ Trung Quốc.

Huguang's curriculum vitae (i.e. President Ho Chi Minh) in training course in Xinan province. 1939. Huguang - In-charge of radio transmission - 38 years old - Guangdong - Majority - graduated from Linh Nam university - teacher of secondary school, ability of foreign languages, national language.

Source: Chinese Archives.

A Vietnamese professor teaching in Taiwan named Hồ Tuấn Hùng has popularized this theory in his 2008 book Hồ Chí Minh Sinh Bình Khảo. Why has it gained traction? Because the current tension in the South China Sea / East Sea as well as contentious issues related to Chinese bauxite mines in Vietnam has brought increased attention to the Vietnamese Communist Party's close relationship with the Chinese Communist Party. They are tapping into this anti-Chinese sentiment both among Vietnamese in Vietnam and abroad.

According to them, there is the Hồ Chí Minh/Nguyễn Ái Quốc that was an active revolutionary in France and southern China until the early 1930s. Hồ was arrested by the Chinese Kuomintang government and while he was imprisoned fell ill with tuberculosis. Rumors of his death appeared in both the Vietnamese press in Vietnam and France. You can find headlines declaring 'Nguyễn Ái Quốc is dead!' during this time.

So, these authors say that a Chinese imposter was the Hồ Chí Minh was the one that led the DRV government after 1945. They call him Hồ Chú Ba Tàu, which is difficult to translate into English but essentially means the 'Chinese Hồ'.

After Hồ Chí Minh was freed from jail in 1932/1933, he went to study at the Comintern in the Soviet Union. However, the above author says Hồ is already dead. Instead an official named Vera Vasilieva took a Chinese man named Hồ Tập Chương and trained him for five years to become a perfect copy of the real Hồ.

They use this theory to explain the Vietnamese relationship with Mao and communist China. It is true that Ho and the communist party were subordinate to the Chinese, and carried out a bloody land reform campaign based on a near copy of Chinese land reform. Chinese advisor controlled many parts of the program in Vietnam. But the explanation for this is that Hồ and the communists very much wanted membership in the communist bloc and the support they could offer them in their fight against France and the non-communist State of Vietnam. Land reform and other programs were necessary to join Mao and Zhou Enlai (who had to vouch for Hồ and the Vietnamese before Stalin fully accepted them as allies).

There are other myths about Hồ, both ones intended to valorize or denounce him. One example is that communist party historians say that Hồ led peasant tax protests in 1908 and was thus expelled from the Quốc Học school in Huế, before fleeing the colonial police and going to Saigon. This is false. Hồ was not even enrolled during the protests. Conversely, non-communist Vietnamese popularized a theory that Hồ had betrayed Phan Bội Châu to the French police to earn a monetary reward. Though Hồ and Châu were rivals at this time, the evidence all points to someone else having betrayed Châu. You can probably guess that authors ideologically opposed to Hồ and the Vietnamese Communist Party do not care for that evidence. They continue to say that Hồ betrayed Châu.

Another reason why this theory is accepted by overseas Vietnamese (not by historians, though) is because there is and was a cult of personality around Hồ. Many myths and larger than life ideas were propagated by the party. Still today students in Vietnam must study Hồ Chí Minh Thought is schools. So, for example, despite the party saying Hồ was a celibate figure devoted totally to the nation, he had several wives. Yet a professor in Vietnam who mentioned this recently was demoted as punishment. You can see how people having learned about fabrications like that are quick to embrace any theory that breaks down the cult of Hồ and the party.

TL;DR: Hồ was rumored to have died in China in 1932. He did not. Vietnamese writers ideologically opposed to the communist party use this theory to discredit the party and--midst tensions as China expands its presence in the South China Sea--to heighten criticisms of the Vietnamese communist party's close relationship to China.

For the best book on Hồ in this period see Sophie Quinn Judge, Ho Chi Minh: The Missing Years, 1919-1941 (Berkeley: UC Press, 2003).

Ho Chi Minh is a difficult figure to analyze because he deliberately cultivated at least two different personalities. The first was of the kindly, elder nationalist and father to the nation. But he also was a committed communist internationalist. He was both. Not one or the either. But, this is precisely why the Indochinese Communist Party chose him as their leader. Men like Tran Phu and Truong Chinh, ('Long March') were committed internationalists that would alienate potential non-communist allies.

The debate about Ho Chi Minh is tied up in the politics of the war. In the late 1960s-70s scholars opposed to the Vietnam War, consciously and subconsciously, used their scholarship on Vietnam as a means to oppose American policies in Indochina. Following the orientalist work of a French scholar Paul Mus, Frances Fitzgerald wrote Fire in the Lake. This became the 'Orthodox' view of the war. Ho Chi Minh represented the only authentic nationalism in Vietnam, combining nationalism with Confucian values. He and other Vietnamese had adopted communism only as a means to liberate their country. But they were not really communists. All Vietnamese understood this, and therefore the artificial South Vietnamese regime and US were fighting against the course of history. At the same time, there were writers like Douglas Pike producing much more critical studies of Vietnamese communism that supported US policies. More recently, a 'Revisionist' group of writers, most well known in Mark Moyar's Triumph Forsaken, that argues that Washington had it right all along. Their policies in Vietnam were wrong, only in that they gave up too soon. Ho was just a brutal autocrat.

Both views are inadequate. Frances Fitzgerald and the Orthodox view is orientalist and simplistic. It's rather insulting to Ho and other Vietnamese. They were intelligent, rational, and believed in socialist modernity -- to say they chose communism because it was their only choice is false and insulting. And the Revisionist view of Ho as communist Asian despot is just as simplistic and problematic.

Before I get to Ho's actions, I want to note that during the period you reference in your question, the American period of Vietnam's civil war from ~1965-1972, Ho Chi Minh was only a figurehead. He held no real power. It was a man from southern Vietnam named Le Duan who held control. Le Duan was transparently aggressive both in escalating the Vietnam war, and domestically against opponents in the communist Vietnamese Workers Party that opposed his war in South Vietnam. Ho at this time was limited to making public trips to visit allies like Mao, Kim Il-Sung, etc, serving as the regime's kind public face, and little else. But he chose to continue on as the figure head.

However, Ho was never all powerful, not even in the 1940s. He faced strong domestic pressure from the Indochinese Communist Party (ICP) members who wanted a more communist regime from the start. Ho's ambassador to France, Tran Ngoc Danh, even defected to the Soviet bloc and wrote scathing reports to the USSR citing Ho's lack of commitment to communism. There were factions inside Vietnam opposed to Ho's attempts to form a united front that could attract non-communists as well.

This would soon change after 1949. But first, I want to note that the Viet Minh front group, run by the ICP, was indeed brutal towards its opponents. From the moment the Vietnamese civil war began in 1945, before the French returned, the ICP was killing Vietnamese rivals (and some of their rivals were killing ICP and Viet Minh). Many were executed in the first weeks, and fighting between the Viet Minh and rival religious and political groups persisted. Ho was complicit in this, but certainly was not deeply involved, and in some cases would have opposed it. Local ICP leaders were often running their own show. While Ho was in Paris negotiating in 1946, Vo Nguyen Giap attacked the armed forces of non-communist revolutionary groups (with the complicity of the French army). After that point, there was no real opposition to the ICP within the revolutionary Democratic Republic of Vietnam (DRV) government.

The other main charge against Ho comes from the bloody land reform that took place in 1953-54. After 1949, China began supplying the DRV with weapons and advisors. Not long after China and the USSR formally recognized Ho's government. No longer needing the support of the non-communists in the countryside, the ICP came back into the open as the Vietnam Workers Party (VWP) and began instituting communist policies. Much control was ceded to the Chinese 'experts', who guided the VWP's policies and held ultimate control. But the VWP was also an enthusiastic participant, eager to embark on its path to modernization.

The land reform was a vicious affair. Based on the Chinese land reform model, a set percentage of the Vietnamese population was determined to be exploitative landowners. Cadres went into the countryside and met this quota. They incited the population to denounce landowners, coached their opinions. After this a staged trial took place under portraits of Stalin, Mao, and Ho. The cadres then carried out a death sentence on behalf of the people. The method varied, sometimes employing a sword or gun, in some cases people were burned alive. Even revolutionary figures who had owned land were targeted. A woman named Nguyen Thi Nam was one of the first executions — the intended message that even if you supported the revolution, it would not absolve your class crimes. The toll of this is unknown. Based on research in Vietnamese archives, it's likely at least 20,000 were killed. It could be higher toward 50,000. We won't know unless the current regime falls and we have access to all the records.

Where is Ho in all of this? Well we know very little about decision-making in the government. For 'Orthodox' writers favorable to Ho in their critiques of US policy, the tendency is to downplay these abuses, eliminate their ideological character, and and say that Ho was powerless at this time. I should note that these are often Americanists who do not know much about Vietnam and haven't researched there. Perhaps representative, in his Pulitzer winning book Embers of War, Fredrik Logevall writes that land reform was to end food shortages, and Ho was powerless, overtaken by extreme elements (no mention of the Chinese advisors), and opposed Nguyen Thi Nam's execution. Yet another historian Alex-Thai Vo, has shown that Ho Chi Minh published a vicious denunciation of Nguyen Thi Nam that approved of her execution. He may have even attended the trial.

Did Ho full-hearted approve of this, or was he simply falling in line? Much like the assassinations of non-communist rivals, perhaps he was not enthusiastic about these things. But nevertheless he participated and lent his support. The same can be said of the DRV/North Vietnam's suppression of academic freedom. In an infamous incident called the Nhan Van Giai Pham affair, the regime arrested or ostracized some of the country's most prominent writers and intellectuals because they had called for freedom of expression or mild reforms in 1955-56.

Was the DRV an oppressive police state? Yes. It remained so after the war, though much less so than the 1940s-80s. Was American involvement driven by that rationale? No. It had much more to do with geopolitics. And while the government of South

Vietnam was a freer society than its northern counterpart, it still committed its fair share of abuses and arrested opponents for nothing more than speaking against it. That however did not dissuade the US from supporting South Vietnam

Countrystudies.us/Vietnam/18.htm

Ho Chi Minh and the Communist Movement

Vietnam Table of Contents

The year 1925 also marked the founding of the Viet Nam Thanh Nien Cach Menh Dong Chi Hoi (Revolutionary Youth League) in Guangzhou by Ho Chi Minh. Born Nguyen Sinh Cung in Kim Lien village, Nghe An Province in May 1890, Ho was the son of Nguyen Sinh Sac (or Huy), a scholar from a poor peasant family. Following a common custom, Ho's father renamed him Nhuyen Tat Thanh at about age ten. Ho was trained in the classical Confucian tradition and was sent to secondary school in Hue. After  working for a short time as a teacher, he went to Saigon where he took a course in navigation and in 1911 joined the crew of a French ship. Working as a kitchen hand, Ho traveled to North America, Africa, and Europe. While in Paris from 1919-23, he took the name Nguyen Ai Quoc (Nguyen the Patriot). In 1919 he attempted to meet with United States President Woodrow Wilson at the Versailles Peace Conference in order to present a proposal for Vietnam's independence, but he was turned away and the proposal was never officially acknowledged. During his stay in Paris, Ho was greatly influenced by Marxist-Leninist literature, particularly Lenin's *Theses on the National and Colonial Questions* (1920), and in 1920 he became a founding member of the French Communist Party. He read, wrote, and spoke widely on Indochina's problems before moving to Moscow in 1923 and attending the Fifth Congress of the Communist International, also called the Comintern, in 1924. In late 1924, Ho arrived in

Guangzhou, where he spent the next two years training more than 200 Vietnamese cadres in revolutionary techniques. His course of instruction included study of Marxism-Leninism, Vietnamese and Asian revolutionary history, Asian leaders such as Gandhi and Sun Yat- sen, and the problem of organizing the masses. As a training manual, Ho used his own publication *Duong Cach Menh* (The Revolutionary Path), written in 1926 and considered his primer on revolution. Going by the name Ly Thuy, he formed an inner communist group, Thanh Nien Cong San Doan (Communist Youth League), within the larger Thanh Nien (Youth) organization. The major activity of Thanh Nien was the production of a journal, *Thanh Nien*, distributed clandestinely in Vietnam, Siam, and Laos, which introduced communist theory into the Vietnamese independence movement. Following Chiang Kai-shek's April 1927 coup and the subsequent suppression of the Communists in southern China, Ho fled to Moscow.

In December of that year, a teacher from a Vietnamese peasant family, Nguyen Thai Hoc, founded Viet Nam Quoc Dan Dang, (VNQDD, Vietnamese Nationalist Party), in Hanoi. With a membership largely of students, low-ranking government employees, soldiers, and a few landlords and rich peasants, VNQDD was patterned after the Chinese Nationalist Party (Kuomintang), from which it received financial support in the 1930s. Another source of funds for the VNQDD was the Vietnam Hotel in Hanoi, which it opened in 1928 as both a commercial enterprise and the party headquarters. The hotel restaurant, however, provided French agents with an easy means of penetrating the party and monitoring its activities. At various times, the VNQDD attempted, without success, to form a united front with Thanh Nien and other independence organizations. Thanh Nien, being two years older, however, had had a head start over VNQDD in organizing in schools, factories, and local government, which it had done with patience and planning. The VNQDD therefore concentrated instead on recruitment of Vietnamese soldiers and the overthrow of French rule through putschist-style activities.

In February 1929, the French official in charge of recruiting coolie labor was killed by an assassin connected with the VNQDD. The French immediately arrested several hundred

VNQDD leaders and imprisoned seventy-eight. VNQDD leaders Nguyen Thai Hoc and Nguyen Khac Nhu escaped, but most members of the Central Committee were captured. The remaining leadership under Nguyen Thai Hoc decided to stage a general uprising as soon as possible. All dissent to the plan was overridden, and the party began manufacturing and stockpiling weapons. On February 9, 1930, a revolt instigated by the VNQDD broke out at Yen Bai among the Vietnamese garrison, but it was quickly suppressed. Simultaneous attacks on other key targets, including Son Tay and Lam Thu, were also unsuccessful because of poor preparation and communication. The Yen Bai uprising was disastrous for the VNQDD. Most of the organization's top leaders were executed, and villages that had given refuge to the party were shelled and bombed by the French. After Yen Bai, the VNQDD ceased to be of importance in the anticolonial struggle. Although more modernist and less bound by tradition than the scholar-patriots of the Phan Boi Chau era, the VNQDD had remained a movement of urban intellectuals who were unable to involve the masses in their struggle and too often favored reckless exploits over slow and careful planning.

On June 17, 1929, the founding conference of the first Indochinese Communist Party (ICP--Dang Cong San Dong Duong) was held in Hanoi under the leadership of a breakaway faction of Thanh Nien radicals. The party immediately began to publish several journals and to send out representatives to all parts of the country for the purpose of setting up branches. A series of strikes supported by the party broke out at this time, and their success led to the convening of the first National Congress of Red Trade Unions the following month in Hanoi. Other communist parties were founded at this time by both supporting members of Thanh Nien and radical members of yet another party revolutionary with Marxist leavings but no direct tie with the Comintern, called the New Revolutinary Party or Tan Viet Party. At the beginning of 1930, there were actually three communist parties in French Indochina competing for members. The establishment of the ICP prompted remaining Thanh Nien members to transform the Communist Youth Leaque into a communist party - the Annam Communist Party (ACP, Annam Cong San Dang), and Tan Viet Party members followed suit by renaming their organization the Indochinese Communist League (Dong Duong Cong San Lien Doan). As a result, the Comintern issued a highly critical indictment of the factionalism in the Vietnamese revolutionary movement and urged the Vietnamese to form a united communist party. Consequently, the Comintern leadership sent a message to Ho Chi Minh, then living in Siam, asking him to come to Hong Kong to unify the groups. On February 3, 1930, in Hong Kong, Ho presided over a conference of representatives of the two factions derived from Thanh Nien (members of the Indochinese Communist League were not represented but were to be permitted membership in the newly formed party as individuals) at which a unified Vietnamese Communist Party (VCP) was founded, the Viet Nam Cong San Dang. At the Comintern's request, the name was changed later that year at the first Party Plenum to the Indochinese Communist Party, thus reclaiming the name of the first party of that named founded in 1929. At the founding meeting, it was agreed that a provisional Central Committee of nine members (three from Bac Bo, two from Trung Bo, two from Nam Bo, and two from the overseas Chinese community) should be formed and that recognition should be sought from the Comintern. Various mass organizations including unions, a peasants' association, a women's association, a relief society, and a youth league were to be organized under the new party. Ho drew up a program of party objectives, which were approved by the conference. The main points included overthrow of the French; establishment of Vietnamese independence; establishment of a workers', peasants', and soldiers' government; organization of a workers' militia; cancellation of public debts; confiscation of means of production and their transfer to the proletarian government; distribution of French-owned lands to the peasants; suppression of taxes; establishment of an eight-hour work day; development of crafts and agriculture; institution of freedom of organization; and establishment of education for all.

The formation of the ICP came at a time of general unrest in the country, caused in part by a global worsening of economic conditions. Although the size of the Vietnamese urban proletariat had increased four times, to about 200,000, since the beginning of the century, working conditions and salaries had improved little. The number of strikes rose from seven in 1927 to ninety- eight in

1930. As the effects of the worldwide depression began to be felt, French investors withdrew their money from Vietnam. Salaries dropped 30 to 50 percent, and employment, approximately 33 percent. Between 1928 and 1932, the price of rice on the world market decreased by more than half. Rice exports totaling nearly 2 million tons in 1928 fell to less than 1 million tons in 1931. Although both French colons and wealthy Vietnamese landowners were hit by the crisis, it was the peasant who bore most of the burden because he was forced to sell at least twice as much rice to pay the same amount in taxes or other debts. Floods, famine, and food riots plagued the countryside. By 1930 rubber prices had plummeted to less than one-fourth their 1928 value. Coal production was cut, creating more layoffs. Even the colonial government cut its staff by one-seventh and salaries by one- quarter.

EARLY SPRING TIME
(Hanoi 1920-1935)

This Springtime reminds me the yesteryear season,

I come back among the cherry blossom breezy…

The Unexpected Visitors

Doctor NQH, a surgeon at Phu Doan hospital in Hanoi just finished a composite leg fracture of an automobile accident. Walking out from the operation room, the doctor hurried pedaling his old bicycle toward home. Under the evening sun, Hanoi in rush hour with subways, automobiles, pedicabs, bicycles…and pedestrians created an incessant noise. About half hour pedaling, NQH felt the sweating on his back and his forehead. Taking a deep breath, he made a hand signal for a left turn onto Fifth street; he was home after a long day at work. The doctor was the only child of Mr. and Mrs. NTP- Mr. NTP was a businessman, he had hundreds of hectares mulberry of silk worms in Son Tay. Silk was in demand of the European markets at this time. Mr. and Mrs. NTP tried to arrange for doctor NQH meetings with daughters from a hierarchy officers, NQH refused, "Please pardon me, Father and Mother, I'd not want to think about that. My heart belongs to my country, Vietnam." Doctor NQH was an under covered member of Việt Nam Quốc Dân Đảng; his goal was to regain the independence for Vietnam.

Doctor NQH inherited a large house in Hanoi from his parent where he lived with a manservant, Cam - a cook, and also a gardener. For supper, Cam prepared rice, fish, vegetables and a cup of soup. The best part of was at night watching the moon in a recliner with a cup of tea under the grape vines while the wind whispering through the bamboo leaves.

Today, doctor NQH entered the gate, Cam told him there were a man and a maiden waiting to meet the doctor. The doctor greeted his guests,

"How may I help you? Whom are you looking for, please?"

"Doctor!" the man ran up to NQH, he said, "Please help us, NQH, do you remember me? I met you when you were just a school boy swimming in the Đà Giang river..."

Doctor NQH kowtowed in respect to the guest,

"Please pardon me, Prince Nguyễn Phước Dân- Cường Để. I'd never forget the Prince who saved me from drowning."

Years ago, Prince Nguyễn Phước Dân- Cường Để was on a boating retreat in the northern area, on the Đà Giang river. The Prince saw a drowning boy screaming for help in the rushing waves; the prince ordered his soldier to rescue the boy- who was doctor NQH today.

"Stand up, doctor, "the prince requested, "Would you help me?"

"With all my heart. "the doctor replied

"Doctor NQH, may we have tea with you?" the prince said

"Of course, Cam-please bring some tea." the doctor told the house keeper; toward the guests, he said, "Prince Cuong De, it's an honor to have you at my home. And, who is this young lady, please?"

"This is Tôn Nữ My Khanh, my niece, she's 12 years old. "the prince said

The maiden bowed her head," Good evening, Doctor."

Tôn Nữ Mỹ Khanh went to look at the gold fish in a pond while the prince talked with doctor NQH. The identity of the prince: [https://cuongde/en.wikipedia.org/wiki/] Cường Để-born Nguyễn Phước Dân, 11 January 1882 – died 5 April 1951) was an early 20th-century Vietnamese revolutionary who, along with Phan Bội Châu, unsuccessfully tried to liberate Vietnam from French colonial occupation. He was a royal relative of the Nguyễn dynasty and, according to the rule of primogeniture, was the heir of the dynasty, directly issued from the line of first-born descendants of Emperor Gia Long and his son Prince Cảnh. He was officially an "external marquis" (Ky Ngoai Hau). Prince Cường Để went in secret to Japan at the end of 1905, leaving a pregnant wife and two young sons in Indochina. He attended a military academy in the Kanda district of Tokyo, followed by Waseda University, where he learned to speak perfect, accentless Japanese. He also married a Japanese woman. While in Japan, he supported and became the figurehead for the Phong Trao Dong Du ("On the Way to the East" movement), led by the revolutionary Phan Bội Châu in support of Indochinese independence from France. The organization was encouraged by the victory of Japan over Russia in the Russo-Japanese War, and received financial support from Sun Yat-sen, Liang Qichao as well as Inukai Tsuyoshi and Kashiwabara Buntaro. Between 1905 and 1910, it sponsored some 200 Vietnamese to study in Japan.

Prince Cường Để (left) with Phan Bội Châu (right), circa 1907

However, after the Franco-Japanese Treaty of 1907, French colonial authorities applied diplomatic pressure against Japan to suppress the organization and many of its members were deported by 1910. Prince Cường Để made a trip to Siam from November 1908-March 1909, returning to Japan in May 1909. However, his presence in Japan was reported by the French government to the Japanese, who issued a warrant for his arrest. He hid until September, at one point escaping out a hotel window in Kobe as the police came in through the door. However, he was

finally deported to Shanghai at the end of October. Prince Cường
Để then went to Beijing, where the Chinese warlord Duan Qirui
offered financial support if he would start an uprising against the
French in Indochina as leader of the 1911 Vietnam Restoration
Organisation (Việt Nam Quang Phục Hội). He traveled to Hong
Kong and then to Bangkok in 1911, but was apprehended by
Siamese authorities and deported back to China. He then traveled
via Singapore to Europe, visiting Berlin and London. However,
in 1913, he was sentenced to death in absentia as the French
started to suppress pro-independence agitation more harshly.
Returning to Japan, Prince Cường Để found help from the Pan-
Asian movement, including Tōyama Mitsuru and was given a
monthly allowance by his old friend Inukai Tsuyoshi. However,
he was devastated by the news of the arrest of Phan Bội Châu in
Shanghai in 1925.

[Continued the meeting of Dr. NQH and his unexpected
guests.]

"I admire your patriot and loyalist with our country. "Doctor
NQH kowtowed to Prince Cường Để.

"I came here to ask you a favor. Would you please care for
Tôn Nữ My Khanh? Her father- my brother was arrested by the
French colonialists because he was against the cruelty of the French
recruiters of laborers for the rubber plantations in S Vietnam; her
mother died in sorrow and illness. Would you please care for her,
for I still have a mission: Independence Vietnam to fulfil?" the
prince kowtowed to the doctor

"Prince, please...." the doctor lifted the prince up- in a
moment, he was hesitated- he was an under covered member of
Việt Nam Quốc Dân Đảng with the same goal to get Vietnam out
of the French domination; his life was in danger every minute.
"Doctor NQH told himself, "How could I take care of a young
girl? Yet how could I refuse to help the man who saved me
from drowning?" The doctor glanced at the young girl in her
sad situation, and he answered the prince, "You saved my life, I
promise I will do my best to take care of Miss."

"Thank you very much," the prince whispered a secret,
"Now, I can concentrate my mind on my work. One more thing,

doctor NQH: please never reveal the identity and relationship between me and Tôn Nữ My Khanh." And he called out for the niece and gave the young girl his last talk with an advice,

"For now, sojourn at the doctor's home and be a good girl! As God's will, we'll meet again!"

The girl hugged her uncle with tears running down her cheeks, "I'll keep your words within my heart."

"Good bye, Prince Cường Đê!" the doctor and the young girl said

"Good bye, doctor NQH! Good bye, Tôn Nữ My Khanh!" the prince waved back with a smile

A gentle breeze spread as Prince Cường Để disappeared in the night. We follow the prince's steps according to [https: // cuongde/en.wikipedia.org/wiki/] From 1930 to 1951. Prince Cuong Để founded Phuc Quoc (Vietnam Restored Allied Kingdom, "Vietnam Recovery Alliance. He approached the Japanese army, hoping to restore the throne in Vietnam because Puyi was restore the throne at Manchukuo. Following the collapse of the Vichy French government, the Japanese staged a coup de main, creating the independent Empire of Vietnam. Prince Cường Để brought forth a five-member provisional government, which was sponsored by the IJA 38th Army; however, Tokyo made the surprising decision to retain Emperor Bảo Đại as nominal head of state, and Prince Cường Để's efforts to return as ruler of Vietnam were frustrated.

Under Japanese rule

Prince Cuong De lived in Taiwan from 1939 to May 1940, he released a four-hour radio program daily. Later that year, Japan invaded Indochina, but retained the Vichy French colonial government to maintain stability and maintain essential war documents. However, Prince Cuong De was faithful to the concept of the Commonwealth of East Asia and communicated with the leaders of the Cao Dai movement, who were interested in a monarchy led by Prince Cuong De.

Final years

Following the end of World War II, Prince Cường Để became a Japanese citizen, taking the name of Masao Ando. He gave a press conference in August 1949, vowing to return to Vietnam to oppose Bảo Đại, should Bảo Đại sign agreements granting France colonial rights in Vietnam again. However, as a Japanese subject, he was not permitted a Vietnamese passport. His attempts to return to Vietnam via Thailand and via Hong Kong disguised as a Chinese with a fake passport were foiled in 1950. Prince Cường died of cancer in 1951 at the Nippon Medical School Hospital in Tokyo.

Now, should we return to doctor NQH's story in Hanoi from 1925 to 1930?

After saying "Good bye!" to the prince, the doctor told the young girl

"Ah, Miss, please come in…"

"Thank you…" the girl bowed her head, "The prince said…"

"We're not supposed to mention about the prince anymore," the doctor said

"Yes, doctor. "the girl replied

From that day, My Khanh stayed at the doctor's house. She went to middle school, where her name was on the Honors List; yet her mind was up to something more important: revenge for her father; to fight against the French in order taking back Independence for Vietnam. My Khanh learned that doctor NQH was an under covered member of Việt Nam Quốc Dân Đảng. My Khanh asked the doctor if she could join the party.

"No. It's very dangerous; I'm a member of Việt Nam Quốc Dân Đảng, my life is on the verge of death or imprison at any moment. I don't want you to involve in this mission. "he said

"I must revenge for my father, Doctor would you help me?" the girl looked up at NQH

"You don't have to address me as a "Doctor" when we're at home; consider me as your older brother. Your goal is revenge for your father; I have the mission to fight for the Independence of our country, Vietnam. We have a common dream. I hate the French so much in my heart, I want to revenge- not for my happiness, but I'd like them to suffer in repaying their cruelty to the Vietnamese people. How about you? Could you be happy; your father was deceased? Supposedly we succeed, which is still in a faraway road?" Doctor NQH asked

"Yes, I'd be very happy when we defeated the French." the girl said, "I also hate the French; my father was no longer with me, but I think about the future of Vietnam. What else could I do to be accepted in Việt Nam Quốc Dân Đảng?"

"I'm glad to hear that! When you're 18 years old, after high school graduation; I'll introduce you to Việt Nam Quốc Dân Đảng." Doctor NQH said

"Yes, Doctor! Thank you!" the girl bowed her head

Living under the same roof and being trained and protected by doctor NQH, Tôn Nữ Mỹ Khanh admired the doctor who devoted the care to the patients and committed his life for VNQDĐ; and she also dreamed about him!

After the high school graduation, doctor NQH explained Mỹ Khanh about Việt Nam Quốc Dân Đảng [VNQDĐ]. https://www.tinparis.net › chanhtri › vnqd_ls

12/25-1927: Day Of Establishing VNQDĐ

December 25, 1927 is an important day in the history of the modern nation: The birth of Việt Nam Quốc Dân Đảng, a National Revolutionary Force with the first rigorous, democratic and scientific organization system in Viet Nam. (The Cộng Sản Đông Dương (CSĐD) was founded in 1930).

At that time, the VNQDĐ advocated a "violent revolution to gain independence" and a "national and democratic revolution".

The Preparatory Committee for the Meeting, chaired by student Nguyễn Thái Học, was composed of a draft sub-committee of the program and regulations, which were attended by young people under the age of 25 such as Hoang Van Tung and Nguyen Ngoc Son (who had just graduated from a college in France), and writer Nhuong Tong.

The meeting hall was at home of party member Le Thanh Vy, The Giao village, suburban Hanoi. On the wall hung a 4-meter-long, 20-meter-long banner with a solemn Fatherland altar: "Warmly welcome the Conference the First Representative and The Founding Party Day 25 - December 1927 ".

Nguyen Thai Hoc was elected President of the Ministry.

Vice Chairman: Nguyen The Nghiep

Organizing Committee: Deputy Duc Chinh, Head of the Committee.

Le Van Phuc, Deputy Head of the Department.

Propaganda Committee: Nhuong Tong, Chairman.

Foreign Affairs Committee: Nguyen Ngoc Son, Ho Van Mich.

Finance Committee: Dang Dinh Dien, Head of the Committee.

Doan Manh Che, Deputy Head.

Supervisory Committee: Nguyen Huu Dat, Head of the Committee.

Hoang Trac, Vice Chairman.

Reconnaissance Committee: Truong Dan Bao, Pham Tiem.

Assassination Committee: Hoang Van Tung.

Military Service Committee: (Disabled. The Second Congress is conducted by Tran Van Mon, the Flying Squadron).

More than 5 am, 16 Dong Chi aged 60, 70 to 20, 30, solemnly sworn in front of the Altar of the Fatherland with the wish:

"Determined to fulfill the mission given, eager to bring revolutionary career to perfect success. Absolutely sacrifice all for the country and for the Party. If the wrong oath, please plead for the death penalty".

The General Assembly voted the Nam Dong Thu Xa to be the UNIQUE BRANCH, which was the first nuclear branch of the VNQDĐ, expressing the collective leadership of the Party, Do Van Sinh is the Chief of the Party cell, governed by the General Department.

Việt Nam Quốc Dân Đảng [https://en.wikipedia.org/wiki/Việt_Nam_Quốc_Dân_Đảng] The Việt Nam Quốc Dân Đảng (Vietnamese: [vìət naːm kwə́wk zən ɗã:ŋ]; chữ Hán: 越南國民黨; Vietnamese Nationalist Party), abbreviated VNQDĐ or Việt Quốc, was a nationalist and moderate socialist political party that sought independence from French colonial rule in Vietnam during the early 20th century. Its origins lie in the mid-1920s, when a group of young Hanoi-based intellectuals began publishing revolutionary material. In 1927, after the publishing house failed because of French harassment and censorship, the VNQDD was formed under the leadership of Nguyễn Thái Học. Modelling itself on the Republic of China's Kuomintang (the same 3 characters in chữ Hán: 國民黨) the VNQDD gained a following among northerners, particularly teachers and intellectuals. The party, which was less successful among peasants and industrial workers, was organised in small clandestine cells. From 1928, the VNQDD attracted attention through its assassinations of French officials and Vietnamese collaborators. A turning point came in February 1929 with the Bazin assassination, the killing of a French labour recruiter widely despised by local Vietnamese people. Although the perpetrators' precise affiliation was unclear, the French colonial authorities held the VNQDD responsible. Between 300 and 400 of the party's approximately 1,500 members were detained in the resulting crackdown.

Doctor NQH was a member of Việt Nam Quốc Dân Đảng [VNQDĐ], he was a liaison- connecting enthusiastic students of Hanoi University from different faculties to VNQDĐ; especially students in Science faculty [Chemistry, Physics, Mechanic Engineering]. Doctor NQH had a plan: creating bombs and guns to fight against the French. Working with all the hearts and souls, young men and women of VNQDĐ aimed at the ultimate goal: Independence for Vietnam. Under doctor NQH's protection, Tôn Nữ My Khanh respected and cherished the image of doctor in her heart and asked the doctor to introduce her to VNQDĐ.

"Why do you want to join the party?" Doctor NQH looked at the young girl

"I wish to be by your side in the revolution." My Khanh replied

"Oh, silly girl! On the contrary, I'd think you should not..."

"No. Doctor! I've decided to follow you."

Doctor NQH introduced Tôn Nữ My Khanh to VNQDĐ. The young girl kneeled down in front of the Vietnam altar and the party flag to make the solemn oath,

1.   Resolutely achieve the devoted mission.

2.   Ardently lead the revolutionary affairs to perfect success.

3.   Absolutely sacrifice for the State and the Party.

4.   Die if the promise was broken

[Viet Nam Quoc Dan Dang: A Contemporary History of a National Struggle: 1927-1954-By Văn Đào Hoàng, page 23] flag of the party with the solemn oath,

Tôn Nữ My Khanh met comrade Nguyễn thị Giang, an important member of VNQDĐ; she was also Leader Comrade Nguyễn Thái Học's fiancée. My Khanh loved and admired Miss Nguyễn thị Giang. Walking in the garden in the early spring time, the birds chirping on the branches; the wind was still briskly cold, yet the cherry bloomed already, the pink petals fluttering in the breeze then dropped on the green grass. As catching the flowers My Khanh shared her thought with them.

"Miss Nguyễn thị Giang is so talented, and she's also lucky to have Leader Comrade Nguyễn Thái Học as her fiancée! Both of them love the country so much and they dedicate their lives for VNQDĐ. Oh, how much do I wish to be doctor NQH's fiancée!"

"What are you mumbling about, My Khanh?"

My Khanh turned her head, Doctor NQH was in front of her. Where did he come from? Did he overhear the secret of her heart?

"Nothing… How are you, Doctor NQH?" My Khanh covered her face in her hands

"Should I arrange a marriage for you? What kind of suitor are you looking for?" the doctor asked with an elfin smile

"Oh, no, Doctor NQH!"

A gentle breeze of early spring time blew through the trees, the pinkish petals of the cherry followed the wind and rested on My Khanh's tunique. The young girl picked up the petals and asked doctor NQH, "The cherry blossoms … aren't they pretty?"

"Ah! Early Spring time! Yes, the flowers are beautiful. How precious is this moment!" the doctor said

"I wish that we could be like this for a long time." My Khanh whispered under her breathe

"We have a mission to do. I had a meeting with the Leader, Comrade Nguyễn Thái Học," doctor NQH said, "My Khanh, don't ever forget this in your mind, our Leader, Comrade Nguyễn Thái Học said, "Even if a man fails to succeed, he'll become virtuous. "

"Is there anything I could do for VNQDĐ party, please?" My Khanh asked

"Would you like to be a member in the propaganda team?"

"Yes, with my heart!" My Khanh called out joyfully

Tôn Nữ My Khanh was enthusiastic and eagerly in the propaganda "Joining Việt Nam Quốc Dân Đảng!". Involving in this mission, My Khanh had opportunities to get acquainted with other young members of VNQDĐ as Nguyễn văn Kính- who was also a student. The two of them spread around the flyers to recruit more members for VNQDĐ. One evening, Nguyễn văn Kính walked Tôn Nữ My Khanh home. He coaxed her,

"You're my girl, beautiful one. I love you. Will you be submissive to me?"

My Khanh was speechless; she changed the subject,

"I live with uncle NQH, he's a surgeon at Phủ Doãn hospital… and he's also a member of VNQDĐ."

"Is he home?" Nguyễn văn Kính asked

"No. He usually gets home around 7pm." My Khanh shared with Nguyễn văn Kính, "He has involved in the creating bombs and guns for the revolution…."

Entering the house, Mr. Cam- the housekeeper greeted My Khanh,

"Good evening, Miss. Who's this gentleman with you?"

"Mr. Cam, this's Nguyễn văn Kính; he's at the same college with me." My Khanh said

"Did you ask Doctor NQH's permission to let your friend come in our home?" Mr. Cam starred at My Khanh and her friend

"He's a member of VNQDĐ." My Khanh whispered to Mr. Cam

"I don't know…" Mr. Cam hesitantly said

The youngsters walked in the living room. Nguyễn văn Kính inquired,

"Do you know the documents of the bomb factories?"

"I'm not quite sure…" My Khanh said, "Probably in his study room…"

"Let's take a look." Nguyễn văn Kính suggested as he about opening the studio door; he gently kissed My Khanh, "I love you.

We share everything, right? Could you show me the Doctor's documents about the locations of the bomb factories?"

"I've heard about the preparation for the Revolution…Here are the papers…" Mỵ Khanh showed Nguyễn văn Kính the drawer where Doctor NQH kept his materials.

"Stop right where you are!" Doctor NQH appeared in front of them

"Where did Doctor NQH come from?" Nguyễn văn Kính was surprised; however, he tried to be polite,

"Good evening, Doctor. How are you?" Nguyễn văn Kính said

"I think you better leave. "the Doctor firmly ordered the young man.

"No need, Doctor," Nguyễn văn Kính smirked, "Look out to see who are coming in your house!"

Doctor NQH pulled Tôn Nữ Mỵ Khanh's hand; and he unplugged the light; in the dark they ran out of the house by the back door.

"We fell into the betrayal Nguyễn văn Kinh's trap!" the doctor said, "Run faster, Mỵ Khanh!"

Behind them, the French soldiers offshot toward them vigorously but the darkness of the night made the bullets missed the victims.

"It's my fault. I didn't know that Nguyễn văn Kính was a spy for the French." Mỵ Khanh cried, "Doctor, NQH please forgive me…"

"No time to talk about that at this moment. "the doctor said as they hid themselves in a bush along the dyke of Đà Giang river.

"What could we do now?" Mỵ Khanh sobbed quietly

"Once we made the oath to be a member of VNQDĐ; we sacrifice everything, we accept everything-including death-the death for our country, Vietnam. It's an honor" Doctor NQH said "About tomorrow don't worry, my dear. "he whispered, "We'll contact Comrade Nguyễn Khắc Nhu…and he helps us…"

"From now on, I'll not do anything by myself; I must tell you." My̱ Khanh promised

The French soldiers and Nguyễn văn Kính were still searching for the two VNQDĐ members, they had hunting dogs as helpers. The French soldiers ordered the dogs scouting along the hedge close to where the doctor and the young girl hiding; Nguyễn văn Kính pointing to a bush, "Over here, quick!"

Gazing at the river, the doctor told the girl, "Ready, we jump into the water now!"

The French soldiers came to the spot, but all they saw was some bubbles flashing back by the water as the victims dived into the river. A gentle breeze of early spring time blew through the trees, the pinkish petals of the cherry followed the wind and rested on the waves of the river.

Viet Nam Quoc Dan Dang: A Contemporary History of a National Struggle: 1927-1954- By Văn Đào Hoàng [page 63/ Nguyen van Kinh] In June of 1929, the French Security Service arrested Nguyen van Kinh, a youth member of VNQDD. After torturing him, Bribes [Chief French Security Service-Northern Administrative and Economic Inspector] discovered that Nguyen van Kinh was a liaison of Nguyễn Thái Học and Brides turned Nguyen van Kinh into a tool against the VNQDD party. For a young and inexperienced as Nguyen van Kinh, Brides' offers seemed attractive; he revealed Nguyễn Thái Học's movements which led to the searching of many VNQDD members' houses.

On July 13, 1929 French Security Service agents searched the house of vice village chief, Dương Quang in Bắc Ninh province. On July 18, they searched Quan Khê's home, also in Bắc Ninh; on their way back to Hà Nội, they searched Vũ Ngọc Sơn's wife home, but there was no trace of Nguyễn Thái Học.

Although the French Security Service could not arrest Nguyễn Thái Học based on Kinh's information, they decided Kinh would be useful for their future policies. They released Kinh from prison, hoping that Kinh would help the French to fight against VNQDD, but Kinh didn't do anything as he returned to Phủ Lạng Thương; Brides re-arrested him and trained Kinh to be a professional spy.

By that time, many important VNQDD members, such as Phó Đức Chính and Nguyễn Xuân Đài were arrested and released fairly often without suspicion; likewise, Kinh met with little misgiving with his comrades about his times in and out of prison, a situation that he used for the French advantage to catch Nguyễn Thái Học later. As soon as Nguyen van Kinh knew Nguyễn Thái Học had left Võng La for the elder comrade, Nguyễn Tiến Nguyên in Liễu Ngạn, Bắc Ninh. Nguyen van Kinh went to visit Nguyễn Thái Học and informed him that Kinh had been arrested twice. Not only did Nguyễn Thái Học believed Kinh, yet also encouraged Kinh and allowed Kinh to serve Nguyễn Thái Học side by side. The consequences were damaging.

https://en.wikipedia.org › wiki › Yên_Bái_mutiny The Yên Bái mutiny (Vietnamese: Tổng khởi-nghĩa Yên- Bái) was an uprising of Vietnamese soldiers in the French colonial army on 10 February 1930 in collaboration with civilian supporters who were members of the Việt Nam Quốc Dân Đảng (VNQDĐ, the Vietnamese Nationalist Party).

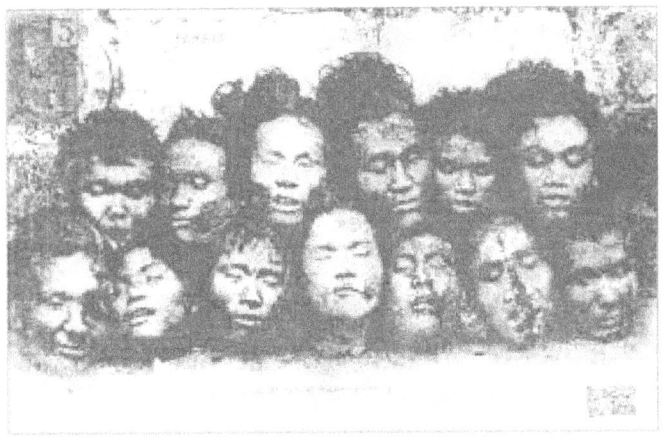

Nguyễn Thái Học and 12 comrades were guillotined on June 17, 1930

The aim of the revolt was to inspire a wider uprising among the general populace in an attempt to overthrow the colonial regime and establish independence. The VNQDĐ had previously attempted to engage in clandestine activities to undermine French rule, but increasing French scrutiny on their activities led to their leadership group taking the risk of staging a large-scale military attack in the Red River Delta in northern Vietnam.

Shortly after midnight on 10 February, about 50 Vietnamese soldiers (Tirailleurs indochinois) of the 4th Regiment of Tonkinese Rifles within the Yên Bái garrison turned on their French officers with assistance from about 60 civilian VNQDĐ members who invaded the camp from the outside. The mutiny failed within 24 hours when the majority of the Vietnamese soldiers in the garrison refused to participate and remained loyal to the colonial army. Further sporadic attacks occurred across the Delta region, with little impact. French retribution to the attack was swift and decisive. The main leaders of the VNQDĐ were arrested, tried and put to death, effectively ending the military threat of what was previously the leading Vietnamese nationalist revolutionary organisation.

THE WIND BLEW THAT EVER NIGHT

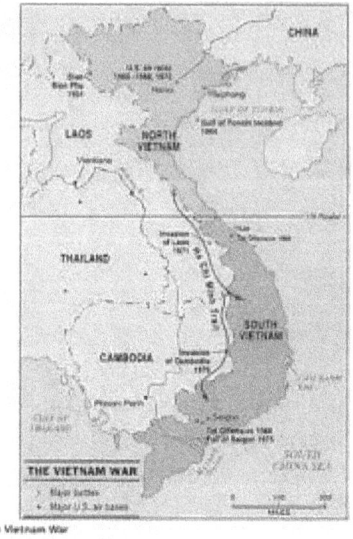

Hung Yen, a province in norther Vietnam, 1954

Luu thi Nguyet whispered to her sons, "Run away! Never tell anybody about your parents." She pushed Nguyen van Giap, Nguyen van Hai away and told the comrade, "I do not know these boys. Take me and my daughter with you." Nguyen van Giap and Nguyen van Hai scurried themselves into a bush, they gawked at the scenario. Pointing the rifle toward Luu thi Nguyet, the comrade yelled,

"Don't you recognize me? I'm Bui van Ty- one of the peasants who worked for your husband's rice field - Nguyen van Ba. When I was sick, I begged you for money to buy the medications. You refused to help…. Now I'll send you to hell!"

"No! No!" the little girl yelled out loud

The comrade shot at Luu thi Nguyet's chest, she fell down on the ground with her daughter. The comrade kicked on the body of the woman, it fell into a ditch; he shot one more bullet into her head. The little girl screamed; the comrade threw her up in the air then left. Nguyen van Giap and Nguyen van Hai ran out from the bush to grab their sister- Nguyen Hoa Le. The little girl dropped down on the ground, she cried in pain, "Mama…Mama…"

Nguyen van Giap embraced his little sister, the little girl was trembling in fear.

"I'll take care of you. Don't cry. "the elder brother said

"My leg, the right one, it hurts..." the girl kept on moaning

"Can you raise it up?" Hai asked

"No! It hurts...." Hoa Le cried

Giap looked at his sister's legs, the right leg was twisted. The brothers glanced at the little sister in pain; while they didn't know what to do in the field surrounded by gun shots and fire, they heard the sound of an airplane.

"Lie down!" Giap called out loud to Hai as he covered the little sister with his body.

The airplane torn the air with the deadly sound combined with chains of bombs dropping down. Why did the airplanes from a foreign country bomb his hometown, Giap- an eleven years old boy- was not able to understand the reasons of war, all he knew at this moment was, "Run for life!". Giap was the elder brother of Nguyen van Hai and Nguyen Hoa Le. Didn't his parents teach him that his duty was taking care of his siblings? The airplane was gone, not too far away, the village where Giap was born and spent his child hood was on fire. Father- Nguyen van Ba- inherited one hectare of rice field from Grandfather...there were people worked on the field with the buffaloes. Nguyen van Giap remembered his house with the blue door, the almendron by the window where he climbed up to find the bird's nest....the pond with the gold fish swimming among the lotus flowers... Nguyen van Giap and Nguyen van Hai chased the butterflies while baby Nguyen Hoa Le slept in a crib.... Nguyen van Hai fell into a hole, and Mother took him to the medical man at the temple... Those were the peaceful days until the Viet Minh Party [Communism] took control of Hung Yen. During the Land Reform Regime, the Viet Minh comrades claimed that Nguyen van Ba- Nguyen van Giap's father committed a great crime as being a "Landowner", they tortured him by having his feet tied by a rope that hung him to the ceiling. This hurt him so much, and he cried wildly; they stuffed cloth into his mouth and beat him to death. The mother escaped with the children but they were caught back.

Nguyen Hoa Le, his little sister was not able to walk. Nguyen van Giap carried his sister on his back and Nguyen van Hai by his side, they walked across the field among the snipers' shots of the militia of the Communist party. The rain fluttered on the grass with the crescent moon spread dimming light on the three orphans. Nguyen van Giap felt the cold wind blowing the rain on his face, on his body as pushing him backward. He comforted the little girl,

"I'll take care of you. I promise. "

A group of peasants hurried passing the three orphans, Giap asked a man,

"Tell me, please…Where're you going?"

"We're heading to Hai Phong harbor where the US Operation of Freedom ship would take us the South."

"Hai, go with them." Giap told his younger brother

"Huh?" Hai gazed at Giap, "How about you and Hoa Le?"

"I'll take care of Hoa Le; we might join you later. Listen, go with them so you may have a life." Giap pushed Nguyen van Hai, a nine years old boy- into the refugee crowd. Nguyen van Hai turned his head to glance at his brother and sister but he couldn't see them. [Nguyen van Giap lay down on the grass next to the injured sister Nguyen Hoa Le avoiding the sad parting moment.] A man in the refugee group screamed at Nguyen van Hai, "Run for your life, kid!". The young boy hurried to catch up with the crowd into an arduous, unknown journey.

Nguyen van Giap carried Nguyen Hoa Le on his back crossing the field. Nguyen van Giap knew with the injured little sister, all three of them couldn't make the flight. Under the diming light from the crescent moon above the bamboo bushes and listening to the wind blowing through the bamboo leaves, Nguyen van Giap wondered at the wind whispered to the leaves. Oh, he would never forget sound of the wind blew through the bamboo leaves that ever night!

Ho Chi Minh's Land Reform: Mistake or Crime? - www. paulbogdanor.com › Vietnam › land reform

NB: The following is an analysis of the bloodbath resulting from Ho Chi Minh's land reform in North Vietnam. For decades, totalitarian apologists such as Gareth Porter and Edwin Moise have denied that the bloodbath took place. They have claimed that the death toll was in the low thousands and that the killings were a "mistake." They rely on official North Vietnamese publications, which they take at face value. This is what passes for scholarship on the "anti-imperialist" left.

The bloodbath deniers simply ignore or dismiss the evidence from dissident publications, communist defectors and foreign witnesses. Below, Lam Thanh Liem, a major authority on land issues in Vietnam, concludes that the communists perpetrated a huge bloodbath and that the death toll was in the hundreds of thousands. Translated from Vietnamese.

[From Lam Thanh Liem, "Chinh sach cai cach ruong dat cua Ho Chi Minh: sai lam hay toi ac?" in Jean-Francois Revel et al., Ho Chi Minh: Su that ve Than the & Su nghiep (Paris: Nam A, 1990), pp. 179-214. This excerpt is from pp. 200-5.] The Result of the Land Reform

The 5-phase land reform resulted in a bloodbath all over North Vietnam. Unfortunately, because of the techniques of falsification and censorship under the "closed door" policy implemented by Ho's regime from 1954, the world was completely unaware of this catastrophe. Genuine information related to this land reform is extremely scarce, and even inaccurate and vague. As a result, it is almost impossible to establish a clear picture of this internecine massacre.

A recent memoir by Hoang Van Hoan – a former member of the Hanoi communist Politburo who fled the country in September 1979 and is presently in exile in China – partly uncovered the disastrous situation the government had created for the population. Like the Vietnamese Communist Party's other leaders, Hoang Van Hoan dwelt lightly on the "errors" and "deviations" of the lower levels. He never revealed the real number of victims who suffered in this reform campaign or the number of innocent people wrongly accused by people's tribunals and later executed.

In 1987, the Institute of Marxist-Leninism in Hanoi published a book entitled Ho Chi Minh: The Era of 1954-7 (simultaneous with the progression of the land reform). However, the book failed to provide anything useful and only touched on the incident briefly in 2 pages.

Vo Nhan Tri, at the request of the Hanoi government, wrote a book, Croissance économique de la Répubique démocratique du Vietnam (Economic Growth in the Democratic Republic of Vietnam). Having been given this task, the author was allowed to access the documents in the Prime Minister's archives, where he "found and read a top-secret report on the number of communist cadres falsely accused and executed: 15,000." Ho Chí Minh, in an attempt to hide the truth, reduced this number to 10,000 when he addressed an assembly of Party members, confessing to having killed a number of "innocent victims." "Of course, this number of so-called 'innocent victims' would be much greater," according to Vo Nhan Tri

In South Vietnam, Nguyen Van Canh, a former Deputy Minister of the Ministry of Information and Amnesty (1969-70), sought an answer to this problem by interviewing returnees

from Chieu Hoi programs and interrogating POWs, including communist cadres, soldiers, and officers from the North. These interviews and interrogations produced a great deal of valuable and reliable information. Ultimately Nguyen Van Canh was able to generate an estimate of 200,000 victims, which he divided into 2 main categories:

— 100,000 accused and murdered during the period before 1955, excluding another 40,000 victims who were sent to various concentration camps in the mountain areas. Here most of them died of malaria or other epidemic diseases. Those who were able to survive and were released became crippled mentally as well as physically. They have led a dog's life ever since.

— 100,000 killed during phase 5, the last phase of the reform campaign, known as the Dien Bien Phu General Offensive, which ended in summer 1956. Thousands of others, most of them rich farmers and land owners, were sent to concentration camps for "reeducation."

Of more than 200,000 victims executed, 40,000 (20%) were communist cadres, according to Nguyen Van Canh.

During work visits to the Mekong Delta (assigned by Ho Chi Minh City's agriculture department), we had opportunities to talk to a number of Northern cadres working in scientific and technological areas as part of the "agricultural collectivization policy" in 1978-9. The discussions eventually touched on the land reform campaign in the North. Two of the cadres admitted that they were participants in the campaign in 1955-6.

— One estimated that 120,000 victims were falsely accused and executed. This number included 40,000 communist cadres.

— The other gave a larger figure: 150,000-160,000 victims killed, among them 60,000 communist cadres.

In general, the conclusions and estimates are similar; especially the number of communist cadres, which ranged from 20-30% of the total number of victims. Though the numbers of victims falsely accused may be different, the acceptable figure is 120,000-200,000 (including cadres and Party members).

According to official statistics, the outcome of the land reform was an award of more than 800,000 hectares of land and rice paddies, plus 100,000 cows and water buffalo, redistributed to 2 million farmers. Nearly 150,000 houses and huts were allocated to new occupants. These estates had been in the possession of people classified as "indigenous oppressors, reactionaries, or traitorous elements." These figures are quite significant in relation to the number of murdered victims. Another estimate for the period 1952-6 was about 150,000 victims (of which 30% were communist cadres and Party members).

Let us note how Hoang Van Hoan described the situation in that period: Unjust and false verdicts imposed on the victims were concealed and were never brought to light for verification. Those who had been erroneously classified and accused were never exonerated. Grievances against the Party accumulated during the reform campaign have taken root in everyone's heart and have remained intense to this moment.

Land reform in North Vietnam – Wikipedia- en.wikipedia. org › wiki › Land_reform_in_Vietnam

Land reform in North Vietnam (Vietnamese: Cải cách ruộng đất tại miền Bắc Việt Nam) can be understood as an agrarian reform in northern Vietnam throughout different periods, but in many cases, it only refers to the one within the government of Democratic Republic of Vietnam (DRV) in the 1950s. The reform was one of the most important economic and political programs launched by the Viet Minh government during the years 1953-1956.

The project of land reform in North Vietnam was a product of the interplay of complex internal and external factors. On 9 March 1945, several years after occupation in Indochina, Japan instigated a military coup, overthrew the French administration in Indochina and established a puppet indigenous government headed by Tran Trong Kim. However, five months later, Japan unconditionally surrendered. Taking the political vacuum, Viet Minh seized power by launching a nationwide revolution, and founded the DRV in Hanoi in September 2, 1945.

Soon after that, Vietnam saw an influx of foreign power. The

Kuomintang Chinese armies accepted the surrender of Japan in Vietnam North of the 16th parallel, with the British in the south. Both of them negotiated and facilitated the French return. After negotiations between the Viet Minh and the French broke down, the war between them started from late 1946 until 1954; this is called the First Indochina war (1946-1954).

In the whole of the 1940s, the Viet Minh fought solely against the French army. In terms of military capability, the Viet Minh was in a position of clear-cut disadvantage; this did not change until the establishment and involvement of the People's Republic of China.

During this period of time, the DRV government was dominated by the Viet Minh who were popular among the indigenous political force; its domestic policy was to unite all possible forces for a resistance war. It also embraced peasants, workers, students and some merchants and intellectuals. On 11 November 1945, the ICP declared its dissolution, aiming at downplaying the role of communist ideology by dissolving and forcing the ICP underground in order to garner more support from the masses.

In October 1949, the Chinese Communist Party (CCP) established the People's Republic of China by winning its political rivalry with the KMT, which had a major impact on the political landscape of the region in general and Vietnam in particular. From the CCP's perspective, the Chinese revolutionary model was intended to be exported to the Asian countries, Vietnam included. Moreover, the increasing influence in its southern periphery was also for national defense and security. From the perspective of the DRV, communist China was a good ally who shared the same ideology and similar approaches to complete communist revolution. They were glad to conduct a binary revolution at the same time: externally anti-colonialism and internally anti-feudalism. Thus Ho Chi Minh pled proactively for Chinese aid After establishing formal diplomatic relations with the PRC in early 1950, Luo Guibo became the first Chinese ambassador to the DRV, and Chinese aid also flooded into the DRV, the most significant of which was the Chinese advisory group, which was later sent to North Vietnam in the same year. Basically, Chinese advisory groups had a double mission. The most important one was to provide advice on military affairs. After winning victories in a series of military campaigns with considerable help from August 1950 onward, the DRV not only gradually turned around the war situation but also expanded its controlled areas. This conducive environment facilitated the DRV to carry out its land reform plan.

As a government dominated by the communists, land reform was an integral part of its revolution. After its first trial failed in the 1930s, Vietnamese communists never had a real chance to carry it out, even during a long time after the foundation of the DRV. For the sake of war, communist slogans were even diminished. Instead, they needed support from landowners and landlords. However, Chinese assistance outweighed domestic support from feudal classes and communism was re-emphasized. The Indochinese party was divided along national lines and the Vietnamese Worker's party (VWP) was officially formed in early 1951. Simultaneously, land reform was put on its agenda. More comprehensive and stricter land policies were formulated, and class struggle was emphasized as inseparable from the military struggle for the first time.

On the other hand, the French and American-sponsored Quoc Gia Viet Nam (the State of Vietnam) emerged and was recognized by western powers. Particularly after the Bao Dai interval, the DRV faced a competent rival regime which contested its monopolistic representation of the Vietnamese people. In this situation, Truong Chinh in his report to the party Congress in 1951 pointed out that as soon as the Bao Dai regime was set up, the landlord class aligned itself with the State of Vietnam.

Excepting international and domestic political factors, as

Bernard B. Fall pointed out, land reform was also necessary for economic reasons. 90 percent of the population lived by agriculture, but the problem was the enormous population pressure put upon the relatively small fertile areas. In the Red River delta, 9 million people were crowded into an area of 5790 square miles. The majority of population under the DRV were peasants but did not have land to till, which was an unjust situation. After the end of WWII in Indochina, people suffered a lot from famine and lack of sufficient food due to continuous conflict. Improving their welfare would consolidate the Viet Minh's regime by garnering more support. Collective ownership as a palliative to landlessness has been a century-old practice throughout Vietnam and as for individuals, they were deprived of rice fields and had to turn to support from communal land.

In Vietnam, there is a saying called "Phép Vua Thua Lệ Làng", literally meaning that the emperor is secondary to village customs and implicitly indicating that national rule at the village level was giving way to autonomous rule by village itself. This was also true for the DRV government; their influence at the grass roots level was relatively weak. Land reform served as a good way to cement its power at the grass roots level.

Implementation: Land reform in North Vietnam was a grand project. At the beginning, it was a relatively mild campaign; later on, it was radicalized and caused serious effects. When the top leaders notices the side effects, they tried to rectify the caused errors.

Pre-1953 communist land policy in DRV: Social revolution is part of revolution led by the Communist Party. However, for a long time, the regime failed to grasp the essential tasks of Vietnamese national democratic revolution and placed too much emphasis on unity with landlords in the interest of national resistance, and did not pay much attention to the peasant and land issues. What they did was to adopt a middle way: landlords agreed to decrease the land rent and the peasants still needed to pay rent but with a lower rate. The land rent reduction was formulated in July 1949. Also, all pre-1953 policy had failed in breaking through the landlord's economic and political power and in serving the interests of the peasants. According to VWP's mouthpiece Nhan Dan, even landlords were allowed to join the party, which somehow dominated the party chapters in many areas. DRV gradually abandoned its former policy toward landlords and peasants. From 14 to 23 November 1953, VWP organized a national conference, in this meeting, anti-feudalism was put much emphasis on. The most important change was that a new approach was adopted, which was mass mobilization for class struggle.

Land reform constituted two successive campaigns: land rent reduction campaign (1953-1954) and land reform campaign proper (1954-1956). The first campaign included eights waves and the second had five waves. According to Hoang Van Chi who was a former member of DRV and fled to South Vietnam in the mid-1950s, these two campaigns had but one purpose, namely the liquidation of the landowning class and the subsequent establishment of a proletarian dictatorship in the countryside. The only notable difference between them was the degree of violence and the nature of the wealth confiscated.

Land Rent Reduction Campaign: After being trained by Chinese, through the local party-cell, Vietnamese cadres were sent to the village and lived with a few landless peasants. They practiced the "Three Together System", namely, worked together, ate together and lived together. By doing so for two to three months, they had amassed much information of the peasants and that village, and also arouse awareness of social class by posing questions to the peasants like why they were poor.

After this survey by professionally trained cadres, the reduction campaign officially began, and there were six successive stages. The first stage was to classify population during which peasants were categorized according to their possession, this was followed by classification of landlords. Theoretically speaking, there were three classes of landlords: traitorous; ordinary; resistance and "democratic personalities". Those landlords, if found not comply with rent reduction decree, would be arrested. In this case, they had to pay back the excess land rent within time limit, this is the third stage of extortion of money and valuables. The fourth stage is crime revelation, the peasants were made to attend a special course and taught how to publicly reveal crimes of landlords, and they would have a role of denouncing crimes in the front of a number of people in the fifth stage, but the problem was that they denounced for appearing faithful and obedient to the party, so they may denounce as much as they can rather than considered the reality.

On 12 April 1953, a special people's tribunal court, composed of peasants who knew nothing about law, was formed according to decree 150/SL. Sentences varied from the death penalty to years' hard labor, for this point, the most well-known case was Nguyen Thi Nam, a patriotic landlord who joined the resistance war against the French but was sentenced to death. The label of landlord is dangerous. According to Hoang's memoir, as soon as a man was defined as landlord, he and his family were isolated from their fellow human beings and nobody was permitted to talk to them or even have any contact with them. This policy of isolation even caused a number of deaths.

Land Reform Campaign Proper: In the year of 1953, a series of decrees and laws on land reform were released. VWP central committee assessed the possibility of moving on to the last phase of land revolution: redistribution of agricultural land, which was followed by the most crucial land reform law publicized on 19 December 1953, which can be regarded as the platform for land reform. Very soon after the law was passed in national congress, the experimental wave of land reform took place between December 1953 and March 1954 in Thai Nguyen province. This experiment was fruitful according to the official, and a Central Land Reform Committee was established on 15 March 1954 which was headed by Pham Van Dong.

Compared to the prior campaign, land reform campaign proper was carried out more violently and in larger areas especially after the Geneva Conference because the VWP leaders realized that the Geneva Agreement was impossible to be implemented; and feared that Diem's "March North" may start a fire at its backyard. Five times the number of landlords than the first campaign was fixed by the party, thus it provoked increased internal conflict. According to Hoang, the DRV authorities never stated the number of dispossessed landlords in any of their official publications. Expropriation was occasional during the first campaign but it was universally practiced during the second. As soon as the confiscation ceremony was over, an exhibition of the confiscated personal belongings of the landlord was organized, and in doing so, class awareness was intentionally provoked by illustrating the sharp contrast in living standards between peasants and landlords. However, this is not the end, the next big question was the apportionment of land and other properties. Normal practice should distribute them among peasants, however, it lacked accurate information.

Chinese Involvement: Due to the traditionally close connection between China and Vietnam in general, and the enormous tie between Chinese and Vietnamese communists since 1949 in particular, right from the early 1950s onward, communist China's influence over DRV increased dramatically. There were three kinds of Chinese advisory groups in North Vietnam providing assistance in the aspect of military, politics and logistics. Chinese military advisory group was headed firstly by Wei Guoqing (July 1950- May 1951) providing directly consultation to the top commander of DRV. Chinese political advisory group was headed by Luo Guibo. Land reform was part of political issue, and Luo played a big role in it. Under political advisory group, a financial team was established in early 1951 to help North Vietnam formulate regulations on how to collect tax and rice. Since 1953, for facilitating mass mobilization and rent reduction campaign, more than 100 North Vietnamese cadres was sent to China to participate training class. Later on, in spring 1953, a particular institution exclusively in charge of helping DRV to conduct land reform was called the Land Reform and Party Consolidation Section which was headed by Zhang Dequn. According to his memoir, more land reform specialists of Chinese cadres were responsible for training. Similar to Chinese experience, social organizations such as peasant, youth, and women's league were established. Cadres were trained to practice Vietnamese version of Chinese "three together system" while peasants were mobilized and encouraged to "pour out grievances suffering from landlords and French collaborators". For the case of North Vietnam, some soldier was also affected due to their family background, and among the army, there were some degree of dissatisfaction. Considering this and from Chinese experience, Chinese advisors proposed to carry out a land reform education campaign among DRV's army. On February 1953, Luo Guibo sent a report to the Chinese leadership proposing a political consolidation campaign in order to make them aware of class distinction. On December 1953, the third National Congress passed land reform law which put forward route of land reform: step by step wipe out feudal system by relying on poor peasants, uniting middle and rich peasants. The Chinese pattern of land reform in DRV was successful in meeting the need of the poor peasants for land and thus increased the prestige of the new Communist authorities. However, it also produced significant negative consequences for the party due to that Mao's pattern of land reform emphasized the excessive class struggle and repression. This was an important reason for the later Vietnamese criticism of the Chinese model.

Repression: Executions and imprisonment of persons classified as "landlords" or enemies of the state were contemplated from the beginning of the land reform program. A Politburo document dated 4 May 1953 said that executions were "fixed in principle at the ratio of one per one thousand people of the total population." That ratio would indicate that communist Vietnam contemplated the execution of about 15,000 "reactionaries and evil landlords" in carrying out the program. On July 9, 1953, the first landlord executed was the woman Nguyễn Thị Năm, who had in fact been an active supporter of the Vietnamese Communist resistance.

The scale of the ensuing repression has proved difficult and controversial to quantify, with estimates of the number of executions ranging from 800 to 200,000. Testimony from North Vietnamese witnesses suggested a ratio of one execution for every 160 village residents, which extrapolated nationwide would indicate nearly 100,000 executions. Because the campaign was concentrated mainly in the Red River Delta area, a lower estimate of 50,000 executions became widely accepted by scholars at the time. A Saigon communique put the figure at 32,000 executions (12,000 party members and 20,000 others), based on the testimony of an ex-party member involved in the campaign. However, declassified documents from the Vietnamese and Hungarian archives indicate that the number of executions was much lower than reported at the time, although likely greater than 13,500. Economist Vo Nhan Tri reported uncovering a document in the central party archives which put the number of wrongful executions at 15,000. From discussions with party cadres, Vo Nhan Tri concluded that the overall number of deaths was considerably higher than this figure. According to the Vietnam Institute for Economics, 172,008 individuals were designated as landlords and rich peasants, of whom 71.66% were mistakenly categorized. Although it is impossible to know how many of them were executed, this suggests that the scale of errors committed "was undeniably dramatic."

"Rectification of errors": As soon as the reform was completed by 1956 and the so-called peasants' authority well-established in the villages, the party quite unexpectedly admitted to having made many serious mistakes during the reform when the "masses" had been "given a free hand".[46] VWP developed a campaign called "Rectification of Errors" from January 1957 till mid-1957. This campaign was divided into three phases. The first phase was a crash operation to survey the damage done and release from prison incorrectly classified peasants and falsely accused cadres. The second phase, more deliberate and the real heart of the campaign, was divided into two steps. Step I was the re-classification of peasants, and step II was the restitution of property erroneously expropriated or else making suitable compensation. The third phase of the mistake's correction was to be a review, inventory and concentrated re-indoctrination of local personnel.

Significance: As one of the most important events of DRV in the 1950s, as well as the first radical political campaigns of Vietnamese communists as an exclusive power-holder, this program has produced much controversial effect on North Vietnamese society, the government itself, as well as relations between peasants and the DRV regime. The reform also reached very considerable ends in terms of economic and social transformation. Economically speaking, collective ownership prevailed and the rural population was more or less equal. From the perspective of social transformation, it radically changed the traditional pattern of village: formerly, the landlords played a leading role in the village affairs but now they were eliminated and replaced by peasants. However, partly due to the land reform and other radical campaigns, nearly one million North Vietnamese moved to the South. Because of the use of violence and excessive emphasis over class struggle, land reform in the 1950s caused much negative impact. For this reason, it is still a sensitive topic even today. It also constitutes a considerable part of oversea Vietnamese political dissents criticizing today's communist party of Vietnam and its dependence on China. The aims of the reform were military, economic, political and social, the most important of which, until the decisive victory at Dien Bien Phu in May 1954, was the military objective. Ho Chi Minh once listed in 1956 achievements of land reform, nearly ten million peasants had received land; tens of thousands of new cadres had been trained in the countryside. The organization of the Party, the administration and peasants' associations in the communes have been readjusted. The Viet Minh regime gained its control over the grass village and its ability to influence and mobilize the mass was consolidated. Land reform is an agrarian project but also a political campaign. Through mass mobilization and classification, anti-revolutionary and reactionary enemies were suppressed economically and politically. This had a nearly profound impact for wars in the latter years. One, this paved the way for the socialist construction in the North, which could provide southern communists with logistical support. Two, the reform can be regarded as a preparatory step for a large-scale war. The regime opened the door to enlightenment by completely altering the existing patterns of production; but also provided the masses with an ideology which would modify their attitude to work even before the economic conditions were fundamentally changed.

Dommen, Arthur J. (2001), The Indochinese Experience of the French and the Americans, Indiana University Press, p. 340.

"Newly released documents on the land reform". Vietnam Studies Group. Archived from the original on 2011-04-20. Retrieved 2016-07-15. "Vu Tuong: There is no reason to expect, and no evidence that I have seen to demonstrate, that the actual executions were less than planned; in fact, the executions perhaps exceeded the plan if we consider two following factors. First, this decree was issued in 1953 for the rent and interest reduction campaign that preceded the far more radical land redistribution and party rectification campaigns (or waves) that followed during 1954-1956. Second, the decree was meant to apply to free areas (under the control of the Viet Minh government), not to the areas under French control that would be liberated in 1954-1955 and that would experience a far more violent "

Let's follow Nguyen van Hai's journey, shall we?

Operation of Freedom- The Evacuation from North to South Vietnam 1954

Anticommunist Vietnamese refugees moving from a French LSM landing ship to the USS Montague during Operation Passage to Freedom in August 1954. [en.wikipedia.org › wiki › 1954_Geneva_Conference]- 1954 Geneva Conference – Wikipedia

THE BLOWING OF THE WIND
ACROSS THE GRASS FIELD

Nguyen van Giap carried his little sister, Nguyen Hoa Le on his back and walked with Nguyen van Hai, the younger brother by his side; they walked across the field among the snipers' shots of the militia of the Communist party. The rain fluttered on the grass with the crescent moon spread dimming light on the three orphans. Nguyen van Giap felt the cold wind blowing the rain on his face, on his body as pushing him backward. He comforted the little girl, "I'll take care of you. I promise. "

A group of peasants hurried passing the three orphans, Nguyen van Giap asked a man,

"Tell me, please…Where're you going?"

"We're heading to Hai Phong harbor where the US Operation of Freedom ship would take us the South."

"Nguyen van Hai, go with them." Nguyen van Giap told his younger brother

"Huh?" Nguyen van Hai gazed at Nguyen van Giap, "How about you and Hoa Le?"

"I'll take care of Hoa Le; we might join you later. Listen, go with them so you may have a life." Nguyen van Giap pushed Nguyen van Hai, a nine years old boy- into the refugee crowd. Nguyen van Hai turned his head glancing at his brother and sister but he couldn't see them. [Nguyen van Giap lay down on the grass next to the injured sister Nguyen Hoa Le avoiding Nguyen van Hai's parting moment.] A man in the refugee group screamed at Nguyen van Hai, "Run for your life, kid!". The young boy hurried to catch up with the crowd into an arduous, unknown journey.

At sunset, immigrant group rested under the roof of an abandoned temple; at dawn, they traveled again. Early in the morning, when the grass field was still wet with dew, the refugees continued their flight. Nguyen van Hai looked at the meadow, the green grass stretched out toward the horizon. Oh, the green grass field of home! The village with thatched roofs along the bamboo hedge, the wild flowers under the blue sky full with birds' singing where the Nguyen van Hai chased the butterflies…. now the village was on fire, killing, and deaths happened everywhere. A cold strong wind blew by the field pressing the green grass, the green fragile blades bowed down toward the gale direction. The young boy Nguyen van Hai compared himself to a green grass blade, the fragile épée lowered itself under the strong blowing wind. The orphan young boy didn't know the reason of the country's chaos, he struggled for survival in this world by following the waves of thousands of people in the Operation of Freedom- The Evacuation from North to South Vietnam 1954 with no idea about their future.

The refugees entered the - "big open-mouthed ship"-sponsored by the Administration of President Eisenhower of the United States of America taking the Northern refugees to the South Vietnam. The homeless people were greeted friendly "Hello!" by the American soldiers on the ship.

Anticommunist Vietnamese refugees moving from a French LSM landing ship to the USS Montague during Operation Passage to Freedom in August 1954. [en.wikipedia.org › wiki › 1954_Geneva_Conference]

Standing in the line waiting for food, Nguyen van Hai was given a can of soup with some crackers by an American sailor,

"What do you like to drink? "the sailor asked

Nguyen van Hai starred at him as he didn't understand English.

The sailor smiled and gave him a bottle of orange juice and two slices of bread, "Here, you go!"

The boy walked to a corner on the deck of the ship among the Vietnamese northern evacuees who held on tightly to their belongings: a few bags of clothes, hats, shoes, pots and pans....The blowing of the Pacific ocean wind created high waves and flashed the water on the refugees made them shivering; a Vietnamese man approached him with a sweater and said, "Put it on, child."

"Thank you. "the boy said

"Where're your parents or relatives?" the man inquired

"I lost my parents when Viet Minh took control."

"I'm Tran van Phu. I and my wife have a one-year old boy. My parents are also with me, how about you stay with our family? "the man put his hand on Nguyen van Hai's shoulders, "How old are you?"

"I'm nine years old, I'm happy to be with you family." The boy looked up at the man

"Come with me, carry these soups and crackers to our family." the man said

They walked to an old man and an old woman huddled themselves in a torn canvas under the chilly wind from the Pacific ocean [Tran van Phu's parents]; nearby, a middle age woman [Truong thi Cuc- Tran van Phu's wife] with a young child[Tran San], Truong thi Cuc grumbled as she saw Nguyen van Hai,

"One more mouth to feed? Why did it take so long for the food?"

"Here're your supper," the man gave the soup to his wife and whispered to her, "The Americans feed us on this ship. When we are in the South, with a healthy orphan; isn't it nice that you have a helper for the baby?" turning to the old couple, he said, "And here're yours. Ma and Pa, are you alright? And here's Nguyen van Hai lost his parents. It's fine for him to be with us, right?"

"Everything has a reason," the old man said while the old woman added, "Adopt him, you'll obtain blessings from the Buddha."

"Thank you, Ma and Pa." Tran van Phu said

"The soup warms us up a little bit!" the old couple mumbled

"Take care of your little brother San." the middle age woman ordered Nguyen van Hai

"Yes, Mom. "the young boy bowed his head and sat next to the baby; he gave San a spoon of soup.

"Mash the potato and the meat first, he doesn't swallow very well yet. "the woman yelled and slapped Nguyen van Hai

"Don't do that, Cuc!" the older woman stopped Truong thi Cuc before she gave Nguyen van Hai another slap, "He's just a young child lost his parents..." and she told Nguyen van Hai, "Take the baby here, I'll show you how to feed him."

"Yes, Grandma. "Nguyen van Hai replied.

After supper, they retired on the mats. Homesick, Nguyen van Hai cried himself to sleep. How were Nguyen van Giap and Hoa Le doing? Oh! The boy missed his family so much. How could the young boy Nguyen van Hai understand the cause of his leaving home to get in an American ship to south Vietnam, knowing nobody, and an unknown future?

Let's take a look at the Geneva Treaty which divided Vietnam into two parts, North and South Vietnam by the 17th parallel. [Excerpt from en.wikipedia.org › wiki › 1954_Geneva_Conference/1954 Geneva Conference. Translation: Pham ThuDzung]

The Geneva Conference started in April, 1954 the discussions on Indochina did not begin until May 8, 1954 after Viet Minh- the army directed by Vo Nguyen Giap fought a guerrilla war, against [and defeated] the French military [by] employed traditional Western technology. The Eisenhower administration of the United States had considered air strikes in support of the French at Dien Bien Phu but was unable to obtain a commitment to united action from key allies such as the United Kingdom. However, the Viet Minh achieved the upmost decisive victory over the French Union forces at Dien Bien Phu on May 7th, 1954.

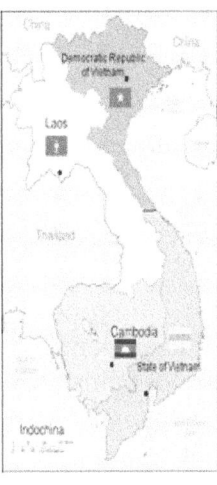

The Western allies (the United States, the United Kingdom, and France colonialism) did not have a unified position on what the Conference was to achieve in relation to Indochina. Anthony Eden, leading the British delegation, favored a negotiated settlement to the conflict. Georges Bidault, leading the French delegation, vacillated and was keen to preserve something of France's position in Indochina to justify past sacrifices, even as the nation's military situation deteriorated. The US had been supporting the French in Indochina for many years and the Republican Eisenhower administration wanted to ensure that it could not have "lost" Indochina to the Communists. Three successor states were created: The Kingdom of Cambodia, the Kingdom of Laos, and the Democratic Republic of Vietnam, the state led by Ho Chi Minh and the Viet Minh. The State of Vietnam was reduced to the southern part of Vietnam. The division of Vietnam at the 17th parallel was intended to be temporary, with elections planned for in 1956 to reunify the country.

Behind the scenes, the US and the French governments continued to discuss the terms for possible US military intervention in Indochina. Eisenhower, President of the US at that time (1953-1961) would seek Congressional approval for military intervention in Indochina, but US failed to have the approval of Australian and New Zealand governments in supporting US military intervention forces in Vietnam. By mid-June, the US began to consider the possibility that rather than supporting the French in Indochina, it might be preferable for the French to leave and for the US to support the new Indochinese states. Phạm Văn Đồng, the leader of the Democratic Republic of Vietnam (DRV) delegation the Viet Minh had tried to ensure that the Pathet Lao and Khmer Issarak would join the governments in Laos and Cambodia, respectively, under the leadership of the DRV. The Chinese also sought to ensure that Laos and Cambodia were under China's preventing Vietnam's future influence in these countries.

On June 16, 1954 twelve days after France granted full independence to the State of Vietnam, Bao Dai [the last Emperor of Vietnam] appointed Ngo Dinh Diem as Prime Minister of Vietnam. Diem was a staunch nationalist, both anti-French and anticommunist, with strong political connections in the US. Diem agreed to take the position if he received all civilian and military powers. On June 23, 1954 Mendès France secretly met with Zhou Enlai at the French embassy in Bern. Zhou outlined the Chinese position that an immediate ceasefire was required, the three nations should be treated separately, and that two governments existed in Vietnam would be recognized. They agreed that the Bao Dai government would need time to consolidate its position and that US assistance would be vital while Viet Minh might have prolonged the negotiations and continued fighting to achieve a more favorable position militarily. In addition, there was a widespread perception that the Diem government would collapse, leaving the Viet Minh free to take control of the State of Vietnam.

On July 20, 1954 the partition line of north and south Vietnam was settled at the 17th parallel and that the elections for reunification should be in July 1956, two years after the ceasefire. The "Agreement on the Cessation of Hostilities in Vietnam" was signed only by French and Viet Minh military commands, completely bypassing the State of Vietnam. Based on a proposal by Zhou Enlai, an International Control Commission (ICC) was in charge of supervising the ceasefire and the elections. The Viet Minh never accepted ICC authority over these matters.

Provisions: The accords, issued on July 21, 1954, set out the following terms in relation to Vietnam:

1) the "provisional military demarcation line" running approximately along the 17th Parallel "on either side of which the forces of the two parties shall be regrouped after their withdrawal".

2) 3 miles (4.8 km) wide demilitarized zone on each side of the demarcation line.

3) French Union forces to regroup to the south of the line and Viet Minh to the north.

4) free movement of the population between the zone for three hundred days.

5) neither zone to join any military alliance or seek military reinforcement establishment of the International Control Commission, comprising Canada, Poland and India as chair, to monitor the ceasefire.

Reactions: The DRV at Geneva accepted a much worse settlement than the military situation on the ground indicated. "For Ho Chi Minh, there was no getting around the fact that his victory [Dien Bien Phu], however unprecedented and stunning was incomplete and perhaps temporary. The vision that had always driven him on, that of a 'great union' of all Vietnamese, had flickered into view for a fleeting moment in 1945–46, then had been lost in the subsequent war. Now, despite vanquishing the French military, the dream remained unrealized..." That was partly as a result of the great pressure exerted by China (Pham Van Dong is alleged to have said in one of the final negotiating sessions that Zhou Enlai double-crossed the DRV) and the Soviet Union for their own purposes, but the Viet Minh had their own reasons for agreeing to a negotiated settlement, principally their own concerns regarding the balance of forces and fear of US intervention.

Aftermath: On October 9, 1954, the tricolored flag [French flag in Indochina] was lowered for the last time at the Hanoi Citadel and the last French Union forces left the city, crossing the Paul Doumer Bridge on their way to Haiphong for embarkation. For the communist forces, which were instrumental in the defeat of the French, the ideology of communism and nationalism were linked. Many communist sympathizers viewed the South Vietnamese as a French colonial remnant and later an American puppet regime. On the other hand, many others viewed the North Vietnamese as a puppet of Communist International.

After the cessation of hostilities, a large migration took place. North Vietnamese, especially Catholics, intellectuals, business people, land owners, anti-communist democrats, and members of the middle-class moved south of the Accords-mandated ceasefire line during Operation Passage to Freedom. The ICC reported that at least 892,876 North Vietnamese were processed through official refugee stations, while journalists recounted that as many as 2 million more might have fled without the presence of Viet Minh soldiers, who frequently beat and occasionally killed those who refused to turn back. The CIA attempted to further influence Catholic Vietnamese with slogans such as "the Virgin Mary is moving South". At the same time, 52,000 people from the South went North, mostly Viet Minh members and their families.

The US replaced the French as a political backup for Ngo Dinh Diem, the Prime Minister of the State of Vietnam, who asserted his power in South Vietnam. [In 1954 Diem began serving as prime minister in what would become the Republic of Vietnam (South Vietnam). Diem defeated Bao Dai in a referendum in October 1955, ousted the emperor, and made himself president.[Excerpt from Ngo Dinh Diem | Facts, Vietnam War, & Death | Britannica/ www.britannica.com › Presidents & Heads of States] [Excerpt from en.wikipedia.org › wiki › 1954_Geneva_Conference/1954 Geneva Conference]The Geneva conference had not provided any specific mechanisms for the national elections planned for 1956, and Diem refused to hold them by citing that the South had not signed and were not bound to the Geneva Accords and that it was impossible to hold free elections in the communist North. Instead, he went about attempting to crush communist opposition. North Vietnam violated the Geneva Accords by failing to withdraw all Viet Minh troops from South Vietnam, stifling the movement of North Vietnamese refugees, and conducting a military buildup that more than doubled the number of armed divisions in the North Vietnamese army while the South Vietnamese army was reduced by 20,000 men. US military advisers continued to support the Army of the Republic of Vietnam, which was created as a replacement for the Vietnamese National Army. The failure of reunification led to the creation of the National Liberation Front (better known as the Viet Cong) by Ho Chi Minh's government. They were closely aided by the Vietnam People's Army (VPA) of the North, also known as the North Vietnamese Army. The result was the Vietnam War [1954-1975]. Historian John Lewis Gaddis said that the Geneva accords 1954 "were so hastily drafted and ambiguously worded that, from the standpoint of international law, it makes little sense to speak of violations from either side."

Land reform in South Vietnam- en.wikipedia.org ›

Following World War II [1945], the communist Việt Minh (the predecessor of Viet Cong) fought against the French colonialists and their local supporters (mainly landowners) in the First Indochina War. At the time, a large percentage of agricultural land was owned by powerful landowners and the majority of the rural population of Vietnam owned only small plots of land (with little legal assurance) or were simply landless peasants. The early success of the land reform program under the Viet Minh gave the communists a strong base of support among the 80% of the Vietnamese people who lived in rural areas.

Early reforms enacted by the South Vietnamese government in the 1950s largely failed, as the ordinances prescribed by the government often attempted to directly undo the already-popular land reforms of the Việt Minh, requiring poor peasants to pay to acquire land that the communists had already given to them. During the 1960s, such programs were rendered defunct and unenforceable due to the South Vietnamese army's inability to control farmland territories against the Viet Cong. In the 1970s, South Vietnam implemented the "Land to the Tiller" reform with the aid of the United States. This program was more successful than earlier programs, and was almost entirely underwritten by the United States. The reform program was discontinued in 1975 following South Vietnam's defeat in the Vietnam War and the unification of Vietnam.

Bernard B. Fall a prominent war correspondent, historian, political scientist, and expert on Indochina during the 1950s and 1960s, claimed that delayed land reform in South Vietnam had played such a fundamental role in the Vietnam War that it was as important as "ammunition for howitzers." South Vietnam's ally and financial supporter, the United States, either failed to realise the importance of land reform in a timely fashion or was not able to persuade the South Vietnamese government of its importance. Andrew Biggs, at researcher at the University of Washington argues that the "Land to the Tiller" program of the early 1970s was too little, too late to swing the war in the favour of the US. In the words of an American official, Robert Samson "The Americans (lost the war because) they offered the peasant a constitution; the Viet Cong offered him his land and with it the right to survive".

(Continued by The Wind Teases the Falling Leaves)

THE WIND TEASES THE FALLING LEAVES

Life is a leaf in the innocent wind
South Vietnam from 1940 to 1950

In the French rule period [1945], Mr. Vo Thanh was a wealthy landowner in the Tien Giang area, his father inherited a prosperous 150-hectare- rice field from his great grandfather and passed it down to his son, Vo Hung. Under the revolution of Vietnam Army [Communist- Viet Minh, the predecessors of Viet Cong] regime, Vo Hung lost most of his land since Communist-Viet Minh took it away from him and redistributed to the peasants in 1949. Why was Mr. Vo Hung not beheaded as Mr. Nguyen van Ba? [Tran van Hai's biological father, Nguyen van Ba named his son- Nguyen van Hai at birth. Later, Nguyen van Hai by adoption by Tran van Phu, his named was changed to Tran van Hai.] Mr. Nguyen van Ba was a wealthy landowner in the North Vietnam; he was sentenced and beheaded by the People Court when Communist- Viet Minh took over the government in North Vietnam, in 1949] while Mr. Vo Hung a wealthy landowner in South Vietnam was able to keep a large portion of his rice land.

Vo Kiet, the only son of Mr. Vo Hung, in the 1940's, Vo Kiet was the "My Tho's Childe" in My Tho. He had a lavish life: Mr. Vo Hung sent Vo Kiet to study in Hanoi College de France, a privilege institute for students from wealthy families. One day, Vo Kiet drove the Peugeot in the suburb of Hanoi. Vo Kiet was neither familiar with this road nor had experience of driving on a winding course. He couldn't totally control the car, it swerved into the shoulder of the road where the flower girl displayed her bouquets, she ran off and fell on the ground. Vo Kiet walked out from the Peugeot to her,

"I'm sorry, Miss. I'm Vo Kiet. What's your name? Did you get hurt?" Childe asked

"Nguyen thi Lan" she said

The flower girl quietly collected the lotuses and chrysanthemums scattered on the ground. Vo Kiet saw some bleeding cuts in her right arm, he told her,

"Miss, you're bleeding. Let me take you to a doctor."

The girl shook her head and went to look for some herbs. Vo Kiet followed her. The girl picked up some special grass. After washing the cuts, she rubbed the leaves over the lesion. Vo Kiet was amazed: no more bleeding. He helped her to bandage the cuts by tearing his handkerchief into stripes.

"How do you what kind of grass will stop the bleeding?" Childe asked in curiosity

"My grandfather is an herbalist," the girl replied with a smile

108

"Please let me take you home." he said

"Leave me alone." she hurriedly walked away

Vo Kiet followed her. The flower girl entered a brick home by the back door. Vo Kiet hid behind a bush. A man looked much older than the flower girl opened the door, the man yelled and beat the flower girl,

"Why are you so late? Give me the money you earned today."

She gave him the money. Putting the money into his wallet, he said, "Now, I go for a drink, back later."

Vo Kiet waited until the man disappeared, he asked Nguyen thi Lan,

"How is that man related to you?"

"He's the landowner- Mr. Ta Tri. I'm his concubine." The flower girl burst into tears

She told Vo Kiet: Nguyen Quy and Le thi Dau, her father and mother- both were peasants who worked for the landowner Ta Tri on his rice field, and her younger brother, Nguyen Cam tended the buffalo. Ta Tri, a married 47 years old land owner, he had one and a 50 hectares of rice field, a wife and two children, cattle, and houses. Ta Tri paid the peasants' labor by a few bags of rice for their work. A few years ago, a gale that blew the roof of Nguyen Quy's hut away. Nguyen Quy borrowed Ta Tri one hundred "dongs" to repair the roof. Ta Tri calculated the interest and insisted to have the loan paid off this year or Ta Tri would drag Nguyen Quy to court to be imprisoned. Nguyen thi Lan, 17 years old daughter of Nguyen Quy, submitted herself to be TaTri's concubine to release her father from trouble. Ta Tri liked drinking; he beat Nguyen thi Lan for money "to have a good time at the pub".

"Please don't do anything, otherwise he'll beat me." Nguyen thi Lan begged

"I help you out of here. Nobody will hurt you anymore." Childe Vo Kiet promised

While they were talking, Ta Tri's wife called out loud, "Lan, prepare some tea!"

"Go away, right now!" Nguyen thi Lan hastily pushed Vo Kiet out of the door

"I'll help you." Vo Kiet repeated

Vo Kiet found the land owner, Ta Tri in a pub, he arranged to pay Nguyen thi Lan's parents' debt to set her free. Ta Tri agreed [he said the debt was 150 "dongs" while it was only 100 "dongs"]. Vo Kiet paid in full, 150 "dongs". Grabbing the money, Ta Tri laughed out loud, "Idiot, you know how many times I had sex with her?"

"Please let her go." Vo Kiet requested

"Go get her, she's yours now. "Ta Tri raised the money to the bartender, "Pour for everybody a shot, my treat today."

"Bravo Ta Tri!" folks at the pub roared

Vo Kiet took Nguyen thi Lan to her parents' house, a thatched hut in that village. Nguyen Quy and Le thi Dau were moved by Vo Kiet's kindness to save their daughter from the land owner, Ta Tri. The flower girl told her parents about Childe Vo Kiet's noble action to rescue her.

"Mom and Dad, I'd not be able to repay him in this life time, next life I will!" Nguyen thi Lan cried

"Please don't say that," Vo Kiet said, "I love you. Will you go with me to My Tho, south Vietnam?"

"Wherever you're are, I'll be with you." The flower girl Nguyen thi Lan said

"I'm Nguyen Quy. I and my wife, Le thi Dau appreciated your kindness to free our daughter Nguyen thi Lan from the landowner, Ta Tri. What is your plan for her?" Nguyen Quy inquired

"Mr. Nguyen Quy, I'm Vo Kiet, 20 years old." Vo Kiet said, "I've just graduated from College de France in Hanoi. I want to give Nguyen thi Lan a better life. My father, Vo Hung, was inherited 150 hectares of rice field in My Tho, south Vietnam. Will you accept me as your son in law? May I take her to My Tho introducing to my family?"

"Very good!" Nguyen Quy patted on Vo Kiet's shoulder, "It's fate that my daughter met you. The favor you did for her, I'll never forget. The walls here have ears, you should return to Hanoi. I will arrange for my daughter to meet you later and both of you can go to the South."

"Thanks to the Buddha." Le thi Dau- the mother said in tears

"Thank you, Mom and Dad." Vo Kiet bowed his head and he told Nguyen thi Lan, "I return to Hanoi, then I'll go to My Tho to talk to my parents about you. I'll be back. I love you."

"Take care!" Nguyen thi Lan held Vo Kiet's hands in hers, "I love you, too."

"When is the wedding?" Nguyen Cam asked

"Cam, be quiet!" Le thi Dau reprimanded her son

"Good bye Mom and Dad." Vo Kiet waved to Nguyen Cam, "See you later!"

Nguyen Quy and Le thi Dau have worked for Ta Tri over twenty years, however; they have nothing and the family was constantly not having enough food to eat. Nguyen Quy loathed Ta Tri and he vowed to revenge. Three years ago, Nguyen Quy secretly joined the Viet Minh Party. Why did Nguyen Quy and many young men from North Vietnam voluntarily enlisted in the North Vietnamese People's Army of Vietnam (PAVN) and the Viet Minh? Let's take a look at Viet Minh-www.britannica. com ›-Vietnamese revolutionary organization- The Editors of Encyclopaedia Britannica: League for the Independence of Vietnam, Viet Nam Doc Lap Dong Minh Hoi. [Excerpt from www.britannica.com by Pham ThuDzung]

Viet Minh, in full Viet Nam Doc Lap Dong Minh Hoi, [English: League for the Independence of Vietnam] the organization that led the struggle for Vietnamese independence from French rule. The Viet Minh was formed in China in May 1941 by Ho Chi Minh. Although led primarily by communists, the Viet Minh operated as a national front organization open to persons of various political persuasions. In late 1943, members of the Viet Minh, led by General Vo Nguyen Giap, began to infiltrate Vietnam to launch guerrilla operations against the Japanese, who occupied the country during World War II. The Viet Minh forces liberated considerable portions of northern Vietnam, and after the Japanese surrender to the Allies, Viet Minh units seized control of Hanoi and proclaimed the independent Democratic Republic of Vietnam. The French at first promised to recognize the new government as a free state but failed to do so. On November 23, 1946, at least 6,000 Vietnamese civilians were killed in a French naval bombardment of the port city of Haiphong, and the First Indochina War began [1946-1954]. The Viet Minh had popular support and was able to dominate the countryside, while the French strength lay in urban areas. As the war neared an end, the Viet Minh was succeeded by a new organization, the Lien Viet, or Vietnamese National Popular Front. In 1951 the majority of the Viet Minh leadership was absorbed into the Lao Dong, or Vietnamese Workers' Party (later Vietnamese Communist Party), which remained the dominant force in North Vietnam. Elements of the Viet Minh joined with the Viet Cong against the U.S.-supported government of South Vietnam and the United States in the Vietnam War (Second Indochina War [1956-1975]) of the late 1950s, the '60s, and the early '70s. After the reunification of the country (1976), Viet Minh leaders continued to take an active role in Vietnamese politics.

Excerpt from VietCong – Wikipedia- en.wikipedia.org › wiki ›Việt Cộng was also known as the National Liberation Front of South Vietnam or FNL (from French Front National de Libération), was a mass political organization in South Vietnam and Cambodia with its own army – the Liberation Army of South Vietnam (LASV) – that fought against the United States and South Vietnamese governments during the Vietnam War[1956-1975], eventually emerging on the winning side. It had both guerrilla and regular army units, as well as a network of cadres who organized peasants in the territory it controlled. Many soldiers were recruited in South Vietnam, but others were attached to the People's Army of Vietnam (PAVN), the regular North Vietnamese army. During the Vietnam War, the Communist Party in North Vietnam and anti-war activists insisted the Việt Cộng was an insurgency indigenous to the South, while the U.S. and South Vietnamese governments portrayed the group as a tool of Hanoi. Although the terminology distinguishes northerners from the southerners, communist forces were under a single Communist command structure set up in 1958, in Hanoi.

North Vietnam established the National Liberation Front on December 20, 1960, to foment insurgency in the South. Many of the Việt Cộng's core members were volunteer "regroupees", southern Việt Minh who had resettled in the North after the Geneva Accord (1954). Hanoi gave the regroupees military training and sent them back to the South along the Ho Chi Minh trail in the early 1960s. The National Liberation Front [NLF] called for southern Vietnamese to "overthrow the camouflaged colonial regime of the American imperialists" and to make "efforts toward the peaceful unification". The Liberation Army of South Vietnam's [LASV] best-known action was the Tet Offensive, a gigantic assault on more than 100 South Vietnamese urban centers in 1968, including an attack on the U.S. embassy in Saigon. The offensive riveted the attention of the world's media for weeks, but also overextended the Việt Cộng. Later communist offensives were conducted predominantly by the North Vietnamese. The organization was dissolved in 1976 when North and South Vietnam were officially unified under a communist government.

South Vietnam 1948

On the way back to Hanoi, Vo Kiet realized in an impulse he spent money lavishly. How could he explain and introduce Nguyen thi Lan to his Mom and Dad? However, Vo Kiet kept his promise with Nguyen thi Lan. A month later, he took Nguyen thi Lan to My Tho to meet his family. Mr. Vo Hung was upset when Vo Kiet, asked for a wedding with Nguyen thi Lan. Mr. Vo Hung raised his voice,

"Last week, Viet Minh warned me about land reform. We're going to lose our land; I don't even know about our fate. Do you know how much I paid for your tuition and expenses in Hanoi? Now you bring home a northerner, is this your piety to your parents?"

"We've arranged an engagement for you and Tran Kim Hoa this summer." Mrs. Vo Hung said

"I'll go back home in the North. Pardon me, Mr. and Mrs. Vo Hung." Nguyen thi Lan bowed her head

"No, you stay here." Vo Kiet told Nguyen thi Lan, he begged his father, "Dad, I love her. Please give me half a hectare at the far east of your rice field. I'll live there with my wife."

"You can plough?" Mr. Vo Hung walked out, but he confronted with a stranger,

"Not so rush, Mr. Vo Hung." Mr. Nguyen Quy said,

"Who are you? How did you know my name?" Mr. Vo Hung inquired

"My name is Nguyen Quy, Nguyen thi Lan is my daughter. I've met your son, Vo Kiet." Mr. Nguyen Quy said, "Did Bui Than talk to you about land reform?"

"How is it concerned you?" Vo Hung was irritated, "I have it until the end of the month to give up 10% of my land to the peasants, do you need to remind me?"

"I appreciate your son, Vo Kiet recued my daughter from the landowner Ta Tri in north Vietnam. I'd like to repay his kindness." Nguyen Quy said, "I suggest ..."

"Viet Minh wants 10%, you also want 10%; how much land will I lose?" Vo Hung was angry

"No," Nguyen Quy explained, "totally only 10%. You give to me, I'm a Viet Minh comrade. I volunteered to the South in the land reform project. As I receive the land from you, I let Vo Kiet, Nguyen thi Lan, and my family live there. Vo Kiet is your only son, you give him 10% of the inheritance- it's reasonable; otherwise, that part of the land would belong to a stranger- any peasant in this area. What would you rather do? Give it to your son is better, would you agree with me?"

"Northerners are very cunning, you win anyway!" Vo Hung burst into laughing

"Should we lean on one another for survival?" Nguyen Quy said

"Welcome, my in- law!" Vo Hung said, "Vo Kiet only knows his text books, no idea about life."

"We, the Viet Minh provides rice land for the peasants and pay them for their labor. Vo Kiet will receive the benefit from the rice land somewhat little bit less than you have got before the reform." Nguyen Quy smiled, "On the other hand, you gain a daughter- in- law!"

"Thank you, Mom and Dad," Vo Kiet bowed to his parents and to Nguyen Quy, "Thank you, Dad."

"Thank you, Mom and Dad." Nguyen thi Lan bowed to Mr. and Mrs. Vo Hung and to her father, "Thank you, Dad."

"Let's have dinner together." Mrs. Vo Hung said and she called the servants, "Prepare meal!"

A servant helped Mrs. Vo Hung up because her left knee hurt.

"Mom, I know an herb can ease off your pain. My grandfather was an herbalist." Nguyen thi Lan said,

"I don't have a daughter, now I have one. Thanks to the Buddha." Mrs. Vo Hung laughed with her husband

"Let's have dinner together!" Mr. Vo Hung invited the guests

Vo Kiet took care of his father's [Vo Hung] rice field business, and his wife practiced herbal medicine to care for the sick in the village. At that time, there were only medical doctors and hospitals in big cities like Sai Gon. In the rural areas, people still went to see an herbalist in case they were sick.

South Vietnam 1960- 1970

Vo Kiet and Nguyen thi Lan had a son and twin daughters: Vo Hoang, Vo thi Thu and Vo thi Tam. In 1960, after graduation from High school, Vo Hoang obtained the Fulbright scholarship to study Mechanics Engineering at the University of Austin, Texas. Vo thi Thu and Vo thi Tam attended tenth grade at My Tho high school. The family was so excited that Vo Hoang go to study in America! This was a wonderful opportunity for the young Vietnamese to explore the world, to build his promising future. The neighbors came to congratulate the parents and wish Vo Hoang all the best in his future. On the day Vo Hoang flew to America, the whole family: the parents, Vo Kiet, Nguyen thi Lan, and the twin girls, Vo thi Thu, Vo thi Tam went to Tan Son Nhất Airport in Saigon to say "Good Luck!" to Vo Hoang. "We're proud of you." They said and hugged him,

"I know you will be a good student." The twin girls told their brother

Vo Hoang was overjoyed about a promising future, yet he was a bit anxious about living in a foreign country, far away from home. Embracing his family, he said, "I love you all."

"We love you, too! When we see you again, you'll be famous!" Vo Hung said

The announcement called the passengers to board the plane to America. Vo Hoang waved to his family as walking toward the gate, "I'll come back." he promised

Vo Hoang left in on the first week of August to prepare for

the academic year in America; the twin girls were still in summer vacation time, for school year started the day after Labor Day September 7th in Vietnam. Vo thi Tam went to visit a relative in Khanh Hoa [Aunt Truong thi Hoa was Truong thi Cuc's sister. Truong thi Cuc's husband- Tran van Phu adopted Nguyen van Hai and changed his name to Tran van Hai.] Vo thi Thu preferred to stay in My Tho [she volunteered to teach an adult class The Vietnamese Alphabet: Read & Write"]. One day, Vo thi Thu went to work, she saw a young man got stuck in a ditch. She asked, "What happened?"

"I fell into the ditch. Could you give me some water?" the man said with the central accent

Seeing his uniform, Vo thi Thu realized that he was one of the Communist Viet Minh- Viet Cong comrades who mingled in with the southern people, she had nothing to do with him. When she just about to walk away, the comrade called out, "Please give me some water. I'm very thirsty."

Vo thi Thu hesitated for a few seconds then she gave him some water,

"Hold on, I have to find somebody to pull you out of the mud."

"I got shot in arm in a conflict with the QLVNCH [ARSVN Army of Republic South Vietnam], I can't get out. "the comrade said, "Please go to the house number 5 in the village ask comrade Le van Xuan to help me. I'm comrade Truong van Mai, from Central Vietnam." The comrade gawked at the girl, "Do you want to help or call the Republic Police to put me in jail?"

"I don't want you to be in jail. I'll go to comrade Le van Xuan. Wait here. I'll be back." Vo thi Thu waved her hand

"Could I trust you?" Truong van Mai asked

"My grandfather is comrade Nguyen Quy." Vo thi Thu said in a soft voice to Truong van Mai

Vo thi Thu went to comrade Le van Xuan's home, who lived not too far from Mr. Vo Kiet's house; Vo thi Thu did not know there were Communist Viet Minh- Viet Cong's in the neighborhood. Vo thi Thu told comrade Le van Xuan about comrade Truong van Mai. Immediately comrade Le van Xuan said, "Take me to where he is."

When comrade Truong van Mai saw comrade Le van Xuan, he said, "Comrade Le van Xuan, last night, the VNCH soldiers [South Vietnam military under Ngo Dinh Diem administration] attacked us. I got shot; I fell in to this ditch so they didn't see me. My arm is broken; I can't get out. Would you help me out from the ditch?"

"Hold on onto me, Comrade Truong van Mai!" Comrade Le van Xuan lifted comrade Truong van Mai when Vo thi Thu helped with the wounded arm.

Comrade Le van Xuan put comrade Truong van Mai on the ground, Vo thi Thu looked at the saw the injury, she said,

"Please take him to my home; my parents can help him."

Comrade Le van Xuan stared at comrade Truong van Mai for the decision, comrade Truong van Mai said,

"Take me there."

When they arrived at Mr. Vo Kiet's home, Vo thi Thu signaled the two comrades,

"Please wait here. I'll ask my father."

"I'll not forget your favor." Comrade Truong van Mai said

Vo thi Thu told her father about the wounded comrade, at first Mr. Vo Kiet was hesitated to help, for he lived in My Tho-South Vietnam, [South Vietnam at that time was under the Ngo Dinh Diem administration; this government only controlled Saigon and other big cities, the rural and countryside were a mixture of Viet Cong and Southerners of Vietnam which were uncontrollable by the military of the Republic of South Vietnam. Communist-Viet Minh [Viet Cong] received military support by China trafficked through Laos and Cambodia.]

"Help him, father." Vo thi Thu begged, "Grandfather is also

a comrade from the North."

Mr. Vo Kiet saw the compassion of his daughter toward comrade Truong van Mai. Did Vo Kiet also fall in love with a communist's daughter in north Vietnam?

"Let's ask Grandpa Nguyen Quy for help." Mr. Vo Kiet said

Comrade Nguyen Quy came to see comrade Truong van Mai, he said,

"The left arm is broken. I'll take care of this," Comrade Nguyen Quy said, "I have connection with the surgeon."

After a few minutes, somebody took Truong van Mai away. Vo thi Thu worried,

"Grandpa, when could I see him again?"

"Ah, it's fate…. how mysterious life is!" Mr. Vo Kiet said

Comrade Truong van Mai was secretly transferred to a place with a sign "Seamstress" with some models of traditional Vietnamese clothing's, but inside was the operation room of Dr. Bui and the assistants to treat wounded Viet Minh [Viet Cong] comrades. Vo thi Thu was anxious to hear about comrade Truong van Mai, but Grandpa Nguyen Quy had gone for two days, without any news. At last, Grandpa returned, he said, "Luckily, it was not too serious. Dr. Bui operated it and put a cast over the upper left arm. He will be there for a week to recover." Turning to Vo thi Thu, he added, "Comrade Truong van Mai said "Thanks" to your kindness."

"Thanks to the Buddha." Vo thi Thu said in joy, "Thank you, Grandpa. I've prayed a lot for him," and she asked her father and mother, "May I come to see him?"

"It's better if I go with you. "the mother [Le thi Lan] said

Vo thi Thu visited comrade Truong van Mai every day. She inquired the mother, "Mom, you're an herbalist, which herbs should I use for him get well very soon?"

"Ah! Tell me if you love that comrade?" the mother asked

"Oh, Mom! Please help me with the herbs..." Vo thi Thu was blushing

After a month, comrade Truong van Mai was recovered. He represented to his superior [a Viet Minh/Viet Cong comrade] and was assigned a task "Guerrilla combatants with the task of disrupting the transmission line of the QLVNCH Quân Lực Việt Nam Cộng Hòa [ARVN]". Before going on the mission, comrade Truong van Mai proposed to Vo thi Thu, "Would you ve my wife when I come back?"

"When will you be back?" she asked

"Someday...I'll be back.... when the two Vietnams be united into one, we are completely independent from the Empire America!" comrade Truong van Mai proudly said

"I'll wait for you ...... I love you." Vo thi Thu leaned her head on the comrade's shoulder

Due to the relationship of Vo thi Thu and Truong van Mai, Communist Viet Minh [Viet Cong] didn't execute land owner Vo Kiet as other land owners in north Vietnam. Instead, Communist Viet Minh [Viet Cong] had an agreement with Vo Kiet: when soldiers QLVNCH of the Republic of South Vietnam checked up on the village, Vo Kiet would say that his family, included his son in law- Truong van Mai- were Catholics and they devoted themselves to President Ngo Dinh Diem and his regime in south Vietnam.

Khanh Hoa 1955

Truong van Mai was Truong thi Cuc's younger brother, their parents were Mr. and Mrs. Truong Van. They lived in Thank Hoa, a province in the North- Central Vietnam. Truong van Mai joined the Communist Party- Viet Minh, he was assigned a special role in the guerrilla militia [referred as Viet Cong by the US Military] to attack QLVNCH military creating chaos in Ngo Dinh Diem's administration. Truong thi Cuc married to Tran Phu; the couple had a son, Tran San. They followed the northern refugees embarked a US ship on the Operation of Freedom leaving Thank Hoa to settle in Khanh Hoa, a province in the central part of Vietnam.

On the ship, Tran Phu adopted Nguyen van Hai. Nguyen van Hai, the orphan young boy from Hung Hoa, a province of north Vietnam who entered the "Open Mouth" US ship to immigrate in south Vietnam in 1954. Nguyen van Hai became a member of Tran Phu's family, they renamed him, Tran van Hai. Tran Phu's family settled in Khanh Hoa, a province of the central Vietnam along the South Pacific coast. Tran Phu worked as an officer in Khanh Hoa province while his wife- Truong thi Cuc did some seamstress in the neighborhood. One day, when returning an altered tunique for a customer, Truong thi Cuc met Le thi Thanh, this woman asked,

"How much do you make a day?"

"Only a few piastres." Truong thi Cuc said

"There's a way to make a lot of money!" Le thi Thanh whispered to Truong thi Cuc as she showed a deck of four-colored card, "Gambling!"

"I don't know how...." Truong thi Cuc hesitantly replied

"I'll show you." Le thi Thanh laughed

The next day, Truong thi Cuc told Tran van Hai to take care of the two years old boy- Tran San, for the baby's mother "went to visit a relative". Tran van Hai carried Tran San on his back and walked on the village lane toward Minh Tam Elementary school. In the North, Nguyen van Hai [his former name] was a good pupil in Third grade; his favorite subject was Mathematics. Nguyen van Hai wanted to become a teacher, now it was just a dream.

Every day, when Tran Phu's sight on the bicycle disappeared by the curve of the street, his wife- Truong thi Cuc put a deck of the four- colored- card in her bag, and a snack, she was ready to "visit the nearby relatives". Tran van Hai carried Tran San on his back walking around the neighborhood. He liked to listen to the teaching at Minh Tam Elementary school. Oh, how much he wished if he could be in that classroom! Tran van Hai saved the sheets of paper Tran Phu threw in the waste basket, because- sometimes there was a blank side on the sheets, which Tran van Hai wrote the lessons he learned behind the windows at Minh Tam Elementary school when taking care of the little boy, Tran San.

One day, Mr. Bui Chau- the teacher- taught the pupils about "Measurement"; he asked the class,

"15 deciliters = how many liters? Who knows the answer?"

The whole classroom of 25 pupils no body raised his hand up. It was so quiet that you could even hear the rustles of the bamboo leaves. Then, a head jutted out from the window with a voice, "It's 1.5 liters." The teacher and the pupils turned their eyes to the window, but they saw nobody. Mr. Bui Chau walked out; he brought in Tran van Hai with the young boy Tran San on his back. The pupils burst into laughing, they pointed to the poor northern immigrant,

"He has to babysit his younger brother!"

Mr. Bui slapped the big ruler on the desk to reprimand the children,

"Order! Sit down and be quiet!"

In a flash, the whole class was in silence. The teacher reprimanded the pupils,

"Shouldn't you all be ashamed of yourselves? A boy listens to my teaching by the window, yet he understands "Measurements" while I've taught you for over a week, there's nothing in your brain!" turning to Tran van Hai, the teacher continued, "Child, go to the blackboard and show my class how you got that answer."

Tran van Hai wrote on the blackboard, "10 deciliters = 1 liter; 15 deciliters = 1.5 liters."

"Correct!" the teacher put his hand on Tran van Hai's shoulder, "I'll talk to your parents and help you going to school."

Mr. Bui Chau-the teacher, came "to have a talk" with Mr. Tran Phu and the outcome was good news, Tran van Hai would be in Mr. Bui's class, Third grade of Minh Tam Elementary in the province of Khanh Hoa, central part of Vietnam. Mrs. Tran Phu [Truong thi Cuc] was upset at the decision,

"Who will take care of Tran San? Why should we feed an orphan who does nothing for us?"

"You can take Tran San with you when you visit the relatives, dear." Mr. Tran Phu justified the situation, "Tran van Hai cooks supper and does the house works after school."

The next day, Tran van Hai put on a shirt, Tran Phu's old shirt, which his wife altered it to fit Tran van Hai, and dark blue trousers with tire-recycled sandals. Tran van Hai didn't have a school bag, he used a brown paper bag to put a note book, and a pen. Carried in his hand, a non-spilled ink pot, Tran van Hai went to Minh Tam Elementary School.

Khanh Hoa 1963

Tran Phu became the supervisor of the Civil Office in town while his wife, Truong thi Cuc involved deep into the gambling, she owed the relatives a lot of money. Many times, the "loan sharks" stopped by the house collecting the money, Truong thi Cuc had to hide at a friend's home in the next villages for a few days. Tran San, the little boy Tran van Hai used to take care of, went to Minh Tam Elementary School while Tran van Hai attended Vo Tanh Middle & High School. Tran van Hai was a hard-working student; he was outstanding in Mathematics. At the age of 18, he graduated from Vo Tanh high school, Baccalaureate Part II with "Excellente" remark, the valedictorian of Khanh Hoa province. Tran San started sixth grade of a Middle school of Khanh Hoa. The District Chief of Mai Dien, Khanh Hoa province- Mr. Duong Quang and his wife, Mrs. Duong Quang, maiden name: Nguyen thi Hoa, had a daughter, Duong Kim Ngan. When Mrs. Duong Quang learned about the valedictorian, she discussed with the District Chief about planning a banquet to invited the famous student- Tran van Hai- who passed the Baccalaureate Part II with "Excellente" remark; the purpose behind the feast was to choose the future husband for Duong Kim Ngan, the only child of the District Chief and his wife. Avoiding the rumor, Mrs. Duong Quang also included some high ranked officers of the City Hall and other graduates with the "Bien/ Good" remarks. Duong Kim Ngan, a 20 years old girl graduated from École Secondaire de France [French High School] last year. This was a co-ed private school for the privilege children from wealthy families in the province of Khanh Hoa. The curriculums from sixth to twelve grades were in French with a few hours a week in Vietnamese for students. Duong Kim Ngan enjoyed wearing blue jeans, miniskirts, swim suits…at MyDzung fashion boutique owned by her mother. Mrs. Duong Quang displayed the western outfits among the Vietnamese traditional clothing. Duong Kim Ngan fell in love in a class mate Ngo Vien, but this young man was more interested in pursuing his future- to become a medical doctor, he was accepted in the Medical school in Hue- than staying in Khanh Hoa to be the District Chief's son in law. At that time, there were only colleges and universities in the big cities as Saigon and Hue for students who wanted higher education and professional careers after high school. Duong Kim Ngan was not a good student, even with private tutoring, she struggled through high school with a "Passable" remark on the Baccalaureate Part II. She enjoyed partying and shopping than studying. When Mrs. Duong Quang told her about the meeting with the valedictorian Tran van Hai at the banquet and the future wedding, Duong Kim Ngan laughed out loud,

"Do you know that we're in the 20th century! You insist in the old traditional arranged marriage?"

"Aye! Tran van Hai is the best guy in Khanh Hoa." Mrs. Duong Quang told her daughter

"His family is middle class. We give him an opportunity to make his dream comes true, so he will be with you forever. "the father, District Chief Duong Quang, revealed the plan.

Duong Kim Ngan had a different idea, she searched for a partner who would dance and enjoy rock music with her, not a "bookworm". Duong Kim Ngan thought about the "cousin from the country", Vo thi Tam to place her role to meet the valedictorian since Duong Kim Ngan had a date with Phan Don after Ngo Vien and her broke up. Vo thi Tam, a sixteen years old girl from My Tho, a province in Southern Vietnam, Duong Kim Ngan's cousin [Vo thi Tam's father- Vo Kiet, he married to Nguyen thi Lan. Nguyen thi Hoa [Nguyen thi Lan's elder sister] married to Duong Quang, the District Chief of Mai Dien in Khanh Hoa province.] –

124

Vo thi Tam attended tenth grade in a public school in My Tho, in the summer of 1960 she spent the vacation at her aunt's- the District Chief mansion in Khanh Hoa, a province by the seaside of Central Vietnam. Vo thi Tam was about to go to the beach, then Duong Kim Ngan called her,

"Hey, could you do me a favor? Mom and Dad arranged for a "bookworm" to meet me this evening, would you please see him instead? I have a dance with someone else…"

"Did you tell Uncle and Aunt?" Vo thi Tam was surprised

"I didn't have time. See you later!" Duong Kim Ngan waved to Vo thi Tam on her way out. The District Chief and Mrs. Duong Quang came downstairs, they were startled as hearing Vo thi Tam mumbled, "Uncle and Aunty, Duong Kim Ngan asked me to substitute for her to meet someone, she went dancing this evening."

Mrs. Duong Quang pulled Vo thi Tam next to her and whispered to her niece, "Put on a tunique."

"I only have the school uniform." Vo thi Tam said

"Put it on, right now!" Mrs. Duong Quang insisted and she turned to the District Chief, "What else could we do?"

The doorbell rang. The servants announced, "The guests arrive!"

The District Chief and Mrs. Duong Quang with Vo thi Tam greeted the guests,

"Thank you for coming to the banquet. We hope you enjoy the foods."

"Yes, Sir, Madam and Miss." the guests shook hands with the District Chief and Mrs. Duong Quang while the valedictorian Tran van Hai bowed his head to the Mayor, Mrs. Duong Quang, and glanced at Vo thi Tam. The District Chief introduced Tran van Hai to some officers of the City Hall and the Commerce Bureau of Khanh Hoa province. Tran van Hai didn't have any formal garments for special occasions except the uniforms for school: navy-blue trousers, and white long-sleeved shirts. The valedictorian was nervous, he thought to receive a medal of achievement from the District Chief of Mai Dien- Khanh Hoa province then went home to show it to his family; but there was a banquet with a lovely girl! The District Chief called Mrs. Duong Quang, "Should we check on the main dish?", he whispered to his wife, "Explain to me, what is Duong Kim Ngan dancing tonight?" then both of them disappeared behind the door.

A servant brought out liquors, appetizers, and fruit juice. Tran van Hai and Vo thi Tam glanced at each other; the high ranked officers enjoyed the liquors. Vo thi Tam initiated,

"Valedictorian... please take a seat..."

Looking around, Tran van Hai was not quite sure where to sit; he didn't move.

"Valedictorian...please take a seat..." Vo thi Tam repeated

The District Chief and Mrs. Duong Quang returned, and the banquet dinner was served. Mrs. Duong Quang set Tran van Hai's seat next to her niece, Vo thi Tam. The valedictorian enjoyed the different dishes. What a difference compared to rice, vegetables, and dried fish that he had every day at home! Tran van Hai was a little bit curious about the timid girl sitting next to him.

"Please have some tea, Valedictorian." Vo thi Tam gave Tran van Hai the tea, he reached for it; she saw a long scar on the dorsum of his left hand.

"You and my mother are left-handed. What happened to your hand?" she smiled with a dimple

"I fell off a tree when I was a boy to get a bird nest." he said, "Thank you for the tea."

Tran van Hai had never tasted these special dishes in his life, and what a wonderful evening with a lovely girl by his side! After dinner, the District Chief invited the guests to the pavilion for tea and desserts. The District Chief seemed not happy so Mrs. Duong Quang told Vo thi Tam took the officers and the valedictorian for a tour of the Mayor's mansion while the District Chief and his wife retired. Vo thi Tam wished that Duong Kim Ngan had not left for dancing, for Vo thi Tam was not familiar with the mansion! Vo thi Tam walked to the garden and Tran van Hai went with her. The summer evening with the breeze from the Pacific Ocean spread the Chinese cherry petals all over the green grass. They sat down on a bench near the gold fish pond. The wind blew Vo thi Tam's hair ribbon away, she tried to catch it back but it got caught on a branch of a tree. Tran van Hai got it and gave it back to her. "Thank you" she said

"What's your name?" Tran van Hai asked

"Vo thi Tam" she replied

"Vo thi Tam?" he repeated in doubting, "I thought that you're the District Chief's daughter?"

"I'm Mrs. Duong Quang's niece. I'm here for a visit." Vo thi Tam said

"My name is Tran van Hai. I live in Khanh Hoa," the valedictorian asked, "Where's your home town?"

"My parents are in My Tho. After summer, I'll be in eleventh grade at My Tho high school." Vo thi Tam said, "Have you had Vinh Long milk puff cake, it's very delicious!"

"In Khanh Hoa. We have sesame candy; I think you'd like it." Tran van Hai said

Suddenly, they heard loud rock n' roll music and Duong Kim Ngan's screaming, "I went to dancing, but Phan Don had a girlfriend already." She ran into the garden before Mrs. Duong Quang could intervene. Vo thi Tam enclosed a piece of paper into Tran van Hai's hand, he put that in the pocket of his trousers as a young woman in a leather short skirt and a V neck blouse approached him,

"Je suis Duong Kim Ngan, unique fille du Maire. Danses avec moi?" ["I'm Duong Kim Ngan, the District Chief's only daughter. Dance with me?"]

The valedictorian looked at Duong Kim Ngan and replied,

"Désolé, mademoiselle. Je ne sais pas danser."{ Sorry, Miss. I don't know how to dance}

Seeing Tran van Hai and Vo thi Tam together made Duong Kim Ngan angry,

"Mom, please discipline your niece! She bad mouth me to the valedictorian."

"What did Vo thi Tam say to you?" Mrs. Duong Quang requested Tran van Hai

"She didn't say anything about Miss." Tran van Hai replied

"Mom! Don't you see he covered up for her!" Duong Kim Ngan yelled, "Vo thi Tam, you're back to My Tho!"

"I'm sorry if I cause any troubles," Tran van Hai told Mrs. Duong Quang, "Thank you for the dinner. May I go home now?" Tran van Hai said "Good bye!" to the District Chief's family and some pertinent figures of the Khanh Hoa province then walked toward the gate. Putting his hand into the trousers' pocket, he found a piece of paper: Vo Thi Tam's address in My Tho.

A week after graduation, Tran van Hai worked at a grocery store in town, he had no financial resource to attend college either in Hue or Saigon. Mr. Tran Phu was a civil officer, his salary was enough to provide food on the table, pay the utility expense, and sundries for his wife and children. Mrs. Tran Phu [Truong thi Cuc]- with the habit of gambling- had a huge debt with the sharp loan brokers; they came to the house and took away furniture "these are just for the interests, we'll come back by no time." Avoiding the shameful situation, Mr. Tran Phu stayed at a friend's house while Mrs. Tran Phu went into hiding for a few days. Thursday afternoon, Mr.& Mrs. Tran Phu received an invitation for tea at the District Chief's mansion. Tran van Hai looked at the card and wondered about the second encounter; right now, all he wanted was something to eat, he had a long day at work. Tran van Hai sat down at the table, he opened a package: some rice and a piece of dried fish. Tran San went to the back yard to pick up some vegetables. This was their supper, for a few days the parents were not home. There was a rustle behind the door,

Mrs. Tran Phu came in,

"I haven't eaten for days!" she gulped the boys' supper; yet she hadn't swallowed it down the loan sharp brokers entered and pulled her out,

"We've waited for this moment. We put you in jail until you pay off the debts. "they shouted and pushing her into a van, Tran San cried, "Mom! Mom!". Tran van Hai was speechless; he comforted Tran San, "Don't cry…"

That evening, Mr. Tran Phu came home. Listening to the sharp loan incident and the District Chief's invitation, he told Tran van Hai, "We must go the District Chief's mansion."

"What is the reason, Dad?" Tran van Hai inquired, Mr. Tran Phu sighed, "Who knows?"

The second time coming to the District Chief's mansion, Tran van Hai had no idea what the meaning of "having a cup of tea with us" was; he just followed Mr. Tran Phu. To his surprise, the District Chief and his wife greeted them at the gate. The District Chief shook hands with both of them in cordially and Mrs. Duong Quang insisted them to enter. In the immense hall, with a coffee table by each other window and a nacre salon set in the middle of the room with a beautiful flower vase full of red roses. Tran van Hai startled when he saw Mrs. Tran Phu in a tunique appeared. Mrs. Duong Quang said,

"Mrs. Tran Phu and I are friends a long time. It's the will the Buddha to unite us into one family."

Tran van Hai felt uncomfortable, he asked for looking at the gold fish pond in the garden,

"Excellent! Duong Kim Ngan is waiting for you outside, have a good time!" the District Chief smiled

Tran van Hai walked out to the pond, he saw a young woman in tight stretch pants jeans and a tied knot blouse. Tran van Hai recognized this was the one demanded him to dance when he came to the District Chief's mansion the first time.

"Do you have a light? I want to smoke a cigarette. "she asked

"Sorry, Miss. I don't smoke." Tran van Hai said

Mrs. Duong Quang and Mrs. Tran Phu appeared by the door, Mrs. Duong Quang stroked her daughter's hair, "Sweetheart, would you be nice to your fiancée?"

"What are you saying, Madam? I don't understand." Tran van Hai gawked at Mrs. Duong Quang

"Everything has settled," Truong thi Cuc told Tran van Hai "Your father and I have asked the District Chief's and Mrs. Duong Quang for their daughter- Miss Duong Kim Ngan's hand- and they accepted the proposal. Now, will you pay curtesy to your in- laws? And thank them for the honor to be a member of the high-class family."

"No! I do not agree..." Tran van Hai had not finished the sentence, the District Chief and Mr. Tran Phu joined the conversation,

"Congratulations to the valedictorian! The wedding comes soon!"

"Please explain to me…." Tran van Hai moaned

"It's better to discuss this matter at home with your parent. Mr. Tran Phu, see you next week. "the District Chief said

…

As soon as they got home, Tran van Hai repeated the request,

"Please explain to me…."

"You saved my life!" Truong thi Cuc - Tran Phu's wife- embraced Tran van Hai, "Thank you."

"Sit down," Mr. Tran Phu gave him a glass of water, "the District Chief paid 2,500 piasters to bail Mom out from jail. You know we never could have that money to repay the District Chief. Therefore, the District Chief and his wife agreed to exchange the debt by the wedding of you and their daughter, Duong Kim Ngan."

"You're my adopted parents! I lost my biological parents during the war! You traded me for your own benefits...." Tran van Hai's voice was tearful

"Calm down," Mr. Tran Phu said, "you wish to attend college in Hue, but we're not able to afford it. The District Chief lets you to be the Manager of his wife's fashion shop. What could we dream more?"

"Even with a college degree, you can't find a better job than that position." Truong thi Cuc added, "the District Chief also bought the house we're in now. We do not have to pay rent...."

"Oh! God...Oh! God..." Tran van Hai collapsed on the floor

The wedding of Tran van Hai and Duong Kim Ngan was a great important event in Khanh Hoa province, the major officers of the province, towns, and the school children performed music bands and parade to celebrate the wedding of the young couple. Standing next to Duong Kim Ngan in a white bridal gown, the groom Tran van Hai in a dark blue tuxedo walking as a body without a soul. On the nuptial night, Tran van Hai insisted to have a talk with Duong Kim Ngan alone

"Tell me, Miss. Did you plan this, why?"

"Idiot," Duong Kim Ngan laughed, "What's up?"

"Legally, I'm your husband," Tran van Hai was irritated, "at least show some respect when we talk."

"D'accord! [Agree] May I remind you? I didn't plan this marriage. My parents did." Duong Kim Ngan said, "I was pregnant, eight weeks..."

"What?" Tran van Hai raised his voice

"I didn't say you're the father," Duong Kim Ngan blew some cigarette smoke into Tran van Hai's face, "Idiot, take hold of yourself. I slept with a classmate, that jerk denied it and my parents were terrified..."

"And now I'm the legal father of your baby?" Tran van Hai smirked

"Don't worry, Idiot!" Duong Kim Ngan guffawed at the remark, "I already had an abortion."

"Why there was the wedding?" Tran van Hai was perplexed

"Ask the District Chief!" Duong Kim Ngan had another cigarette, "Mom and Dad have to face the public, do you understand? I'm not interested in you. To everybody, we're husband and wife; however, I live my life and you should do the same, do not bother me, D'accord? [agree?]"

"D'accord et merci." [Agree and Thank you] Tran van Hai said

In 1964, Tran van Hai became the Supervisor of MyDzung fashion boutique {Mrs. Duong Quang was the owner) down town Khanh Hoa province. He was a hard worker; he provided ideas to improve the business, the shop had more customers. The District Chief and Mrs. Duong Quang obtained more benefits than before. Duong Kim Ngan enjoyed the new, up to date designs at the parties while Vo thi Tam [Duong Kim Ngan's cousin] graduated from the Nursing School in Saigon. She was transferred to work at the Emergency Room at General Hospital in Dalat, a province in the central of Vietnam. Tran van Hai seemed settled down at the District Chief's mansion in Khanh Hoa, but the Tran family was in turmoil. One morning, Tran van Hai rode the bicycle to work, abruptly he was attacked by a gang of thugs.

"Stop!" Tran van Hai moaned, "Why did you beat me up?"

"We kidnap you to exchange for a large ransom from the District Chief, you're his son in law, right? "the gang leader said, "Your mother and brother owe us 4,200 piastres."

"How did it happen?" Tran van Hai questioned

"We gave them some marijuana worth 4,200 piastres to sell, they got caught by the police and the stuff was confiscated. Your mother and brother are in jail." The gang leader punched Tran van Hai, "We got you to exchange a deal with the District Chief- your father in law- Tell the District Chief close the case, Police reports no marijuana, only baking soda; we'll release you."

"How many times I've been used for trading! "Tran van Hai cried

"I don't know what you're mumbling about", the gang leader said, "We'll drop you near by the mansion gate, go and tell the District Chief about the deal. Exactly this time tomorrow, the case is closed otherwise you will be dead meat."

"Understood." Tran van Hai said

The thugs dropped the victim by the sidewalk, Tran van Hai walked toward the District Chief's mansion. He met the District Chief, Mrs. Duong Quang and Duong Kim Ngan by the gate,

"Do you know that your mother and brother are in jail …" they said

"District Chief, Mrs. Duong Quang, and Miss Duong Kim Ngan. Let me tell you the truth," Tran van Hai said, "My name was Nguyen van Hai, I was born in Hung Yen, a province in north Vietnam. I lost my parents, my brother and sister when Viet Minh took the control of the government. I followed the refugees on the American ship to South Vietnam, I met Tran Phu family; they adopted me [I was nine years old]. They changed my name to Tran van Hai. Living with that family: as soon as Mr. Tran Phu went to work, Mrs. Tran Phu [Truong thi Cuc] went to play cards. I took care of baby Tran San; I did all the house work…. Through the kindness of a school teacher, I went to elementary school… and high school then graduated at the top of all the candidates of the Baccalaureate Part II. I have fulfilled my duty as your son in law… now the gangsters want to use me for a deal with you: close the marijuana or I'd be dead!"

"We didn't know that you were adopted." Mrs. Duong Quang said

"We'll meet the gangster leader and take care of your mother and brother's crime." the District Chief told Tran van Hai

"I'm not related to the Tran family," Tran [Nguyen] van Hai explained, "and your daughter Duong Kim Ngan knows that I've never had intimacy with her; I fulfilled the duty of the son in law makes your business more prosperous. Hence- I'll walk out of here. Thank you and Good Bye!"

"It'd be better if you stay here." Mrs. Duong Quang said, "Duong Kim Ngan is pregnant."

"Why?" Tran van Hai stared at Duong Kim Ngan, "Didn't you said "Each lives his/her own life? You know very well that I've never touched you."

"Calm down, Idiot," Duong Kim Ngan said, "You're not the father, but legally I can claim Tran van Hai is the father of the baby as we're legally husband and wife. This is Don Phan's baby; I want to keep the baby and he/she will have you as a legal father."

"To use me again?" Tran van Hai cried out loud, "No, no more...I came here with a pair of trousers and a shirt, I got out here the same. I do not want anything from you, Duong Kim Ngan, please sign the divorce paper. I truly appreciate it."

"Only in your dream, Idiot!" Duong Kim Ngan laughed into Tran van Hai's face

Tran van Hai went to his bedroom and changed his clothes into the pair of blue trousers and a white shirt. When he got out, Mrs. Duong Quang winked her eyes with her daughter, the District Chief sighed, "Sorry, Tran van Hai. We have no other choice!"

Tran van Hai ran out of the District Chief's mansion gate, not too far away from the mansion, a group of thugs knocked him down. They beat and stabbed him while yelling, "Why didn't you follow our deal? You have your wish: dead meat."

"Let me tell you who I'm" the gang leader kicked Tran van Hai, "My name Phan Don. Miss Duong Kim Ngan and I, we love each other but the District Chief and his wife never accept me as their son in law. We need you to cover up for us as we cover up for your mother and brother, do you understand?"

"No...no...they're not my family...I was adopted..." Tran van Hai moaned

"Whatever...we don't care." The thugs yelled

"Drop dead meat on our way to Dalat, we have to pick up vegetables and fruits in Dalat this morning." Phan Don told his gangsters when he saw the police vehicle at the corner of the street by the District Chief's mansion, Phan Don told the gangsters pulled Tran van Hai into their truck and they drove off. The gang used a truck that transferred vegetables and fruits from Central Vietnam- Dalat to Saigon, sometimes, they sneaked marijuana for "big bugs". They threw the body of Tran van Hai on the high way near Dalat. The gang leader Phan Don asked his followers,

"Are you sure that he's dead?"

"He didn't move, dead meat for sure." a thug responded

"Good, keep on driving!" the gang leader, Phan Don ordered

At dawn, Nurse Vo thi Tam yawned, "Lucky, I'm on call but it has not too busy last night; only one more hour then I can go home!" The phone rang, Vo thi Tam picked it up, "Hello! This is the ER Nurse; how may I help you?"

"Nurse, Vo thi Tam, the ambulance just picked up a beaten and collapsed man. Get your team ready, I'll be there, too!" Doctor Huynh said

"Yes, Doctor!" Nurse Vo thi Tam replied and transferred the message to the colleagues. The paramedics brought in a badly injured man. Nurse Vo thi Tam listened to the information from the paramedics, "Some body found this man in the city dumpster. No ID, no paper, he was beaten up severely injured but still has a weak pulse...." Nurse Vo thi Tam tried to find a vein for the IV line, she saw a long scar on the left dorsal hand; something just flashed back her mind...

"Loosen his clothes." Doctor Huynh said, "I'll exam the whole body."

Two nurse-assistants changed the patient into the hospital gown, one pulled out from the pocket of his trousers, it was a piece of paper with a few words "Vo thi Tam, address in My Tho". Nurse Vo thi Tam saw it, she cried "The Valedictorian of Khanh Hoa!"

GONE WITH THE WIND

The wind twirls the sorrowful leaves

Hue - a province of north central Vietnam 1963

Dieu My, a fifteen years old girl rode a bicycle on Trang Tien bridge to Dong Khanh Middle & High school for girls, she was born and grew up in Hue, a province of north central of Vietnam. She was the second child of Mr. Thai Khiem, a French professor-he was a member of Thua Thien-Hue City Council; Mrs. Thai Khiem was a music teacher. Dieu My's older brother, Quoc Binh joined the VNCH Marine Force, he stationed in Quang Tri. Every morning, Dieu My rode a bicycle along the Trang Tien bridge to school along her best friend, Dan Thanh- the only child of Major Cao Van in QLVNCH, her mother was a homemaker. Dan Thanh loved the Vietnamese literature and wished to become a high school teacher. On recession at school, Dieu My and Dan Thanh shared salted dry apricots- their mothers said these homemade lozenges were very good in prevention against cold and flu, especially in winter time. When the flamboyant royal poinciana displayed their bright red petals under the blue sky filled with the cicadas' singing, the girls of Dong Khanh exchanged "School Days Memory Notes" with best wishes for the future…. Every Thursday evening, Dieu My went to Tu Dam temple, she enrolled in a class "Buddhism's Basic Teachings" where Trong Hung a 26-year-old- novice was a teacher assistant for the Elder monk, Master Thich Hue Tam. Dieu My learned that ten years ago when Hue and the nearby area were flooded, the young boy Trong Hung lost his parents. A monk at Tu Dam raised up Trong Hung in a charity program of the temple; the old monk wished that the young man would follow his footstep; however, Trong Hung somehow didn't fit in the monastery; he was more an artist [he played the flute and had a nice voice], or a poet rather than a Buddhist. The philosophy of Buddhism was denial of passion, but Trong Hung allowed himself get lost in the woods when spring came with the wild flowers spread on the green grass toward the horizon…For this reason, Trong Hung was not selected to be a monk, the monastery kept him as an assistant for other official works. He dressed in casual clothes and didn't not shaved his head. One time, during a short break Dieu My went to the pond to burn incense at the Bodhisattva's alter, the wind blew her hair band away. The maiden tried to get it back, yet the wind put it up on a Chinese cherry branch. Dieu My looked up at the blue hair band fluttering among the cherry flowers, she sighed and walking back inside then she heard somebody asked her,

"Excuse me, is this yours?"

Turning back, Dieu My saw the Instructor assistant, Trong Hung with the hair band. "Thank you" the girl mumbled as her cheeks turned pinkish. She changed the subject,

"The teaching of pāramī: renunciation is so difficult to learn; would you explain a little more…"

"Ah! I also have problems in that area...Master Thich Hue Tam will help you, please ask him." Trong Hung said with a witty smile.

After class, Trong Hung and Dieu My volunteered helping in decoration the temple for the Buddha's Birthday next week with all the joyful festival and parade at Tu Dam Temple on this special occasion. Oh! What a nice day that Dieu My and some class mates came to give a hand, too! Dieu My and Dan Thanh's families were Buddhists, they prepared to offer the best fruits and incents to the altar of the Buddha where they prayed for good health and best wishes for their families. Quoc Hoc High School- the famous institute for young men for centuries where the best young men of the north central provinces were chosen and trained to be mandarins or high positions in the government- sent a group of students to contribute their parts at Tu Dam Temple today. This morning Trong Hung and two other students from QuocHoc High School approached the school girls with some flyers,

"Hello! How are you?" they said

"Fine, thank you." Dan Thanh asked, "What's up?"

"Take some and pass them around, would you?" Trong Hung gave the girls the flyers, "The government oppresses the Buddhists..."

"President Ngo Dinh Diem prohibited the display of the Buddhism religious flags on Vesak, the birthday of Gautama Buddha on May 8th..." the other students added, "My father said last week, the Catholic churches had been encouraged to display Vatican flags at the government-sponsored celebration for President Ngo Dinh Diem's brother, Archbishop Ngô Đình Thục..."

The youngsters saw a police office walking toward them, in a flash, they scattered into different directions. In the evening, the students and the returned to the temple preparing for the grand celebration on May 8th. How lovely to work side by side with the Instructor assistant, Trong Hung- Dan Thanh thought as she gave him the lanterns to hang them up along the eaves of the temple roofs. The evening breeze brought the michella alba fragrance from the garden toward the Buddha's altar, a nun announced, "It's refreshment time!" The volunteer youngsters joyfully ran to the lemonade stand for a biscuit and fresh citrus punch. Trong Hung made his hands into two fists of the game "What hand is it in?" and showed them to Dan Thanh,

"Which one has it, do you know?"

"Oh! How could I know?" Dan Thanh said sheepishly. "What is it, please?"

"You'll know, just make a guest...come on..." Trong Hung insisted

Dan Thanh pointed to the right hand, Trong Hung opened it with a smile, "It's a Michella alba for you..."

"Ah! I love this flower very much, "she said, "Thank you."

"I also love this flower, I picked it for you." Trong Hung said

"Assistant Trong Hung, please come and help me." A nun walked by, she frowned at the young man

"Yes, Sister!" Trong Hung hurried following the nun; however, his soul was lingering at the michella alba which Dan Thanh put it on her hair clip.

May 8, 1963, the waiting and expecting day of the Buddha's birthday celebration arrived with musical parades, preaching and prayers at Tu Dam temple. The assistant instructor eagerly ushered the believers into the seats of the auditorium as Mater Thich Hue Tam started the ceremony. The children came up to offer flowers to the altar of the Gautama Buddha, the faithful adults kneeled along the site, then suddenly the armed policemen and soldiers of Ngo Dinh Diem's government with machine guns started shooting at the Buddhists,

"Idolatries! You do not worship God; we'll eliminate you all from the face of the earth!"

The armed policemen pulled the Buddhists out, and hit them with the batons and guns...At the other corner of the temple, the soldiers used tear gases and other chemicals spraying at harmless women and children...Dan Thanh saw it clearly with her very own eyes, the instructor assistant-Trong Hung distributed the sermons to the believers,

"We have the right to worship the Buddha, don't be shy. South Vietnam is the land of freedom, freedom to worship the Buddha...." he hadn't finished the sentence, the armed agents of Ngo Dinh Nhu's Secret Agents poured in the auditorium. They clubbed, punched into Trong Hung's face while the other hit his head with batons. The yelling's, screaming's in panic of the Buddha worshipers roared up from Tu Dam temple echoed from several areas of the province of Hue as the other temples were also attacked by the armed soldiers. A group of Buddhists escaped by the back door, Dan Thanh followed them, but she was pulled back, "I saw her with the Instructor assistant." A secret agent told the police and they arrested Dan Thanh. They blind folded her including a group of other Buddhists and shoveled them into armored vehicles. The attackers and their equipment disappeared into the night amidst the believers' screaming in panic, taking with them Trong Hung, Dan Thanh and other Dong Khanh and QuocHoc high school students and other Buddhists for torturing and imprisonments according to Ngo Dinh Diem's order Buddhist crisis – Wikipedia/en.wikipedia.org › wiki › Buddhist crisis

May 1963 - Huế Phật Đản shootings

A rarely enforced 1958 law—known as Decree Number 10—was invoked in May 1963 to prohibit the display of religious flags. This disallowed the flying of the Buddhist flag on Vesak, the birthday of Gautama Buddha. The application of the law caused indignation among Buddhists on the eve of the most important religious festival of the year, as a week earlier Catholics had been encouraged to display Vatican flags at a government-sponsored celebration for Diem's brother, Archbishop Ngô Đình Thục, the most senior Catholic cleric in the country.[18][19] On May 8, in Huế, a crowd of Buddhists protested against the ban on the Buddhist flag. The police and army broke up the demonstration by firing guns at and throwing grenades into the gathering, leaving nine dead

Vietnam, Diem, the Buddhist Crisis | JFK Library - JFKLibrary.org

In the spring of 1963, South Vietnamese forces suppressed Buddhist religious leaders and followers, which led to a political crisis for the government of President Ngo Dinh Diem.

The suppression of Buddhists in South Vietnam became known as the "Buddhist crisis." President Ngo Dinh Diem did little to ease the tensions, though he later promised reforms. Many people suspected that his brother and closest advisor, Ngo Dinh Nhu, was the actual decision maker in the Saigon government and the person behind the Buddhist suppression.

The Buddhist demonstrations continued throughout spring and summer and culminated in June when a Buddhist monk publicly lit himself on fire. The photograph of the event made news around the world.

In August, Diem declared martial law and his forces raided the pagodas of the Buddhist group behind the protests. e volunteered in a group helping with decoration for the Gautama Buddha's birthday celebration; Trong Hung was also in this group. Dan Thanh gave Trong Hung the lanterns and the Buddhist flags, they hang them along the eaves of the temple and on the street poles. The afternoon breeze st, 8, Djin Huế, a crowd of Buddhists protested against the ban on the Buddhist flag. The police and army broke up the demonstration by firing guns at and throwing grenades into the gathering, leaving nine dead.

A rarely enforced 1958 law—known as Decree Number 10—was invoked in May 1963 to prohibit the display of religious flags. This disallowed the flying of the Buddhist flag on Vesak, the birthday of Gautama Buddha. The application of the law caused indignation among Buddhists on the eve of the most important religious festival of the year, as a week earlier Catholics had been encouraged to display Vatican flags at a government-sponsored celebration for Diem's brother, Archbishop Ngô Đình Thục, the most senior Catholic cleric in the country.[18][19] On May 8, in Huế, a crowd of Buddhists protested against the ban on the Buddhist flag. The police and army broke up the demonstration by firing guns at and throwing grenades into the gathering, leaving nine dead. Life is a leaf in the playful wind

Ngô Đình Diệm: 3 January 1901 – 2 November 1963) was a Vietnamese politician. He was the final prime minister of the State of Vietnam (1954–55), and then served as President of South Vietnam (Republic of Vietnam) from 1955 until he was deposed

Ngo Dinh Diem
- Wikipediahttps://
en.wikipedia.org › wiki ›
Ngo_Dinh_Diem

and assassinated during the 1963 military coup.

Diệm was born into a prominent Catholic family, the son of a high-ranking civil servant, Ngô Đình Khả. He was educated at French-speaking schools and considered following his brother Ngô Đình Thục into the priesthood, but eventually chose to pursue a civil-service career. He progressed rapidly in the court of Emperor Bảo Đại, becoming governor of Bình Thuận Province in 1929 and interior minister in 1933. However, he resigned the latter position after three months and publicly denounced the emperor as a tool of the French. Diệm came to support Vietnamese nationalism, promoting an anti-communist and anti-colonialist "third way" opposed to both Bảo Đại and communist leader Hồ Chí Minh. He established the Can Lao Party to support his political doctrine of Person Dignity Theory.

Diệm, accompanied by US Secretary of State John Foster Dulles,
arrives at Washington National Airport in 1957.
Diệm is shown shaking hands with US President Dwight D. Eisenhower.

After several years in exile, Diệm returned home in July 1954 and was appointed prime minister by Bảo Đại, the head of the Western-backed State of Vietnam. The Geneva Accords were signed soon after he took office, formally partitioning Vietnam along the 17th parallel. Diệm soon consolidated power in South Vietnam, aided by his brother Ngô Đình Nhu. After a rigged referendum in 1955, he proclaimed the creation of the Republic of Vietnam, with himself as president. His government was supported by other anti-communist countries, most notably the United States. Diệm pursued a series of nation-building schemes, emphasising industrial and rural development. From 1957, he was faced with a communist insurgency backed by North Vietnam, eventually formally organized under the banner of the Việt Cộng. He was subject to a number of assassination and coup attempts, and in 1962 established the Strategic Hamlet Program as the cornerstone of his counterinsurgency effort.

Diệm's favoritism towards Catholics and persecution of South Vietnam's Buddhist majority led to the "Buddhist crisis" of 1963. The violence damaged relations with the United States and other previously sympathetic countries, and his regime lost favour with the leadership of the Army of the Republic of Vietnam. On 1 November 1963, the country's leading generals launched a coup d'ég'tat with assistance from the CIA. He and his younger brother Nhu initially escaped, but were recaptured the following day and assassinated on the orders of Dương Văn Minh, who succeeded him as president. Diệm has been a controversial historical figure in historiography on the Vietnam War. Some historians have considered him a tool of the United States, while others portrayed him as an avatar of Vietnamese tradition. Some recent studies have portrayed Diệm from a more Vietnamese-centred perspective as a competent leader focused on nation building and the modernisation of South Vietnam.[3][4][page needed]

The Fall of Diem (1963) | Encyclopedia.comhttps://www. encyclopedia.com › history › fall-diem-1963 |

During 1963, American dissatisfaction with Ngo Dinh Diem's (1901–1963) government in South Vietnam continued to grow. At the beginning of the year, the United States' policy of providing military and financial aid to Diem remained in place. But as the months passed, U.S. President John Kennedy (1917–1963; president

1960–1963) and his administration reluctantly concluded that the Diem government was too deeply flawed to survive. One primary reason for American unhappiness with Diem was the growing strength of Viet Cong Communists operating in South Vietnam. But an even bigger cause for alarm was Diem's response to a massive uprising by the country's Buddhist majority population, which finally became fed up with Diem's anti-Buddhist views and policies. Diem's brutal crackdown against the demonstrators kept him in power for another few months. But it also convinced the United States that Diem would never be able to rally his people against the Communist threat. As a result, the United States did not interfere when several South Vietnamese generals engineered the overthrow of Diem's government in November 1963.

Viet Cong gains in the country side

During the early 1960s the Communist guerrillas known as the Viet Cong continued to make military gains throughout South Vietnam (guerrillas are small groups of fighters who launch surprise attacks). Relying on terrorism and widespread dissatisfaction with Ngo Dinh Diem's government, the Viet Cong successfully recruited large numbers of South Vietnamese from both rural villages and urban areas. They also launched periodic attacks on targets throughout South Vietnam, including government installations, military outposts, villages, and strategic hamlets (fortified villages created by the Diem government). All of these efforts were actively supported by the Communist government of North Vietnam. Around this same time, the performance of the South Vietnamese army came under increasingly harsh criticism. Many U.S. military advisors stationed in the country complained that Diem and the military leadership of the South Vietnamese army—formally known as the Army of the Republic of Vietnam or ARVN—were reluctant to move aggressively against the Viet Cong. The advisors also noted that South Vietnamese officers were afraid that Diem would punish them if their troops suffered many casualties. Some U.S. observers even came to believe that the ARVN contained significant numbers of secret Viet Cong agents. "The whole country had been penetrated [by the Viet Cong], from the palace down to the platoons," claims historian Bruce Palmer in The 25-Year War: America's Military Role in Vietnam. "The Vietnamese could not put out their orders the way we would. They did not trust their own chain of command. They wouldn't tell the troop commanders where they were going until the last minute. And I think that when we [the United States] went in there, we didn't really realize the extent of the subversion.'"

By early 1963, the United States had stationed more than 12,000 American advisors and pilots in South Vietnam to help the country defend itself from the Communists. Despite this assistance, however, the ARVN continued to struggle in its campaign against the Viet Cong. "One had a sense on all sides of the... incompetence and unpopularity of the [Diem] government at the time," recalled presidential advisor John Kenneth Galbraith. "Here were just a few thousand Vietcong guerrillas scattered over that still quite huge country and a vast array of armed men already incapable of doing anything about them."

Battle of Ap Bac

American concern about the capabilities of South Vietnam's army intensified after an early 1963 clash known as the Battle of Ap Bac. This battle took place on January 2, 1963, at the small town of Ap Bac, about thirty-five miles southwest of Saigon. During the course of this fight, a Viet Cong battalion defeated a much larger South Vietnamese force that was supported by armored vehicles, heavy artillery, and U.S. Army helicopters. The South Vietnamese army performed very poorly in this battle, and the Viet Cong escaped after shooting down several helicopters and inflicting heavy casualties.

American military advisor John Paul Vann witnessed the entire battle at Ap Bac. After the fight was over, he submitted an angry report in which he harshly criticized the South Vietnamese army for its "damn miserable" performance. He charged that the officers were cowards and claimed that the entire ARVN force showed no willingness to fight. A few days later, Vann became further outraged when he learned that the South Vietnamese military lied about what happened in order to claim victory.

It then became clear that U.S. Ambassador Frederick Nolting and other American officials in Vietnam had no intention of telling the public the true story. So Vann secretly informed several American reporters about the disastrous battle. After hearing

Vann's account, these reporters began to doubt the word of U.S. and South Vietnamese military officials, who continued to insist that the war against the Viet Cong was going well.

Armed with Vann's inside information, reporters told the American public about the loss at Ap Bac. The news stunned the American people, many of whom had paid little attention to U.S. involvement in Vietnam until this time. "Ap Bac... was a decisive battle," writes New York Times reporter Neil Sheehan in A Bright Shining Lie. "Ap Bac was putting Vietnam on the front pages and on the television evening talk shows with a drama no other event had yet achieved. The dispatches, [full of] details of cowardice and bumbling, were describing the battle as the worst and most humiliating defeat ever inflicted on the Saigon [South Vietnamese] side."

American worries about Diem continue

As America's worries about South Vietnam's military increased, so did U.S. concerns about the stability of President Ngo Dinh Diem's government. Throughout the spring of 1963, American officials tried to convince Diem to make changes in the way he was ruling South Vietnam. They wanted him to introduce policies that would help the nation's struggling peasant population and stamp out widespread corruption in the military and other branches of government. They also urged Diem, who was Catholic, to show respect for Buddhism, the religion practiced by most South Vietnamese families. The United States hoped that by making these changes, the Diem government could reverse its drop in popularity and strengthen its grip on power.

But Diem ignored most U.S. efforts to get him to change his ways, and the military situation continued to deteriorate. "The military leadership of the ARVN seemed more interested in preserving its own privileges than in fighting the war," states Robert D. Schulzinger in A Time for War: The United States and Vietnam, 1941–1975. "For his part, Diem worried more about disloyal army officers threatening his regime [government] than he did about fighting the Vietcong."

By mid–1963, members of the Kennedy administration were fiercely divided over whether the United States should continue to support Diem's presidency. "We had a big battle all that summer between [the Department of] State and the National Security Council," former Central Intelligence Agency (CIA) Director William Colby recalls in The Bad War: An Oral History of the Vietnam War. "State's position was that you cannot hope to win with Diem because he cannot generate popular support. That was an honest appreciation. The other side, people at Defense and in CIA who'd been there, believed you weren't going to get much different government from anybody else." General Maxwell D. Taylor agreed that "there was a strong group [of Kennedy advisors] that had picked up the slogan 'You can't win with Diem.' The other group, to which I belonged, argued maybe we can't win with Diem, but if not Diem—who? And the answer was complete silence."

The Buddhist crisis

In early May President Diem traveled to the city of Hue to celebrate the 25th anniversary of his brother Ngo Dinh Thuc's promotion to archbishop in the Catholic Church. As part of the celebration, Catholic-themed flags were strung along the city's streets. A few days later, however, the Diem government banned members of the city's majority Buddhist population from flying their own banners in celebration of one of their religious holidays. This discriminatory treatment outraged the Buddhists in Hue, one of the historical centers of Vietnamese Buddhism. Thousands of Buddhist demonstrators soon took to the streets in a major protest against Diem's government. On May 8, 1963, the protest in Hue ended in terrible violence. Diem's soldiers attacked the crowds with clubs, tear gas, and gunfire, killing a number of people (reports range from eight to forty people killed) and wounding and jailing many others.

The Diem government blamed Viet Cong guerrillas for the violence in Hue and never admitted responsibility for its actions. But the nation's general population was not fooled, and new demonstrations organized by Buddhist leaders quickly spread throughout the country. Within a matter of days, the Buddhists were joined by several other South Vietnamese groups who opposed Diem's government. In The Making of a Quagmire: America and Vietnam during the Kennedy Era, New York Times reporter David Halberstam describes these protests against the Diem regime as an ominous sign of "deeprooted discontent [anger] among a religious group [the Buddhists] that constitutes about 70 percent of the country's population. What started as a religious protest has become predominantly political... the Buddhists are providing a spearhead for other discontented [groups]."

Buddhist suicide shocks the world

On the morning of June 11, 1963, a 73-year-old Buddhist bonze (monk) named Quang Duc sat down in the middle of a busy Saigon intersection. He folded his hands in prayer and crossed his legs in the lotus position of meditation, while another monk poured gasoline over his shaven head and orange robe. The old monk then lit a match and set himself on fire to protest Diem's repression of the Buddhist religion.

Shocking pictures of the monk's suicide quickly appeared in the United States and all around the world. The photographs persuaded many stunned Americans to focus greater attention on their country's involvement in South Vietnam. The pictures also triggered a wave of intense international criticism against Diem's government and its treatment of Vietnamese Buddhists. U.S. President John Kennedy commented that "no news picture in history has generated as much emotion around the world as that one."

President Diem and his ruling family reacted defiantly to the criticism, however. Diem's brother Ngo Dinh Nhu (1910–1963) insulted the country's followers of Buddhism and proclaimed that "if the Buddhists want to have another barbecue, I will be happy to supply the gasoline." Diem's sister-inlaw, Madame Nhu, made similar statements. She indicated that she would cheer if other monks committed suicide, adding that "if they [the Buddhists] burn thirty women we shall go ahead and clap our hands."

These remarks horrified President Kennedy and other U.S. officials. They told Diem that "Madame Nhu is out of control" and urged him to send her out of the country. U.S. diplomats also told Diem that Ngo Dinh Nhu should be removed from the government, citing his corrupt ways and his brutal use of the nation's secret police to silence political opposition. American advisors warned the South Vietnamese president that if he did not exercise greater control over Madame Nhu and Ngo Dinh Nhu, his government would become even more unpopular. But Diem relied heavily on his brother and sister-in-law, and he disregarded the warnings.

Demonstrations across South Vietnam

Over the next several weeks, six other monks and nuns in South Vietnam committed suicide by setting themselves on fire in ritual ceremonies. As the summer months passed, the demonstrations against the Diem regime continued to grow in size and intensity. On July 30, for instance, Buddhists and university students launched massive protests in Saigon and four other cities in South Vietnam. "The Buddhist movement became a rallying point for all of the discontent that had been accumulating against the ruling family among urban Vietnamese since 1954," explains Neil Sheehan in A Bright Shining Lie.

During this time, the Diem government used violence in an effort to stop the unrest. Peaceful demonstrators were sometimes attacked by soldiers and police armed with rifles, clubs, and tear gas. Other protestors, including monks and students who were believed to be leaders of the demonstrations, were kidnaped in the middle of the night and never seen again. Nonetheless, the government was unable to stop the demonstrations. According to Sheehan, Diem and the other members of his ruling family "did not understand that each act of repression bred more followers for the Buddhists."

On August 21, 1963, the Diem government declaredmartial law (meaning that the military took charge of the nation) and launched a massive crackdown across South Vietnam in an effort to stamp out the Buddhist-led demonstrations once and for all. Ngo Dinh Nhu's U.S.trained military troops stormed Buddhist temples—known as pagodas—all across the country. They arrested approximately 1,400 monks and nuns in these raids. The attacks were especially bloody in Hue. About 30 monks and student followers were shot or clubbed to death in assaults on Buddhist temples in the ancient city. Madame Nhu personally observed a raid on one of the main Buddhist temples in Saigon. She later called it "the happiest day of my life."

But the government crackdown failed to silence the anti-Diem protestors. Instead, riots broke out at several places across the country, including Saigon University. Diem promptly closed the university, only to see several Saigon high schools erupt in riots. Many of these schoolchildren were the children of important Vietnamese officials and businessmen. Around this same time, Madame Nhu's father, Tran Van Chuong, resigned from his post as ambassador to the United States. He announced that there was "not one chance in a hundred for victory" over the Communists with his daughter, her husband, and brother-in-law in power.

Observers saw these developments as further signs that Diem's rule was in grave danger.

Henry Cabot Lodge arrives in Vietnam

In August 1963, the same month that Diem and his ruling family launched their desperate crackdown on the demonstrators, a new U.S. ambassador to South Vietnam arrived in the country. Henry Cabot Lodge (1902–1985) replaced Frederick Nolting, a longtime defender of Diem's government. After reviewing the situation in Saigon, Lodge quickly concluded that Diem's regime was doomed. A week after his arrival, he sent President Kennedy a top-secret message in which he said, "We are launched on a course from which there is no respectable turning back: the overthrow of the Diem government. There is no possibility, in my view, that the war [against the Communists] can be won under a Diem administration."

Lodge's report disturbed Kennedy, who had hoped that the Diem government could be saved. But other reports confirmed Lodge's view of the situation. The entire length of South Vietnam, from its riot-torn cities to its Viet Cong-threatened rural areas, seemed to be on the verge of collapse. Some intelligence reports even suggested that Diem and his brother Nhu had entered into secret negotiations with North Vietnam in an effort to hold on to their positions. Determined to keep the country out of Communist hands, the Kennedy administration began preparing for the end of the Diem regime.

Diem's last days

In early September 1963, Kennedy publicly expressed his concerns about events in South Vietnam during an interview with newsman Walter Cronkite. "I don't think that unless a greater effort is made by the government to win popular support that the war can be won out there [in South Vietnam]," Kennedy said. "In the final analysis, it is their war. They are the ones who have to win it or lose it. We can help them, we can give them equipment, we can send our men out there as advisors, but they have to win it, the people of Vietnam, against the Communists. We are prepared to continue to assist them, but I don't think that the war can be won unless the people support the effort and, in my opinion, in the last two months, the government has gotten out of touch with the people."

Around this same time, a group of South Vietnamese military officers joined together in a plot to overthrow Diem and take control of the government. The leaders of this group were General Duong Van Minh, General Tran Van Don, and General Le Van Kim. In October, Lodge secretly informed the officers that the United States would not oppose a change of leadership of the South Vietnam government. "It seems at least an even bet that the next government would not bungle and stumble as much as the present one has," Lodge told the Kennedy administration.

After the United States extended its promise not to interfere in the coup (attempt to overthrow the government), the generals set their plan in motion. On November 1, 1963, they used a strong military force to seize control of several strategically important outposts in Saigon and other areas of South Vietnam. Initially, Diem and his brother refused to surrender. When it became clear that they could not stop the coup from succeeding, however, the brothers used a secret exit to escape the presidential palace after dark. But they proved unable to elude their pursuers, and were captured a few hours later at a Catholic church in Saigon. A short time later, Duong Van Minh—also known as "Big Minh"—ordered the execution of both men and assumed leadership of the country. Madame Nhu, meanwhile, escaped capture and possible execution only because she was in the United States at the time of the coup.

Ngô Đình Diệm after being shot and killed in the 1963 coup

President Kennedy was stunned and upset when he learned of Diem's murder. He believed that South Vietnam was better off with new leadership, but he had wanted the South Vietnamese generals to simply remove Diem from office, not assassinate him. "It was a shock to all of us," said General Maxwell Taylor. "But I think perhaps to the President more than any of us—because he didn't realize that we were all playing with fire when we were at least giving tacit [implied or understood] encouragement to the overthrow of this man."

Today, the United States' role in the overthrow of the Diem government continues to be fiercely debated by government officials and historians alike. Some people claim that it was necessary for the Kennedy administration to withhold support for Diem during the coup. They insist that the Communists probably would have seized control of South Vietnam in a matter of months if Diem had remained in power. But other observers strongly disagree. For example, General William C. Westmoreland called the U.S. approval for the overthrow of the Diem government a "grievous mistake." Westmoreland, who commanded U.S. military forces in Vietnam from 1964 to 1968, claimed that "action morally locked us in Vietnam. If it had not been for our involvement in the overthrow of President Diem, we could perhaps have gracefully withdrawn our support when South Vietnam's lack of unity and leadership became apparent."

CROSSING WIND AT THE CHAPARRAL

Probably you did not forget Nguyen van Hai? The orphan boy got in the US ship to South Vietnam in 1954 after the Geneva Treaty. He was adopted by Tran Phu, grew up in Khanh Hoa and the gangster dumped him since he refused to cooperate with them.

Khanh Hoa 1966

The gangster kicked Tran van Hai off the truck, he fell on the shoulder of a highway and rolled down into a ditch in a meadow on the way to Dalat, Central Vietnam while Phan Don and the thugs kept on driving.

"Drop dead meat on our way to Dalat, we have to pick up vegetables and fruits this morning." Phan Don told his gangsters, "Accomplish two tasks in one trip!"

"Bravo, Leader!" the followers laughed out loud

The gang used a truck that transferred vegetables and fruits from Central Vietnam: Khanh hoa- Dalat to Saigon; sometimes, they sneaked marijuana for "big bugs". The gang leader, Phan Don asked his followers,

"Are you sure that he's dead?"

"He didn't move, dead meat for sure." a thug responded

"Good, keep on driving!" the gang leader, Phan Don ordered

In the meantime, at the Emergency Dept in the General hospital in Dalat. About six in the morning, Vo thi Tam, a nurse yawned,

"Lucky, I'm on call but it has not too busied last night; only one more hour then I can go home!"

[Vo thi Tam was Vo Kiet's daughter, a land owner in My Tho. She met Tran van Hai at the banquet in Khanh Hoa. After graduation from high school, Vo thi Tam went to Nursing school and worked as a nurse in the Emergency Dept at Dalat General Hospital.]

The phone rang, Vo thi Tam picked it up, "Hello! This is the ER Nurse; how may I help you?"

"Nurse, Vo thi Tam, the ambulance just picked up a beaten and collapsed man. Get your team ready, I'll be there, too!" Doctor Huynh Yen said

"Yes, Doctor!" Nurse Vo thi Tam replied and transferred the message to the colleagues. The paramedics brought in a badly injured man. Nurse Vo thi Tam listened to the information from the paramedics, "Some body found this man in the ditch near Da Lat. No ID, no paper, he was beaten up severely injured and has a weak pulse...." Nurse Vo thi Tam tried to find a vein for the IV line, she saw a long scar on the left dorsal hand; something just flashed back her mind…

"Loosen his clothes." The Doctor said, "I'll listen to the heart, lungs, and exam the body."

Two nurse-assistants changed the patient into the hospital gown, a white cloth fell out from the trouser pocket. It was a handkerchief with a few words "Vo thi Tam, address in My Tho". Nurse Vo thi Tam saw it, she cried "The Valedictorian, Tran van Hai!"

"CBC with electrolytes panel, hydrate with elements accordingly as needed. CXR and R ankle to rule out fracture…" Dr. Huynh Yen ordered

A couple days later, Nguyen [Tran] van Hai was able to eat and drink. He remembered what happened and realized how lucky he was in Da Lat hospital due to the trauma. It was the best dream of his life, meeting Vo thi Tam again!

One evening, Vo thi Tam visited Nguyen [Tran] van Hai, she showed him a scarf she knitted for him.

"Do you like it?" she asked

"When I was in Khanh Hoa, we never used scarfs. It's useful to me now as it's cold in Dalat," he smiled

"Today I brought some mangosteen, would you try some?"

"Ah, it's delicious!" Nguyen [Tran] van Hai enjoyed the fruit from the South

"They're from my family garden in My Tho," Vo thi Tam said, "Come to the south and see… Dad has a large rice field and a lot of vegetables and fruits…. milk apples, annona… At harvest time, Dad hires a Reformed theater…Oh, a lot of fun! You must come, right?"

"You've been very nice to me. I can't repay your kindness. I'm homeless, no job…I truly don't want to bother you." Nguyen [Tran] van Hai said

"Don't think like that, please…." Vo thi Tam cried

"I was married and leaned on my wife's family to have a position in the society.... At last, they kicked me out, for I refused their order. I don't want to be in the same situation again." Nguyen [Tran] van Hai explained

"I'm not like that. I love you, sincerely." Vo thi Tam ran out of the room

"Ah.... You should not love me, Miss." Nguyen [Tran] van Hai sighed

Da Lat 1967

Nguyen [Tran] van Hai was transferred to the Rehabilitation center for convalescence where he met Do Thanh, a Marine Lieutenant of the Republic of Vietnam (South Vietnam) RVN. Do Thanh was recuperating after the injury in a military operation a months ago. They became good friends. Listening to Do Thanh's life in the military, Nguyen [Tran] van Hai thought about joining the Marine Corp of the RVN.

"The Marine Corp- RVN trains you for the combat. You will have a salary." Do Thanh advised

"Probably this is the best solution for me." Nguyen [Tran] van Hai replied

"I started as a Sergeant; I aim to be a Major someday!" Do Thanh said, "You at least- could be a Captain."

"Indeed!" Nguyen [Tran] van Hai laughed out loud

After being discharged from the Rehabilitation center, Nguyen [Tran] van Hai enlisted in the Marine Corps of the RVN used his name at birth, Nguyen van Hai- as he wanted to forget all about those days with the Tran family and at the Duong's mansion.

Nguyen van Hai made up his mind. Definitely, he'd use all his mind and strength to become a Captain someday. He'd build up his future by himself, not depending on anyone else.... And, he decided to forget about Vo thi Tam since he was training in the Marine Corps in military and technical skills. During this time,

Nguyen van Hai learned English; he was good so they gave him an opportunity to interpret for platoon. He graduated from the Marine Corps with the Sublieutenant rank.

At the graduation ceremony, the Supervisor-Captain Le Trung said,

"Congratulations to you all! Enjoy yourself with your families and loved ones, in two weeks, we'll all be deployed to Quang Tri, ready for the Battle of Khe Sanh."

The newly graduates shouted in joy,

"Hurray, we're free to see girlfriends!"

"Girlfriend?" Nguyen van Hai asked himself, "What would I do in two weeks off before the deploy to the Battle of Khe Sanh? How many times I've tried not to think about Vo thi Tam? The more I put it out of my mind, the more I miss her!"

It was a forgotten love

Yet, you've been still in my heart

I thought you were long far away

but you're still somewhere near by

Nguyen van Hai planned to see Vo thi Tam and tell her about his achievement; especially the English interpreter role to communicate with the American advisors! Happy and proud in the Marine uniform, Nguyen van Hai went to see Vo thi Tam. Nguyen van Hai and Vo thi Tam went for a stroll in the autumn woods. The falling leaves with beautiful colors among the whispering pines; if one listens, he could hear the babbles of the stream running down from the Truong Son mountain toward the meadows of the valley where the wild flowers fluttering their petals and spread the perfume far to the horizon of autumn season. Seeing a rabbit running across, Nguyen van Hai ran after it; he lost it.

"Sublieutenant, people don't catch a rabbit that way." Vo thi Tam laughed

"But I've got you." Nguyen van Hai put his arms around her, "I love you."

"I love you, too." Vo thi Tam whispered

"Next week, I'll be in the crossing wind at the chaparral Khe Sanh, Quang Tri." Nguyen van Hai said

"Remember to put on the scarf I made for you, will you?" Vo thi Tam was about to cry

Feeling her trembling body in his arms, he said,

"Yes. I will. Please smile- today I'm so happy that we have each other…"

She smiled, Nguyen van Hai said,

"I will have your smile- as beautiful as a fairy- in my heart all the times at the battle field."

"Will you be back?" she asked

"I'll be back some day, I promise. "he responded

They looked at the dandelions floating in the air under blue sky toward the Da-tang-la fall. The crystal water slightly touches the rocks then rushes down the cliffs it performs a spectacular view of torrential waters with wonderous sound as this was a fairy tale.

Battle of Khe Sanh - Wikipedia en.wikipedia.org › wiki › Battle_of_Khe_Sanh

The Battle of Khe Sanh (21 January – 9 July 1968) was conducted in the Khe Sanh area of northwestern Quảng Trị Province, Republic of Vietnam (South Vietnam), during the Vietnam War. The main US forces defending Khe Sanh Combat Base (KSCB) were two regiments of the United States Marine

Corps supported by elements from the United States Army and the United States Air Force (USAF), as well as a small number of Army of the Republic of Vietnam (ARVN) troops. These were pitted against two to three divisional-size elements of the North Vietnamese People's Army of Vietnam (PAVN).

The US command in Saigon initially believed that combat operations around KSCB during 1967 were part of a series of minor PAVN offensives in the border regions. That appraisal was later altered when the PAVN was found to be moving major forces into the area. In response, US forces were built up before the PAVN isolated the Marine base. Once the base came under siege, a series of actions was fought over a period of five months. During this time, KSCB and the hilltop outposts around it were subjected to constant PAVN artillery, mortar, and rocket attacks, and several infantry assaults. To support the Marine base, a massive aerial bombardment campaign (Operation Niagara) was launched by the USAF. Over 100,000 tons of bombs were dropped by US aircraft and over 158,000 artillery rounds were fired in defense of the base. Throughout the campaign, US forces used the latest technology to locate PAVN forces for targeting. Additionally, the logistical effort required to support the base once it was isolated demanded the implementation of other tactical innovations to keep the Marines supplied.

On 24 April 1967, a patrol from Bravo Company became engaged with a PAVN force of an unknown size north of Hill 861. That action prematurely triggered a PAVN offensive aimed at taking Khe Sanh. The PAVN forces were in the process of gaining elevated terrain before it launched of the main attack. The 2nd and 3rd battalions of the 3rd Marine Regiment, under the command of Colonel John P. Lanigan, reinforced KSCB and were given the task of pushing the PAVN off of Hills 861, 881 North, and 881 South. PAVN forces were driven out of the area around Khe Sanh after suffering 940 casualties. The Marines suffered 155 killed in action and 425 wounded. To prevent PAVN observation of the main base at the airfield and their possible use as firebases, the hills of the surrounding Khe Sanh Valley had to be continuously occupied and defended by separate Marine elements. In the wake of the hill fights, a lull in PAVN activity occurred around Khe Sanh. By the end of May, Marine forces were again drawn down from two battalions to one, the 1st Battalion, 26th Marines. Lieutenant General Robert E. Cushman Jr. relieved Walt as commander of III MAF in June.

On 14 August, Colonel David E. Lownds took over as commander of the 26th Marine Regiment. Sporadic actions were taken in the vicinity during the late summer and early fall, the most serious of which was the ambush of a supply convoy on Route 9. That proved to be the last overland attempt at resupply for Khe Sanh until the following March. In December and early January, numerous sightings of PAVN troops and activities were made in the Khe Sanh area, but the sector remained relatively quiet.

In March 1968, an overland relief expedition (Operation Pegasus) was launched by a combined Marine–Army/ARVN task force that eventually broke through to the Marines at Khe Sanh. American commanders considered the defense of Khe Sanh a success, but shortly after the siege was lifted, the decision was made to dismantle the base rather than risk similar battles in the future. On 19 June 1968, the evacuation and destruction of KSCB began. Amid heavy shelling, the Marines attempted to salvage what they could before destroying what remained as they were evacuated. Minor attacks continued before the base was officially closed on 5 July. Marines remained around Hill 689, though, and fighting in the vicinity continued until 11 July until they were finally withdrawn, bringing the battle to a close.

In the aftermath, the North Vietnamese proclaimed a victory at Khe Sanh, while US forces claimed that they had withdrawn, as the base was no longer required. Historians have observed that the Battle of Khe Sanh may have distracted American and South Vietnamese attention from the buildup of Viet Cong (VC) forces in the south before the early 1968 Tet Offensive. Nevertheless, the US commander during the battle, General William Westmoreland, maintained that the true intention of Tet was to distract forces from Khe Sanh.

The village of Khe Sanh was the seat of government of Hương Hoa district, an area of Bru Montagnard villages and coffee plantations, situated about 7 miles (11 km) from the

Laotian frontier on Route 9, the northernmost transverse road in South Vietnam. The badly deteriorated Route 9 ran from the coastal region through the western highlands, and then crossed the border into Laos. The origin of the combat base lay in the construction by US Army Special Forces of an airfield in August 1962 outside the village at an old French fort. The camp then became a Special Forces outpost of the Civilian Irregular Defense Groups, whose purpose was to keep watch on PAVN infiltration along the border and to protect the local population.

James Marino wrote that in 1964, General Westmoreland, the US commander in Vietnam, had determined, "Khe Sanh could serve as a patrol base blocking enemy infiltration from Laos; a base for... operations to harass the enemy in Laos; an airstrip for reconnaissance to survey the Ho Chi Minh Trail; a western anchor for the defenses south of the DMZ; and an eventual jumping-off point for ground operations to cut the Ho Chi Minh Trail." In November 1964, the Special Forces moved their camp to the Xom Cham Plateau, the future site of Khe Sanh Combat Base.

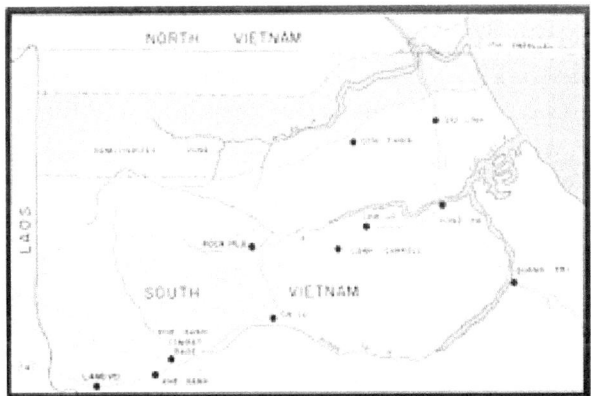

During the winter of 1964, Khe Sanh became the location of a launch site [the area on which a rocket stands for launching, typically consisting of a platform with a supporting structure] for the highly classified Military Assistance Command, Vietnam – Studies and Observations Group (the site was first established near the village and was later moved to the French fort). From there, reconnaissance teams were launched into Laos to explore and gather intelligence on the PAVN logistical system known as the Ho Chi Minh Trail (also known as "Truong Son Strategic

Supply Route" to the North Vietnamese soldiers). According to Marino, "by 1966, Westmoreland had begun to consider Khe Sanh as part of a larger strategy". With a view to eventually gaining approval for an advance through Laos to interdict the Ho Chi Minh Trail, he determined, "it was absolutely essential to hold the base", and he gave the order for US Marines to take up positions around Khe Sanh. Military Assistance Command, Vietnam subsequently began planning for incursion into Laos, and in October, construction of an airfield at Khe Sanh was completed. The plateau camp was permanently manned by the US Marines during 1967, when they established an outpost next to the airstrip. This base was to serve as the western anchor of Marine Corps forces, which had tactical responsibility for the five northernmost provinces of South Vietnam known as I Corps. The Marines' defensive system stretched below the Demilitarized Zone (DMZ) from the coast, along Route 9, to Khe Sanh. During 1966 the regular Special Forces troops had moved off the plateau and built a smaller camp down Route 9 at Lang Vei, about half the distance to the Laotian border. During the second half of 1967, the North Vietnamese instigated a series of actions in the border regions of South Vietnam. All of these attacks were conducted by regimental-size PAVN/VC units, but unlike the usual hit-and-run tactics used previously, these were sustained and bloody affairs.

Combat on Hill 875, the most intense of the battles around Dak To

In early October, the PAVN had intensified battalion-sized ground probes and sustained artillery fire against <u>Con Thien</u>, a hilltop stronghold in the center of the Marines' defensive line south of the DMZ in northern Quảng Trị Province. Mortar rounds, artillery shells, and 122 mm rockets fell randomly, but incessantly, upon the base. The September bombardments ranged from 100 to 150 rounds per day, with a maximum on 25 September of 1,190 rounds. Westmoreland responded by launching Operation Neutralize, an aerial and naval bombardment campaign designed to break the siege. For seven weeks, American aircraft dropped from 35,000 to 40,000 tons of bombs in nearly 4,000 airstrikes.

On 27 October, a PAVN regiment attacked an Army of the Republic of Vietnam (ARVN) battalion at Song Be, capital of Phước Long Province. The PAVN fought for several days, took casualties, and fell back. Two days later, the PAVN 273rd Regiment attacked a Special Forces camp near the border town of Loc Ninh, in Bình Long Province. Troops of the US 1st Infantry Division were able to respond quickly. After a ten-day battle, the attackers were pushed back into Cambodia. At least 852 PAVN soldiers were killed during the action, as opposed to 50 American and South Vietnamese dead. The heaviest action took place near Dak To, in the central highlands province of Kon Tum. There, the presence of the PAVN 1st Division prompted a 22-day battle that had some of the most intense close-quarters fighting of the entire conflict. American intelligence estimated between 1,200 and 1,600 PAVN troops were killed, while 362 members of the US 4th Infantry Division, the 173rd Airborne Brigade, and ARVN Airborne elements were killed in action. Nonetheless, three of the four battalions of the 4th Infantry and the entire 173rd were rendered combat ineffective during the battle. American intelligence analysts were quite baffled by this series of enemy actions. For them, no logic was apparent behind the sustained PAVN/VC offensives, other than to inflict casualties on the allied forces. This they accomplished, but the casualties absorbed by the North Vietnamese seemed to negate any direct gains they might have obtained. The border battles did, however, have two significant consequences that were unappreciated at the time: they fixed the attention of the American command on the border regions, and they drew American and ARVN forces away from the coastal lowlands and cities, in preparation for the Tet Offensive.

The Hill Fights

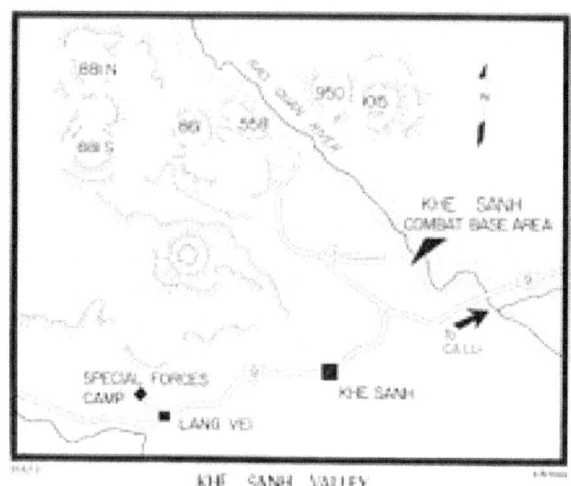

The Khe Sanh Valley

Things remained quiet in the Khe Sanh area through 1966. Even so, Westmoreland insisted that it not only be occupied by the Marines, but that it also be reinforced. He was vociferously opposed by General Lewis W. Walt, the Marine commander of I Corps. Walt argued heatedly that the real target of the American effort should be the pacification and protection of the population, not chasing the PAVN/VC in the hinterlands. Westmoreland won out, however, and the 1st Battalion, 3rd Marine Regiment (1/3 Marines) was dispatched to occupy the camp and airstrip on 29 September. By late January 1967, the 1/3 returned to Japan and was relieved by Bravo Company, 1st Battalion, 9th Marines (1/9 Marines). A single company was replacing an entire battalion.

On 24 April 1967, a patrol from Bravo Company became engaged with a PAVN force of unknown size north of Hill 861. This action prematurely triggered a PAVN offensive aimed at taking Khe Sanh. The PAVN forces were in the process of gaining elevated terrain before the launching of the main attack. The 2nd and 3rd Battalions of the 3rd Marine Regiment, under the command of Colonel John P. Lanigan, reinforced KSCB and were given the task of pushing the PAVN off of Hills 861, 881 North, and 881 South. PAVN forces were driven out of the area around Khe Sanh after suffering 940 casualties. The Marines suffered

Marines of Company C, 2d Battalion, 3d Marines inch their way toward the summit of Hill 881N during the Hill fights. (USMC Photo A189161)

Close air support strikes of the 1st Marine Aircraft Wing and massive artillery fires paved the way for infantry assaults. (USMC Photo A371952)

155 killed in action and 425 wounded. To prevent PAVN observation of the main base at the airfield (and their possible use as firebases), the hills of the surrounding Khe Sanh Valley had to be continuously occupied and defended by separate Marine elements. In the wake of the hill fights, a lull in PAVN activity occurred around Khe Sanh. By the end of May, Marine forces were again drawn down from two battalions to one, the 1st Battalion, 26th Marines. Lieutenant General Robert E. Cushman, Jr. relieved Walt as commander of III MAF in June.

On 14 August, Colonel David E. Lownds took over as commander of the 26th Marine Regiment. Sporadic actions were taken in the vicinity during the late summer and early fall, the most serious of which was the ambush of a supply convoy on Route 9. This proved to be the last overland attempt at resupply for Khe Sanh until the following March. During December and early January, numerous sightings of PAVN troops and activities were made in the Khe Sanh area, but the sector remained relatively quiet.

A decision then had to be made by the American high command: either commit more of the limited manpower in I Corps to the defense of Khe Sanh or abandon the base. Westmoreland regarded this choice as quite simple. In his memoirs, he listed the reasons for a continued effort, "Khe Sanh could serve as a patrol base for blocking enemy infiltration from Laos along Route 9; as a base for SOG operations to harass the enemy in Laos; as an airstrip for reconnaissance planes surveying the Ho Chi Minh Trail."

Khe Sanh could serve as a patrol base for blocking enemy infiltration from Laos along Route 9; as a base for SOG operations to harass the enemy in Laos; as an airstrip for reconnaissance planes surveying the Ho Chi Minh Trail; as the western anchor for defenses south of the DMZ; and as an eventual jump-off point for ground operations to cut the Ho Chi Minh Trail. Leading Marine officers, however, were not all of the same opinion. Cushman, the new III MAF commander, supported Westmoreland (perhaps wanting to mend Army/Marine relations after the departure of Walt). Other concerns raised included the assertion that the real danger to I Corps was from a direct threat to Quảng Trị City and other urban areas; that a defense would be pointless as a threat to infiltration, since PAVN troops could easily bypass Khe Sanh; that the base was too isolated and that the Marines "had neither the helicopter resources, the troops, nor the logistical bases for such operations". Additionally, Shore argues that the "weather was another critical factor because the poor visibility and low overcasts attendant to the monsoon season made such operations hazardous." Brigadier General Lowell English (assistant commander 3rd Marine Division) complained that the defense of the isolated outpost was ludicrous. "When you're at Khe Sanh, you're not really anywhere. You could lose it and you really haven't lost a damn thing."

As far as Westmoreland was concerned, however, all he needed to know was that the PAVN had massed large numbers of troops for a set-piece battle. Making the prospect even more enticing was that the base was in an unpopulated area where American firepower could be fully employed without civilian casualties. The opportunity to engage and destroy a formerly elusive enemy that was moving toward a fixed position promised a victory of unprecedented proportions.

In early December 1967, the PAVN appointed Major General Tran Quy Hai as the local commander for the actions around Khe Sanh, with Le Quang Dạo as his political commissar. In the coming days, a campaign headquarters was established around Sap Lit. Two divisions, the 304th and the 325th, were assigned to the operation: the 325th was given responsibility for the area around the north, while the 304th was given responsibility for the southern sector. In attempting to determine PAVN intentions

Marine intelligence confirmed that, within a period of just over a week, the 325th Division had moved into the vicinity of the base and two more divisions were within supporting distance. The 324th Division was located in the DMZ area 10–15 miles (16–24 km) north of Khe Sanh while the 320th Division was within easy reinforcing distance to the northeast. They were supported logistically from the nearby Ho Chi Minh Trail. As a result of this intelligence, KSCB was reinforced on 13 December by the 1st Battalion, 9th Marine Regiment. According to the official PAVN history, by December 1967 the North Vietnamese had in place, or within supporting distance: the 304th, 320th, 324th and 325th Infantry Divisions, the independent 270th infantry Regiment; five artillery regiments (the 16th, 45th, 84th, 204th, and 675th); three AAA regiments (the 208th, 214th, and 228th); four tank companies; one engineer regiment plus one independent engineer battalion; one signal battalion; and a number of local force units.

At positions west of Hill 881 South and north of Co Roc Ridge, across the border in Laos, the PAVN established artillery, rocket, and mortar positions from which to launch attacks by fire on the base and to support its ground operations. The PAVN 130 mm and 152 mm artillery pieces, and 122 mm rockets, had a longer range than the Marine artillery support which consisted of 105 mm and 155 mm howitzers. This range overmatch was used by the PAVN to avoid counter-battery fire. They were assisted in their emplacement efforts by the continuing bad weather of the winter monsoon. During the rainy night of 2 January 1968, six men dressed in black uniforms were seen outside the defensive wire of the main base by members of a listening post. After failing to respond to a challenge, they were fired upon and five were killed outright while the sixth, although wounded, escaped. This event prompted Cushman to reinforce Lownds with the rest of the 2nd Battalion, 26th Marines. This marked the first time that all three battalions of the 26th Marine Regiment had operated together in combat since the Battle of Iwo Jima during the Second World War. To cover a defilade near the Rao Quan River, four companies from 2/26 were immediately sent out to occupy Hill 558, with another manning Hill 861A. On 20 January, La Thanh Ton, a PAVN lieutenant from the 325th Division, defected and laid out the plans for an entire series of PAVN attacks. Hills 881

South, 861, and the main base itself would be simultaneously attacked that same evening. At 00:30 on 21 January, Hill 861 was attacked by about 300 PAVN troops, the Marines, however, were prepared. The PAVN infantry, though bracketed by artillery fire, still managed to penetrate the perimeter of the defenses and were only driven back after severe close-quarters combat. The main base was then subjected to an intense mortar and rocket barrage. Hundreds of mortar rounds and 122-mm rockets slammed into the base, levelling most of the above-ground structures. One of the first enemy shells set off an explosion in the main ammunition dump. Many of the artillery and mortar rounds stored in the dump were thrown into the air and detonated on impact within the base. Soon after, another shell hit a cache of tear gas, which saturated the entire area. The fighting and shelling on 21 January resulted in 14 Marines killed and 43 wounded. Hours after the bombardment ceased, the base was still in danger. At around 10:00, the fire ignited a large quantity of explosives, rocking the base with another series of detonations.

At the same time as the artillery bombardment at KSCB, an attack was launched against Khe Sanh village, seat of Hướng Hóa District. The village, 3 km south of the base, was defended by 160 local Bru troops, plus 15 American advisers. At dawn on 21 January, it was attacked by a roughly 300-strong PAVN battalion. A platoon from Company D, 1/26 Marines was sent from the base but was withdrawn in the face of the superior PAVN forces. Reinforcements from the ARVN 256th Regional Force (RF) company were dispatched aboard nine UH-1 helicopters of the 282nd Assault Helicopter Company, but they were landed near the abandoned French fort/former FOB-3 which was occupied by the PAVN who killed many of the RF troops and 4 Americans, including Lieutenant colonel Joseph Seymoe the deputy adviser for Quang Tri Province and forcing the remaining helicopters to abandon the mission. On the morning of 22 January Lownds decided to evacuate the remaining forces in the village with most of the Americans evacuated by helicopter while two advisers led the surviving local forces overland to the combat base.

To eliminate any threat to their flank, the PAVN attacked Laotian Battalion BV-33, located at Ban Houei Sane, on Route 9 in Laos. The battalion was assaulted on the night of 23 January by three PAVN battalions supported by seven tanks. The Laotians were overrun, and many fled to the Special Forces camp at Lang Vei. The Battle of Ban Houei Sane, not the attack three weeks later at Lang Vei, marked the first time that the PAVN had committed an armored unit to battle. PAVN artillery fell on the main base for the first time on 21 January. Several rounds also landed on Hill 881. Due to the arrival of the 304th Division, KSCB was further reinforced by the 1st Battalion, 9th Marine Regiment on 22 January. Five days later, the final reinforcements arrived in the form of the 37th ARVN Ranger Battalion, which was deployed more for political than tactical reasons. The Marines and ARVN dug in and hoped that the approaching Tết truce (scheduled for 29–31 January) would provide some respite. On the afternoon of 29 January, however, the 3rd Marine Division notified Khe Sanh that the truce had been cancelled. The Tet Offensive was about to begin.

Westmoreland's plan to use nuclear weapons

Nine days before the Tet Offensive broke out, the PAVN opened the battle of Khe Sanh and attacked the US forces just south of the DMZ. Declassified documents show that in response, Westmoreland considered using nuclear weapons. In 1970, the Office of Air Force History published a then "top secret", but now declassified, 106-page report, titled *The Air Force in Southeast Asia: Toward a Bombing Halt, 1968*. Journalist Richard Ehrlich writes that according to the report, "in late January, General Westmoreland had warned that if the situation near the DMZ and at Khe Sanh worsened drastically, nuclear or chemical weapons might have to be used." The report continues to state, "this prompted Air Force chief of staff, General John McConnell, to press, although unsuccessfully, for JCS (Joint Chiefs of Staff) authority to request Pacific Command to prepare a plan for using low-yield nuclear weapons to prevent a catastrophic loss of the U.S. Marine base." Nevertheless, ultimately the nuclear option was discounted by military planners. A secret memorandum reported by US Secretary of Defense Robert McNamara, sent to US President Lyndon B. Johnson on 19 February 1968, was declassified in 2005. It reveals that the nuclear option was discounted because of terrain considerations that were unique to South Vietnam, which would have reduced the effectiveness of tactical nuclear weapons.

McNamara wrote: "because of terrain and other conditions peculiar to our operations in South Vietnam, it is inconceivable that the use of nuclear weapons would be recommended there against either Viet Cong or North Vietnamese forces". McNamara's thinking may have also been affected by his aide David Morrisroe (later VP at Cal Tech where McNamara later served as Trustee), whose brother Michael Morrisroe (1960 New York State Chess Champion) was serving at the base.

During January, the recently installed electronic sensors of Operation Muscle Shoals (later renamed "Igloo White"), which were undergoing test and evaluation in southeastern Laos, were alerted by a flurry of PAVN activity along the Ho Chi Minh Trail opposite the northwestern corner of South Vietnam. Due to the nature of these activities, and the threat that they posed to KSCB, Westmoreland ordered Operation Niagara I, an intense intelligence collection effort on PAVN activities in the vicinity of the Khe Sanh Valley.

US Navy OP-2E Neptune of VO-67, a variant of a naval patrol bomber and antisubmarine warfare aircraft specifically developed for the Muscle Shoals mission

Niagara I was completed during the third week of January, and the next phase, Niagara II, was launched on the 21st, the day of the first PAVN artillery barrage. The Marine Direct Air Support Center (DASC), located at KSCB, was responsible for the coordination of air strikes with artillery fire. An airborne battlefield command and control center aboard a C-130 aircraft, directed incoming strike aircraft to forward air control (FAC) spotter planes, which, in turn directed them to targets either located by themselves or radioed in by ground units. When weather conditions precluded FAC-directed strikes, the bombers were directed to their targets by either a Marine AN/TPQ-10 radar installation at KSCB or by Air Force Combat Skyspot MSQ-77 stations. Thus, began what was described by John Morocco as "the most concentrated application of aerial firepower in the history of warfare". On an average day, 350 tactical fighter-bombers, 60 B-52s, and 30 light observation or reconnaissance aircraft operated in the skies near the base. Westmoreland had already ordered the nascent Igloo White operation to assist in the Marine defense. On 22 January, the first sensor drops took place, and by the end of the month, 316 acoustic and seismic sensors had been dropped in 44 strings. The sensors were implanted by a special naval squadron, Observation Squadron Sixty-Seven (VO-67). The Marines at KSCB credited 40% of intelligence available to their fire-support coordination center to the sensors. By the end of the battle, USAF assets had flown 9,691 tactical sorties and dropped 14,223 tons of bombs on targets within the Khe Sanh area. Marine Corps aviators had flown 7,098 missions and released 17,015 tons. Naval aircrews, many of whom were redirected from Operation Rolling Thunder strikes against North Vietnam, flew 5,337 sorties and dropped 7,941 tons of ordnance in the area. Westmoreland later wrote, "Washington so feared that some word of it might reach the press that I was told to desist, ironically answering what those consequences could be: a political disaster."

Meanwhile, an interservice political struggle took place in the headquarters at Phu Bai Combat Base, Saigon, and the Pentagon over who should control aviation assets supporting the entire American effort in Southeast Asia. Westmoreland had given his deputy commander for air operations, Air Force General William W. Momyer, the responsibility for coordinating all air assets during the operation to support KSCB. This caused problems for the Marine command, which possessed its own aviation squadrons that operated under their own close air support doctrine. The Marines were extremely reluctant to relinquish authority over their aircraft to an Air Force general. The command and control arrangement then in place in Southeast Asia went against Air Force doctrine, which was predicated on the single air manager concept. One headquarters would allocate and coordinate all air assets, distributing them wherever they were considered most necessary, and then transferring them as the situation required. The Marines, whose aircraft and doctrine were integral to their operations, were under no such centralized control. On 18 January, Westmoreland passed his request for Air Force control up the chain of command to CINCPACCINCPAC Fleet Headquarters, also known as Commander in Chief Pacific Fleet Headquarters or COMPACFLT Headquarters, is a historic military building on Makalapa Drive in Joint Base Pearl Harbor–Hickam, on the island of Oahu in the US state of Hawaii. Wikipedia in Honolulu. Heated debate arose among Westmoreland, Commandant of the Marine Corps Leonard F. Chapman, Jr., and Army Chief of Staff Harold K. Johnson. Johnson backed the Marine position due to his concern over protecting the Army's air assets from Air Force co-option. Westmoreland was so obsessed with the tactical situation that he threatened to resign if his wishes were not obeyed. As a result, on 7 March, for the first time during the Vietnam War, air operations were placed under the control of a single manager.

National Security Advisor Walt W. Rostow *showing President* Lyndon B. Johnson *a model of the Khe Sanh area, 15 February 1968*

Westmoreland insisted for several months that the entire Tet Offensive was a diversion, including, famously, attacks on downtown Saigon and obsessively affirming that the true objective of the North Vietnamese was Khe Sanh. The Tet Offensive was launched prematurely in some areas on 30 January. On the following night, a massive wave of PAVN/VC attacks swept throughout South Vietnam, everywhere except Khe Sanh. The launching of the largest enemy offensive thus far in the conflict did not shift Westmoreland's focus away from Khe Sanh. A press release prepared on the following day (but never issued), at the height of Tet, showed that he was not about to be distracted. "The enemy is attempting to confuse the issue ... I suspect he is also trying to draw everyone's attention away from the greatest area of threat, the northern part of I Corps. Let me caution everyone not to be confused." Not much activity (with the exception of patrolling) had occurred thus far during the battle for the Special Forces of Detachment A-101 and their four companies of Bru CIDGs stationed at Lang Vei. Then, on the morning of 6 February, the PAVN fired mortars into the Lang Vei compound, wounding eight Camp Strike Force soldiers. At 18:10 hours, the PAVN followed up their morning mortar attack with an artillery strike from 152 mm howitzers, firing 60 rounds into the camp. The strike wounded two more Strike Force soldiers and damaged two bunkers. The situation changed radically during the early morning hours of 7 February. The Americans had forewarning of PAVN armor in the area from Laotian refugees from camp BV-33. SOG Reconnaissance teams also reported finding tank tracks in the area surrounding Co Roc mountain. Although the PAVN was known to possess two armored regiments, it had not yet fielded an armored unit in South Vietnam, and besides, the Americans considered it impossible for them to get one down to Khe Sanh without it being spotted by aerial reconnaissance. It still came as a shock to the Special Forces troopers at Lang Vei when 12 tanks attacked their camp. The Soviet-built PT-76 amphibious tanks of the 203rd Armored Regiment churned over the defenses, backed up by an infantry assault by the 7th Battalion, 66th Regiment and the 4th Battalion of the 24th Regiment, both elements of the 304th Division. The ground troops had been specially equipped for the attack with satchel charges, tear gas, and flame throwers. Although the camp's main defenses were overrun in only 13 minutes, the fighting lasted for several hours, during which the Special Forces men and Bru CIDGs managed to knock out at least five of the tanks.

The Marines at Khe Sanh had a plan in place for providing a ground relief force in just such a contingency, but Lownds, fearing a PAVN ambush, refused to implement it. Lownds also rejected a proposal to launch a helicopter extraction of the survivors. During a meeting at Da Nang at 07:00 the next morning, Westmoreland

and Cushman [I Corps (ROK/US) Group United States Army Command and General Staff College 101st Airborne Division Fort Devens 2d Brigade, 101st Airborne Division] accepted Lownds' decision. Army Lieutenant Colonel Jonathan Ladd (commander, 5th Special Forces Group), who had just flown in from Khe Sanh, was reportedly, "astounded that the Marines, who prided themselves on leaving no man behind, were willing to write off all of the Green Berets and simply ignore the fall of Lang Vei."

Ladd and the commander of the SOG [Military Assistance Command, Vietnam – Studies and Observations Group was a highly classified, multi-service United States special operations unit which conducted covert unconventional warfare operations prior to and during the Vietnam War. Wikipedia] compound (whose men and camp had been incorporated into the defenses of KSCB) proposed that, if the Marines would provide the helicopters, the SOG reconnaissance men would go in themselves to pick up any survivors. The Marines continued to oppose the operation until Westmoreland actually had to issue an order to Cushman to allow the rescue operation to proceed. The relief effort was not launched until 15:00, and it was successful. Of the 500 CIDG troops at Lang Vei, 200 had been killed or were missing and 75 more were wounded. Of the 24 Americans at the camp, 10 had been killed and 11 wounded. Lownds infuriated the Special Forces personnel even further when the indigenous survivors of Lang Vei, their families, civilian refugees from the area, and Laotian survivors from the camp at Ban Houei Sane arrived at the gate of KSCB. Lownds feared that PAVN infiltrators were mixed up in the crowd of more than 6,000, and lacked sufficient resources to sustain them. Overnight, they were moved to a temporary position a short distance from the perimeter and from there, some of the Laotians were eventually evacuated, although the majority turned around and walked back down Route 9 toward Laos. The Lao troops were eventually flown back to their homeland, but not before the Laotian regional commander remarked that his army had to "consider the South Vietnamese as enemy because of their conduct."

Ontos, officially the Rifle, Multiple 106 mm, Self-propelled, M50

At the end of January, General Rathvon M. Tompkins had ordered that no Marine patrols proceed more than 500 meters from the Combat Base. Regardless, the SOG reconnaissance teams kept patrolling, providing the only human intelligence available in the battle area. This, however, did not prevent the Marine tanks within the perimeter from training their guns on the SOG camp. Lownds estimated that the logistical requirements of KSCB were 60 tons per day in mid-January and rose to 185 tons per day when all five battalions were in place. The greatest impediments to the delivery of supplies to the base were the closure of Route 9 and the winter monsoon weather. For most of the battle, low-lying clouds and fog enclosed the area from early morning until around noon, and poor visibility severely hampered aerial resupply. 5Making matters worse for the defenders, any aircraft that braved the weather and attempted to land was subject to PAVN antiaircraft fire on its way in for a landing. Once the aircraft touched down, it became the target of any number of PAVN artillery or mortar crews. The aircrew then had to contend with antiaircraft fire on the way out. As a result, 65% of all supplies were delivered by paradrops delivered by C-130 aircraft, mostly by the USAF, whose crews had significantly more experience in airdrop tactics than Marine air crews. The most dramatic supply delivery system used at Khe Sanh was the Low Altitude Parachute Extraction System, in which palletized supplies were pulled out of the cargo bay of a low-flying transport aircraft by means of an attached parachute. The pallet slid to a halt on the airstrip while the aircraft never had to actually land. The USAF delivered 14,356 tons of supplies to Khe Sanh by air (8,120 tons by paradrop). 1st Marine Aircraft Wing records claim that the unit delivered 4,661 tons of cargo into KSCB.

The resupply of the numerous, isolated hill outposts was fraught with the same difficulties and dangers. The fire of PAVN antiaircraft units took its toll of helicopters that made the attempt. The Marines found a solution to the problem in the "Super Gaggle" concept. A group of 12 A-4 Skyhawk fighter-bombers provided flak suppression for massed flights of 12–16 helicopters, which would resupply the hills simultaneously. The adoption of this concept at the end of February was the turning point in the resupply effort. After its adoption, Marine helicopters flew in 465 tons of supplies during February. When the weather later cleared in March, the amount was increased to 40 tons per day. As more infantry units had been assigned to defend KSCB, artillery reinforcement kept pace. By early January, the defenders could count on fire support from 46 artillery pieces of various calibers, five tanks armed with 90-mm guns, and 92 single or Ontos-mounted 106-mm recoilless rifles. The base could also depend on fire support from US Army 175-mm guns located at Camp Carroll, east of Khe Sanh. Throughout the battle, Marine artillerymen fired 158,891 mixed rounds. In addition, over 100,000 tons of bombs were dropped until mid-April by aircraft of the USAF, US Navy] and Marines onto the area surrounding Khe Sanh. This equates to roughly 1,300 tons of bombs dropped daily — 5 tons for every one of the 20,000 PAVN soldiers initially estimated to have been committed to the fighting at Khe Sanh. Marine analysis of PAVN artillery fire estimated that the PAVN gunners had fired 10,908 artillery and mortar rounds and rockets into Marine positions during the battle. Communications with military command outside of Khe Sanh was maintained by an U.S. Army Signal Corps team, the 544th Signal Detachment from the 337th Signal Company, 37th Signal Brigade in Danang. The latest microwave/tropospheric scatter technology [Troposcatter (short for tropospheric scatter) technology uses particles that make up the Earth's atmosphere as a reflector for microwave radio signals. Those signals are aimed just above the horizon in the direction of a receiver station] enabled them to maintain communications at all times. The site linked to another microwave/tropo site in Huế manned by the 513th Signal Detachment. From the Huế site the communication signal was sent to Danang headquarters where it could be sent anywhere in the world. The microwave/tropo site was located in an underground bunker next to the airstrip.

On the night of the fall of Lang Vei, three companies of the PAVN 101D Regiment moved into jump-off positions to attack Alpha-1, an outpost just outside the Combat Base held by 66 men of Company A, 1st Platoon, 1/9 Marines. At 04:15 on 8 February under cover of fog and a mortar barrage, the PAVN penetrated the perimeter, overrunning most of the position and pushing the remaining 30 defenders into the southwestern portion of the defenses. For some unknown reason, the PAVN troops did not press their advantage and eliminate the pocket, instead throwing a steady stream of grenades at the Marines. At 07:40, a relief force from Company A, 2nd Platoon set out from the main base and attacked through the PAVN, pushing them into supporting tank and artillery fire. By 11:00, the battle was over, Company A had lost 24 dead and 27 wounded, while 150 PAVN bodies were found around the position, which was then abandoned. On 23 February, KSCB received its worst bombardment of the entire battle. During one 8-hour period, the base was rocked by 1,307 rounds, most of which came from 130-mm (used for the first time on the battlefield) and 152-mm artillery pieces located in Laos. Casualties from the bombardment were 10 killed and 51 wounded. Two days later, US troops detected PAVN trenches running due north to within 25 m of the base perimeter. The majority of these were around the southern and southeastern corners of the perimeter, and formed part of a system that would be developed throughout the end of February and into March until they were ready to be used to launch an attack, providing cover for troops to advance to jumping-off points close to the perimeter. These tactics were reminiscent of those employed against the French at Dien Bien Phu in 1954, particularly in relation to entrenching tactics and artillery placement, and the realization assisted US planners in their targeting decisions. Nevertheless, the same day that the trenches were detected, 25 February, 3rd Platoon from Bravo Company 1st Battalion, 26th Marines was ambushed on a short patrol outside the base's perimeter to test the PAVN strength.

The Marines pursued three enemy scouts, who led them into an ambush. The platoon withdrew following a three-hour battle that left six Marines dead, 24 missing, and one taken prisoner.

Marine Corps sniper team

In late February, ground sensors detected the 66th Regiment, 304th Division preparing to mount an attack on the positions of the 37th ARVN Ranger Battalion on the eastern perimeter. On the night of 28 February, the combat base unleashed artillery and airstrikes on possible PAVN staging areas and routes of advance. At 21:30, the attack came on, but it was stifled by the small arms of the Rangers, who were supported by thousands of artillery rounds and air strikes. Two further attacks later in the morning were halted before the PAVN finally withdrew. The PAVN, however, were not through with the ARVN troops. Five more attacks against their sector were launched during March. By mid-March, Marine intelligence began to note an exodus of PAVN units from the Khe Sanh sector. The 325C Divisional Headquarters was the first to leave, followed by the 95C and 101D Regiments, all of which relocated to the west. At the same time, the 304th Division withdrew to the southwest. That did not mean, however, that battle was over. On 22 March, over 1,000 North Vietnamese rounds fell on the base, and once again, the ammunition dump was detonated. On 30 March, Bravo Company, 26th Marines, launched an attack toward the location of the ambush that had claimed so many of their comrades on 25 February. Following a rolling barrage fired by nine artillery batteries, the Marine attack advanced through two PAVN trench lines, but the Marines failed to locate the remains of the men of the ambushed patrol. The Marines claimed 115 PAVN killed, while their own casualties amounted to 10 dead, 100 wounded, and two missing. At 08:00 the following day, Operation Scotland was officially terminated. Operation Scotland II – [Wikipediahttps://en.wikipedia.org] was a U.S. Marine Corps security operation that took place in northwest Quảng Trị Province from 15 April 1968 to 28 February 1969.

At 08:00 on 15 April, following the relief of Khe Sanh Combat Base in Operation Pegasus the 3rd Marine Division resumed responsibility for Khe Sanh Combat Base from the 1st Cavalry Division and Operation Scotland II began with the Marines seeking out the People's Army of Vietnam (PAVN) forces on the Khe Operation Scotland II concluded on 28 February 1969 with the subordinate units remaining in place. In early April outgoing 3rd Marine Division commander MG Raymond G. Davis stated that "we totally control Quảng Trị Province. Khe Sanh plateau and across the operational area which comprised the western third of Quảng Trị Province. Operational control of the Khe Sanh area was handed over to the US Army's 1st Air Cavalry Division for the duration of Operation Pegasus. Cumulative friendly casualties for Operation Scotland, which began on 1 November 1967, were: 205 killed in action, 1,668 wounded, and 25 missing and presumed dead. These figures do not include casualties among Special Forces troops at Lang Vei, aircrews killed or missing in the area, or Marine replacements killed or wounded while entering or exiting the base aboard aircraft. As far as PAVN casualties were concerned, 1,602 bodies were counted, seven prisoners were taken, and two soldiers defected to allied forces during the operation. American intelligence estimated that between 10,000 and 15,000 PAVN troops were killed during the operation, equating to up to 90% of the attacking 17,200-man PAVN force. The PAVN acknowledged 2,500 men killed in action. They also reported 1,436 wounded before mid-March, of which 484 men returned to their units, while 396 were sent up the Ho Chi Minh Trail to hospitals in the north. The fighting at Khe Sanh was so volatile that the Joint Chiefs and MACV commanders were uncertain that the base could be held by the Marines. In the US, the media following the battle drew comparisons with the 1954 Battle of Dien Bien Phu, which proved disastrous for the French. Nevertheless, according to Tom Johnson, President Johnson was "determined that Khe Sanh [would not] be an 'American Dien Bien Phu'". He subsequently ordered the US military to hold Khe Sanh at all costs. As a result, "B-52 Arc Light strikes originating in Guam, Okinawa, and Thailand bombed the jungles surrounding Khe Sanh into stubble fields" and Khe Sanh became the major news headline coming out of Vietnam in late March 1968. Planning for the overland relief of Khe Sanh had begun as early as 25 January 1968, when Westmoreland ordered General John J. Tolson, commander, First Cavalry Division, to prepare a contingency plan. Route 9, the only practical overland route from the east, was impassable due to its poor state of repair and the presence of PAVN troops. Tolson was not happy with the assignment, since he believed that the best course of action, after Tet, was to use his division in an attack into the A Shau Valley. Westmoreland, however, was already planning ahead. Khe Sanh would be relieved and then used as the jump-off point for a "hot pursuit" of enemy forces into Laos. On 2 March, Tolson laid out what became known as Operation Pegasus, the operational plan for what was to become the largest operation launched by III MAF thus far in the conflict. The 2nd Battalion, 1st Marine Regiment (2/1 Marines) and the 2/3 Marines would launch a ground assault from Ca Lu Combat Base (16 km east of Khe Sanh) and head west on Route 9 while the 1st, 2nd, and 3rd Brigades of the 1st Cavalry Division, would air-assault key terrain features along Route 9 to establish fire support bases and cover the Marine advance. The advance would be supported by 102 pieces of artillery. The Marines would be accompanied by their 11th Engineer Battalion, which would repair the road as the advance moved forward. Later, the 1/1 Marines and 3rd ARVN Airborne Task Force (the 3rd, 6th, and 8th Airborne Battalions) would join the operation.

Westmoreland's planned relief effort infuriated the Marines, who had not wanted to hold Khe Sanh in the first place and who had been roundly criticized for not defending it well. The Marines had constantly argued that technically, Khe Sanh had never been under siege, since it had never truly been isolated from resupply or reinforcement. Cushman was appalled by the "implication of a rescue or breaking of the siege by outside forces." Regardless, on 1 April, Operation Pegasus began. Opposition from the North

Vietnamese was light and the primary problem that hampered the advance was continual heavy morning cloud cover that slowed the pace of helicopter operations. As the relief force made progress, the Marines at Khe Sanh moved out from their positions and began patrolling at greater distances from the base. Things heated up for the air cavalrymen on 6 April, when the 3rd Brigade encountered a PAVN blocking force and fought a day-long engagement. On the following day, the 2nd Brigade of the 1st Air Cavalry captured the old French fort near Khe Sanh village after a three-day battle. The link-up between the relief force and the Marines at KSCB took place at 08:00 on 8 April, when the 2nd Battalion, 7th Cavalry Regiment entered the camp. The 11th Engineers proclaimed Route 9 open to traffic on 11 April. On that day, Tolson ordered his unit to immediately make preparations for Operation Delaware, an air assault into the A Shau Valley. At 08:00 on 15 April, Operation Pegasus was officially terminated. Total US casualties during the operation were 92 killed, 667 wounded, and five missing. Thirty-three ARVN troops were also killed and 187 were wounded. Because of the close proximity of the enemy and their high concentration, the massive B-52 bombings, tactical airstrikes, and vast use of artillery, PAVN casualties were estimated by MACV as being between 10,000 and 15,000 men. Lownds and the 26th Marines departed Khe Sanh, leaving the defense of the base to the 1st Marine Regiment. He made his final appearance in the story of Khe Sanh on 23 May, when his regimental sergeant major and he stood before President Johnson and were presented with a Presidential Unit Citation on behalf of the 26th Marines.

April, the 3rd Marine Division resumed responsibility for KSCB, Operation Pegasus ended, and Operation Scotland II began with the Marines seeking out the PAVN in the surrounding area. Operation Scotland II would continue until 28 February 1969 resulting in 435 Marines and 3304 PAVN killed. Author Peter Brush details that an "additional 413 Marines were killed during Scotland II through the end of June 1968". He goes on to state that a further 72 were killed as part Operation Scotland II throughout the remainder of the year, but that these deaths are not included in the official US casualty lists for the Battle of Khe Sanh. Twenty-five USAF personnel who were killed are also not included. The evacuation of Khe Sanh began on 19 June 1968 as Operation Charlie. Useful equipment was withdrawn or destroyed, and personnel were evacuated. A limited attack was made by a PAVN company on 1 July, falling on a company from the 3rd Battalion, 4th Marines, who were holding a position 3 km to the southeast of the base. Casualties were heavy among the attacking PAVN, who lost over 200 killed, while the defending Marines lost two men. The official closure of the base came on 5 July after fighting, which had killed five more Marines. The withdrawal of the last Marines under the cover of darkness was hampered by the shelling of a bridge along Route 9, which had to be repaired before the withdrawal could be completed. Following the closure of the base, a small force of Marines remained around Hill 689 carrying out mopping-up operations. Further fighting followed, resulting in the loss of another 11 Marines and 89 PAVN soldiers, before the Marines finally withdrew from the area on 11 July. According to Brush, it was "the only occasion in which Americans abandoned a major combat base due to enemy pressure" and in the aftermath, the North Vietnamese began a strong propaganda campaign, seeking to exploit the US withdrawal and to promote the message that the withdrawal had not been by choice. The PAVN claim that they began attacking the withdrawing Americans on 26 June 1968 prolonging the withdrawal, killing 1,300 Americans and shooting down 34 aircraft before "liberating" Khe Sanh on 15 July. The PAVN claim that during the entire battle they "eliminated" 17,000 enemy troops, including 13,000 Americans and destroyed 480 aircraft. Regardless, the PAVN had gained control of a strategically important area, and its lines of communication extended further into South Vietnam. Once the news of the closure of KSCB was announced, the American media immediately raised questions about the reasoning behind its abandonment. They asked what had changed in six months so that American commanders were willing to abandon Khe Sanh in July. The explanations given out by the Saigon command were that "the enemy had changed his tactics and reduced his forces; that PAVN had carved out new infiltration routes; that the Marines now had enough troops and helicopters to carry out mobile operations; that a fixed base was no longer necessary." While KSCB was abandoned, the Marines continued to patrol the Khe Sanh plateau, including reoccupying the area with ARVN forces from 5–19 October 1968 with minimal opposition. On 31 December 1968, the 3rd Reconnaissance Battalion was landed west of Khe Sanh to commence Operation Dawson River West, on 2 January 1969 the 9th Marines and 2nd ARVN Regiment were also deployed on the plateau supported by the newly established Fire Support Bases Geiger and Smith; the 3-week operation found no significant PAVN forces or supplies in the Khe Sanh area. From 12 June to 6 July 1969, *Task Force Guadalcanal* comprising 1/9 Marines, 1st Battalion, 5th Infantry Regiment and 2nd and 3rd Battalions, 2nd ARVN Regiment occupied the Khe Sanh area in Operation Utah Mesa. The Marines occupied Hill 950 overlooking the Khe Sanh plateau from 1966 until September 1969 when control was handed to the Army who used the position as a SOG operations and support base until it was overrun by the PAVN in June 1971. The gradual withdrawal of US forces began during 1969 and the adoption of Vietnamization meant that, by 1969, "although limited tactical offensives abounded, US military participation in the war would soon be relegated to a defensive stance." According to military historian Ronald Spector, to reasonably record the fighting at Khe Sanh as an American victory is impossible. With the abandonment of the base, according to Thomas Ricks, "Khe Sanh became etched in the minds of many Americans as a symbol of the pointless sacrifice and muddled tactics that permeated a doomed U.S. war effort in Vietnam".

Commencing in 1966, the US had attempted to establish a barrier system across the DMZ to prevent infiltration by North Vietnamese troops. Known as the McNamara Line, it was initially codenamed "Project Nine" before being renamed "Dye Marker" by MACV in September 1967. This occurred just as the PAVN began the first phase of their offensive, launching attacks against Marine-held positions across the DMZ. These attacks hindered the advancement of the McNamara Line, and as the fighting around Khe Sanh intensified, vital equipment including sensors and other hardware had to be diverted from elsewhere to meet the needs of the US garrison at Khe Sanh. Construction on the line was ultimately abandoned and resources were later diverted towards implementing a more mobile strategy. The precise nature of Hanoi's strategic goal at Khe Sanh is regarded as one of the most intriguing unanswered questions of the Vietnam

War. According to Gordon Rottman, even the North Vietnamese official history, *Victory in Vietnam*, is largely silent on the issue. This question, known among American historians as the "riddle of Khe Sanh" has been summed up by John Prados and Ray Stubbe: "Either the Tet Offensive was a diversion intended to facilitate PAVN/VC preparations for a war-winning battle at Khe Sanh, or Khe Sanh was a diversion to mesmerize Westmoreland in the days before Tet." In assessing North Vietnamese intentions, Peter Brush cites the Vietnamese theater commander, Võ Nguyên Giáp's claim "that Khe Sanh itself was not of importance, but only a diversion to draw U.S. forces away from the populated areas of South Vietnam". This has led other observers to conclude that the siege served a wider PAVN strategy; it diverted 30,000 US troops away from the cities that were the main targets of the Tet Offensive. Whether the PAVN actually planned to capture Khe Sanh and whether the battle was an attempt to replicate the Việt Minh triumph against the French at the Battle of Dien Bien Phu has long been a point of contention. Westmoreland believed that the latter was the case and this belief was the basis for his desire to stage "Dien Bien Phu in reverse". Those who agree with Westmoreland reason that no other explanation exists as to why Hanoi would have committed so many forces to the area instead of deploying them for the Tet Offensive. The fact that the North Vietnamese only committed about half of their available forces to the offensive (60–70,000), the majority of whom were VC, is cited in favor of Westmoreland's argument. Other theories argued that the forces around Khe Sanh were simply a localized defensive measure in the DMZ area, or that they were serving as a reserve in case of an offensive American end run in the mode of the American invasion at Inchon during the Korean War. However, North Vietnamese sources claim that the Americans did not win a victory at Khe Sanh, but they were forced to retreat to avoid destruction. The PAVN claimed that Khe Sanh was "a stinging defeat from both the military and political points of view": Westmoreland was replaced two months after the end of the battle and his successor explained the retreat in different ways. General Creighton Abrams has also suggested that the North Vietnamese may have been planning to emulate Dien Bien Phu. He believed that the PAVN's actions during Tet proved it. He cited the fact that it would have taken longer to dislodge the

North Vietnamese at Hue if the PAVN had committed the three divisions at Khe Sanh to the battle there (although the PAVN did commit three regiments to the fighting from the Khe Sanh sector), instead of dividing their forces. Another interpretation was that the North Vietnamese were planning to work both ends against the middle. This strategy has come to be known as the Option Play. If the PAVN could take Khe Sanh, all well and good for them. If they could not, they would occupy the attention of as many American and South Vietnamese forces in I Corps as they could to facilitate the Tet Offensive. This view was supported by a captured (in 1969) North Vietnamese study of the battle. According to it, the PAVN would have taken Khe Sanh if they could, but the price they were willing to pay had limits. Their main objectives were to inflict casualties on US troops and to isolate them in the remote border regions. Another theory is that the actions around Khe Sanh (and the other border battles) were simply a feint, a ruse meant to focus American attention (and forces) on the border. General and historian Dave Palmer accepts this rationale: "General Giap never had any intention of capturing Khe Sanh ... [it] was a feint, a diversionary effort. And it had accomplished its purpose magnificently." Marine General Rathvon M. Tompkins, commander of the 3rd Marine Division, has pointed out that had the PAVN actually intended to take Khe Sanh, PAVN troops could have cut the base's sole source of water, a stream 500 m outside the perimeter of the base. Had they simply contaminated the stream; the airlift would not have provided enough water to the Marines. Marine Lieutenant General Victor Krulak seconded the notion that there was never a serious intention to take the base by also arguing that neither the water supply nor the telephone land lines were ever cut by the PAVN. One argument leveled by Westmoreland at the time (and often quoted by historians of the battle) was that only two Marine regiments were tied down at Khe Sanh compared with several PAVN divisions. At the time Hanoi made the decision to move in around the base, though, Khe Sanh was held by only two (or even just one) American battalions. Whether the destruction of one battalion could have been the goal of two to four PAVN divisions was debatable. Yet, even if Westmoreland believed his statement, his argument never moved on to the next logical level. By the end of January 1968, he had moved half of all US combat troops—nearly 50 maneuver battalions—to I Corps. [I Corps-Wikipediahttps://en.wikipedia.org › wiki › I_Corps_ General Hoàng Xuân Lãm was given responsibility for the I Corps Tactical Zone in 1967. He coordinated the South Vietnamese Operation Lam Son 719 offensive which aimed at striking the North Vietnamese logistical corridor known as the Ho Chi Minh trail in southeastern Laos during 1971.] On 30 January 1971, the ARVN and US forces launched Operation Dewey Canyon II, which involved the reopening of Route 9, securing the Khe Sanh area and reoccupying of KSCB as a forward supply base for Operation Lam Son 719. On 8 February 1971, the leading ARVN units marched along Route 9 into southern Laos while the US ground forces and advisers were prohibited from entering Laos. US logistical, aerial, and artillery support was provided to the operation. Following the ARVN defeat in Laos, the newly re-opened KSCB came under attack by PAVN sappers and artillery and the base was abandoned once again on 6 April 1971.

Posts Tagged 'Super Gaggle' June 15, 2013- On Super Gaggles, CH-46s and Re-Supplying Khe Sanh

CH-46 Re-Supplying Khe Sanh   *F4 Phantom*

My name is Michael Phillips, and I was a Marine Corps pilot with HMM-364 Purple Foxes helicopter squadron during the siege at Khe Sanh. Every day during the siege, we sent 8 CH-46's to resupply the hills and Khe Sanh between 24 February 1968 until 9 April 1968. This came to be known as the "Super Gaggle" in aviation history. Our day began with a 05:30 briefing at Phu Bai, then up to Quang Tri to be briefed again by General Hill. After that we flew over to Dong Ha and picked up our externals. Since it was IFR (Instrument Flight Rules) at Dong Ha, our first aircraft took off on a heading for Khe Sanh, aircraft # 2 took off 10 degrees to the left, aircraft # 3 10 degrees to the right, etc., until all 8 were airborne. We normally punched out around 8,000 feet, on to Khe Sanh where we would orbit for 30-40 minutes while the artillery, F4 Phantoms, A6 Intruders and A4's provided gun support for the hill that we would resupply. One of our biggest concerns was that of a mid-air collision. We had so much air support that F4's was constantly zipping in front of us. At that altitude and at our weight, we barely had enough power to maintain elevation, so when we flew thru their exhaust it was not unusual for us to lose control and drop 3-400 feet prior to regaining control.

When the command was given for us to begin our run, we had to lose 8,000 feet of altitude but still maintain enough power to land at the LZ. On the way down our gunners would begin firing their .50 caliber guns, careful not to hit the Marines on the ground. The NVA AK-47 was not very dangerous to us until we reached around 1,500 feet in elevation above the LZ. The major problem for us was maintaining proper spacing between aircraft, or we might have to attempt to hover at 900 feet. We simply did not have enough power to do so. It was essential that aircrafts #1, 2 and 3 get on to the hill or the LZ at Khe Sanh and off without wasting any time. Or else the balance of the flight was trying to hover, and a pilot could not do so. Hill 881 South was our most difficult as we owned that hill and the NVA owned 881 North. We could always count on intense fire from there. One hill that did not receive much publicity was 558. This hill was in a slight ravine and there must have been 100 mortar tubes there. Keeping them supplied with ammo was a fulltime job. After we completed the resupply, we left for Quang Tri, refueled and flew back to Phu Bai. Every Marine base in I Corps was surrounded. When we got back, our gunners took the .50 caliber guns out of the A/C down to the perimeter as we got hit by the NVA each night. Our crew chiefs worked all night to fix the battle damage to our A/C. We could have done nothing without the crew chiefs. They were superb.

It was not unusual for us to take 50 rockets at a whack. Afterwards the NVA would always put a round in every half hour, so out to the bunkers we went. This ensured that we got very little sleep. Flying that CH-46 lacking sleep was a chore and all of our pilots became extremely rude, ugly, tense and it did have an effect on how efficient we were. Approaching Hill 881 South (or any of the other Khe Sanh LZ's) was somewhat more sophisticated than I mentioned earlier. When we began our descent, it always reverted back to the individual pilot's skill and his ability to shoot a good approach. Controlling the rate of descent, controlling spacing, controlling air speed, maintaining turns (RPM's = Rotations per Minute's), running out of ground speed and altitude at the same time over the LZ was imperative. Dropping the external as "softly" as possible was a never-ending challenge. If any of the A/C in front of you did not do these things, you had to make adjustments, quickly. We simply did not have enough power to hover at 1,000 feet so sometimes one had to drop out of the sequence and go to the Khe Sanh Combat Base airstrip to hover, then air taxi to the hill. This was not a good thing as the Combat Base runway always took a lot of rockets and mortars, and you were exposed to more fire than desired.

The recon team with a bayonet on M16

Prior to flight school, I went to Basic School in Quantico. There I studied tactics, explosives, rifle range (M14).45 pistol, everything that a Second Lieutenant is supposed to know. (Not much, huh?) As a result, I had many friends provided me with a very good understanding of what the grunts were going through. Since I was not there with them, I could not actually experience in depth their plight, but I did have enough knowledge to admire their courage, never giving up, never leaving a wounded man in a hot zone. During and after Tet, I had occasion to fly many medevac missions. Some of these required that I land in a rice paddy, 100 meters from the tree line where we were taking intense fire. The plexiglass cockpit and 1/8-inch aluminum skin of the A/C did not slow down an AK-47 round, and we paid a price. I am proud to say that in the Marine tradition, we never left a wounded man in a hot zone. Never. He was coming out, and was going to be on a hospital ship in 20 minutes. It was not that I was a hero, all of our pilots, and all of the pilots from other squadrons did the same. All in a day's work to support the Private with a bayonet on the ground. The same was true if one of our recon teams was compromised. They might have to run for a mile to find a LZ big enough for us to land, but we took them out. [Michael Phillips]

Footnote

The McDonnell Douglas F-4 Phantom II [Wikipedia] is a tandem two-seat, twin-engine, all-weather, long-range supersonic jet interceptor and fighter-bomber originally developed by McDonnell Aircraft for the United States Navy. Proving highly adaptable, it first entered service with the Navy in 1961 before it was adopted by the United States Marine Corps and the United States Air Force, and by the mid-1960s it had become a major part of their air arms. Phantom production ran from 1958 to 1981 with a total of 5,195 aircraft built, making it the most produced American supersonic military aircraft in history, and cementing its position as an iconic combat aircraft of the Cold War. The F-4 was used extensively during the Vietnam War. It served as the principal air superiority fighter for the U.S. Air Force, Navy, and Marine Corps and became important in the ground-attack and aerial reconnaissance roles late in the war. During the Vietnam War, one U.S. Air Force pilot, two weapon systems officers (WSOs), one U.S. Navy pilot and one radar intercept officer (RIO) became aces by achieving five aerial kills against enemy fighter aircraft. The F-4 continued to form a major part of U.S. military air power throughout the 1970s and 1980s, being gradually replaced by more modern aircraft such as the F-15 Eagle and F-16 Fighting Falcon in the U.S. Air Force, the F-14 Tomcat in the U.S. Navy, and the F/A-18 Hornet in the U.S. Navy and U.S. Marine Corps.

435th TFS F-4Ds over Vietnam   *An A-6E landing on the aircraft carrier USS America (CV-66)*

USAF F-4 Phantom II destroyed on 18 February 1968, during the enemy attack against Tan Son Nhut, during the Tet Offensive

The Grumman A-6 Intruder [Wikipedia] is an American twinjet all-weather attack aircraft developed and manufactured by American aircraft company Grumman Aerospace that was operated by the U.S. Navy. It was designed in response to a 1957 requirement issued by the Bureau of Aeronautics for an all-weather attack aircraft for Navy long-range interdiction missions and with STOL capability [A short takeoff and landing aircraft has short runway requirements for takeoff and landing. Many STOL-designed aircraft also feature various arrangements for use on runways with harsh conditions. Wikipedia] for Marine close air support. It was to replace the piston-engine Douglas A-1 Sky raider. The requirement allowed one or two engines, either turbojet or turboprop. The winning proposal from Grumman used two Pratt & Whitney J52 turbojet engines. The Intruder was the first Navy aircraft with an integrated airframe and weapons system. Operated by a crew of two in a side-by-side seating configuration, the workload was divided between the pilot and weapons officer (bombardier/navigator (BN)). In addition to conventional munitions, it could also carry nuclear weapons, which would be delivered using toss bombing techniques. On 19 April 1960, the first prototype made its maiden flight. The A-6 was in service with the United States Navy and Marine Corps between 1963 and 1997, multiple variants of the type being introduced during this time. From the A-6, a specialized electronic warfare derivative, the EA-6B Prowler, was developed as well as the KA-6D tanker version. It was deployed during various overseas conflicts, including the Vietnam War and the Gulf War. The Gulf War was a war waged by coalition forces from 35 nations led by the United States against Iraq in response to Iraq's invasion and annexation of Kuwait arising from oil pricing and production disputes. The A-6 was intended to be superseded by the McDonnell Douglas A-12 Avenger II, but this program was ultimately canceled due to cost overruns. Thus, when the A-6E was scheduled for retirement, its precision strike mission was initially taken over by the Grumman F-14 Tomcat equipped with a LANTIRN pod. Low Altitude Navigation and Targeting Infrared for Night, or LANTIRN, is a combined navigation and targeting pod system for use on the United States Air Force fighter aircraft — the F-15E Strike Eagle and F-16 Fighting Falcon (Block 40/42 C & D models). LANTIRN significantly increases the combat effectiveness of these aircraft, allowing them to fly at low altitudes, at night and under-the-weather to attack ground targets with a variety of precision-guided weapons. Low Altitude Navigation and Targeting Infrared for Night, or LANTIRN, is a combined navigation and targeting pod system for use on the United States Air Force fighter aircraft — the F-15E Strike Eagle and F-16 Fighting Falcon (Block 40/42 C & D models). LANTIRN significantly increases the combat effectiveness of these aircraft, allowing them to fly at low altitudes, at night and under-the-weather to attack ground targets with a variety of precision-guided weapons.

OF WINGS, WAVES, AND WINDS

Turn on the pages with me, for when I read the Vietnamese history, my heart cries.

đi trong lịch sử dân ta
luống nghẹn ngào

Time went by.... Vo Kiet and Nguyen thi Lan had a son and twin daughters: Vo Hoang, Vo thi Thu and Vo thi Tam. In 1960, after graduation from High school, Vo Hoang obtained the Fulbright scholarship to study Mechanics Engineering at the University of Austin, Texas. Vo thi Thu and Vo thi Tam attended tenth grade at My Tho high school. The family was so excited that Vo Hoang go to study in America! This was a wonderful opportunity for the young Vietnamese to explore the world, to build his promising future. The neighbors came to congratulate the parents and wish Vo Hoang all the best in his journey. On the day Vo Yen flew to America, the whole family: the parents, Vo Kiet and Nguyen thi Lan, and the twin girls, Vo thi Thu, Vo thi Tam thi Van went to Tan Son Nhất Airport in Saigon to say "Good Luck!" to Vo Hoang. "We're proud of you." They said and hugged him

"I know that you will be the best student in your class." The twin girls told their brother

Vo Hoang was overjoyed about a promising future, yet he was a bit anxious about living in a foreign country, far away from home. Embracing his family, he said, "I love you all."

"We love you, too! When we see you again, you'll be famous!" the father said

The announcement called the passengers to board the plane to America. Vo Hoang waved to his family as walking toward the gate, "I'll come back." he promised

Vo Hoang left in on the first week of August to prepare for the academic year in America; the twin girls were still in summer vacation time, for school year started the day after Labor Day in Vietnam. Vo thi

Truong van Mai was Truong thi Cuc's younger brother, their parents were Mr. and Mrs. Truong Van. They lived in Nghe An, a province in the North- Central Vietnam. Truong van Mai joined the Communist Party- Viet Minh, he was assigned a special role in the guerrilla militia [referred as Viet Cong by the US Military] to attack QLVNCH military creating chaos in Ngo Dinh Diem's administration. Truong thi Cuc married to Tran Phu; the couple had a son, Tran San. They followed the northern refugees embarked a US ship on the Operation of Freedom leaving Ha Tinh to settle in Khanh Hoa, a province in the central part of Vietnam. On the ship, Tran Phu adopted Nguyen van Hai.

Truong Dong was Truong Van's older brother. Truong Dong and his wife, Phan thi My had two children, Truong Nghĩa and Truong thi Huyền. Truong thi Huyền married to Phan Toàn. After the wedding, they moved to Nam Dinh, a province in north Vietnam, they had a daughter, and a son, Phan thi Duyen and Phan van Minh. When the Communist party- Viet Minh- took control of the government of north Vietnam, with the Land Reform in North Vietnam, both Phan Toàn and Truong thi Huyen were beheaded, the two children, Phan thi Duyen (eight years old) and Phan van Minh (six years old) came to live with their uncle, Truong Nghĩa and his wife, Le thi Ngoc. The children took care of the oxen and the pigs in the farm belonged to Mr. and Mrs. Nguyen Khanh. One day, Phan van Minh lost one ox, Mr. Truong Nghĩa beat up the boy while Mrs. Le thi Ngoc hit his head. Phan van Minh's head was bleeding. Phan thi Duyen begged for her brother, but the uncle didn't stop hurting the young boy.

"Do you know how much is an ox? You're not even two pence worth!" Mr. Truong Nghĩa yelled

That night, Phan thi Duyen backpack carried her brother to a comrade's [Viet Minh], she pleaded him for help, "Please save my brother. I'll be your servant all my life."

The comrade, Luu Tuan, was surprised as he knew these were children of the landowners. He inquired,

"What happened? Is this a sort of scheme of the bourgeois? Tell me the truth or I kill both of you!"

Phan thi Duyen tearfully reported the reason Phan van Minh was injured. Comrade Luu Tuan, who was a medical technician in Viet Minh militia, when he saw the boy, he cried out loud,

"Goodness's sake! Is he still alive?"

Luu Tuan stopped the bleeding in the boy's head. He put the boy in a wagon and told the girl,

"I take him to see a doctor."

Walking through the meadow with the younger brother on her back, Phan thi Duyen tried to comfort Phan van Minh while tears were rolling down on her cheeks,

"We're almost there, and the doctor will take care of you...."

Phan van Minh weakly said, "Yes."

Following the fading moon light, Phan thi Duyen prayed, "Merciful Buddha, please help my brother..."

They arrived at Comrade Doctor Nguyen Nhiệm after a long walk. Doctor Nguyen Nhiệm treated the boy that night. To repay the kindness of the Doctor, Phan thi Duyen and Phan van Minh vowed to be Doctor Nguyen Nhiệm's servants. Doctor Nguyen Nhiệm,

"We're sharing the fate of our country. I don't have a family; we live together under the roof of my parent's home."

"Thank you, Doctor. We never forget your kindness and saved us." The children said

A few months later, Phan van Minh's condition was somewhat stable, except sometimes he had a seizure; the doctor enrolled Phan thi Duyen and Phan van Minh in an Elementary School. Just after one month, the teachers informed the doctor that both children were very bright children and should have had better education. Even having episodes of seizure, Phan van Minh studied very hard; Phan thi Duyen's name always was in the

Honor Student Roll. When he was eight years old, Phan van Minh graduated from Elementary school; Phan thi Duyen obtained a scholarship for Middle and High school in the province. They were awarded to see Truong Chinh [an important stateman in the communist party in north Vietnam by that time.] They took the train from Nam Dinh to Hanoi. Stateman, Truong Chinh met the two children, he was impressed by their knowledge and admired the children overcame their hardship. When he learned that they were from Nam Dinh, his hometown, he decided to help them. In the 1960's the north Vietnam Communist Regime accepted military help from the Soviet Union and People of Republic of China [two powerful Communist countries] to fight against the U S military based in South Vietnam.] Stateman Truong Chinh arranged for them to study in Hanoi, especially to learn Russian as he planned to send these children among other gifted children in north Vietnam to Russia to have further education at the university level in the Soviet Union.

Three years later, Phan thi Duyen and Phan van Minh took the plane to Lipetsk, Russia. That night, Phan thi Duyen looked out from the plane window, the silver moon was far away in the sky. Phan thi Duyen wondered with a little bit worry about the future at Lipetsk State Technical University, Phan van Minh studied Technology of mechanical engineering, metal-cutting machines and tools; and Phan thi Duyen registered in Chemistry. Phan van Minh pointed to the moon, he told his sister,

"At home, we see the moon; here we also see the moon, it follows us!"

Phan thi Duyen pulled a blanket to cover her brother, "Our parents are in the moon, they bless us. Close your eyes and sleep. We'll have a long day tomorrow."

Phan thi Duyen glanced at the moon, she remembered the wonderful early childhood years, when her parents were with them, Phan thi Duyen and Phan van Minh played under the shade of the moonlight by the bamboo brushes. She could not forget the time living with Uncle Truong Nghĩa time, and also the school semesters in Hanoi...wherever they were, the moon saw their happiness, suffering, and sorrows; the moon never told anybody about those hardships that Phan thi Duyen and Phan van Minh endured. Phan thi Duyen looked at the moon, she still remembered the parents' advice, "Not giving up, try harder for a better tomorrow."

"Mom and Dad, I'll do my best and I take care of Minh." she promised

The pilot announced, "We'll land in a few minutes. Thank you for choosing the TWA."

"Now, we're in the Soviet Union, thousands of miles far away from home!"

Phan thi Duyen and Phan van Minh followed the passengers to check out the luggage, each of them had only a small suitcase; then they went to the customs before entering Lipetsk. The clerk asked the two foreign students to open their suitcases, Phan van Minh did and went through the security check. Phan thi Duyen had a difficult time, the key got stuck, the young girl was embarrassed, the clerk stared at her

which made her cry, she felt somebody pat gently on her shoulder, "I'll help you." Phan thi Duyen turned her head, the man smiled, "May I?" and he helped Phan thi Duyen open the suit case.

"Thank you very much "she said

"My name is Anton Semyonov," the man said, "nice to meet you. Where's your destination, Miss?"

"Duyen thi Phan," the young girl replied with her best Russian, "I and my brother Minh van Phan go to Lipetsk to study."

"Ah, that's good! I work in Oblast Administration, Belgorod." Anton Semyonov said, "The train will stop at Lipetsk on the way to Belgorod."

"I'm Minh van Phan," Duyen's brother joined the conversation, "Could we take the same train, Mr. Semyonov? We need your help as we're not familiar with Russia yet."

"Call me Anton," the man said, "I'm glad to help you. We're done with custom check, now we take the bus to the train station. Let's go!" Anton carried Duyen's suitcase

"Shall we have dinner on the train?" Minh asked

"Oh, first time to have Russian food!" Duyen added

"What would you like to order, Miss?", Anton proudly said, "Shchi, Okroshka or Ukha?"

"You made me feel hungry!" Minh laughed

"Here comes the bus." Anton pointed to the shuttle

Anton and the two Vietnamese students arrived at the train station, the boarded the night trip to Lipetsk and enjoyed the Russian super before bedtime. Minh was tired, he dozed off after saying "Goodnight!" to Anton and his sister. Duyen said, "Goodnight" to her brother and Anton.

"Goodnight, I'll let you know when we come to Lipetsk." Anton said

Duyen looked out the window to see the moon. "Mom and Dad, I miss both of you and our home very much." Duyen prayed and took off her glasses, she retired in the train seat, next to Minh-her brother. Before closing her eyes, she held them in her hand, "They're expensive, what can I do if I lost them?" and Duyen fell asleep, the girl had no idea that Anton was watching her. Anton Semyonov was the only child from an upper-class family in Belgorod, his parents were doctor and pharmacist. He admired the courage of these two Vietnamese students who could speak Russian almost fluently and went here to study at the university; suddenly Anton felt a brotherly love feeling toward these youngsters. Duyen slept soundly; the glasses dropped out from her hand. Anton picked them up and put them on the tray, he lay in the seat across from hers- before closing his eyes, he covered her up with a blanket. "Ah, these youngsters from a semi tropical climate, how could they face the cold of Russian weather? Tomorrow each of us will go to different way. Could we ever meet again, I always remember the warmness feeling to be with you tonight!" Anton glanced at the moon and smiled in his sleep.

ALONG THE PACIFIC COAST WIND

1) Nguyen van Giap & Nguyen Hoa Le

Nguyen van Giap, the eleven years old boy, carried his little sister- Nguyen Hoa Le, who was injured in the right leg- on his back across the field among the snapshots of the Viet Minh comrades against the French Legions. Nguyen van Giap separated with his younger brother- Nguyen van Hai as the younger brother followed the northern refugees entering an American war ship to settle in south Vietnam while the elder brother and the sister struggled to survive in North Vietnam after the Land Reform of the North Vietnam and the execution of their parents. Exhausted after a long walk through the night, Nguyen van Giap stopped by an abandoned patio, now he entered a town- Hung Yen. Putting down the little sister, who was sleeping, Nguyen van Giap had to find something for both himself and his sister to eat, for his stomach had been empty...for how long? People escaped from the communists and the French soldiers changed Hung Yen into a border town prodigal. There were lootings and poor folks searched for something to eat in the dried fields, garbage, and dumpsters. Followed them, Nguyen van Giap found some yams and a piece of molded rice cake; he brought back to his sister. Nguyen Hoa Le was starving, she grabbed the piece of rice cake and was just about to put it in her mouth. Nguyen van Giap stopped her; he cut off the molded part and gave her the good portion, "Eat this one, and here's some water."

The little girl engulfed the cake in one bite, "It tastes so good!" she said with a mouth full

Nguyen van Giap had a yam and some water. After "dinner", the two children slept on the patio under the light of the crescent moon high up in the sky.

One day in searching for foods, clothing...among the abandoned houses, Nguyen van Giap met Pham Quang- a man lost his wife and son during the chaos of the country- Pham Quang accepted Nguyen van Giap as his son because "You look so much alike Ty, my son!". Nguyen van Giap told him about his little sister. Pham Quang told the young boy that the only way to survive nowadays was to go to Hanoi; even with the war happened all over the country, there were still some business in the capital. Pham Quang was a worker in a newspaper printing shop, he helped Nguyen van Giap have a paper boy job. People were anxious about the fate of the country; newspaper was a "hot job". Nguyen van Giap was delighted, for all his concern was to have money to pay the doctor so the little sister, Nguyen Hoa Le could be able to walk normally again; the little girl was limping due to the injured of her right leg.

Nguyen van Giap went with Pham Quang to "Tieng Dan" newspaper printing shop where Pham Quang got busy with the printing assembly line and Nguyen van Giap put the papers in a bag and said in a loud voice, "Today's Newspaper! Today's Newspaper..." and he worked in downtown Hanoi as a paper boy. The three of them slept under the eaves on an old house at night, during the day, Pham Quang and Nguyen van Giap worked at the printing shop, they asked a woman also homeless as themselves to care for Nguyen Hoa Le, Nguyen van Giap paid the woman by giving her some food to eat. Every morning, Nguyen van Giap waved to the little sister, "See you later!". How many times Nguyen van Giap cried as he thought about his little disabled sister had to struggle through life! The plan of having money to pay for the treatment of the injured leg was a faraway wish!

Time went by.... Hanoi 1969 Pham Quang and Nguyen van Giap had a small house by the riverside, Nguyen Hoa Le went to the Pham Quang and Nguyen van Giap had a small house by the riverside, Nguyen Hoa Le went to the elementary school, just a few blocks away from home. The little girl dragged her right leg along the street toward Lac Hong Grammar school, the boys ran after her yelling, "Hobble! Hobble!", one boy pushed her to fall on the ground. Nguyen van Giap ran to pick his siter up, he warned the nasty boys, "Leave her alone or I will beat you up!"

The boys disappeared in a flash while Nguyen van Giap wiped off his sister's tears. Nguyen Hoa Le asked her elder brother,

"I didn't do anything to them. Why did they hurt me?"

"No reason, no reason..." Nguyen van Giap embraced his little sister, both of them cried quietly

"I'll study hard, I promise." Nguyen Hoa Le said

"Alright. I have to go to work now. See you later!" Nguyen van Giap waved to his sister

In the beginning, the elder brother helped his little sister with reading and writing [Nguyen van Giap finished Grammar school by the time his father was executed], later Nguyen Hoa Le surpassed the elder brother. By the end of each school year, the disabled girl got a reward from school: a few notebooks, three meters of uniform materials for the next school year. Nguyen Hoa Le graduated from high school at the aged of 17, she was accepted to School of Medicine in Hanoi. Nguyen Hoa Le was enthusiastic to work on her dream "No other limping child in Vietnam" while the country was involved in the Civil War between the North and South Vietnam [1955-1975].

Hanoi 1969 Every morning, Nguyen van Giap had breakfast with his sister, Nguyen Hoa Le, before he rode the bicycle to work at the printing shop. Waving to her elder brother, Nguyen Hoa Le also ready to leave for classes at Hanoi Medical School. On weekend, Nguyen Hoa Le tutored a middle school girl with Algebra, and Geometry; she earned some money enough to buy some text books for school. In the evening, the brother and sister shared dinner under the crescent moon hanging among the bamboo leaves. Tonight, after supper, Nguyen Hoa Le sat at the table, she was just about to review her notes for the coming up exam, her elder brother- Nguyen van Giap said in a solemn manner, "I need to tell you something..."

"Is it about mother's death anniversary next week?" Nguyen Hoa Le asked

"Ah, I almost forgot ..." Nguyen van Giap said, "No, I arrange for you to stay with my friend- the Pham Quang family-you're a big girl now, you'll be a medical doctor. I'm proud of you. I'll be gone for, probably a few years. I don't know when I could be back..."

"What happens?" Nguyen Hoa Le's eyes were full of tears

"Don't cry...." Nguyen van Giap stroked his sister's hair, "You're a big girl now. I didn't want to tell you earlier since you're too busy with school. Two years ago, I voluntarily joined Viet Minh and was enlisted in the North Vietnamese People's Army of Vietnam (PAVN). I was trained and classified as a comrade to enter South Vietnam by the Ho Chi Minh Trail with the mission "Liberate South Vietnam from the American Empire.""

"Why...Oh!" Nguyen Hoa Le inquired her brother

"Do you know what the American Empire has done to our country, Vietnam?" Nguyen van Giap explained to his younger sister as he gave her the headlines in the newspaper, "My Lai Massacre". Read it, you will that I took the vows with the Viet Minh Party "to sweep away all the barbarous Americans from our home land."

2) My Lai Massacre- 1968 Vietnam War

The My Lai massacre was one of the most horrific incidents of violence committed against unarmed civilians during the Vietnam War. A company of American soldiers brutally killed most of the people—women, children and old men—in the village of My Lai on March 16, 1968. More than 500 people were slaughtered in the My Lai massacre, including young girls and women who were raped and mutilated before being killed. U.S. Army officers covered up the carnage for a year before it was reported in the American press, sparking a firestorm of international outrage. The brutality of the My Lai killings and the official cover-up fueled anti-war sentiment and further divided the United States over the Vietnam War.

My Lai Massacre - Definition, Facts & Causes -www.history.com ›

The small village of My Lai is located in Quang Ngai province, which was believed to be a stronghold of the communist National Liberation Front (NLF) or Viet Cong (VC) during the Vietnam War. Quang Ngai province was therefore a frequent target of U.S. and South Vietnamese bombing attacks, and the entire region was heavily strafed with Agent Orange, the deadly herbicide. In March 1968, Charlie Company—part of the American Division's 11th Infantry Brigade—received word that VC guerrillas had taken control of the neighboring village of Son My. Charlie Company was sent to the area on March 16 for a search-and-destroy mission. At the time, morale among U.S. soldiers on the ground was dwindling, especially in the wake of the North Vietnamese-led Tet Offensive, which was launched in January 1968. Charlie Company had lost some 28 of its members to death or injuries, and was down to just over 100 men. Army commanders had advised the soldiers of Charlie Company that all who were found in the Son My area could be considered VC or active VC sympathizers, and ordered them to destroy the village. When they arrived shortly after dawn, the soldiers—led by Lieutenant William Calley—found no Viet Cong. Instead, they came across a quiet village of primarily women, children and older men preparing their breakfast rice. The villagers were rounded up into groups as the soldiers inspected their huts. Despite finding only a few weapons, Calley ordered his men to begin shooting the villagers. Some soldiers balked at Calley's command, but within seconds the massacre had begun, with Calley himself shooting many men, women and children.

Mothers who were shielding their children were shot, and when their children tried to run away, they too were slaughtered. Huts were set on fire, and anyone inside who tried to escape was gunned down.

"I saw them shoot an M79 (grenade launcher) into a group of people who were still alive. But it was mostly done with a machine gun. They were shooting women and children just like anybody else," Sgt. Michael Bernhardt, a soldier at the scene, later told a reporter.

"We met no resistance and I only saw three captured weapons. We had no casualties. It was just like any other Vietnamese village—old papa-sans [men], women and kids. As a matter of fact, I don't remember seeing one military-age male in the entire place, dead or alive," Bernhardt said.

In addition to killing unarmed men, women and children, the soldiers slaughtered countless livestock, raped an unknown number of women, and burned the village to the ground. Calley was reported to have dragged dozens of people, including young children, into a ditch before executing them with a machine gun. Not a single shot was fired against the men of Charlie Company at My Lai.

The My Lai massacre reportedly ended only after Warrant Officer Hugh Thompson, an Army helicopter pilot on a reconnaissance mission, landed his aircraft between the soldiers and the retreating villagers and threatened to open fire if they continued their attacks. "We kept flying back and forth ... and it didn't take very long until we started noticing the large number of bodies everywhere. Everywhere we'd look, we'd see bodies. These were infants, two- three-, four-, five-year-old, women, very old men, no draft-age people whatsoever," Thompson stated at a My Lai conference at Tulane University in 1994.

Thompson and his crew flew dozens of survivors to receive medical care. In 1998, Thompson and two other members of his crew received the Soldier's Medal, the U.S. Army's highest award for bravery not involving direct contact with the enemy.

Cover-Up of the My Lai Massacre: By the time the My Lai massacre ended, 504 people were dead. Among the victims were

182 women—17 of them pregnant—and 173 children, including 56 infants. Knowing news of the massacre would cause a scandal, officers higher up in command of Charlie Company and the 11th Brigade immediately made efforts to downplay the bloodshed. The coverup of the My Lai Massacre continued until Ron Ridenhour, a soldier in the 11th Brigade who had heard reports of the massacre but had not participated, began a campaign to bring the events to light. After writing letters to President Richard M. Nixon, the Pentagon, State Department, Joint Chiefs of Staff and several congressmen—with no response—Ridenhour finally gave an interview to the investigative journalist Seymour Hersh, who broke the story in November 1969.

Who Was Responsible for the My Lai Massacre? Amid the international uproar and Vietnam War protests that followed Ridenhour's revelations, the U.S. Army ordered a special investigation into the My Lai massacre and subsequent efforts to cover it up. The inquiry, headed by Lieutenant General William Peers, released its report in March 1970 and recommended that no fewer than 28 officers be charged for their involvement in covering up the massacre. The My Lai trial began on November 17, 1970. Did you know? Hugh Thompson, the helicopter pilot who stopped the My Lai massacre, later told the news program "60 Minutes" that he was ostracized and received death threats upon his return from Vietnam. But in 1998, Thompson attended a memorial service at My Lai on the 30th anniversary of the massacre. The Army would later charge only 14 men, including Calley, Captain Ernest Medina and Colonel Oran Henderson, with crimes related to the events at My Lai. All were acquitted except for Calley, who was found guilty of premeditated murder for ordering the shootings, despite his contention that he was only following orders from his commanding officer, Captain Medina. In March 1971, Calley was given a life sentence for his role in directing the killings at My Lai. Many saw Calley as a scapegoat, and his sentence was reduced upon appeal to 20 years and later to 10; he was paroled in 1974. Later investigations have revealed that the slaughter at My Lai was not an isolated incident. Other atrocities, such as a similar massacre of villagers at My Khe, are less well known. A notorious military operation called Speedy Express killed thousands of Vietnamese civilians in the Mekong Delta, earning the commander of the operation, Major General

Julian Ewell, the nickname "the Butcher of the Delta."

Impact of My Lai: By the early 1970s, the American war effort in Vietnam was winding down, as the Nixon administration continued its "Vietnamization" policy, including the withdrawal of troops and the transfer of control over ground operations to the South Vietnamese. Among the American troops still in Vietnam, morale was low, and anger and frustration were high. Drug use increased among soldiers, and an official report in 1971 estimated that one-third or more of U.S. troops were addicted. The revelations of the My Lai massacre caused morale to plummet even further, as GIs wondered what other atrocities their superiors were concealing. On the home front in the United States, the brutality of the My Lai massacre and the efforts made by higher-ranking officers to conceal it exacerbated anti-war sentiment and increased the bitterness regarding the continuing U.S. military presence in Vietnam.

3) Vo Hoang

Time went by.... Vo Kiet and Nguyen thi Lan had a son and twin daughters: Vo Hoang, Vo thi Thu and Vo thi Tam. In 1960, after graduation from High school, Vo Hoang obtained the Fulbright scholarship to study Mechanics Engineering at the University of Austin, Texas. Vo thi Thu and Vo thi Tam attended tenth grade at My Tho high school. The family was so excited that Vo Hoang go to study in America! This was a wonderful opportunity for the young Vietnamese to explore the world, to build his promising future. The neighbors came to congratulate the parents and wish Vo Hoang all the best in his journey. On the day Vo Yen flew to America, the whole family: the parents, Vo Kiet and Nguyen thi Lan, and the twin girls, Vo thi Thu, Vo thi Tam thi Van went to Tan Son Nhất Airport in Saigon to say "Good Luck!" to Vo Hoang. "We're proud of you." They said and hugged him

"I know that you will be the best student in your class." The twin girls told their brother

Vo Hoang was overjoyed about a promising future, yet he was a bit anxious about living in a foreign country, far away from home. Embracing his family, he said, "I love you all."

"We love you, too! When we see you again, you'll be famous!" the father said

The announcement called the passengers to board the plane to America. Vo Hoang waved to his family as walking toward the gate, "I'll come back." he promised

Vo Hoang left in on the first week of August to prepare for the academic year in America; the twin girls were still in summer vacation time, for school year started the day after Labor Day in Vietnam. Vo thi Tam went to visit a relative in Khanh Hoa, while Vo thi Thu preferred to stay in My Tho [she volunteered to teach an adult class "The Vietnamese Alphabet: Read & Write"]. One day, Vo thi Thu went to work as usual, she saw a young man crying by the road. Coming closer, she saw a young man got stuck in a ditch. She asked, "What happened?"

"I fell into the ditch. Could you give me some water?" the man said with the northern accent

Seeing his uniform, Vo thi Thu realized that he was one of the Communist comrades who mingled in with the southern people, she had nothing to do with him. When she just about to walk away, the comrade called out, "Please give me some water. I'm very thirsty."

Vo thi Thu hesitated for a few seconds then she gave him some water,

"Hold on, I have to find somebody to pull you out of the mud."

"I got shot in my right leg, I can't stand up. "the comrade said, "Please go to the house number 5 on the left of this road, and ask for Mr. Xuan to fetch me. I'm comrade Truong van Dau, from N. Vietnam." The comrade gawked at the girl and inquired, "Do you still want to help or will you call the Republic Police to put me in jail?"

"I'll go to Mr. Xuan. Wait here. I'll be back." Vo thi Thu said

"Why? How could I trust you?" Truong Tan asked

"My grandfather, Nguyen Quy, is also a comrade." Vo thi Thu whispered to him

Vo thi Thu went to Mr. Xuan's home, who lived not too far from Mr. Vo Kiet's house; Vo thi Thu did not know there were Viet Cong's in the neighborhood. Vo thi Thu told Mr. Xuan about comrade Truong Tan. Immediately Mr. Xuan said, "Take me to where he is."

When Truong Tan saw Mr. Xuan, he said, "Comrade Xuan, last night, the QLVNCH soldiers [South Vietnam military under Ngo Dinh Diem administration] attacked us. I got shot; I fell in to this ditch so they didn't see me. Would you pull me out from the ditch?"

"Hold on onto me, Comrade Mai!" Comrade Xuan said

Comrade Xuan put comrade Tan on the ground, Vo thi Thu saw the injury, she asked,

"Please take him to my home; my parents can help him."

Comrade Xuan stared at comrade Truong Tan for the decision.

"Take me there." comrade Truong Tan said,

When they arrived at Mr. Vo Kiet's home, Vo thi Thu signaled the two comrades,

"Please wait here. I'll ask my father."

"I'll not forget your favor." Comrade Truong Tan said

Vo thi Thu told her father about the wounded comrade, at first Mr. Vo Kiet was hesitated to help, for he lived in My Tho- S. Vietnam, [S. Vietnam at that time was under the Ngo Dinh Diem administration; this government only controlled Saigon and other big cities, the rural and countryside were a mixture of Viet Cong and Southerners of Vietnam which were uncontrollable the Ngo family. Viet Cong received military support by China trafficked through Laos and Cambodia.]

"Help him, father." Vo thi Thu begged, "Grandfather is also a comrade from the North."

Mr. Vo Kiet saw the compassion of his daughter toward comrade Truong Tan. Did Vo Kiet also fall in love with a communist's daughter in N. Vietnam?

"How old are you, comrade Truong Tan?" Vo thi Thu's father asked,

"I'm 20 years old. I've been with the Communist Party for seven years now." Truong Tan said

"Ah...my daughter is 16..." Mr. Vo Kiet said, "Let's ask Grandpa Nguyen Quy for help."

Mr. Nguyen Quy came to see comrade Truong Tan,

"I'll take care of this," Mr. Nguyen Quy said, "I have connection with the doctor, and the surgeon."

After a few minutes, somebody came and took Truong Tan away.

"Grandpa, when could I see him again?" Vo thi Thu worried

"Of course, my dear!" Mr. Nguyen Quy assured his grandniece, "You'll see him in good health, OK?"

"Ah, it's fate.... how mysterious life is!" Mr. Vo Kiet mumbled

Due to the relationship of Vo thi Thu and Truong Tan, Viet Cong didn't execute Vo Kiet. Instead, they had an agreement: when soldiers QLVNCH of the Republic of S. Vietnam checked up on the village, Vo Kiet would say that his family, included his son in law- Truong Tan- were Catholics and they devoted themselves to President Ngo Dinh Diem and his regime.

4) Viet Minh | History & Definition | Britannica -https://www. britannica.com › topic ›

Viet Minh, in full Viet Nam Doc Lap Dong Minh Hoi, English League for the Independence of Vietnam, organization that led the struggle for Vietnamese independence from French rule. The Viet Minh was formed in China in May 1941 by Ho Chi Minh. Although led primarily by communists, the Viet Minh operated as a national front organization open to persons of various political persuasions. In late 1943, members of the Viet Minh, led by General Vo Nguyen Giap, began to infiltrate Vietnam to launch guerrilla operations against the Japanese, who occupied the country during World War II. The Viet Minh forces liberated considerable portions of northern Vietnam, and after the Japanese surrender to the Allies, Viet Minh units seized control of Hanoi and proclaimed the independent Democratic Republic of Vietnam.

Ho Chi Minh

The French at first promised to recognize the new government as a free state but failed to do so. On November 23, 1946, at least 6,000 Vietnamese civilians were killed in a French naval bombardment of the port city of Haiphong, and the first Indochina War began. The Viet Minh had popular support and was able to dominate the countryside, while the French strength lay in urban areas. As the war neared an end, the Viet Minh was succeeded by a new organization, the Lien Viet, or Vietnamese National Popular Front. In 1951 the majority of the Viet Minh leadership was absorbed into the Lao Dong, or Vietnamese Workers' Party (later Vietnamese Communist Party), which remained the dominant force in North Vietnam.

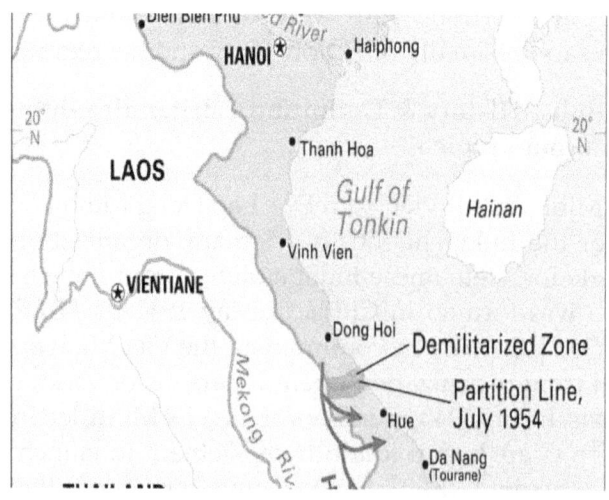

N. Vietnam (1954–75) Encyclopædia Britannica, Inc.

214

Elements of the Viet Minh joined with the Viet Cong against the U.S.-supported government of South Vietnam and the United States in the Vietnam War (or Second Indochina War) of the late 1950s, the '60s, and the early '70s. After the reunification of the country (1976), Viet Minh leaders continued to take an active role in Vietnamese politics. [The Editors of Encyclopaedia Britannica/ Michael Ray.]

World War II & The Independence Of Indochina

For five years during World War II, Indochina was a French-administered possession of Japan. On September 22, 1940, Jean Decoux, the French governor-general appointed by the Vichy government after the fall of France to the Nazis, concluded an agreement with the Japanese that permitted the stationing of 30,000 Japanese troops in Indochina and the use of all major Vietnamese airports by the Japanese military. The agreement made Indochina the most important staging area for all Japanese military operations in Southeast Asia. The French administration cooperated with the Japanese occupation forces and was ousted only toward the end of the war (in March 1945), when the Japanese began to fear that the French forces might turn against them as defeat approached. After the French had been disarmed, Bao Dai, the last French-appointed emperor of Vietnam, was allowed to proclaim the independence of his country and to appoint a Vietnamese national government at Hue; however, all real power remained in the hands of the Japanese military commanders. Meanwhile, in May 1941, at Ho Chi Minh's urging, the Communist Party formed a broad nationalist alliance under its leadership called the League for the Independence of Vietnam, which subsequently became known as the Viet Minh. Ho, returning to China to seek assistance, was arrested and imprisoned there by the Nationalist government. After his release he returned to Vietnam and began to cooperate with Allied forces by providing information on Japanese troop movements in Indochina. At the same time, he sought recognition of the Viet Minh as the legitimate representative of Vietnamese nationalist aspirations. When the Japanese surrendered in August 1945, the communist-led Viet Minh ordered a general uprising, and, with no one organized to oppose them, they were able to seize power in Hanoi. Bao Dai, the Vietnamese emperor, abdicated a few days later and declared his fealty to the newly proclaimed Democratic Republic of Vietnam. The Communist Party had clearly gained the upper hand in its struggle to outmaneuver its disorganized rivals, such as the noncommunist VNQDD. The French, however, were determined to restore their colonial presence in Indochina and, with the aid of British occupation forces, seized control of Cochinchina. Thus, at the beginning of 1946, there were two Vietnams: a communist north and a noncommunist south. [Joseph Buttinger, William J. Duiker, and William S. Turley]

First Indochina War [Dec 19, 1946]

Viet Minh soldiers   *French Army*

Negotiations between the French and Ho Chi Minh led to an agreement in March 1946 that appeared to promise a peaceful solution. Under the agreement France would recognize the Viet Minh government and give Vietnam the status of a free state within the French Union. French troops were to remain in Vietnam, but they would be withdrawn progressively over five years. For a period in early 1946 the French cooperated with Ho Chi Minh as he consolidated the Viet Minh's dominance over other nationalist groups, in particular those politicians who were backed by the Chinese Nationalist Party.

Despite tactical cooperation between the French and the Viet Minh, their policies were irreconcilable: the French aimed to reestablish colonial rule, while Hanoi wanted total independence. French intentions were revealed in the decision of Georges-Thierry d'Argenlieu, the high commissioner for Indochina, to proclaim Cochinchina an autonomous republic in June 1946.

Further negotiations did not resolve the basic differences between the French and the Viet Minh. In late November 1946 French naval vessels bombarded Haiphong, causing several thousand civilian casualties; the subsequent Viet Minh attempt to overwhelm French troops in Hanoi in December is generally considered to be the beginning of the First Indochina War. Initially confident of victory, the French long ignored the real political cause of the war—the desire of the Vietnamese people, including their anticommunist leaders, to achieve unity and independence for their country. French efforts to deal with those issues were devious and ineffective. The French reunited Cochinchina with the rest of Vietnam in 1949, proclaiming the Associated State of Vietnam, and appointed the former emperor Bao Dai as chief of state. Most nationalists, however, denounced these maneuvers, and leadership in the struggle for independence from the French remained with the Viet Minh.

French defeated by Viet Minh at Dien Bien Phu, 1954

Meanwhile, the Viet Minh waged an increasingly successful guerrilla war, aided after 1949 by the new communist government of China. The United States, fearful of the spread of communism in Asia, sent large amounts of aid to the French. The French, however, were shaken by the fall of their garrison at Dien Bien Phu in May 1954 and agreed to negotiate an end to the war at an international conference in Geneva.

How the US considered helping France nuke its way out of an embarrassing military defeat?

Benjamin Brimelow- BBC News [5 May 2014]

French Foreign Legion paratroopers land near Dien Bien Phu,
March 16, 1954. [Getty Images]

In March 1954, French troops were in northern Vietnam for what commanders thought would be a decisive blow against the Viet Minh. By May, after weeks of brutal fighting, French forces surrendered, ending the battle of Dien Bien Phu and the French Indochina War. Western countries saw that war as essential to stopping the spread of communism, and the US was willing to take extreme action to win.

Dien Bien Phu: Did the US offer France an A-bomb?

Sixty years ago this week, French troops were defeated by Vietnamese forces at Dien Bien Phu. As historian Julian Jackson explains, it was a turning point in the history of both nations, and in the Cold War - and a battle where some in the US appear to have contemplated the use of nuclear weapons.

"Would you like two atomic bombs?" These are the words that a senior French diplomat remembered US Secretary of State John Foster Dulles asking the French Foreign Minister, Georges Bidault, in April 1954. The context of this extraordinary offer was the critical plight of the French army fighting the nationalist forces of Ho Chi Minh at Dien Bien Phu in the highlands of north-west Vietnam.

The battle of Dien Bien Phu is today overshadowed by the later involvement of the Americans in Vietnam in the 1960s. But for eight years between 1946 and 1954 the French had fought their own bloody war to hold on to their Empire in the Far East. After the seizure of power by the Communists in China in 1949, this colonial conflict had become a key battleground of the Cold War. The Chinese provided the Vietnamese with arms and supplies while most of the costs of the French war effort were borne by America. But it was French soldiers who were fighting and dying. By 1954, French forces in Indochina totaled over 55,000.

Dien Bien Phu [Getty Image]

At the end of 1953, French commander in chief Gen Navarre had decided to set up a fortified garrison in the valley of Dien Bien Phu, in the highlands about 280 miles from the northern capital of Hanoi. The valley was surrounded by rings of forested hills and mountains. The position was defensible providing the French could hold on to the inner hills and keep their position supplied through the airstrip. What they underestimated was the capacity of the Vietnamese to amass artillery behind the hills. This equipment was transported by tens of thousands of laborers - many of them women and children - carrying material hundreds of miles through the jungle day and night. On 13 March the Vietnamese unleashed a massive barrage of artillery behind the hills. This equipment was transported by tens of thousands of laborers - many of them women and children - carrying material hundreds of miles through the jungle day and night. On 13 March the Vietnamese unleashed a massive barrage of artillery and within two days two of the surrounding hills had been taken, and the airstrip was no longer usable. The French defenders were now cut off and the noose tightened around them.

It was this critical situation which led the French to appeal in desperation for US help. The most hawkish on the American aide were Vice-President Richard Nixon, who had no political power, and Admiral Radford, Chair of the Joint Chiefs of Staff. Also quite hawkish was the US Secretary of State John Foster Dulles, who was obsessed by the crusade against Communism. More reserved was President Eisenhower who nonetheless gave a press conference in early April where he proclaimed the infamous "domino theory" about the possible spread of Communism from one country to another.

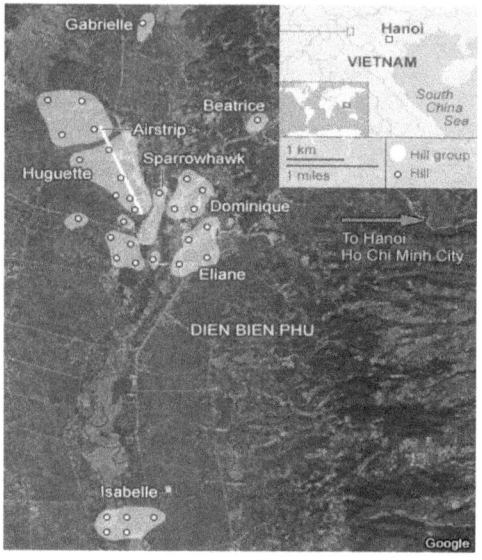

"You have a row of dominoes set up, you knock over the first one, and what will happen to the last one is the certainty that it will go over very quickly," he said. "So you could have a beginning of a disintegration that would have the most profound influences."

"He didn't really offer. He made a suggestion and asked a question. He uttered the two fatal words 'nuclear bomb'," Maurice Schumann, a former foreign minister, said before his death in 1998. "Bidault immediately reacted as if he didn't take this offer seriously."

According to Professor Fred Logevall of Cornell University, Dulles "at least talked in very general terms about the possibility, what did the French think about potentially using two or three tactical nuclear weapons against these enemy positions".

Bidault declined, he says, "because he knew... that if this killed a lot of Viet Minh troops then it would also basically destroy the garrison itself".

In the end, there was no American intervention of any kind, as the British refused to go along with it. The last weeks of the battle of Dien Bien Phu were atrociously grueling. The ground turned to mud once the monsoon began, and men clung to craters and ditches in conditions reminiscent of the battle of Verdun in 1916. On 7 May 1954, after a 56-day siege, the French army surrendered. Overall, on the French side there were 1,142 dead, 1,606 disappeared, 4,500 more or less badly wounded. Vietnamese casualties ran to 22,000. In this year marked by two other major anniversaries - the centenary of the outbreak of World War One and the 70th anniversary of D-Day - we should not forget this other battle that took place 60 years ago. In the history of decolonization, it was the only time a professional European army was decisively defeated in a pitched battle. It marked the end of the French Empire in the Far East, and provided an inspiration to other anti-colonial fighters. It was no coincidence also that a few weeks later a violent rebellion broke out in French Algeria - the beginning of another bloody and traumatic war that was to last eight years. The French army held so desperately on to Algeria partly to redeem the honour it felt had been lost at Dien Bien Phu. So obsessed did the army become by this idea that in 1958 it backed a putsch against the government, which it believed was preparing what the generals condemned as a "diplomatic Dien Bien Phu". This putsch brought back to power Gen de Gaulle who set up the new presidential regime that exists in France today. So, the ripples of Dien Bien Phu are still being felt. It was also in 1954 that France began working on its own independent nuclear deterrent. For the Vietnamese, however, Dien Bien Phu, was only the first round. The Americans, who had refused to become directly involved in 1954, were gradually sucked into war - the second Vietnam War - during the 1960s. [The Siege of Dien Bien Phu written and presented by Julian Jackson]

Viet Minh | History & Definition | Britannica -https://www. britannica.com ›

The two Vietnams (1954–65)

The agreements concluded in Geneva between April and July 1954 (collectively called the Geneva Accords) were signed by French and Viet Minh representatives and provided for a cease-fire and temporary division of the country into two military zones at latitude 17 °N (popularly called the 17th parallel). All Viet Minh forces were to withdraw north of that line, and all French and Associated State of Vietnam troops were to remain south of it; permission was granted for refugees to move from one zone to the other during a limited time period. An international commission was established, composed of Canadian, Polish, and Indian members under an Indian chairman, to supervise the execution of the agreement.

This agreement left the Democratic Republic of Vietnam (henceforth called North Vietnam) in control of only the northern half of the country. The last of the Geneva Accords—called the Final Declaration—provided for elections, supervised by the commission, to be held throughout Vietnam in July 1956 in order to unify the country. Viet Minh leaders appeared certain to win these elections, and the United States and the leaders in the south would not approve or sign the Final Declaration; elections were never held. In the midst of a mass migration of nearly one million people from the north to the south, the two Vietnams began to reconstruct their war-ravaged land. With assistance from the Soviet Union and China, the Hanoi government in the north embarked on an ambitious program of socialist industrialization; they also began to collectivize agriculture in earnest in 1958. In the south a new government appointed by Bao Dai began to build a new country. Ngo Dinh Diem, a Roman Catholic, was named prime minister and succeeded with American support in stabilizing the anticommunist regime in Saigon. He eliminated pro-French elements in the military and abolished the local autonomy of several religious-political groups. Then, in a government-controlled referendum in October 1955, Diem removed Bao Dai as chief of state and made himself president of the Republic of Vietnam (South Vietnam).

Diem's early success in consolidating power did not result in concrete political and economic achievements. Plans for land reform were sabotaged by entrenched interests. With the financial backing of the United States, the regime's chief energies were directed toward building up the military and a variety of intelligence and security forces to counter the still-influential Viet Minh. Totalitarian methods were directed against all who were regarded as opponents, and the favoritism shown to Roman Catholics alienated the majority Buddhist population. Loyalty to the president and his family was made a paramount duty, and Diem's brother, Ngo Dinh Nhu, founded an elitist underground organization to spy on officials, army officers, and prominent local citizens. Diem also refused to participate in the all-Vietnamese elections described in the Final Declaration. With support from the north, communist-led forces—popularly called the Viet Cong—launched an insurgency movement to seize power and reunify the country. The insurrection appeared close to succeeding, when Diem's army overthrew him in November 1963. Diem and his brother Nhu were killed in the coup.

The Second Indochina War

Viet Cong

The government that seized power after Diem's ouster, however, was no more effective than its predecessor. A period of political instability followed, until the military firmly seized control in June 1965 under Nguyen Cao Ky. Militant Buddhists who had helped overthrow Diem strongly opposed Ky's government, but he was able to break their resistance. Civil liberties were restricted, political opponents—denounced as neutralists or pro-Communists—were imprisoned, and political parties were allowed to operate only if they did not openly criticize government policy. The character of the regime remained largely unchanged after the presidential elections in September 1967, which led to the election of Gen. Nguyen Van Thieu as president.

No less evident than the oppressive nature of the Saigon regime was its inability to cope with the Viet Cong. The insurgent movement, aided by a steady infiltration of weapons and advisers from the north, steadily built its fighting strength from about 30,000 men in 1963 to about 150,000 in 1965 when, in the opinion of many American intelligence analysts, the survival of the Saigon regime was seriously threatened. In addition, the political opposition in the south to Saigon became much more organized. The National Front for the Liberation of the South, popularly called the National Liberation Front (NLF), had been organized in late 1960 and within four years had a huge following.

Growing U.S. Involvement in the Vietnam War

Until 1960 the United States had supported the Saigon regime and its army only with military equipment, financial aid, and, as permitted by the Geneva Accords, 700 advisers for training the army. The number of advisers had increased to 17,000 by the end of 1963, and they were joined by an increasing number of American helicopter pilots. All of this assistance, however, proved insufficient to halt the advance of the Viet Cong, and in February 1965 U.S. Pres. Lyndon B. Johnson ordered the bombing of North Vietnam, hoping to prevent further infiltration of arms and troops into the south. Four weeks after the bombing began, the United States started sending troops into the south. By July the number of U.S. troops had reached 75,000; it continued to climb until it stood at more than 500,000 early in 1968. Fighting beside the Americans were some 600,000 regular South Vietnamese troops and regional and self-defense forces, as well as smaller contingents from South Korea, Thailand, Australia, and New Zealand. Three years of intensive bombing of the north and fighting in the south, however, did not weaken the will and strength of the Viet Cong and their allies from the north. Infiltration of personnel and supplies down the famous Ho Chi Minh Trail continued at a high level, and regular troops from the north—now estimated at more than 100,000—played a growing role in the war. The continuing strength of the insurgent forces became evident in the so-called Tet Offensive that began in late January 1968, during which the Viet Cong and North Vietnamese attacked more than 100 cities and military bases, holding on to some for several weeks. After that, a growing conviction in the U.S. government that continuing the war at current levels was no longer politically acceptable led President Johnson to order a reduction of the bombing in the north. This decision opened the way for U.S. negotiations with Hanoi, which began in Paris in May 1968. After the bombing was halted over the entire north in November 1968, the Paris talks were enlarged to include representatives of the NLF and the Saigon regime. The war continued under a new U.S. president, Richard M. Nixon, who began gradually to withdraw U.S. troops. Public opposition to the war, however, escalated after Nixon ordered attacks on the Ho Chi Minh Trail in Laos and on Viet Cong sanctuaries inside Cambodia. In the meantime, the peace talks went on in Paris. [Milton Edgeworth Osborne, William J. Duiker, and William S. Turley]

Viet Cong - Wikipedia https://en.wikipedia.org › wiki ›

National Liberation Front Flag

The Viet Cong, officially known as the National Liberation Front of South Vietnam (Vietnamese: Mặt trận Dân tộc Giải phóng Miền Nam Việt Nam), was an armed communist political revolutionary organization in South Vietnam and Cambodia. Its military force, the Liberation Army of South Vietnam (LASV), fought under the direction of North Vietnam, against the South Vietnamese and United States governments during the Vietnam War, eventually emerging on the winning side. The LASV had both guerrilla and regular army units, as well as a network of cadres who organized peasants in the territory the Viet Cong controlled. During the war, communist fighters and anti-war activists claimed that the Viet Cong was an insurgency indigenous to the South, while the U.S. and South Vietnamese governments portrayed the group as a tool of North Vietnam.

North Vietnam established the National Liberation Front on December 20, 1960, at Tân Lập village in Tây Ninh Province to foment insurgency in the South. Many of the Viet Cong's core members were volunteer "regroupees", southern Viet Minh who had resettled in the North after the Geneva Accord (1954). Hanoi gave the regroupees military training and sent them back to the South along the Ho Chi Minh trail in the early 1960s. The Viet Cong called for southern Vietnamese to "overthrow the camouflaged colonial regime of the American imperialists" and to make "efforts toward the peaceful unification". The LASV's best-known action was the Tet Offensive, an enormous assault on more than 100 South Vietnamese urban centers in 1968, including an attack on the U.S. embassy in Saigon. The offensive riveted the attention of the world's media for weeks, but also overextended the Viet Cong. Later communist offensives were conducted predominantly by the North Vietnamese. The organization officially merged with the Fatherland Front of Vietnam on February 4, 1977, after North and South Vietnam were officially unified under a communist government.

By the terms of the Geneva Accord (1954), which ended the Indochina War, France and the Viet Minh agreed to a truce and to a separation of forces. The Viet Minh had become the government of Democratic Republic of Vietnam since the Vietnamese 1946 general election, and military forces of the communists regrouped there. Military forces of the non-communists regrouped in South Vietnam, which became a separate state. Elections on reunification were scheduled for July 1956. A divided Vietnam angered Vietnamese nationalists, but it made the country less of a threat to China. The Democratic Republic of Vietnam in the past and Vietnam in the present did not and do not recognize the division of Vietnam into two countries. Chinese Premier Zhou Enlai negotiated the terms of the ceasefire with France and then imposed them on the Viet Minh.

About 90,000 Viet Minh were evacuated to the North while 5,000 to 10,000 cadre remained in the South, most of them with orders to refocus on political activity and agitation. The Saigon-Cholon Peace Committee, the first Viet Cong front, was founded in 1954 to provide leadership for this group. Other front names used by the Viet Cong in the 1950s implied that members were fighting for religious causes, for example, "Executive Committee of the Fatherland Front", which suggested affiliation with the Hòa Hảo sect, or "Vietnam-Cambodia Buddhist Association". Front groups were favored by the Viet Cong to such an extent that its real leadership remained shadowy until long after the war was over, prompting the expression "the faceless Viet Cong".

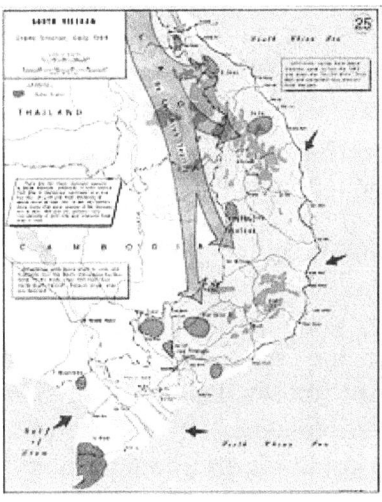

Situation of the Communist forces in South Vietnam in early 1964

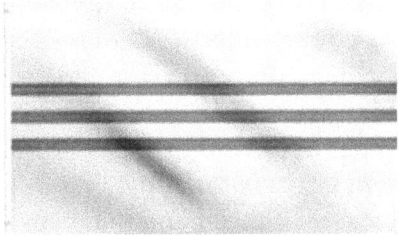

South Vietnam flag

Led by Ngô Đình Diệm, South Vietnam refused to sign the Geneva Accord Arguing that a free election was impossible under the conditions that existed in communist-held territory, Diệm announced in July 1955 that the scheduled election on reunification would not be held. After subduing the Bình Xuyên organized crime

227

gang in the Battle for Saigon in 1955, and the Hòa Hảo and other militant religious sects in early 1956, Diệm turned his attention to the Viet Cong. Within a few months, the Viet Cong had been driven into remote swamps. The success of this campaign inspired U.S. President Dwight Eisenhower to dub Diệm the "miracle man" when he visited the U.S. in May 1957. France withdrew its last soldiers from Vietnam in April 1956. In March 1956, southern communist leader Lê Duẩn presented a plan to revive the insurgency entitled "The Road to the South" to the other members of the Politburo in Hanoi. He argued adamantly that war with the United States was necessary to achieve unification. But as China and the Soviets both opposed confrontation at this time, Lê Duẩn's plan was rejected and communists in the South were ordered to limit themselves to economic struggle. Leadership divided into a "North first", or pro-Beijing, faction led by Trường Chinh, and a "South first" faction led by Lê Duẩn.

As the Sino-Soviet split widened in the following months, Hanoi began to play the two communist giants off against each other. The North Vietnamese leadership approved tentative measures to revive the southern insurgency in December 1956. Lê Duẩn's blueprint for revolution in the South was approved in principle, but implementation was conditional on winning international support and on modernizing the army, which was expected to take at least until 1959. President Hồ Chí Minh stressed that violence was still a last resort. Nguyễn Hữu Xuyên was assigned military command in the South, replacing Lê Duẩn, who was appointed North Vietnam's acting party boss. This represented a loss of power for Hồ, who preferred the more moderate Võ Nguyên Giáp, who was defense minister. An assassination campaign, referred to as "extermination of traitors" or "armed propaganda" in communist literature, began in April 1957. Tales of sensational murder and mayhem soon crowded the headlines. Seventeen civilians were killed by machine gun fire at a bar in Châu Đốc in July and in September a district chief was killed with his entire family on a main highway in broad daylight. In October 1957, a series of bombs exploded in Saigon and left 13 Americans wounded. In a speech given on September 2, 1957, Hồ reiterated the "North first" line of economic struggle. The launch of Sputnik in October boosted Soviet confidence and led to a reassessment of policy regarding Indochina, long treated as a Chinese sphere of influence. In November, Hồ traveled to Moscow with Lê Duẩn and gained approval or a more militant line. In early 1958, Lê Duẩn met with the leaders of "Inter-zone V" (northern South Vietnam) and ordered the establishment of patrols and safe areas to provide logistical support for activity in the Mekong Delta and in urban areas. In June 1958, the Viet Cong created a command structure for the eastern Mekong Delta. French scholar Bernard Fall published an influential article in July 1958 which analyzed the pattern of rising violence and concluded that a new war had begun.

The Communist Party of Vietnam approved a "people's war" on the South at a session in January 1959 and this decision was confirmed by the Politburo in March. In May 1959, Group 559 was established to maintain and upgrade the Ho Chi Minh trail, at this time a six-month mountain trek through Laos. About 500 of the "regroupees" of 1954 were sent south on the trail during its first year of operation. The first arms delivery via the trail, a few dozen rifles, was completed in August 1959. Two regional command centers were merged to create the Central Office for South Vietnam (Trung ương Cục miền Nam), a unified communist party headquarters for the South. COSVN was initially located in Tây Ninh Province near the Cambodian border. On July 8, the Viet Cong killed two U.S. military advisors at Biên Hòa, the first American dead of the Vietnam War. The "2d Liberation Battalion" ambushed two companies of South Vietnamese soldiers in September 1959, the first large unit military action of the war. This was considered the beginning of the "armed struggle" in communist accounts. A series of uprisings beginning in the Mekong Delta province of Bến Tre in January 1960 created "liberated zones", models of Viet Cong-style government. Propagandists celebrated their creation of battalions of "long-hair troops" (women). The fiery declarations of 1959 were followed by a lull while Hanoi focused on events in Laos (1960–61). Moscow favored reducing international tensions in 1960, as it was election year for the U.S. presidency. Despite this, 1960 was a year of unrest in South Vietnam, with pro-democracy demonstrations inspired by the South Korean student uprising that year and a failed military coup in November. To counter the accusation that North Vietnam was violating the Geneva Accord, the independence of the Viet Cong was stressed in communist propaganda. The Viet Cong created the National Liberation Front of South Vietnam in December 1960 at Tân Lập village in Tây Ninh as a "united front", or political branch intended to encourage the participation of non-communists. The group's formation was announced by Radio Hanoi and its ten-point manifesto called for, "overthrow the disguised colonial regime of the imperialists and the dictatorial administration, and to form a national and democratic coalition administration." Thọ, a lawyer and the Viet Cong's "neutralist" chairman, was an isolated figure among cadres and soldiers. South Vietnam's Law 10/59, approved in May 1959, authorized the death penalty for crimes "against the security of the state" and featured prominently in Viet Cong propaganda. Violence between the Viet Cong and government forces soon increased drastically from 180 clashes in January 1960 to 545 clashes in September. By 1960, the Sino-Soviet split was a public rivalry, making China more supportive of Hanoi's war effort. For Chinese leader Mao Zedong, aid to North Vietnam was a way to enhance his "anti-imperialist" credentials for both domestic and international audiences. About 40,000 communist soldiers infiltrated the South in 1961–63. The Viet Cong grew rapidly; an estimated 300,000 members were enrolled in "liberation associations" (affiliated groups) by early 1962. The ratio of Viet Cong to government soldiers jumped from 1:10 in 1961 to 1:5 a year later.

Viet Cong soldiers   *QLVNCH [S. VN Army]*

The level of violence in the South jumped dramatically in the fall of 1961, from 50 guerrilla attacks in September to 150 in October. U.S. President John F. Kennedy decided in November 1961 to substantially increase American military aid to South Vietnam. The

USS *Core* arrived in Saigon with 35 helicopters in December 1961. By mid-1962, there were 12,000 U.S. military advisors in Vietnam. The "special war" and "strategic hamlets" policies allowed Saigon to push back in 1962, but in 1963 the Viet Cong regained the military initiative. The Viet Cong won its first military victory against South Vietnamese forces at Ấp Bắc in January 1963. A landmark party meeting was held in December 1963, shortly after a military coup in Saigon in which Diệm was assassinated. North Vietnamese leaders debated the issue of "quick victory" vs "protracted war" (guerrilla warfare). After this meeting, the communist side geared up for a maximum military effort and the troop strength of the People's Army of Vietnam (PAVN) increased from 174,000 at the end of 1963 to 300,000 in 1964. The Soviets cut aid in 1964 as an expression of annoyance with Hanoi's ties to China. Even as Hanoi embraced China's international line, it continued to follow the Soviet model of reliance on technical specialists and bureaucratic management, as opposed to mass mobilization. The winter of 1964–1965 was a high-water mark for the Viet Cong, with the Saigon government on the verge of collapse. Soviet aid soared following a visit to Hanoi by Soviet Premier Alexei Kosygin in February 1965. Hanoi was soon receiving up-to-date surface-to-air missiles. The U.S. would have 200,000 soldiers in South Vietnam by the end of the year. In January 1966, Australian troops uncovered a tunnel complex which had been used by COSVN. Six thousand documents were captured, revealing the inner workings of the Viet Cong. COSVN retreated to Mimot in Cambodia. As a result of an agreement with the Cambodian government made in 1966, weapons for the Viet Cong were shipped to the Cambodian port of Sihanoukville and then trucked to Viet Cong bases near the border along the "Sihanouk Trail", which replaced the Ho Chi Minh Trail. Many Liberations Army of South Vietnam units operated at night, and employed terror as a standard tactic. Rice procured at gunpoint sustained the Viet Cong. Squads were assigned monthly assassination quotas. Government employees, especially village and district heads, were the most common targets. But there were a wide variety of targets, including clinics and medical personnel. Notable Viet Cong atrocities include the massacre of over 3,000 unarmed civilians at Huế, 48 killed in the bombing of My Canh floating restaurant in Saigon in June 1965 and a massacre of 252 Montagnards in the village of Đắc Sơn in December 1967 using flamethrowers. Viet Cong death squads assassinated at least 37,000 civilians in South Vietnam; the real figure was far higher since the data mostly cover 1967–72. They also waged a mass murder campaign against civilian hamlets and refugee camps; in the peak war years, nearly a third of all civilian deaths were the result of Viet Cong atrocities. Ami Pedahzur has written that "the overall volume and lethality of Vietcong terrorism rivals or exceeds all but a handful of terrorist campaigns waged over the last third of the twentieth century".

Britain's secret Vietnam war missions Lucy Fisher, Defense Correspondent 1962

An RAF pilot told his family that he flew over Laos
to help fight the Viet Cong rebels

The Handley Page Hastings aircraft were ideal for navigating the Ho Chi Minh Trail's remote terrain, military figures said-ALAMY

Britain provided covert assistance to western forces in the Vietnam War by flying secret missions over Laos, the daughter of a former Royal Air Force navigator has claimed.

Flight Lieutenant Donald Roberts, who was based in Asia with the RAF at the time, confided in his family decades later that he had taken part in flying Handley Page Hastings transport aircraft over Laos in the second half of 1962. The alleged flights were designed to help close off the Ho Chi Minh Trail.

TRANSPACIFIC

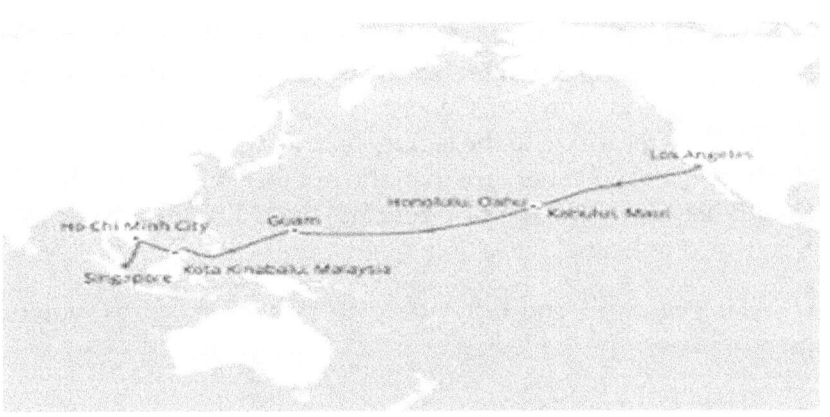

Transpacific-Westward 1975

USS Brule AKL 28

That day... Saigon, Vietnam Thursday April 24, 1975

Ngày qua giã từ đất Mẹ mà đi
Tình quê, tình nước đôi bề...

The day I felt my homeland
Oh! My beloved country....

Suddenly, unprepared, un announced. the wind changed its direction. Off, it sent Le thi Lan across the Pacific Ocean. A third-year medical student of Saigon Medical School involved in the Transpacific journey to a strange land with an unknown destiny.

Le thi Lan, 21 years old, third year medical student of Saigon Medical School, S. Vietnam just finished the morning rounds with Doctor K. at Binh Dan General Hospital. The students took a break before returning to the lecture hall. Le thi Lan took a pocket mirror and looked at her face then she put on a thin layer of lotion around her eyes, now she saw her class mate, Dang van Huynh's visage next to her,

"Hi Beautiful! You don't need to put on makeups, you're already pretty." he smiled

"Hey! Who needs your advice?" timidly, she put the mirror away as feeling her cheeks were blushing, she changed the subject,

"Today we learn a lot of new subjects, don't we?"

"Yes! The most interesting was the cirrhosis of the liver case." Dang van Huynh said, "I'm not quite sure I understand the causes of this condition. I remember Doctor K. said one of the reasons is hepatitis, do you remember what are the others?"

"And alcoholism!" Le thi Lan said, "This year we'll learn a lot about Pathology, don't we? This afternoon, I go to OB/GYN clinic, how about you?"

"Orthopedics." Dang van Huynh said and gave her a small bag, "I have something for you."

"What's that?" Le thi Lan asked with twinkles in her eyes

"Ah! I'll keep your smile in my heart forever." Dang van

Huynh waved, "See you later!"

"See you later!" she said

In the afternoon, third year Medical student Le thi Lan went to Clinics for assisting the OB/GYN Doctor N. The Doctor asked the pregnant patient,

"I'm Doctor N. Do you mind if my Medical student here to observe?"

The woman nodded her head. Le thi Lan put on the mask, gown, and gloves, "Thank you" she said and ready to watch Doctor N.'s performance. A nurse came in, she told the Doctor,

"Pardon me, Doctor. May I have a word with the medical student- Le thi Lan, for her brother asked your permission let her go home, her family has an emergency situation."

"That's fine. Le thi Lan, you may leave now. See you tomorrow!" Doctor N. said

"Thank you, Doctor." Le thi Lan left, never did she know that was the last time she saw Doctor N. When she got home, her father, mother, sister and brothers were at the door; they cried. Le Anh Duy- her brother- told her, "Your elder sister, Le thi Minh is leaving us to Vung Tau harbor to S. Korea!"

"What happened?" Le thi Lan inquired worriedly while Le thi Minh tearfully couldn't utter a word.

A jeep stopped by the house, the driver- a S. Korean- said in English,

"Anh Duy, I'll help Le thi Minh, your sister."

"Thank you, Kim Bu Muk." Anh Duy waved to the S. Korean brother-in-law and helped Le thi Minh got in the jeep. Faster than a blink of the eye, the mother thrust Le thi Lan into the vehicle with Le thi Minh. The driver drove off before Le thi Lan could sit down. Next to her, Le thi Minh [the elder sister] covered her face with her hands, crying, "Oh! Papa, Mama, Anh Duy..." Le thi Lan embraced her sister, "Tell me, why..." the older sister didn't answer. After a few minutes, Le thi Minh composed herself.

Wiping off her tears, she discussed with her husband, Kim Bu Muk, in English about something seemed important. Le thi Lan didn't understand the conversation, since her English was poor. There were five people in the jeep: three S. Korean men: the driver, a technician, and Kim Bu Muk; and two Vietnamese women: Le thi Minh and Le thi Lan. Le thi Minh graduated from the University of Saigon, Faculty of Letters with the BA degree in English Literature. The Le family had three children: Anh Duy, Minh, and Lan. Mr. Le Khoa, the father, a lawyer married Mrs. Tran thi Mai, an Elementary teacher. Their oldest child, Le Anh Duy, a mechanic engineer, worked with the S. Korean military in construction project of bridges since 1970 as the S. Korean military force involved in Vietnam War fought against the N. Vietnam Communist force.

Sometimes, Le Anh Duy invited his Manager, Kim Bu Muk home for dinner. Le Anh Duy thought that Kim Bu Muk was a bachelor, far away from home, Le Anh Duy wanted Kim Bu Muk tasted the Vietnamese cuisine, and his younger sister, Le thi Minh enjoyed showing her cooking skills. Coincidentally, the foreigner from S. Korea, Kim Bu Muk liked the Vietnamese dishes and fell in love with Le thi Minh. On April 1, 1975, Kim Bu Muk whispered to Le Anh Duy a secret, "S. Korean military got an order from the White House Administration to withdraw their force from S Vietnam gradually in contingent with the US military, for the Communists from N. Vietnam would take over S. Vietnam by the end of April 1975." For that reason, Le Anh Duy arranged the marriage between Kim Bu Muk and Le thi Minh so Kim Bu Muk would take her back to S. Korea with him when the military force of S. Korea withdrew from S. Vietnam. Kim Bu Muk agreed and promised to take care of Le thi Minh in S. Korea, for he knew the dangerous situation of the Vietnamese in S. Vietnam when the N. Vietnam Communist party took over the country. Le thi Lan overheard the arranged marriage, but she didn't know when it happened as she was too busy with school. Then, on the spur of the moment, her mother thrust her into a vehicle to an unexpected voyage to an unknown future. Yet, the main problem she had to resolve right now was: what would happen tomorrow? No documents to enter S. Korean, how could she be accepted to sojourn in that country? Would they kick her out of the jeep on the way to Vung Tau harbor or deport her back to Vietnam when they arrive in S. Korea? By that time, Vietnam was under the control of the Communist Party, what would be her fate? Someone put his hand on Le thi Lan's shoulder,

"Don't worry. We have a way to help you." It was Kim Bu Muk- her brother in law.

"We'll take care of you." Le thi Minh explained to her younger sister, "From now on you are Kim Bu Muk's assistant; you'd be allowed to sojourn in S. Korea. After that, we'll find a way for you to go to France, Uncle Quynh and his family live in Paris. You might continue Medicine there, right?"

Kim Bu Muk gave the Le sisters two stickers and he wrote something in Korean which the sisters didn't understand. He said, "the stickers say both women belong to the Kim Bu Muk family. Keep them with you when we entered Pusan harbor."

Le thi Lan embraced her sister, both said in tears to Kim Bu Muk, "Thank you very much."

By the evening, they arrived at Vung Tau harbor. There were a huge crowd of S. Korean military men, professional and skill workers came to work in S. Vietnam and their families waiting to board the warship USS Brule AKL 28 heading back to Pusan harbor of S. Korea. On the ship, besides the S. Korean military and their families returned home, there were some Vietnamese men and women in similar situations as the Le sisters. The cruise officers, the sailors, the S. Koreans worked in S. Vietnam, including 45 refugee passengers were about 350 people. Kim Bu Muk and Le thi Minh had a cabin on board, they let Le thi Lan stayed with them. Kim Bu Muk told his wife, "You and your sister take the bed, I'll sleep on the floor."

"I sleep on the floor with you." Le thi Minh said

Kim Bu Muk hugged his wife while Le thi Lan mumbled in English to Kim Bu Muk, "Thank you" and she told her sister [in Vietnamese], "I'll sleep outside with the refugees. You need your privacy."

The Korean sailors dispensed sleeping bags to the refugees,

Le thi Lan joined them to sleep in tents on the deck of the ship. The refugees people made a line to received supper: noodles, dried fish, seaweeds, and tea or water. Le thi Lan had some noodles with sea weeds. She was hungry, but couldn't eat her food. The first time on the ship floating on the Pacific Ocean, even though tired, she was not able to sleep. Opening the backpack, she saw her white coat with her name tag and three red stars [At Saigon Medical School, a first-year student had one red star above name, he/she had five red stars on their last year. A after the graduation, they did the internship two more years in a hospital to be a specialist.], a note book, two pens, a pocket mirror, and a small bag from Dang van Huynh gave her this morning. She unwrapped the gift, some sesame candies and a piece of paper with "I love you". Le thi Lan pressed it to her heart. Dang van Huynh and Le thi Lan studied together for three years. She also liked Dang van Huynh and dreamed about a future with: after graduation from medical school, both of them worked to treat the sick in Vietnam. Le thi Lan stared at herself in the mirror, just this morning: there were two images in the screen, Dang van Huynh with a smile with Le thi Lan, but now there was only bewildered Le thi Lan. Where was Dan van Huynh? And they were nautical miles away from each other? She tried to reason logically in finding an answer or the truth of her situation at this moment,

"How come all of sudden I became insane, left school, home, family, and friends boarding a war ship to S. Korea? If I do not feel pain, I definitely must be in a very strange dream; on the other hand, if I feel the pain, then I'm sailing on the Pacific." And she pinched herself. Le thi Lan felt the pain. With tears rolling on her face, she cried, "Oh! Papa, Mama, and Anh Duy.... Oh, God! Please take me out of this maze...."

The announce on the USS Brule AKL 28 took her back to reality, "We're now heading to Pusan harbor- S. Korea. I pray that God bless and give us a safe trip to our homeland."

The waves rapped into the hulk of the ship, the sky was high with twinkled stars, but no moon light. Le thi Lan was still in a daze. She remembered exactly this morning, she was in the hospital following the Doctors in their rounds, she said, "See you later!" to her classmate, Dang van Huynh. They were in the same class at Saigon Medical School … tonight, she was floating on the Pacific to S. Korea! And, what would happen to father, mother, and her brother? Could she see Dang van Huynh again? What would be the fates of people in the south when the Communists from N. Vietnam took over S. Vietnam?

Next morning, when the sun rays reflected the colors on the window glass; Le thi Lan told herself,

"Today is Friday, April 25: Morning at Nhi Dong Hospital; Afternoon: Pharm and GI Clinic…Ah! Why am I here?"

The bell rang for breakfast on the USS Brule AKL 28 reminded her the reality: she was one in the Vietnamese refugees on the way to S. Korea…Then, the bell for lunch…. The bell for supper…The bell announced breakfast time… The medical student gazed blankly into the vast blue Pacific Ocean under the immense blue sky.

Let's take a look at S. Vietnam who escaped from the country when the Communist Party form the N. Vietnam took over the country in April 1975 and a few years after the collapse of S. Vietnam.

Wikipedia- en.wikipedia.org › wiki › Vietnamese_boat_people "Boat people" redirects here.

Vietnamese boat people awaiting rescue.

Vietnamese boat people (Vietnamese: *Thuyền nhân Việt Nam*), also known simply as **boat people**, refers to the refugees who fled Vietnam by boat and ship following the end of the Vietnam War in 1975. This migration and humanitarian crisis were at its highest in 1978 and 1979, but continued through the early 1990s. The term is also often used generically to refer to the Vietnamese people who left their country in mass exodus between 1975 and 1995 (see Indochina refugee crisis). This article uses the term "boat people" to apply only to those who fled Vietnam by sea. The number of boat people leaving Vietnam and arriving safely in another country totaled almost 800,000 between 1975 and 1995. Many of the refugees failed to survive the passage, facing danger from pirates, over-crowded boats, and storms. According to the United Nations High Commission for Refugees, between 200,000 and 400,000 boat people died at sea. The boat people's first destinations were the Southeast Asian locations of Hong Kong, Indonesia, Malaysia, the Philippines, Singapore, and Thailand. External tensions stemming from Vietnam's dispute with Cambodia and China in 1978 and 1979 caused an exodus of the majority of the Hoa people from Vietnam, many of whom fled by boat to China. The combination of economic sanctions, the legacy of destruction left by the Vietnam War, policies of the Vietnamese government, and further conflicts with neighboring countries caused an international humanitarian crisis, with Southeast Asian countries increasingly unwilling to accept more boat people on their shores. After negotiations and an international conference in 1979, Vietnam agreed to limit the flow of people leaving the country. The Southeast Asian countries agreed to admit the boat people temporarily, and the rest of the world, especially more developed countries, agreed to assume most of the costs of caring for the boat people and to resettle them in their countries. From refugee camps in Southeast Asia, the great majority of boat people were resettled in more developed countries. Significant numbers resettled in the United States, Canada, Italy, Australia, France, West Germany, and the United Kingdom. Several tens of thousands were repatriated to Vietnam, either voluntarily or involuntarily. Programs and facilities to carry out resettlement included the Orderly Departure Program, the Philippine Refugee Processing Center, and the Comprehensive Plan of Action.

The Vietnam War ended on April 30, 1975 with the fall of Saigon to the People's Army of Vietnam and the subsequent evacuation of more than 130,000 Vietnamese closely associated with the United States or the former government of South Vietnam. Most of the evacuees were resettled in the United States in Operation New Life and Operation New Arrivals. The U.S government transported refugees from Vietnam via aircraft and ships to temporarily settle down in Guam before moving them to designated homes in the contiguous United States. Within the same year, communist forces gained control of Cambodia and Laos, thus engendering a steady flow of refugees fleeing all three countries. In 1975, President Gerald Ford signed the Indochina Migration and Refugee Assistance Act, budgeting roughly 415 million dollars in the effort of providing transportation, healthcare, and accommodations to the 130,000 Vietnamese, Cambodian, and Laos refugees. After the Saigon evacuation, the numbers of Vietnamese leaving their country remained relatively small until mid-1978. A number of factors contributed to the refugee crisis, including economic hardship and wars among Vietnam, China, and Cambodia. In addition, up to 300,000 people, especially those associated with the former government and military of South Vietnam, were sent to re-education camps, where many endured torture, starvation, and disease while being forced to perform hard labor. In addition, 1 million people, mostly city dwellers, "volunteered" to live in "New Economic Zones" where they were to survive by reclaiming land and clearing jungle to grow crops. Repression was especially severe on the Hoa people, the ethnic Chinese population in Vietnam. Due to increasing tensions between Vietnam and China, which ultimately resulted in China's 1979 invasion of Vietnam, the Hoa were seen by the Vietnamese government as a security threat. Hoa people also controlled much of the retail trade in South Vietnam, and the communist government increasingly levied them with taxes, placed restrictions on trade, and confiscated businesses. In May 1978, the Hoa began to leave Vietnam in large numbers for China, initially by land. By the end of 1979, resulting from the Sino-Vietnamese War, 250,000 Hoa had sought refuge in China and many tens of thousands more were among the Vietnamese boat people scattered all over Southeast Asia and in Hong Kong. The Vietnamese government and its officials profited from the outflow of refugees, especially the often well-to-do Hoa. The price for obtaining exit permits, documentation, and a boat or ship, often derelict, to leave Vietnam was reported to be the equivalent of $3,000 for adults and half that for children. These payments were often made in the form of gold bars. Many poorer Vietnamese left their country secretly without documentation and in flimsy boats, and these were the most vulnerable to pirates and storms while at sea.

There were many methods employed by Vietnamese citizens to leave the country. Most were secret and done at night; some involved the bribing of top government officials. Some people bought places in large boats that held up to several hundred passengers. Others boarded fishing boats (fishing being a common occupation in Vietnam) and left that way. One method used involved middle-class refugees from Saigon, armed with forged identity documents, traveling approximately 1,100 kilometres (680 mi) to Danang by road. On arrival, they would take refuge for up to two days in safe houses while waiting for fishing junks and trawlers to take small groups into international waters. Planning for such a trip took many months and even years. Although these attempts often caused a depletion of resources, people usually had several false starts before they managed to escape. Exodus in 1978–1979: Although a few thousand people had fled Vietnam by boat between 1975 and mid-1978, the exodus of the boat people began in September 1978. The vessel Southern Cross unloaded 1,200 Vietnamese on an uninhabited island belonging to Indonesia. The government of Indonesia was furious at the people being dumped on its shores, but was pacified by the assurances of Western countries that they would resettle the refugees. In October, another ship, the Hai Hong, attempted to land 2,500 refugees in Malaysia. The Malaysians declined to allow them to enter their territory and the ship sat offshore until the refugees were processed for resettlement in third countries. Additional ships carrying thousands of refugees soon arrived in Hong Kong and the Philippines and were also denied permission to land. Their passengers were both ethnic Vietnamese and Hoa who had paid substantial fares for the passage. As these larger ships met resistance to landing their human cargo, many thousands of Vietnamese began to depart Vietnam in small boats, attempting to land surreptitiously on the shores of neighboring countries. The people in these small boats faced enormous dangers at sea and many thousands of them did not survive the voyage. The countries of the region often "pushed back" the boats when they arrived near their coastline and boat people cast about at sea for weeks or months looking for a place where they could land. Despite the dangers and the resistance of the receiving countries, the number of boat people continued to grow, reaching a high of 54,000 arrivals in the month of June 1979 with a total of 350,000 in refugee camps in Southeast Asia and Hong Kong. At this point, the countries of Southeast Asia united in declaring that they had "reached the limit of their endurance and decided that they would not accept any new arrivals". The United Nations convened an international conference in Geneva, Switzerland in July 1979, stating that "a grave crisis exists in Southeast Asia for hundreds of thousands of refugees". Illustrating the prominence of the issue, Vice President Walter Mondale headed the U.S. delegation. The results of the conference were that the Southeast Asian countries agreed to provide temporary asylum to the refugees, Vietnam agreed to promote orderly departures rather than permit boat people to depart, and the Western countries agreed to accelerate resettlement. The Orderly Departure Program enabled Vietnamese, if approved, to depart Vietnam for resettlement in another country without having to become a boat person. As a result of the conference, boat people departures from Vietnam declined to a few thousand per month and resettlements increased from 9,000 per month in early 1979 to 25,000 per month, the majority of the Vietnamese going to the United States, France, Australia, and Canada. The worst of the humanitarian crisis was over, although boat people would continue to leave Vietnam for more than another decade and die at sea or be confined to lengthy stays in refugee camps. Pirates and other hazards. Boat people had to face storms, diseases, starvation, and elude pirates. The boats were not intended for navigating open waters, and would typically head for busy international shipping lanes some 240 kilometres (150 mi) to the east. The lucky ones would succeed in being rescued by freighters or reach shore 1–2 weeks after departure. The unlucky ones continued their perilous journey at sea, sometimes lasting a few months long, suffering from hunger, thirst, disease, and pirates before finding safety.

A typical story of the hazards faced by the boat people was told in 1982 by a man named Le Phuoc. He left Vietnam with 17 other people in a boat 23 feet (7.0 m) long to attempt the 300-mile (480 km) passage across the Gulf of Thailand to southern Thailand or Malaysia. Their two outboard motors soon failed and they drifted without power and ran out of food and water. Thai pirates boarded their boat three times during their 17-day voyage, raped the four women on board and killed one, stole all the possessions of the refugees, and abducted one man who was never found. When their boat sank, they were rescued by a Thai fishing boat and ended up in a refugee camp on the coast of Thailand. Another of many stories tell of a boat carrying 75 refugees which were sunk by pirates with one person surviving. The survivors of another boat in which most of 21 women aboard were abducted by pirates said that at least 5 merchant vessels passed them by and ignored their pleas for help. An Argentine freighter finally picked them up and took them to Thailand. United Nations High Commissioner for Refugees (UNHCR) began compiling statistics on piracy in 1981. In that year, 452 boats carrying Vietnamese boat people arrived in Thailand carrying 15,479 refugees. 349 of the boats had been attacked by pirates an average of three times each. 228 women had been abducted and 881 people were dead or missing. An international anti-piracy campaign began in June 1982 and reduced the number of pirate attacks although they continued to be frequent and often deadly until 1990. Estimates of the number of Vietnamese boat people who died at sea can only be estimated. According to the United Nations High Commission for Refugees, between 200,000 and 400,000 boat people died at sea. Other wide-ranging estimates are that 10 to 70 percent of Vietnamese boat people died at sea.

Refugee camps

In response to the outpouring of boat people, the neighboring countries with international assistance set up refugee camps along their shores and on small, isolated islands. As the number of boat people grew to tens of thousands per month in early 1979, their numbers outstripped the ability of local governments, the UN, and humanitarian organizations to provide food, water, housing, and medical care to them. Two of the largest refugee camps were Bidong Island in Malaysia and Galang Refugee Camp in

Indonesia. Bidong Island was designated as the principal refugee camp in Malaysia in August 1978. The Malaysian government towed any arriving boatloads of refugees to the island. Less than one square mile (260 ha) in area, Bidong was prepared to receive 4,500 refugees, but by June 1979 Bidong had a refugee population of more than 40,000 who had arrived in 453 boats. The UNHCR and a large number of relief and aid organizations assisted the refugees. Food and drinking water had to be imported by barge. Water was rationed at one gallon per day per person. The food ration was mostly rice and canned meat and vegetables. The refugees constructed crude shelters from boat timbers, plastic sheeting, flattened tin cans, and palm fronds. Sanitation in the crowded conditions was the greatest problem. The United States and other governments had representatives on the island to interview refugees for resettlement. With the expansion of the numbers to be resettled after the July 1979 Geneva Conference, the population of Bidong slowly declined. The last refugee left in 1991. Galang Refugee Camp was also on an island, but with a much larger area than Bidong. More than 170,000 Indochinese, the great majority Boat People, were temporarily resident at Galang while it served as a refugee camp from 1975 until 1996. After they became well-established, Galang and Bidong and other refugee camps provided education, language and cultural training to boat people who would be resettled abroad. Refugees usually had to live in camps for several months—and sometimes years—before being resettled. In 1980, the Philippine Refugee Processing Center was established on the Bataan Peninsula in the Philippines. The center housed up to 18,000 Indochinese refugees who were approved for resettlement in the United States and elsewhere and provided them English language and other cross-cultural training.

Between 1980 and 1986, the outflow of boat people from Vietnam was less than the numbers resettled in third countries. In 1987, the numbers of boat people began to grow again. The destination this time was primarily Hong Kong and Thailand. On June 15, 1988, after more than 18,000 Vietnamese had arrived that year, Hong Kong authorities announced that all new arrivals would be placed in detention centers and confined until they could be resettled. Boat people were held in prison-like conditions and education and other programs were eliminated. Countries in Southeast Asia were equally negative about accepting newly arriving Vietnamese boat people into their countries. Moreover, both asylum and resettlement countries were doubtful that many of the newer boat people were fleeing political repression and thus merited refugee status. Another international refugee conference in Geneva in June 1989 produced the Comprehensive Plan of Action (CPA) which had the aim of reducing the migration of boat people by requiring that all new arrivals be screened to determine if they were genuine refugees. Those who failed to qualify as refugees would be repatriated, voluntarily or involuntarily, to Vietnam, a process that would take more than a decade. The CPA quickly served to reduce boat people migration. In 1989, about 70,000 Indochinese boat people arrived in five Southeast Asian countries and Hong Kong. By 1992, that number declined to only 41 and the era of the Vietnamese Boat People fleeing their homeland definitively ended. However, resettlement of Vietnamese continued under the Orderly Departure Program, especially of former re-education camp inmates, Amerasian children, and to reunify families. Resettlement and repatriation: The boat people comprised only part of the Vietnamese resettled abroad from 1975 until the end of the twentieth century. A total of more than 1.6 million Vietnamese was resettled between 1975 and 1997. Of that number more than 700,000 were boat people; the remaining 900,000 were resettled under the Orderly Departure Program in

China or Malaysia. (For complete statistics see Indochina refugee crisis). UNHCR statistics for 1975 to 1997 indicate that 839,228 Vietnamese arrived in UNHCR camps in Southeast Asia and Hong Kong. They arrived mostly by boat, although 42,918 of the totals arrived by land in Thailand. 749,929 were resettled abroad. 109,322 were repatriated, either voluntarily or involuntarily. The residual caseload of Vietnamese boat people in 1997 was 2,288, of whom 2,069 were in Hong Kong. The four countries resettling most Vietnamese boat people and land arrivals were the United States with 402,382; France with 120,403; Australia with 108,808; and Canada with 100,012.

The refugees faced prospects of staying years in the camps and ultimate repatriation to Vietnam. They were branded, rightly or wrongly, as economic refugees. By the mid-1990s, the number of refugees fleeing from Vietnam had significantly dwindled. Many refugee camps were shut down. Most of the well-educated or those with genuine refugee status had already been accepted by receiving countries.

Bronze plaque in the Port of Hamburg dedicated by Vietnamese refugees giving thanks to Rupert Neudeck and the rescue ship Cap Anamur

There appeared to be some unwritten rules in Western countries. Officials gave preference to married couples, young families, and women over 18 years old, leaving single men and minors to suffer at the camps for years. Among these unwanted, those who worked and studied hard and involved themselves in constructive refugee community activities were eventually accepted by the West by recommendations from UNHCR workers. Hong Kong was open about its willingness to take the remnants at its camp, but only some refugees took up the offer. Many refugees would have been accepted by Malaysia, Indonesia, and the Philippines, but hardly any wanted to settle in these countries. The market reforms of Vietnam, the imminent handover of Hong Kong to the People's Republic of China by Britain scheduled for July 1997, and the financial incentives for voluntary return to Vietnam caused many boat people to return to Vietnam during the 1990s. Most remaining asylum seekers were voluntarily or forcibly repatriated to Vietnam, although a small number (about 2,500) were granted the right of abode by the Hong Kong Government in 2002. In 2008, the remaining refugees in the Philippines (around 200) were granted asylum in Canada, Norway, and the United States, marking an end to the history of the boat people from Vietnam.

Now, should we continue with Le thi Lan's story?

The journey from S. Vietnam to S. Korea took 18 days.

Le thi Lan shared the cabin with her sister and brother-in-law, Kim Bu Muk said that she could sleep in the bed while the couple retired on the floor, but Le thi Lan stayed with the Vietnamese refugees so Le thi Minh could have some privacy with her husband. There were about fifty man, women, and children in the Vietnamese refugee group. Some were Vietnamese women married to S. Korean soldiers, officers while these men on their tour of duty in S. Vietnam; some just followers as Le thi Lan's case. The sailors helped the refugees set up the canvas tents on the deck, distributed blankets and clothes, and gave them food. In this war ship, there were: The Captain and his sailor team, three Navy S. Korean Doctors and nurses, cooks...

One day, the Pacific Ocean had wind gust, the high waves flashed the water upon the deck, the ship was waggled; some refugees and Le thi Lan got severe sea sick. She vomited and vomited until she was exhausted; then she was extremely thirsty. There was no more water, she drank all water in the bottle which was given to each person on board. Water was more precious than gold on the trip across the Pacific! Her sister, Le thi Minh gave her some water, she swallowed and said, "Thank you!". Later, she vomited again. About fifteen minutes later, Le thi Lan felt extremely thirsty. She saw the water bottle of the couple refugees in the same tent by their sleeping bags. Bui van Phuoc and Tran thi Chau [the husband was a student of Pharmacy School and the wife was a student of Education Dept] went out of the tent for some fresh air. Looking around once more: everything was clear. Nobody saw Le thi Lan quickly grabbed the water bottle and gulped the water down her throat. The couple returned, they stared at Le thi Lan. Bui van Phuoc yelled, "Disgusting!" Tran thi Chau added, "You said that you are a Medical student, and you stole water, no shame?"

"Sorry, I'm so thirsty." Le thi Lan mumbled and passed out

Some body called the sailors, other went to Kim Bu Muk & Le thi Minh's cabin. Kim Bu Muk called the doctor. A S. Korean Doctor on the USS AKL 28 came to examined Le thi Lan and administered the Normal saline through IV line and he kept Le thi Lan in the Infirmity ward of the ship for one day. Le thi Minh and Kim Bu Muk, Bui van Phuoc and Tran thi Chau came to visit. Le thi Lan apologized, the couples embraced her then all of them wept. At the same time, one woman and two children got sick [Le thi Lan didn't know the diagnoses, for they spoke Korean]; unfortunately, one child died. They wrapped the boy in bed sheets, put him in a box and let it go down to the bottom of the sea. The refugees watched the scene, the mother of the boy cried her heart out, the father was speechless.

Every day Le thi Lan looked at the waves rapped into the hulk of the ship, the sea gulls soared up high in the sky... the bubbles in the waves reflected the rainbow colors of the sun rays, then broken and disappeared in a brink of the eye. In one bubble, there was the image of her family: father, mother, Anh Duy... then the image dissolved; in another bubble, there was the Saigon Medical School where Le thi Lan and Dang van Huynh studied together...then the bubble evaporated.... Le thi Lan- a 21 years old medical student just realized that everything was just an illusion, including the USS ALK 28, and Life is but a dream?

On May 12, 1975, the Captain announced, "We now arrived at Pusan, harbor, S. Korea. The Koreans will be transferred to the S. Korean Navy Dept, and the refugees stay in the ship for 14 days of quarantine for Medical purpose." Le thi Minh hugged her sister and said, "Stay here, the S. Korean Home Office will review your situation and would temporarily allow you to stay in this country. Then, I will take you home with us, this is our address and telephone numbers in Seoul. Call anytime if you need us. On my part, I'll contract Uncle Quynh in France for you to live there with his family and continue Medicine."

"The goal of my life is to be a Medical doctor. I have to go to France, for at least I know this language. If I stay here, probably it'd take me years to learn the Korean language!" Le thi Lan told her sister

"We will take you to our home for visiting after the quarantine." Kim Bu Muk said

"Thank you very much." Le thi Lan bowed her head

After the quarantine, the Vietnamese refugees moved to an old elementary school in Pusan which the S. Koran government transformed it to a refugee camp. In June, 1975, the International Rescue Committee and the UN Refugee Agency came to assigned the Vietnamese evacuees in S. Korean to non-communist countries all over the world. Le thi Lan was interviewed by the agents [with telephonic interpreters] of these organizations; she filled the immigration forms for France and the USA. She and other evacuees were told that they would know their situations in a few weeks or a few months.

Seoul Pusan

On September 27 [Le thi Lan's birthday], the Vietnamese refugee told herself, "A day as any day, I'm still in the Refugee Camp. I enjoy eating seaweeds and Kimchee....". A guard let Le thi Lan know that she had visitors: Le thi Minh and Kim Bu Muk took her to Seoul and Daegu for scenery viewing. What a beautiful country with gentle people; Le thi Lan kept this gratitude in her heart all her life.

THE WIND BLOWS YOUR HAIR

In October, 1975 Bui van Phuoc and his wife Tran thi Chau were accepted by the Catholic Relief Services to settle in Michigan, USA through the kindness of the Priest of St. Ann Church in Detroit, Michigan. The immigration Office of the USA provided them with the Five-Year-Immigration cards, the Social Security cards, and Work Permits in the US. The Priest of St. Ann's parish in Detroit showed them an apartment paid by St Ann Church for the Vietnamese refugee couple. People from St. Ann contributed clothing, linen, tables, chairs…for the new comers. The refugees appreciated their kindness in helping them to sojourn in the US after the strenuous escape from the Communists. The Social Services of Detroit provided the food stamps for the family. St. Ann's parish gave the refugees clothes and furniture. The Priest brought Bui van Phuoc and Tran thi Chau to Synergy Solutions Company. The Supervisor of the electronic assembly line productions. Mr. John Smith agreed to train the refugee couples, he helped them to fill out the employment forms and told them to return next week to work.

Saigon 1974

253

That night, Tran thi Chau could not sleep, her mind went back two years ago, Bui van Phuoc and Tran thi Chau were students of University of Saigon, S. Vietnam. Bui van Phuoc was in Pharmacy School and Tran thi Chau belonged to Education Dept since she wished to be a Middle School teacher of Vietnamese literature. One afternoon, when Tran thi Chau rode her bicycle home from school, the wind blew away her ribbon and made her hair spread over her shoulders, she heard someone singing, "Gió có còn làm tóc em bay…" [The wind blows your hair…] Bui van Phuoc rode his bicycle next to her asked with a smile, "Lovely hair, how are you?"

And, he followed her after school every day. They dated and got married in March, 1975. In April, 1975, during the chaos of the S. Vietnam collapse, they escaped for freedom from the Communism. In that frantic moment, Bui van Phuoc and Tran thi Chau didn't take the Certification of Marriage, Pharmacy Student ID, Education Dept Student ID with them. All they had was clothes on their bodies…Then, 18 days floating on the Pacific Ocean to S. Korea…Then, from S. Korea, they flew across the East Pacific Coast to the West Pacific Coast to Alaska then transferred to Michigan, the Midwest of the USA. They lived together as husband and wife, but not legally married in the US. Bui van Phuoc told Tran thi Chau,

Detroit

"I want to continue Pharmacy study."

"How could you get in Pharmacy School in the US?" Tran thi Chau wondered

"I have to ask the Priest for help." Bui van Phuoc said, "And you? I'd think you still want to be a Middle school teacher?"

"I want you to concentrate on Pharmacy study only. You don't have to work, I'll work to support you," Tran thi Chau said, "After you become a Pharmacist, I'll go back to school." Tran thi Chau leaned on Bui van Phuoc's shoulder, "I can wait because I love you. With the help of Social Services by giving us food stamps and clothes, and furniture from St. Ann, we can make it."

"I love you, too. First of all, both of us have to learn English!" Bui van Phuoc hugged his wife

"Yes!" Tran thi Chau laughed happily

Three years passed by…. Bui van Phuoc and Tran thi Chau got acquainted with the weather, especially the snow and the cold of the Midwest winter. "Cold to the bone!" Tran thi Chau told her husband when she dropped her husband at school then went to work. They learned and were able to speak English [the husband's English was better than his wife]. They made friends with the neighbors, got along with the customs, holidays, and culture in America. At work, Tran thi Chau earned the title "Lead Person" in the electronic board assembly line at Synergy Solutions Company due to her hard working and perfect attendance record. Bui van Phuoc passed the pre-Pharmacy examination and waited to be accepted in the first year of Pharmacy school at Michigan State University.

Ten years later…. They had two children, a girl [Bui thi Mai] Mia t Bui was born in 1981 and a boy [Bui van Loc] Luke v Bui, born in 1984. Tran thi Chau was very happy to announced at work that her husband, Bui van Phuoc graduated from Pharmacy School with the BS in Pharmacy and he was accepted to do one-year internship at the CVS Pharmacy downtown Detroit. Oh! America, land of opportunities and dreams came true! [Bui thi Mai] Mia Bui and [Bui van Loc] Luke v. Bui were good students at Chrysler Elementary School. Tran thi Chau invited the assemblers and the supervisor at Synergy Solutions Company to come to the celebration at St. Ann church. Mrs. Jane Brown, a member of St. Ann's parish gave Tran thi Chau a dress for this banquet and put on some make ups on Tran thi Chau. Ah, what a long time that

Tran thi Chau paid attention to her appearance! In the mirror, she saw: an old assembler in blue collar uniform woman with crow feet lines by the ends of the eye lids, deep nasal labial folders and wrinkles at the chin. At the age 35, she looked like a woman in her menopause. Oh, that was not important. She was contented with her husband's and her children's achievement in the USA.

That night, after washing the dishes and put a load of clothes in the washer, and the children were in bed, Tran thi Chau embraced her husband, "I'm so proud of you!"

"Wait a minute," Bui van Phuoc said as he gently pushed her away, "We need to talk."

Tran thi Chau looked up at her husband in surprise, "What's up, dear?"

"I'm going to move to California." Bui van Phuoc said

"Ah, that's good. We'll all go together. Where are you going to work?" Tran thi Chau asked

"Sit down, please," Bui van Phuoc said, "I do not go with you and the children. I found someone I love- my true love, VTL, Vietnamese. She's just graduated in Nursing and has a job at St. Joseph's Hospital in LA, California. It's not too hard for me to work as a pharmacist there; I'd have to take the Boards of Pharmacist in California and...I'll marry VTL...."

Tran thi Chau couldn't believe what she heard. Broken heart, tearful in her eyes, she ran into her daughter's bed room. She cried and hugged the girl tightly, "Oh, Bui thi Mai...."

Bui van Loc woke up, he came toward the mother, "Mom, why do you cry? "

"You keep the children," Bui van Phuoc walked in and continued, "I don't think we need to divorce as we don't have the Marriage Certificate in the US, the one in Vietnam wouldn't count as no trace of it by now. I hope we resolve this case peacefully. Thank you" then he walked away

"Oh, my God!" Tran thi Chau cried out loud

The Wind Flows The Leaves Along The Stream

Spring arrives on the green grass
The wind flows the leaves along the stream

Michigan 1990

How many days did Tran thi Chau live in a state of stunned confusion or bewilderment? Bui van Phuoc was right. No Marriage Certificate in the US, no need to file a divorce, and she had the custody of the children. It was a fair bargain, wasn't it? Over ten years her work to support her husband in Pharmacy school went down the drain. Tran thi Chau wiped off the tears on her face and vowed not to cry again. She kept on working at Synergy Solutions and took care of her children, the purpose of her living. She moved to another apartment, two bed rooms upstairs for the children, for Bui thi Mai told the mother, "I'm a big girl now, I should have my own bed room." Bui van Loc also said, "I don't want to share room with a girl." The mother explained to them that she grew up in a large family. At night, everybody slept on cots on the floor. The children responded, "Sorry! Mom, you're Chinese, we're Americans." So, at night Tran thi Chau put a screen in front of the sofa, this was her bed room. Tran thi Chau had to confront with another problem, which was not less challenging. Luke v. Bui [Bui van Loc] and Mia t. Bui [Bui thi Mai] were born in Michigan, USA. They went to American schools here and they spoke English fluently while Tran thi Chau's English was at the beginner level with a heavy accent. When she talked to her children, she had to scratch her head to find an English word.

This year, a Vietnamese family, Phan Thanh and his wife, Nguyen thi Kim at St. Ann parish planned to go back to Vietnam in two weeks for visiting their parents and relatives. Tran thi Chau asked them,

"May I and my two children Mia and Luke take the same trip with you?"

"We go to Saigon [Ho Chi Minh City]." Nguyen thi Kim smiled

"I go to Gia Dinh, the suburb of Saigon." Tran thi Chau said

"We'll go together, no problems." Phan Thanh told her

"That's wonderful! I can ask for vacation time off work." Tran thi Chau said

"Good!" Phan Thanh added, "Phan Hieu [Hughes Phan] goes to High school, he speaks English very well; that would help us to find the right flights as we need to change airplanes on the way home."

"Exactly!" Everybody laughed

Time has been flying! Tran thi Chau could not imagine that it was 15 years since the day she left Saigon, Vietnam. Everything has been changing, from a student who knew nothing but the text books to be the Lead person of the electronic assembling line at Synergy Solution company, a wife, a mother of two children, and the husband left her to be with another woman. And now, Tran thi Chau returned to Vietnam to visit her family. Oh, how excited was the trip home from across the Pacific Ocean! Today, after work, she stopped by Liberty Bank of Detroit to withdraw $2,000 USD. That was her savings for the whole year of hard work, she planned to give the money to her family as a gift.

January 19th 1990

"We'll go to Vietnam to celebrate the Lunar New Year. You'll see the country of your parents, Vietnam- the place where I was born. You visit grandparents and relatives." Tran thi Chau announced to her children, "I asked school two weeks off permission for both of you."

"How about to Disney's world, Mom?" the children asked, "Bobby's family go to Disney world, there're lots of fun!"

Tran thi Chau stared at her children and took a deep breath, then she said, "Listen! Both of you go with me to Vietnam." She added, "January 27 is the Lunar New Year. We'll celebrate Year of the Horse in Vietnam. You should learn how to greet your grandparents. Repeat after me, Chào Ông, Chào Bà [Greeting to Grandpa, Grandma]."

"I don't know what you're talking about." Mia and Luke giggled to imitate their mother speak Vietnamese, Chào Ông, Chào Bà."

"You'll have plenty of very good foods and sweets for this special occasion." Tran thi Chau continued, "Rice cakes, coconut jams, Southern pastry- you'd love them…Uncle Bao or Aunt Hoa will pick us up at the airport. We stay two days in Gia Dinh, Ho Chi Minh city then we'll go to Vinh Long, to see Grandpa and Grandma. Vinh Long, where I was born. Oh, you will eat Southern noodle soup; there are a lot of stuff in this special soup: chicken or beef, or even seafood with delicious spices.... And you'll see the green rice field spreads toward the horizon.... Do you know that we have the best rice in the world? And the meadows with the green grass for the cattle.... Ah! Nowhere you can find greener grass than the one at home...."

Tran thi Chau looked around, the children were not there; she was talking to herself for how long?

January 22, 1990

"We pack up clothes and gifts for our relatives," Tran thi Chau told her children, "Tomorrow, we'll go to...Ah, Mia...I can't read this, please read for me..." She gave her daughter the itinerary of the trip.

"Start at Detroit Metropolitan Wayne International Airport- DTW, flight by Qatar airline at 6:15 am, January 24, 1990" Mia read, "fly to O'Hare International Airport, Chicago- Illinois USA then Toronto Pearson International Airport- YYZ in Ontario, Canada transfer to Air Vietnam at Hamad International Airport-

DOH Qatar to Tan Son Nhat Airport-SGN, Ho chi Minh City, Vietnam at 6:45 pm January 26, 1990."

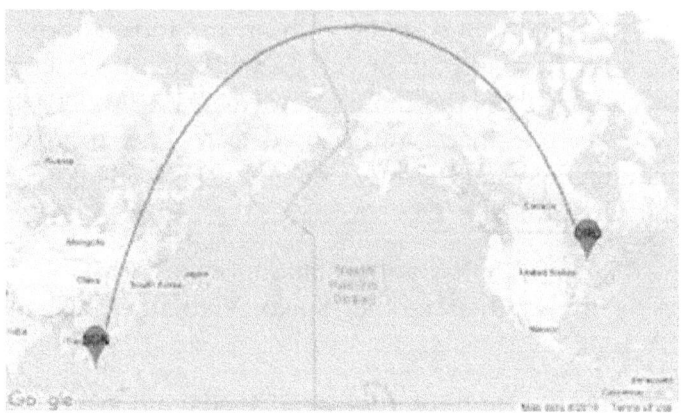

Transpacific-Eastward 1990

"How long is the flight?" Luke asked

"21 hours and 45 minutes." Mia answered

"Almost a daylong for the trip!" the mother exclaimed, "Let's pack up. Huh?"

"Yes!" the children said and they went upstairs.

Tran thi Chau gave Mia and Luke each a small suitcase, a bigger one for her. While they were arranging bits and pieces, Luke found some masks of Superman and Spiderman. Mia put it on her brother and herself, they chased each other and laughed happily. Tran thi Chau just remembered she was cooking something in the kitchen. In a hurry, she rushed downstairs, unfortunately, she fell down the stairs: the right side of her head hit the last step of the stairs. She screamed, "Oh! Help!", the children didn't hear the mother but the mother heard them laughing in their play, then she passed out. When she woke up, Tran thi Chau didn't not remember how long she was unconscious; the last thing she knew was the laughing voice of her children as they, they didn't know what happened to their mother. Tran thi Chau put her hand to the back of her head, "It hurts." She told herself, "I'm fine." and got up. It came to her mind that she had to check something in the kitchen. The meat was burned to charcoal, luckily there was no fire. She turned off the burner. She wondered if she should go to the hospital to check out the head injury, then the telephone rang; she picked it up and said, "Hello?"

"Hello! This is Kim, from St. Ann parish. Tomorrow we'll pick you and your children up for the airport. My husband has a van, we all go together. Get ready, we just wait outside, OK?" Nguyen thi Kim said

"Yes. Thank you." Tran thi Chau put the telephone down

There was no time for the hospital, no need to tell her children about the incident. Tran thi Chau took two Tylenol tablets and called the children,

"All set? Let's have dinner, today we rest early as we'll have a very long day tomorrow."

"Yes, Mom." Mia and Luke went down stairs for dinner

That night, Tran thi Chau had a dream. She met her family: parents, brother, and sister. Strangely, everybody wept bitterly around a coffin in the living room. That made no sense at all. She talked to her family three days ago. The parents were fine, her mother had arthritis and knee pain, father had diabetes, he took medicine. Her brother Bao and her sister Hoa- both were in good health, nobody was in a serious condition What was the reason that everybody wept, who was in the coffin?

Tran thi Chau woke up, she was so scared and sweating. To be sure about her family's health condition, she called Tran thi Hoa-her sister, in Vietnam [4am in Detroit, Michigan- USA = 3pm Ho Chi Minh- Vietnam]. She didn't want to tell anybody about her strange dream, "Of course they'd laugh at me." so she only mentioned about the time she and her children would arrive at Tan Son Nhat International Airport, Ho Chi Minh city.

"Hi, Hoa! How are you? How are Mom and Dad? Is everybody OK?" Tran thi Chau asked with running up questions, "I and my children will be at Tan Son Nhat Airport at 6:45pm- your time on January 26. It's the New Year Eve, the lunar calendar. I can't wait to see you all, I miss you so much!"

"Everybody is fine." Tran thi Hoa answered the phone, "Yes, The New Year Eve. It's wonderful to have you for the New Year celebration. We'll pick you up at the airport. Your voice is trembling, are you OK?"

"I'm fine. See you!" Tran thi Chau said

"Take care! See you!" Tran thi Hoa put down the phone

Tran thi Chau assured herself, "Nothing to worry, it was just a weird dream."

January 24 1990

Early in the morning, Phan Thanh and Nguyen thi Kim came to pick Tran thi Chau and her children to Detroit Metropolitan Wayne International Airport. The clerks at the Information desk helped the Vietnamese people with their flight. Settling down in the seat of the airplane, Tran thi Chau felt tired and dizzy. Probably she was excited about the trip, she took a nap while Mia and Luke enjoyed the view by the windows. How many flights, airports they went through….and lots of people who spoke different languages! Tran thi Chau seemed lost in a rapidly current waves of the Pacific Ocean which she had no choice but yield with the flow. By the end of a strenuous journey, Tran thi Chau heard the pilot announced something, for she only recognized the words "Tan Son Nhat".

"What did he say, Mia?" she asked her daughter

"The plane will land at Tan Son Nhat International Airport, Ho Chi Minh city, Vietnam, at local time 6:45 pm, January 26, 1990." Mia explained to her mother

January 26 1990

Oh! How happy it was to meet her family after 15 years of separation! Tran thi Chau didn't cry but tears falling down her cheeks. After checking out the luggage, she and her children followed Phan Thanh and Nguyen thi Kim waiting for their families. Each of them raised up a card written in English and Vietnamese: "My name is …. Looking for…" since they might not recognize their relatives and vice versa after a long separation.

Phan Thanh and Nguyen thi Kim met their relatives and they went home with them. Nguyen thi Kim said,

"We'll get in touch and meet together here on the way back to the US."

"Thank you very much. See you!" Tran thi Chau waved to her friends

She set Mia and Luke standing in front of her, each had a card with his/her name and Tran van Bao's name [Tran thi Chau's brother]. Tran van Bao recognized his sister, he called out loudly, "Over here!" Tran thi Chau ran toward him, she cried, "Ah! My brother...."

Tran van Bao hugged his sister, "I'm so very glad to see you! Mom and Dad are waiting at home, they prepared the foods you love to eat.... Come home on the Lunar New Year Eve, Super!"

"I'm happy to see you," Tran thi Chau said. Turning to the children, she introduced, "This is Mia, nine years old; and this is Luke, six years old. Children, greet your Uncle!"

"Hi!" Mia and Luke said to their uncle, Tran van Bao

"Hello! How are you?" Tran van Bao tried his best English

"Fine." the children said, "It's hot here! It was snowing the day we left Detroit."

"Ah! I don't understand." Tran van Bao said in Vietnamese and laughed

"I don't understand, either." The children said in English and chuckled

How wonderful it was to go back to Vietnam at the Lunar New Year to be with the family! Tran van Bao drove through the street of Ho Chi Minh city [Saigon]. Tran thi Chau was overjoy with the scenery, memory from the past over flowed her heart, the Tet decorations all over the streets of the city, the pagodas with the believers' offering gifts to the Buddha, the markets were full of fruits and flowers... Again, she felt tired and dizzy. She thought it was due to the long flight across the Pacific, and she ignored it, she had so many things to do right now! They arrived at their parents' house in Gia Dinh [a suburb of Ho Chi Minh city]. Her parents were waiting at the door when the car stopped, the Tran thi Chau's mother ran to the driveway to embrace her daughter, both of them were in tears. The father came, he was very happy to see his daughter and the grandchildren. Tran thi Chau reminded the children,

"Greetings to your grandparents. Chào Ông, Chào Bà"

Mia [Bui thi Mai] and Luke [Bui van Loc] repeated after their mother. The grandparents hugged the children, tears were in their eyes. Tran thi Chau's family knew Bui van Phuoc [Tran thi Chau's husband] left his wife for another younger woman after he obtaining the Pharmacist Diplomat, Tran thi Chau had been working as an assembler to support him and the children through all those years. The family didn't mention anything about this matter as it was time to celebrate the Lunar New Year. They had dinner; it was an excellent meal which Tran thi Chau enjoyed the Vietnamese dishes very much. However, Mia and Luke asked for hamburgers and soda to drink. Tran thi Hoa served tea and special home-made cakes after dinner. Tran thi Chau wished that she could stay up to talk to her mother and sister about her life in America, but all her eyes wanted now was to sleep. Oh, it would take days to tell them about America! And she had plenty of time to share with the family. Tran thi Chau's father asked her,

"Tomorrow, we take the bus to Vinh Long. We enjoy Tet [the Lunar New Year] at Grandpa and Grandma's farm. You love to see the country, don't you?"

"We take the boat along the Hau Giang River to see the green rice field and the lotus ponds." The mother joined the conversation

"The green…rice …field…" Tran thi Chau said and she felt very sleepy; she leaned on her mother's shoulder, "I love you, Mom."

"I love you, too." The mother said and told Tran thi Hoa," Help her to bed. She is so tired."

Tran thi Chau slept peacefully. The father, the mother looked at their daughter whom she hasn't seen for 15 years. They hugged her and said, "Goodnight!"

Aunt Tran thi Hoa and Uncle Tran van Bao showed Mia and Luke their bed rooms. The Tran family gathered around the altar waiting for the Lunar New Year, Tran thi Chau's father burned the incent as they prayed in thankfulness to the Buddha and the ancestors for the new year. This year it was so special, their daughter whom they thought was missing but now united with them to celebrate the Tet special occasion.

Next morning… January 27 1990

Tran van Bao started the firecrackers to honor the Lunar New Year, Year of the Horse! Enjoy Tet in the sunny and warm day! Some relatives and their children, the neighbors came to say "Happy New Year!" with warm greetings and presents to the Tran's family. Tran thi Chau's father happily introduced Mia and Luke to the guests. The mother and Tran thi Hoa prepare the ingredients for the southern noodle soup, this was Tran thi Chau's favorite dish. Tran thi Chau was still in bed; everybody understood that she had a long trip so they let her slept in. Mia put on a pink "ao dai" [a traditional Vietnamese tunique for girl] and Luke laughed heartily as he saw himself in the "ao thung" [a traditional tunique for boy] to greet the grandparents and relatives. The children received red envelopes with some money as gifts to them. Mia and Luke loved to munch on the delicious sweets and played some games with their cousins. Suddenly, Tran thi Hoa hear Mia crying, "My Mom!"

"What's wrong, sweetheart?" Aunt Tran thi Hoa came in and she asked but Mia kept on crying,

"Mom does not get up!" Luke called out loud

The children spoke English, Tran thi Hoa didn't understand; she went out to tell Tran van Bao. Tran thi Chau's mother sensed something wrong, she followed them. Tran thi Chau slept soundly and peacefully. The children were crying, the adults were talking, the sounds of the New Year greetings….in the morning of Lunar New Year Tran thi Chau was sleeping.

"What's wrong?" the mother inquired

"I cannot wake my mom up." Mia said in tears

"Let's me try." Tran van Bao said and touched Tran thi Chau's shoulders gently, "Wake up, sister!"

Tran thi Chau did not respond. Tran thi Hoa tickled the sole of her sister's foot, and told everybody, "She will laugh and scold us for disturbing her sleep", but Tran thi Chau did not move. The mother tremblingly put her face close to her daughter's nose, "She's breathing."

"Why doesn't Mom wake up?" Mia and Luke wept

"I'll take her to the Emergency Room of the General Hospital." Tran van Bao decided

"I'll go with you," Tran thi Hoa told her mother, "Please take care of the children."

"No! No! we go with Mom!" the children scream as they took Tran thi Chau away

"It's OK. You stay with grandma." The grandmother said

At the Emergency Room, General Hospital, HCMC, Vietnam

Tran van Bao stopped the car in the entrance to the ER, Tran thi Hoa called out, "Please help!". Some paramedics and nurses asked as they saw the patient, they pulled put a stretcher and put Tran thi Chau on it. A nurse asked Tran van Bao as she checked the vital signs and alarmed the other nurse,

"What happened? Pulse…Heartbeat…Breathing… Get a stretcher, inform the Doctor…"

"My sister- Tran thi Chau, flew from the US to HCMC [Ho Chi Minh City] yesterday." Tran van Bao said, "Last night, we had dinner, she was alert …. This morning, we couldn't wake her up."

The Doctor Nguyen arrived. He examined the patient: listening to the heart and lungs. He opened the patients' eyes with a bright, pin picked to check the sensations…He asked Tran van Bao and Tran thi Hoa for some details about the situation, but they didn't give any further information.

"Was there any trauma?" Doctor Nguyen asked

Tran van Bao and Tran thi Hoa stared at the Doctor, "We don't understand, Doctor?"

"Was there an accident, incident, or did she fall?" Doctor Nguyen inquired

"No! There was none!" Tran thi Hoa denied

"I meant before yesterday," Doctor Nguyen said, "I assumed this is a head trauma, the patient is unconscious so we do not know what happened. We'll have CT scan of the brain to see... and I will let you know. Please go to the waiting room, someone will call your number, later."

"Head injury, CT scan, trauma...unconscious..." Tran van Bao mumbled these words while Tran thi Hoa said, "Thank you, Doctor."

"Chau, Chau..." Tran thi Hoa ran along the stretcher as they rolled it to the Radiology Dept, but they stopped her. Tran van Bao and Tran thi Hoa called home to let the parents know about Tran thi Chau's situation. They heard the mother crying, "Amitabha!"

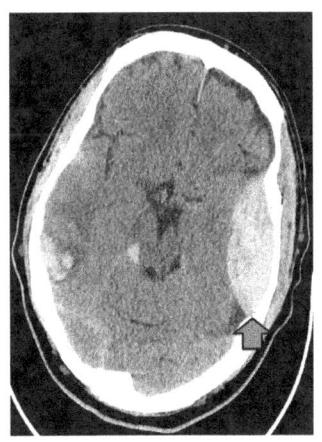

en.wikipedia.org › wiki ›
Epidural hematoma

They waited, the needles of the clock of the hospital seemed not moving. Then Doctor Nguyen appeared, he called Tran van Bao and Tran thi Hoa to his office. On the screen, there were some black and white images. The Doctor pointed to the images and told Tran van Bao and Tran thi Hoa,

"Here's the CT scan of the patient's, we call it head injury with epidural hematoma [Excerpt from en.wikipedia.org › wiki › Epidural hematoma]"

"Epidural hematoma commonly results from a blow to the side of the head." Doctor Nguyen explained, "I believe the patient had a head injury at least three days ago. Probably she didn't tell you the cause? Since she was able to travel and was alert up to last night, I think the hematoma comes from veins and can progress more slowly. A venous hematoma may be acute (occurring within a day of the injury and appearing as a swirling mass of blood without a clot), subacute (occurring in 2–4 days and appearing solid), or chronic (occurring in 7–20 days and appearing mixed or lucent). Epidural hematoma is when bleeding occurs between the tough outer membrane covering the brain (dura mater) and the skull. There is loss of consciousness following a head injury, a brief regaining of consciousness, and then loss of consciousness again. The cause is typically head injury. Many people with epidural hematomas experience a lucid period immediately following the injury, with a delay before symptoms become evident. As blood accumulates, it starts to compress intracranial structures."

"How do you treat my sister, please?" Tran van Bao inquired

"Treatment is generally by urgent surgery in the form of a craniotomy or burr hole. Without treatment, death typically results." Doctor Nguyen said

"Oh, no!" Tran thi Hoa burst into tears

"Many people with epidural hematomas experience a lucid period immediately following the injury, "Doctor Nguyen continued, "without a delay before symptoms become evident. The hematoma is evacuated through a burr hole or craniotomy. If transfer to a facility with neurosurgery is unavailable, prolonged trephination (drilling a hole into the skull) may be performed in the emergency department. Large hematomas and blood clots may require an open craniotomy. As blood accumulates, it starts to compress intracranial structure.... In this case, the blood accumulates, it starts to compress intracranial structures, which has impinged on the third cranial nerve, causing a fixed and dilated pupil on the side of the injury. When I checked her eyes, the pupils are dilated and fixed, it means that the epidural hematoma has gradually caused tonsillar herniation, resulting in respiratory arrest any moment ..."

"I'm deeply sorry. I cannot help." Doctor Nguyen said

"No! No!" Tran van Bao and Tran thi Hoa screamed

Outside the window of the hospital, a gentle breeze blew the yellow ochna petals and spread them on the green grass of spring. Spring came as Tran thi Chau returned her home to celebrate the New Year with her family after a long journal overseas. She was sleeping, what did she dream about? The birds chirped a sweet song calling the Mia and Luke go out to play in the beautiful spring scenery where the wind carried the leaves along the stream going back to the source far away in the mountain heights …

POSTCRIPT

"Papa, I've just finished the last page of Beloved Vietnam-Vol 2!" ThuDzung told her father

"Ah, what do you think?" the father asked

"Truly, I'm confused and lost." ThuDzung sheepishly said, "Born during the Vietnam War and tasted the suffering of the country due to US bombing…"

"…the homeland was devastated by the US bombs from World War II (1945) to the worst in 1968 after the battle of Khe Sanh. … then worked in America and ironically obtained a USA passport, isn't it the maze?" the father added

"Papa, what could I do for my country?" ThuDzung looked up at the father

"Uncountable numbers of the unknown people in that motherland thousands of years ago and up to this moment have been continuously contributing their effort to claim Independence of Vietnam, a gem of the Far-East. I quote here the words from Rabindranath Tagore FRAS was an Indian polymath—poet, writer, playwright, composer, philosopher, social reformer and painter. He reshaped Bengali literature and music as well as Indian art with Contextual Modernism in the late 19th and early 20th centuries. Wikipedia. "In my next life, I still wish to be born as an Indian, for I love my country above everything else in the world." The father gave his daughter a message, "ThuDzung, remember, next life, we'll also be Vietnamese, for we love our country with all our hearts. Try harder, Oh little soldier in the Great Vietnamese Army!"

PHAM THUDZUNG

www.ingramcontent.com/pod-product-compliance
Lightning Source LLC
Chambersburg PA
CBHW050927030726
47503CB00007BB/2498